CUP OF
BLOOD . . .
BREAD OF
SALVATION

CUP OF BLOOD . . .
BREAD OF SALVATION

The Dark Ages Saga of Tristan de Saint-Germain

BOOK FIVE

Robert E. Hirsch

OPEN ROAD
INTEGRATED MEDIA
NEW YORK

Copyright © 2019 by Robert E. Hirsch

ISBN: 978-1-5040-7920-4

This edition published in 2023 by Open Road Integrated Media, Inc.
180 Maiden Lane
New York, NY 10038
www.openroadmedia.com

This book is dedicated in entirety to my loving, compassionate, patient, and supportive wife, Melissa Ann (Lewis) Hirsch. She is the cornerstone from which I launched into writing the Dark Ages Saga of Tristan de Saint-Germain. Her heart and spirit are to be found in one chapter after another of the series in terms of character, philosophy, persona, understanding of people, motives, and political/social point of view. It is so rare in life that one could hope to meet, love, and share their one existence on this earth with a person of identical heart. In that, I have been more than fortunate as Melissa and I, together, have faced life, unanticipated obstacles, unimaginable challenges, and hardships well beyond the normal spectrum of experience. Melissa, you are my anchor, and I thank the stars for you each night.

AUTHOR'S DISCLAIMER

Although deeply steeped in history of the 11th century, the entire five novel series of The Dark Ages Saga of Tristan de Saint-Germain—*Promise of the Black Monks, Hammer of God, A Horde of Fools, God's Scarlet Fury, Cup of Blood . . . Bread of Salvation*—is a work of fiction. All characters, names, incidents and dialogue, whether historical or fictitious, are purely representations of the author's artistic interpretation and imagination.

VANITY

Oh, but vanity . . . wellspring of deception and ruination, disassembling others as well as self. Vanity, rising from the backwater scum of that part of the bosom lying concealed from others—silently feeding those worms of our pride feasting on ambition.

Though we for millennia have spoken of and analogized Achilles' heel, that myth is misdirected; our weakness lies not at the foot, but within the 'heart' where envy is bred, where that ceaseless war of weighing ourselves against others is waged.

So it is, then, that vanity has shaped humanity's fate, recarving maps of civilization while chiseling at history in the same manner that devastating sea storms carve great scars and gaps into stone cliffs once imagined to be immovable and indestructible.

Yes, all this, driven by . . . vanity.

PROLOGUE

By the 5th century, in Western Europe, the ability to trample over and butcher others fueled by an insatiable thirst for blood became so prevalent and irreversible as to give rise to a bleak, merciless period known as the Dark Ages. It was an era punctuated by violence as marauding Vikings, savage Germanic tribes, and roving Muslim hordes scarred the European landscape with invasion, bloodletting, and subjugation. Bludgeoning the enlightenment of the Age of Antiquity and Roman classicism into the fog of history, mankind regressed into the blackness of ignorance, intolerance, and savagery.

The seminal, defining measure of the Dark Ages in Western Europe became a bloody holy war engineered by a coven of high Roman Catholic clerics driven by religious devotion, righteousness, and the heart-fire of liberating the Holy City of Jerusalem from the grasp of Islam. These obsessions placed in motion a bitter wheel of hatred and intolerance precipitating into a cataclysmic disaster ignited by the triple tinderboxes of race, religion, and culture. This conflict, the remnants of which stand to this very day, became known to history as the First Holy Crusade.

The effect of war in shaping global history and national boundaries is evident. Be that as it may, of all factors forging the maps of history, the force of migration has an even greater impact. Just as Romans swarmed out of Italy to establish their vast empire, Vikings and Germanic tribes migrated south, Moors migrated north out of Africa, and Huns and Tartars migrated west from Asia. One particular horde of Tartars, the Seljuk Turks, abandoned their steppes, drove west, and established a powerful empire in Persia. Overcoming the indigenous Saracens of Arabia who made up the Islamic Abbasid caliphate, the Seljuks captured Baghdad in 1055. Having converted to Islam, they ventured further west, invading Anatolia, Asia Minor, and Syria, all belonging to the Christian Byzantine Empire. Defeating the Byzantines at the Battle of Manzikert in 1071, the Seljuks forced the Byzantines from those areas, halting their Islamic advance at the very doorstep of the Christian Byzantine capital, Constantinople, merely twenty miles across the Bosphorus Straight.

The Byzantine Empire at this time was the last vestige of Christianity and the old Roman Empire in the East. Although now more Greek than Roman, and having split with Roman Catholicism during the Great Schism of 1054 into its own rite of the Greek Orthodox Church, the besieged Byzantines begged Western Europe for military help against further Turkish encroachment. Specifically, Byzantine Emperor Alexius Comnenus pleaded with Pope Urban II of Rome to send European knights to stop the Turkish threat. Pope Urban, wishing to establish a state of détente with the Christian Greek Orthodox Church in the wake of the Great Schism of 1054 and recapture Jerusalem from Islam, sent out an incendiary plea to the knights of Western Europe to undertake a holy crusade to help Catholicism's fellow Christians of Byzantium.

Responding to the pope's passionate preaching, a zealous army of 100,000 crusaders marched from France, Germany, and Southern Italy, arriving in Constantinople during the spring of 1097. From there they sailed the Bosphorus, launched into Turkish territory, and twice defeated the Seljuk Sultan of Rüm, Kilij Arslan. By late August, after arduous marches across Asia Minor and Anatolia, the Latin crusaders found themselves in Syria, the last barrier standing in the path of their holy quest to re-conquer Jerusalem from Islam and the Seljuk Turks.

This enormous Christian army perfectly epitomized the arrogance and brutality of the European warrior class of the age. Led by a confederation of dukes and princes intent on halting the aggressive spread of Islam, they saw their foe as dark, godless heathens whose religion had infected Southern Spain, North Africa, and the East.

Beneath the veneer of their professed piety and Catholic faith, many within this Christian horde were driven by the lure of fabled Muslim riches and territory. Thus, obsessed with incongruent motivations and led by an eclectic mix of leadership driven by altruism as well as greed, the crusaders launched the final leg of their struggle to the death over belief, culture, plunder, and dominion against the great Syrian city of Antioch.

CUP OF BLOOD . . . BREAD OF SALVATION

CHAPTER ONE

ANTIOCH: THE MYSTICAL COURT OF YAGHI SIYAN

It was late summer of 1097 when Pope Urban's enormous crush of Christian warriors entered Syria along the northern edges of the Holy Land. Jerusalem, the final target of their quest, merely a few weeks' march to the south, had but one obstacle standing its way—Antioch, the massive city of the Orient.

Antioch, established three centuries before the birth of Christ, in the wake of Alexander the Great's march eastward, had been named after one of his favored generals, Antiochus. Its location as a vital and pulsing trade center between East and West destined it to become the third largest city of the entire Roman empire, with a burgeoning population approaching over 300,000. Of special significance to Christians, it was at Antioch that Peter met Paul and the two agreed to allow gentiles into their religion. Later, in the 6th century, Emperor Justinian constructed a formidable fortification system and encircled the entire city with a massive wall, heightening its glory and significance.

Over time, a series of catastrophes conspired to threaten the city's grandeur and power in the form of three devastating earthquakes, the plague, and the city-wide outbreak of a deadly fire. Next, the Persians attacked, plundering the city. In 638, it was conquered by the Arabians, who allowed it to decline in favor of Aleppo and Damascus. In 969, three centuries later, it was re-conquered by the Christian Byzantines and restored to its former eminence and glory. Then came the Seljuk Turks, sweeping relentlessly in from the steppes of Asia, claiming dominion over Antioch in 1085, just fourteen years after their poignant victory over the Byzantine Empire at the bloody Battle of Manzikert.

The power of the Seljuk hammer in Northern Syria had been wielded by the celebrated Malik Shah, but after his death in 1092 succession wars ruptured Seljuk unity. Shah's son was caught in a vicious fight over control of Baghdad, while Shah's nephews, Ridwan of Aleppo and Duqaq of Damascus, were battling each other over control of Syria. Religious division further fragmented the region. As the area had once been part of the Byzantine Empire, a large Christian Armenian population inhabited the territory, living alongside Syrian Muslims, some of whom had over time converted to Christianity. The conquering Turks themselves were mostly Sunni Muslims, whereas a sizeable portion of Syria's Arab population adhered to the Shia sect.

In the midst of this boiling caldron of Christian-Muslim division, Shia-Sunni feuding, and Turkish infighting, Antioch was governed by the aging but wily Turcoman, Yaghi Siyan. Knowing that survival depended on backing the right horse at the right time, not always the same horse at all times, Yaghi Siyan cleverly vacillated between Ridwan of Aleppo and Duqaq of Damascus as a means of survival.

As the former faithful slave of the celebrated Malik Shah, Yaghi Siyan had earned Shah's full trust and confidentiality, and was rewarded accordingly. In 1090, Malik Shah appointed him governor of Antioch. At the time, it was a common custom among Seljuk clans to appoint the most intelligent and trusted slaves to positions of responsibility and prestige. On Shah's death in 1092, this same respect was extended to Yaghi Siyan by Shah's heir, Tutush, granting even further power and land rights to the former slave. Tutush died in 1095, leaving Yaghi Siyan as the emir of Antioch and its surrounding territories.

Yaghi Siyan, interestingly, was mostly renowned for his unusual appearance. Possessing an "abnormal head of enormous proportions" accompanied by wide and hairy ears, his long, snow-white hair was but a shade from turning stark silver, and his hoary beard of similar thread flowed all the way to his navel. Many claimed he resembled not a man but a strange, plump, feline-like creature lounging on his cushioned throne, gazing forward with that curious confidence of the cat toying with the wounded mouse. Nonetheless, Siyan's destitute past and tortuous ascent to success had colluded to keep him humble and judicious. He had survived and surmounted many tribulations, but only through uncommon guile, intelligence, and perception; qualities others often failed to recognize because of his bizarre visage.

As with many enduring a particular foible, his mien cast him into an isolated lot early on, marking him as "peculiar." This isolation profoundly affected his emotional development, forcing him to question himself and deeply question and weigh the motives, judgments, and reactions of others. More significantly, it drove him to seek comfort in a netherworld of his own devise, a place where fables, dreams, theatre, and the "improbable" served as a salve to assuage his discomfort with reality. Fantasia, therefore, anchored him because he assessed real life to be a scaffold of sorts, and perceived fellow men as willing executioners. Serving as the ruling emir of Antioch, he viewed his own existence as an improbable tale, a living refutation of reality.

In the face of reports of a great foreign army advancing toward his city, Siyan dismissed panic and impending doom, holding court as usual, refusing to emote alarm in the midst of rising fears flooding the streets of Antioch. Sitting there nestled on his lush, exquisite pillows, his throne appeared to be an ornately gilded nest, not a seat of authority. Positioned in a casual recline rather than sitting erect, he called on those seeking audience; greeting visitors, signing proclamations, and dispensing justice each morning of the week.

The palace nobility of Antioch had grown accustomed to the meticulously choreographed but curious entourage surrounding Yaghi Siyan as he held court, but visitors often grew confused, if not startled, by the oddity of it all. Adjacent to Yaghi Siyan's throne-chair sat a tiny man from a land far away; a slave whose face and body were heavily painted various tints of blue. It seems the slave had been painted as he stood on the auction block the year before when Yaghi Siyan happened across him. Amused, captivated by the man's diminutive stature, unusual appearance, and high-pitched elfin voice, Yaghi Siyan purchased him on the spot, insisting that he remain painted from that day forward.

On that first day, unable to properly pronounce the full western name of his new acquisition, Siyan dubbed him with the shortened version of 'Ben', adding 'fazi' to the end, which translated as 'opening.' Siyan felt that the tiny man's appearance opened people's eyes to the realm of other possibilities. Two days later, to further embellish this effect, Siyan ordered that the little man be clothed in a costume of unfamiliar fashion but of Yaghi Siyan's own design, causing one to assume the slave had been relegated to the role of jester or another such position of amusement.

Yet, there was no humor in the little man's eyes as he sat ensconced in court each day next to Yaghi Siyan. As the emir held morning court, it was not uncommon for him to lean over to the "blue man," exchange whispers, then nod, declaring, "Ay, Ben-fazi, I think you may be correct!"

Evidently, clownish as the slave appeared and poor as his mastery of the Turkish tongue was, he had earned his way into carrying sway.

On the opposite side of Yaghi Siyan's throne seated on the floor, a huddle of young boys aged eight to ten was assembled. Wearing elegant slippers and ballooning trousers of exquisite fabric, denoting nobility, they were shirtless and wore no head-cover, contrary to Muslim aristocracy and courtly expectation. The incongruence of their dress was exacerbated by their immediate proximity to the emir. Whereas high court officials were nowhere to be seen within range of the throne-chair, these boys had been given a location of privilege. This, of course, further fueled rumors that Yaghi Siyan possessed a penchant for young boys, yet no such thing had ever actually been confirmed. Further puzzling, this pack of boys was easily distracted amongst themselves, but their occasional flare-ups seemed not to perturb Yaghi Siyan as it did others. Ignoring their disturbances, he sustained business as if they were not even present.

To the back of these boys stood eighteen young women from Yaghi Siyan's brimming harem. Heavily clothed and veiled, the sensuality of their large almond eyes and heavy brows was irresistible, as was the mystery emanating from behind their veils. Standing there, motionless as marble statues, in contrast to the boys at their feet, these perfectly proportioned young maidens embodied the delicate precision of a master sculptor's finely chiseled masterpieces. If not for a rare blink from time to time, it was difficult to tell whether the women were real or statues.

Just beyond their position on the floor, seated in the same fashion as the boys, sat a cluster of old men, all of whom appeared to be beggars. Quietly listening to visitors approaching Yaghi Siyan's throne, bowing, and stating their purpose, these men would at times put their heads together in quiet counsel, assessing the merits of what had just been said, proposed, or requested. On occasion, the eldest of these beggars would stand, advance to Yaghi Siyan's throne, kneel, and exchange whispers with the emir. When done, the old beggar would place his forehead to the floor at Yaghi Siyan's feet, stand, and return briskly to his place amongst his fellow beggars.

Visitors new to court gazed about blankly, astonished by such lack of convention surrounding the throne of a powerful emir. The vignette confronting them seemed surreal in a sense, yet all within the Antioch court behaved as though nothing was out of place, heightening the illusory feel of things. The pretension of courtly Antiochians that nothing was amiss forced newcomers to, in turn, mask their curiosity, joining in on the apparent charade for fear of creating offense.

The first individual summoned before the throne that morning was the city commandant of Antioch, General Ahmet. Face flushed, he could not suppress the urgency that had been pulling at him for days. "Master Siyan," he said, "the first of the foreigners have already approached and the full force is expected to arrive within the week. Their advance contingents are already pitching perimeters at various points before our walls. Our military garrison here is well-numbered at 5,000, but our scouts estimate over 100,000 within the foreign army's ranks!"

"We don't know their intentions, Ahmet," said Yaghi Siyan, looking over at the tiny man to his right already nodding in agreement with the emir, "yet you behave as if they intend to besiege us. Besides, 100,000 men or not, they can't all be men-at-arms, surely."

"No, Master," replied Ahmet. "Perhaps a third are knights and footmen, the others labor in support roles. Nonetheless, we're woefully undermanned before such huge numbers!"

At this, the tiny man whispered something to Yaghi Siyan.

Looking at General Ahmet, Siyan said, "Ben-fazi asks if they have siege equipment, towers, ballistas?"

"No, our scouts report no heavy machinery, but their advance parties are downing trees already. We suspect their army may have battalions of engineers and craftsmen, along with sappers."

"General," nodded Siyan, "despite the enormous size of this foreign army and vague, unconfirmed reports of its defeat of Kilij Arslan in Asia Minor, we command a well-fortified, well-armed, impregnable fortress. Then, too, please know that I've taken precautionary measures. I've already dispatched my sons Shams ad-Daulah and Muhammad on diplomatic missions to, if necessary, seek military assistance from Duqaq in Damascus and Ridwan in Aleppo. Should that not work, then Shams ad-Daulah shall make his way to Mesopotamia to seek help from the great Kerbogha, atabeg of Mosul, a leader mightier than Duqaq, Ridwan, and ourselves combined."

The very mention of Kerbogha of Mosul prompted the huddle of boys to break into chatter, accompanied by a busy exchange from the beggar-men. The young women remained motionless save their eyes, which took on new light, as did the eyes of painted Ben-fazi.

"You spread needless alarm, General," Siyan admonished, stroking his long white beard with deliberation, his eyes narrowing.

Ahmet felt the chastisement. "Yes, Master, I understand!" he lied, snapping to attention. But within, Ahmet was beginning to simmer. He knew the two demented brothers from Aleppo and Damascus despised each other to the bone, being heavily engaged in a deadly duel over control of Syria. The eldest, twenty-year-old Ridwan of Aleppo, had already had two of his younger brothers strangled to death by the Order of the Assassins, and Duqaq of Damascus had barely escaped the same fate by a hair on the night Ridwan's assassins had come looking for him. And even with Duqaq's alliance with Antioch, he was not dependable and reputably flighty.

Worse, Ridwan of Aleppo had openly expressed designs of taking over Antioch despite his marriage, just years earlier, to Yaghi Siyan's own daughter. Siyan had offered her up to avert war, but most Antiochians suspected it was just a matter of time before that ploy collapsed in the face of Ridwan's insatiable greed.

No, thought General Ahmet, neither Ridwan nor Duqaq could be counted on for help. The only prayer would be Kerbogha of Mosul, but he was a long, long distance away in Mesopotamia, and seemed little interested in Syrian affairs.

Spotting General Ahmet's diffidence, Siyan said, "As you know, Ahmet, the bulk of our population here in Antioch is Christian, not Muslim. To calm your fears, tomorrow I shall allow you to expel those Greek and Armenian Orthodox Christians with a history of raising disturbances, and you may also begin keeping a closer eye to the rest, but without getting too heavy-handed, mind you. As you know, we've had to provide refuge for our Artah garrison because Artah's Armenian revolt was instigated by the very approach of this foreign Christian army. Armenians are a different race than us, Ahmet. With a Western army approaching our gates, some of them might incline toward a return to Christian rule."

Siyan's orders placated Ahmet minimally, yet he feared sedition among many Antiochian Christians. Therefore, it forced a question. "And what of the Syrian Orthodox Christians, Master?"

"Yes, Christian, but Syrian," said Siyan, "not Western like the Greeks, Armenians, or the approaching army. Being dark by birth, race alone shall keep Syrian Christians in our corner. They've no interest in a return to Byzantine rule, nor rule by anyone else of a white race. They'll remain true to us, Ahmet, as will our Muslim population. Blood clings to blood of its own kind, Ahmet, as history has shown. Race is the great divider of the world, and the great unifier amongst those of the same color."

As Siyan finished, Ben-fazi leaned into his ear, pointing at the general. Unable to read Ben-fazi's expression through his face paint, Ahmet guessed Ben-fazi was undermining him; the two men had disliked each other immensely since laying eyes on one another. When mysterious Ben-fazi had appeared a year earlier, Ahmet had ridiculed the little man's appearance and odd voice, never suspecting the newcomer would end up earning Yaghi Siyan's affection and trust, becoming a valued pet of sorts.

Issuing Ahmet a cold look, Siyan pulled at his beard, his lips riffling as if engaged in self-conversation. "Ben-fazi believes you fail to recognize this foreign army is engaged in a holy war," he said. "Yes, a Christian jihad against the Islamic takeover of Jerusalem, which is to them, as to us, a cradle of their faith. They view themselves as holy warriors intent on recapturing Jerusalem for Christianity, so says Ben-fazi. Therefore, it's quite possible they have little intention of molesting Antioch. They could simply have come here to negotiate safe passage south, something I would gladly grant since the Seljuk tribes of the Levant are my enemies. Little would I care should they lose Jerusalem."

"But Master," reasoned Ahmet, bowing but holding his ground, "jihad is a word thrown about recklessly by warring Sunni and Shia factions effusing bad blood or staking territory. And Jerusalem has been in Muslim hands for four centuries, going back to our enemies of the Fatimid Caliphate of Arabia and Egypt. What would suddenly incite these Christians to invade after all this time? Not jihad, Master, but plunder and land, just like Ridwan of Aleppo, or Kilij Arslan, or the Byzantines. A holy war, says Ben-fazi? Ha! And how would he know such a thing?"

"Ben-fazi is from the West, Ahmet," replied Siyan, "and he's heard the preaching there. But he's since converted to Islam and is now faithful to Antioch, and to me. But he understands the roots of this unexpected invasion better than we do. It makes little sense to us, but it is what it is, in the eyes of the foreigners at least."

Ahmet sighed, resignation filling his face. He wished to strangle the blue man but instead bowed with deference.

"Be on your way then, Ahmet," said Siyan, flagging the back of his hand at the commandant, "unless you have anything else for my attention?"

"There is one other matter," said Ahmet. "Late last night, a large troop of ghazis maneuvered the approach up Mount Silpius and appeared at our rear gate."

"The Iron Gate?" asked Siyan, surprised.

"Yes, Master. An odd mix of Persians, Turks, and Arabs led by a huge fellow who thought much of himself. He demanded we open the gate immediately and allow his ghazis entry."

"Demanded? Oh? And what was your reply?"

"Because you were asleep, and I had no wish to disturb you, I refused. I told him to have his men sleep on the rocks until morning. Besides, with the rash of Seljuk infighting and feuding gripping the region, I didn't trust the unannounced arrival of such a sizeable force, no matter the claims of seeking refuge from the Western army advancing our direction."

"Ah, well done, Ahmet. But then, did you get their leader's name?"

"After blathering much profanity, the man identified himself as a Persian named Mahmoud Malik. But such an ass, acting like he owned the place!"

Rubbing his beard, Siyan dropped into reflection. "I do believe I've heard the name, actually," he said, brows drawing down. "Go back to the Iron Gate, Ahmet, and tell him that he and his men shall sleep yet another night among the rocks, and another, until he discovers the art of courtesy."

"Yes, Master!" replied Ahmet, pleased for the first time all morning. Bowing in reverence, he left the court, accompanied by his detail.

Looking at Ben-fazi, a tiny flicker issued from Siyan's eye as he said, "Maybe the rocks will teach this rude visitor some manners, eh? I despise men of such grain, as I'm certain you do also."

Ben-fazi shrugged, offering little sign of agreement. Rather, even through the paint, a shadow arrived, darkening his expression.

"What is it?" asked Siyan.

"Nothing, Master Yaghi," lied Ben-fazi, his tone betraying a trace of dread. He, in fact, was well acquainted with the name Mahmoud Malik, and the profound evil of him. "Please," he added, "continue with the many important affairs awaiting you this morning."

CHAPTER TWO

THE CHILDREN OF FIRUZ

When court concluded, the palace hall was cleared of visitors, court officials, and other attendees, including the huddle of boys and beggars, along with the eighteen young women of the emir's harem. Only Yaghi Siyan, Ben-fazi, and a squad of guards remained.

"Bring in the children," ordered Siyan, gesturing to the guard captain.

A boy of ten and his sister, twelve, were ushered into the hall, followed by their father. As they advanced, Yaghi Siyan's eyes brightened a fraction with each footstep taken forward by the two children. "Firuz and his children!" declared the captain, pushing the boy and girl toward the throne, planting them just inches from Yaghi Siyan.

Their father stepped behind them but Siyan frowned. "Ho there," he motioned, "no need for you to come any further, Firuz."

"Yes, Emir Siyan," bowed Firuz, backing away. "I didn't mean to offend."

The boy was afraid, eyes darting downward with furtive glances, unwilling to focus on the emir. One foot awkwardly positioned atop the other, his face was pink with color and the fingers of one hand clung tightly to the grasp of his sister. He was breathing hard, which brought a smile from Yaghi Siyan, but that failed to set the boy at ease.

"There, there, young Garik," cooed Yaghi Siyan, reaching out gently to rumple the boy's dark spill of curly hair, "nothing to be afraid of from old Yaghi here. I'll always be careful with one as fragile as you."

This did little to calm the boy. Trembling, he glanced at his sister, seeking comfort, but found none. Her eyes were anchored on those of Yaghi Siyan, studying him, unsmiling and unafraid. Their steady bead announced that intangibility of youthful but knowing awareness undeterred by authority or age. "Good morning, Master Yaghi," she offered, her voice lacking expression.

"Ah, aha, my sweet blossom, Karine!" chortled Siyan, his eyes glimmering in amusement at the familiarity of her salutation. While others referred to him as 'Master Siyan,' he liked to think that her greeting of 'Master Yaghi' was driven by affection, though any such sentiment was voided by her frigid expression. Still, the lilt of the girl's voice, an ungiving, neutral tone, pleased him for some reason. The only other person allowed to address him as Master Yaghi was Ben-fazi, who now sat erect as a shaft of wheat. Having lost all air of previous perturbation, he was eyeing the children with curiosity.

The children had first been brought to court three weeks earlier. Siyan had come across them incidentally as he toured the Antioch market. Struck by their appearance, he made inquiries about them and learned they were the offspring of his preferred armor maker, an Armenian named Firuz. Firuz had been prosperous as Antioch's premier armorer before the recent Turkish takeover, and was a highly regarded figure within the large Armenian community of the city. As time passed, Yaghi Siyan came to depend on Firuz's iron-working skills and soon became the man's most profitable patron.

Firuz enjoyed another unexpected advancement when Siyan, in a thinly disguised attempt to boost his own influence within the Armenian community, appointed Firuz as Captain of the Guard over the Tower of the Twin Sisters, one of more than 400 towers lining the ramparts of Antioch. This was unusual in that Firuz was the first Armenian appointed to a trusted post beneath the boot of Seljuk rule over Antioch. Siyan's single requirement was that Firuz convert to Islam. A good number of Armenians had already converted from Christianity over the past twelve years, especially of late, but more likely for purposes of trade and stature than purposes of actual faith.

Siyan's insistence to convert had caused Firuz distress since he was actually a devout Greek Orthodox Christian. However, after much soul searching, the nagging of his ambitious Armenian wife overcame Firuz's own objections and he accepted Siyan's proposal. Notwithstanding, there remained within his proud Armenian heart a murky backwater of shame and regret. But no matter how many doors Yaghi Siyan opened for him, Firuz refused to view him and the Turks as nothing more than foreign occupiers.

On discovering Firuz's children in the marketplace, Siyan had them summoned to court a half dozen times for short visits. The lone parties privy to these surreptitious visits were Ben-fazi and a small retinue of palace guards. Their father merely presented the children, then was surreptitiously dismissed.

To Ben-fazi, by now rather familiar with Yaghi Siyan's foibles and eccentricities, the two children had struck a peculiar chord within the old man's heart, much like Ben-fazi had after being spotted painted blue on the auction block. Simply put, Ben-fazi's tiny stature and elfin voice had pricked Yaghi Siyan's imagination, a place where the 'unusual' flourished.

It appeared these children had done the same.

CHAPTER THREE

THE PERSIAN

As court assembled the following morning, the first man presented was accompanied to the throne by General Ahmet. "Emir Siyan," said the commandant, delivering a crisp salute, "Mahmoud Malik, Persian general from Asia Minor and the Sultanate of Rüm."

Even as the Persian advanced, a pall fell over the court. Larger in girth and height than most had ever witnessed, his over-sized skull was meticulously shaved to the scalp, and oiled, fairly gleaming in the light. Onlookers could not help but notice that his thick, muscled neck flesh melded into equally muscled shoulder flesh; his naturally dark skin, further deepened by the desert sun, especially his face and neck, evidenced horrendous war scars. Most striking was his gait; exaggerated and overly imposing for a stranger in a distant court. In a word—frightening.

"Emir," the man said, not bowing but nodding, "I am Mahmoud Malik, warlord, recently arrived here to Antioch. I've brought a force of 700 ghazis of Persian, Seljuk, and Syrian mix, my private army. I've recently been engaged in skirmishes to the north with these invading forces surrounding your gates. As things now stand, and in your own favor, I offer you my services."

"Hmmm . . . Mahmoud Malik . . ." said Siyan, his brows knitting with reflection. "I've heard talk of a mercenary to the far north by that name. Have you not spent time in service to Sultan Kilij Arslan of Nicaea?"

"Yes," Malik stated gruffly, "at his whim and whenever peril threatened his borders."

Cupping his chin, Siyan's fingers disappeared one by one into his hoary bush of a beard. "I've heard the name elsewhere as well. Might you be the same man known as the 'Butcher of Medina'?"

Malik offered no change of expression. "I've been called that," he said. "I was commissioned by the caliphs of Medina in the past to quell a Shia uprising plaguing their domain."

Siyan's eyes dropped, displeased. "It's said that after decapitating several thousand rebels and mounting their heads on lances along the avenues of Medina, you then sought out their women and children, and did the same."

"I was hired to settle an issue, and that's what I did. There had been a string of earlier uprisings also. I merely settled things for good."

"Allah blesses women and children," scowled Siyan, shaking his head.

"Ah, but Allah has also, since my birth, directed me. As such, he has guided my sword as well. Who are we, you and I, to question Allah?"

"If you take comfort in such belief for the benefit of sleeping at night, then so be it. But tell, how is it you've ended up here in Antioch?"

"I was in flight from an enemy of Syrian Seljuks, Lord Abdul Azim, to the north, whose family once ruled much of these lands many years ago."

"Abdul Azim?" echoed Siyan, his thoughts reverting in time. "Ah, yes. His father was among the first Seljuks to enter Syria and claim land here, but his realm was overrun by the clan of Tutush, my former master. As I recall, Abdul was but a boy at the time, barely escaping the massacre of his entire bloodline."

"That's true. As you know then, the boy grew into a man and has never forgotten those days. His hatred for anyone connected to Tutush runs deep, which would subsequently include yourself, Emir Siyan."

"Probably," acknowledged Siyan, "but what's his business with you?"

"Not long ago, I raided his sultanate east of Anatolia and was on my way back to the Sultanate of Rüm. During my retreat, I learned of Kilij Arslan's defeats at Nicaea and Dorylaeum by this same Christian force arriving here in Antioch. You've heard, have you not, that the entirety of Asia Minor has been lost and that Kilij Arslan remains in hiding?"

"We've heard rumors of such. Do you confirm it?"

"Verily. And because of that unexpected turn, my flight from Abdul Azim was forced south. Encountering the invaders as they turned south for Antioch, I battled my way here. I learned from Syrian shepherds along the way about the back path up Mount Staurin to the city's rear gate." Turning, he gave General Ahmet an evil, penetrating stare. "But this damned fellow beside me refused entry, forcing us to sleep on the rocks!" Refocusing on Siyan, he continued, "Now, to your own good fortune, as I said before, I offer you my services."

"Your services?" asked Siyan, his brows drawing down until his eyes appeared shut. "For a price, no?"

"Certainly, but to our mutual benefit." Malik's expression lightened then, and he nearly smiled. "You're not in a favorable position at the moment, Emir. Of course, should you refuse, I'll be on my way."

"On your way?" chortled Siyan, tugging at his beard thoughtfully, taking on that renown expression of the cat lying on its side, lazily toying with a subdued victim. "And just where would that be, General Malik? Your protector, Kilij Arslan, is lost, your path back north is blocked by a foreign army, and because you've plundered Abdul Azim's sultanate, he now stands in your path. Ha! I dare say he'll stop at nothing to see your head separated from those shoulders!"

Unperturbed, Malik stated calmly, "You are far from alone in the face of this threat. Ridwan of Aleppo and Duqaq of Damascus could easily become targets of this Christian invasion. Should you not be interested in my services, I'll simply seek work beneath their banners."

Siyan's lips peeled back into a grin, undetectable beneath the snowy cover of his beard. Glancing at Ben-fazi, catching his eye, he straightened and again faced the Persian. "No, Malik, it seems you are in a bit of a snare, especially since you've already engaged these crusaders—who'll recognize your black banners—and you'll not be able to break out for Aleppo, although it's only three days march from here, and Damascus is even further than that." Here, he crossed his arms and reclined his head back on his pillows, to stare at the palace ceiling, yawning with lost interest. There was a long pause in which everyone held their breath. "But I shall, in honor of Allah's generosity alone, award you temporary refuge here behind my walls . . ." Slowly bringing up his head, his eyes targeted Malik's, and he raised one boney forefinger, saying, "On one condition: that should it become necessary, you will fight for Antioch."

"Should it become necessary!?" shouted Malik, derision washing into his tone as he pivoted full circle, looking at those in court as if the emir had gone daft. "Why do you suppose they've amassed here at Antioch?" he fumed. "Do you not smell invasion though it burns your own nostrils? Ha! Rather than offer me fair compensation to help defend your walls, you ask me to fight for nothing? Oh, but life is too precious a commodity to flitter away in such imbalanced bargains, I say!"

"Say what you wish," sniffed Siyan, pointing to Ben-fazi. "My counselor and I have reached into the basket and pulled from it three possibilities. Granted, invasion is one of them. But respite is another. Antioch is the last large city before Jerusalem, which is, according to Ben-fazi, the ultimate target of these crusaders. They may simply be seeking markets and supplies before their push south. And the third possibility, they may be seeking to negotiate passage, as do many armies passing through new territory to a final destination."

His face contracting with incredulity, Malik laughed aloud, his tone seeping mockery, which settled ill with the old emir. "Ha! They're here to attack you, Siyan! Just as at Nicaea and all along the path through Asia Minor, Anatolia, and Armenia!" His face knotting scorn, he shook his head, pointing to Ben-fazi. "I've no idea who this little blue pigeon sitting there next to you might be, yet you claim him as your, your counselor?" Pointing at the boys, the pack of old men, and the row of silent maidens, he ranted on, "And whatever in the name of Allah is all this absurdity surrounding me? Have I landed in a damned mad-house!?"

At this, General Ahmet advanced, his face coloring. "Watch your words, imbecile!" he hissed, motioning to the guards. Considering his private fears about future siege, part of him knew the Persian's additional troops could prove valuable in the end. His voice lowered to a whisper. "The old cat, despite his appearance, has claws, damn you. He could have you gutted before you blinked. Hold that tongue of yours!"

Having reached the limits of his patience, Yaghi Siyan waved off the guards. Sitting rigid for the first time, his expression evolved from anger into that dubious, antithetical smile of the jackal. "Mah-moud Ma-lik," he purred, elongating each syllable as his jaw tightened, "do you wish to walk from this court in one piece?"

Aware that he was caught standing at the edge of a crumbling precipice, Malik backed a step and bowed. "My pardon," he said with strained humility, "I was merely trying to warn you about what's soon to unfold, Emir Siyan, and I delivered it poorly, apparently. But heed my words, you're in danger. The serpent is gathering his train to coil, then to strike."

Satisfied by Malik's slide into deference, such as it was, Siyan's eyes bored in on him. "Two things then . . ." he said coldly. "First, you shall apologize to Ben-fazi, then you shall vow to fight for Antioch should the necessity arise. Should you refuse, your head shall be plated, your arms and legs shall be parted from your trunk, and your remains shall be fed to my cats within the half hour. And by cats, I refer not to house cats, but my private collection of panthers, lions, tigers, and other exotic felines of which I am quite fond."

Seeing no room to barter, Malik bit his lip, nodding in agreement. "To the blue man," he scowled, "I ask your pardon." He then went silent.

"And?" insisted Siyan.

"And yes," assented Malik, biting back bitterness in favor of a false smile, "I vow to fight for Antioch."

"Very well then," replied Siyan, motioning to General Ahmet. "Ahmet, garrison Malik's ghazis and familiarize him with our defenses." With a flap of his hand, Siyan dismissed the Persian. The thug had accomplished little during his visit but earn the full contempt of Yaghi Siyan, who had struggled against men of such vein his entire existence, and loathed them.

As Malik stalked away, Yaghi Siyan motioned to his guards to have the next visitor approach. But had he taken a closer look at Ben-fazi, he would have seen that beneath the cover of his paint, the little man's face was turning ashen as Mahmoud Malik stepped to the throne; his heart began thumping against the walls of his chest and tiny tremors seized the tips of his fingers as his thoughts reeled back in time . . . to the day the big Persian nearly took his life.

It's him, but he failed to recognize me because of the paint, thought Ben-fazi, shivering to the bone. His eyes locked on Malik as he strutted to the back of the crowd, taking position there, crossing his arms. Like the trapped fly awaiting its fate, staring at the motionless spider beyond, Ben-fazi sat statue-like, his conscience reknitting the moment of his enslavement and conversion to Islam. He had kissed the Koran that day and cried, "Allah!" for the sole purpose of saving his own skin while others about him were being butchered. The ploy worked with witnessing Muslim clerics, even though Malik insisted the little man be killed. Later, fortune snatched him from the scabrous grasp of Mahmoud Malik into the softer palms of Yaghi Siyan.

Yet, in his heart, Ben-fazi felt all of this had been directed, in truth, not by Allah but by his own Christian God.

CHAPTER FOUR

THE CRUSADER ADVANCE

At the very start of the campaign, the Battle of Nicaea against Kilij Arslan, the Holy Crusade would have suffered a resounding defeat if not for the last-minute arrival of Raymond of Toulouse and other Frankish forces that had been dallying too long in Constantinople's court of Emperor Alexius Comnenus. Then yet again, after splitting forces to facilitate foraging and feeding of their vast army, the crusaders narrowly escaped a similar repeat of that first disaster at Dorylaeum, again at the hands of Kilij Arslan. As at Nicaea, none other than a miraculous arrival by the trailing half of the Christian army had averted certain decimation of the advanced half.

Next, the crusaders struggled their way through Anatolia, suffering the effects of Kilij Arslan's scorched-earth retreat of burning crops, killing livestock, and poisoning wells. After a month of barely surviving drought, starvation, and the loss of men, horses, and beasts of burden, the Christian army straggled into Pisidia. There, along the western fringes of Armenian Cilicia, the Latins finally found rest, markets, and recovery. Departing Pisidia, the expedition became far less difficult as it moved through Armenia, coalescing alliances with Christian Armenians and defeating lesser Turkish garrisons along the march.

In sum, the Army of God had now three times narrowly escaped meeting their own end but by the grace of God and good fortune. Having endured all that, approaching Antioch, they were rested and ready for the final trek toward Jerusalem. However, several circumstances had changed since initially departing Constantinople, and these developments were about to impact the future of the Holy Crusade itself and change to a large degree its original direction and impetus.

To begin with, Baldwin of Boulogne, younger brother of Godfrey of Bouillon, had abandoned the crusade in favor of establishing his own kingdom in the County of Edessa. His ugly inclination for personal ambition had actually surfaced early in the crusade, eventually exposing his earlier pretensions of altruism.

Following him, Tancred of Hauteville, Bohemud's nephew, had, to a similar degree, shared Baldwin's lust for nefarious enrichment. Remaining with the crusade, along the path through Armenia, he had laid claim to the city of Mamistra, leaving there a contingent of knights to secure it as 'his.'

These personal acquisitions by Baldwin and Tancred did little to hold together the early unity of the Holy Crusade. Rather, they managed to ignite greed among other crusader princes. Until this point, the Council of Princes had been turning over former Byzantine cities and territory to Taticius, the Byzantine general accompanying them, as instructed by Emperor Alexius and as adhered to by the oath of fealty and allegiance signed at the onset by the Christian princes. Through time and circumstance Raymond of Toulouse, Bohemud of Taranto, and Godfrey of Bouillon grew weary of battling the Turks only to relinquish city after captured city to Taticius and the Byzantine Empire.

Of further significance was the fact these three primary princes felt that Emperor Alexius had contributed little to the war in terms of manpower and military support. Yes, he had awarded lavish gifts upon their arrival to Constantinople to encourage their signing of an oath of fealty and provided substantial subsidies at Nicaea to support the cost of troops and bivouac, on top of promising to send a large Byzantine force to reinforce the crusaders when they reached Antioch. But in truth, he had remained detached, allowing one crusader expectation after another to languish. Other than the small Byzantine contingent led by Taticius, whose main function was to accept captured cities formerly belonging to Byzantium, the crusaders had prosecuted the war entirely on their own. Subsequently, the growing disaffection toward Emperor Alexius by Raymond, Bohemud, and Godfrey festered and began to infect the entire crusade, even with the march nearing its end and Jerusalem now seemingly within their grasp.

This is not to say the entire crusader leadership shared these same resentments or schemes. Many continued to fight exclusively for Pope Urban's cause, the halt of Islamic aggression, and the banner of Christianity. In truth, the makeup of the overall crusader force was extremely eclectic. Significantly, the vast majority of men-at-arms and support personnel had neither designs nor even possibilities of gaining individual kingdoms. Most, in particular the footmen and support personnel, were scarcely earning enough to subsist. The archers, engineers, sappers, and other specialists fared better, but barely. In turn, the knights and minor nobles enjoyed better accommodations and compensation but were fighting out of fealty and obligation to overlords. They stood to gain little but glory, scraps of plunder, and as with others, the Pope's promise of heavenly reward. Knowing this, as the vast Christian army neared Antioch, motivations and intentions were, if nothing else, disparate. Of further note, no decision had actually been agreed to by Bishop Adhémar and the Council of Princes as concerned the actual disposition of Antioch.

Early disorganization and feuding plagued the onset of the crusade, yet the Christian advance on Antioch was well devised, characterized by strategic foresight and well-ordered execution. Nearing the city, the crusaders seized satellite defenses to both the north and the south. Raymond of Toulouse sent Peter of Roaix to control the Ruj Valley, one of two southern approaches to Antioch. Then rather than taking a direct southern route from Baghrās, the crusaders opted to veer east around the Lake of Antioch, securing the fertile plains north-east of the city. And finally, Robert of Flanders, with 1,000 crusaders, was sent to capture Artah, twenty-two kilometers from Antioch at the intersection of ancient Roman roads from Marash, Edessa, and Aleppo. Artah, being the region's most critical Seljuk fortress, was actually known as the 'Shield of Antioch.' Robert of Flanders had expected a pitched battle there, but his approach alone was enough to ignite an Armenian revolt against the Turkish garrison occupying Artah, spurring them to quickly abandoned the fortress and take flight to Antioch.

Making their final advance, the crusaders had to ford the Orontes River, dividing the region north to south. This solitary crossing lay twelve kilometers north of Antioch at a place known as the Iron Bridge, guarded by twin fortresses but defended by a sparse force of 700 Turks. On October 19th, Robert of Normandy led 2,000 troops against the Iron Bridge, overwhelming its defenders and opening the road to Antioch. Holding position, he waited on the eastern bank for the other elements of the crusader army to arrive.

Leading the advance guard and marching one day ahead of the main army, Bohemud was the first to cross the Iron Bridge with troops. Hailing from Italy, as did Bohemud's Italian-Normans, Guillaume de Saint-Germain's Tuscan force had recently joined Bohemud's camp. As things happened, and despite Guillaume's fractious relationship with Bohemud's nephew, Tancred, Guillaume and Bohemud had themselves struck up a firm bond.

While crossing the Iron Bridge, the crusaders heard a commotion arising from the opposite bank. Gaining the other side, they came onto a weathered old man shaking his fist and howling as they passed. Bent horribly at the waist from age, bare of foot, hairless and toothless, he was naked except for sack-cloth loosely knotted about his waist in such a manner that his testicles became exposed from time to time as he moved. Possessing that glazed stare common to the recently bereaved, and scrabbling about with motions of the deranged, he was wailing in Armenian, "Aiee! Go back from whence you came, you poor bastards!" His eyes frogging, pulsing with tiny red rivers streaming up and down the length of their sockets, he ranted, "Do you not smell that rotting stench of death ahead!?" Yowling like an injured cat, turning first one way, then another, he then began pointing out particular knights destined for doom. "You there! Why hasten your own end!?"

"Fool," grunted Bohemud.

"Aye," agreed Guillaume. "He has long ago joined the world of the mad, I suppose. When I was a boy at Cluny, there was a woman that frequented the monastery gates, haranguing all intent on entering, just as this fellow seems to be doing. We called her the "white witch," and this poor old codger brings her to mind."

Riding behind them, the Danes caught sight of the old spastic. Nearing him, Orla and Crowbones reined their horses away from the old wag, as not wishing to be near him.

"Strange that such a man would be waiting here, harping like a bickering crow trying to ward us off," said Orla.

"Ja," nodded Crowbones, a hint of shadow slipping over his face as his eyes followed the man. "Funny thing, Orla," he added, "that you should say such a thing, in those exact terms, I mean."

"Huh? About the man?"

"No. About a 'bickering crow.' Remember the Battle of Hastings? Just before the charge, we spotted crows quarreling in the trees ahead and I told you their bickering was a bad omen."

"Ja, I remember, but you were mistaken, Ivar. We won that day against the Saxons."

"Perhaps, but Loki's ass, Orla. We lost half the Danish Guard to Saxon axes that bloody day. Then ten years later, right before the wolf hunt in DuLacshire, we spotted crows bickering again in the oaks just below the castle. And that's when the Gamekeeper's Revolt broke out and I lost my arm." His expression then waned further. "And now you mention the bickering of a crow, ten years later again, too. Odd, that, huh?"

"Perhaps," said Orla dismissively, "but this howling banshee in our path is no crow. He's but an old fool cast away by others, left to wander the roads and pass time agitating those happening by."

"Maybe, but he could be an ill omen."

Listening to this exchange, Orla's son, Hroc, spoke up, "You're both Christians, Uncle Crowbones. You took the water when we were spared at the last minute from the massacre at Nicodemia a year ago and promised to set aside pagan superstitions that same day. As Father says, the old man's no omen. Simply a madman appearing by chance."

"J-ja," scolded Guthroth the Quiet, who had been listening intently. "you're Chr-Christian, Crowbones. The old be-liefs are d-dead!"

"Oh? But look there then, at Boy!" snapped Crowbones, calling Tristan by his childhood moniker. "Why is he, a high bishop, making the sign of the cross as we pass the old man?"

"Ha," replied Tristan, amused, "certainly not to ward off omens sent by Nordic sorcerers, Crowbones! No, simply to pass along a blessing to one of God's less fortunate souls, at least here in this life. From the looks of it, fate has dealt this unfortunate fellow a cruel hand. I merely pity him and ask God to remember him in His generosity."

As Tristan talked, the old man caught sight of the stub of Crowbones' severed left arm. Doddering forward, he tucked a fist beneath his armpit, waggling his own arm as if severed. With outlandish mockery, he began to spin slowly about, mimicking a broken-winged bird, grounded, unable to move in a straight direction. "You've been bloodied once!" he gibbered. "Have you not lost enough? Keep fighting, you fool, and you'll lose that other arm! Ha! Then what'll you do?"

Having no understanding of Armenian, the old man's disrespectful gestures aimed at his brother infuriated Orla. "Helves jeer!" he swore in Danish, spurring his horse into the man, knocking him to the ground. "God damn you! No one makes fun of my brother, Ivar Crowbones!"

Simultaneously, Crowbones involuntarily shuddered in his saddle, feeling the icy grip of a hereditary cold hand rising from nowhere, clutching his heart. In watching the old man's mimicry, it appeared as if ancient Nordic spirits had suddenly resurrected from a frozen, forgotten past, warning Crowbones that they had refused to die. "Hold there!" he cried, alarmed. "Leave him be, Orla! He's doing what the gods force him to, and they've only given him half a mind! Don't tempt fate!"

"But dammit!" Orla hollered in return, bridling his mount away from the old man as Crowbones instructed. "This old shit pile gives you offense, Ivar, and I'll not tolerate it!"

Looking at Guthroth the Quiet, Hroc whispered, "Uncle Crowbones, to this day, talks of pagan gods, but this is just a madman along the side of the road, not an omen."

Guthroth the Quiet only bowed his head. Having been baptized long before Hroc, Orla, and Crowbones, and having made an earnest effort to embrace Catholicism, he had dismissed his pagan past. Nonetheless, within the depths of his eye, there appeared a momentary speck of vacillation. "J-ja," he muttered, "it's b-but a m-madman."

CHAPTER FIVE

ARRIVAL

Coming within first view of Antioch, the bristling of crusader weapons and clank of armor fell mute. The colossal fortifications standing before them far surpassed anything imaginable.

Stunned, Stephen of Blois, later that evening, dispatched a letter to his wife, writing: "We found the city of Antioch very extensive, fortified with incredible strength and almost impregnable."

Another crusader recorded: "The city could never be captured if the inhabitants, supplied with bread, wished to defend it long enough."

Dismayed by what they encountered, having traveled thousands of kilometers and overcoming one obstacle after another, the Army of God realized Antioch was a formidable challenge.

But perception is a human foible, and as such, in regards to consensus, within sizeable groups, refuses to allow unanimity. The minds of men are too disconnected, one from another, to conjure an identical vision. Even when faced with the commonality of an impossibility, men diverge, taking different directions. Whereas some princes wavered, losing heart beneath this mammoth shadow of a monster rising from the desert floor, others saw no invulnerable fire-breathing dragon threatening extinction and annihilation but an inconceivable prize promising unimaginable rewards and riches, but only for those bold enough to stake their lives on seizing it. Embracing the latter of these two interpretations, such were the judgments of Raymond of Toulouse, Bohemud of Taranto, and Godfrey of Bouillon.

Raymond of Toulouse had embarked on the crusade infected by spiritual fever spurred by concerns brought on by age and conscience. Having advanced in years and enjoying himself of late as a "made man," possessing more wealth than even Philippe, King of France, he found himself struck by the need to "expiate his many past sins." This he had intimated to all, especially his lifelong friend, Bishop Adhémar of Le Puy. But now into a full year from departing France, having witnessed Baldwin of Boulogne's seizure of a kingdom in his name—Edessa—and Tancred's claim to Mamistra, the fire of possession in Raymond had rekindled and was aflame with old ambitions. As his eyes raked over the vastness of Antioch, former instincts of exploitation and acquisition that had driven him earlier began to resurface from the shards of slowly splintering spiritualism. Dammit, I shall have this jewel, he vowed privately.

Not far down the line, standing high in his stirrups, Bohemud stared at the city, his nephew, Tancred, at his side.

"God in Heaven," remarked Tancred, eyes wide with disbelief, "imagine the wealth held within those walls, Uncle. Your step-brother Roger Money-Bags stole from you the Norman kingdom of Southern Italy, but even that lost realm can't match what sits before us!"

"Aye, to be certain," muttered Bohemud, more to himself than in reply, old venom against the Byzantines from years gone by stirring deep within his belly. Having joined the crusade to assist the Byzantines, he had in earlier years battled against Emperor Alexius and the Greeks for decades, hoping to claim Constantinople as his own. But his failure in those bloody campaigns had been disastrous, even causing him to lose favor with his father, the fearsome Duke Robert Guiscard the Wily. In the end, Duke Guiscard disinherited Bohemud as successor to the Italian-Norman Empire over these defeats, even though Bohemud was his first-born son. In his place, Guiscard appointed Roger 'Money Bags' Borsa, son from a second marriage.

This had embittered Bohemud and, as retribution, he had hoped to hatch a conspiracy against the Byzantines during the combined crusader arrival to Constantinople for the Holy Crusade but failed to find other willing Catholic co-conspirators to join his plot. And yes, Alexius had bought him off with incredible awards of bribery in order to secure Bohemud's signature to an oath of fealty for the crusade. A futile endeavor to the emperor, he had since done nothing to advance the crusader effort.

So, eyeing the bounty of Antioch, Bohemud began calculating the worth of the fabled city looming in the distance. The treasury alone, not to mention the plunder, must surely exceed all comprehension!

Beyond Bohemud's position, Godfrey of Bouillon had dismounted and was thinking of his brother. Oh, Baldwin, damnation! If you were here to shore me up, he whistled aloud, then together we'd mount our banner atop those ramparts there and take claim of this fat, ripe bounty! But I am on my own now.

Further down the ranks, Bishop Tristan de Saint-Germain and his brother, Guillaume, sat mounted alongside the Danes, Lord Martin Letellier of Northern France, and Scule, the dwarf monk from Cluny. Seated behind Scule, sharing the saddle, sat nine-year-old Christos Laskaris, the orphaned boy Scule had collected from the road in Armenia.

"Christ alive! Can you believe such a fortress?!" exclaimed Letellier, awed by the massive fortifications staring back at him.

"Aye," nodded Guillaume quietly, his focus punishingly elsewhere; lost within memories, that parasitic realm that devours the insides of faith's most ardent and spiritual adherents. He was being disassembled from within by that hammer of religion. Guilt. As such, Guillaume presented a puzzle of sorts.

It had often been cited, by those close to Guillaume, that 'you, not Tristan, should have become the monk.' But unlike Tristan, as a child, Guillaume missed being indoctrinated by Asta and her troupe of teacher-nuns because he was but four years old when he and Tristan were sent to Cluny Monastery. Also, his upbringing among monks at Cluny did not appear to take hold as it had for Tristan. Rather, it took leaving Cluny and falling beneath the care of la Gran Contessa Mathilda of Tuscany that turned young Guillaume toward obsession with the Catholic faith, and absolute piety.

It was at this time that God began to direct Guillaume's existence, not as a priest or monk, but as God's consummate warrior defending Catholicism, Catholic dogma, and righteousness as seen by the Church. Guillaume even went so far as to embrace and honor the vows of celibacy and chastity, although there was no expectation of it by the Church or others.

But then appeared Queen Irene in Constantinople and Camp Pelekanum where, during a lapse of self-control, Guillaume fell into a carnal union of passion and sexual abandonment, as did she. Briefly, Guillaume lost his mind thinking even to finally understand "love." On departing Irene and Pelekanum, stark reality struck; the gravity of his sins began to call on him. Eternal damnation, he worried. How can God ever forgive my transgressions?

Bold as he was in battle, fearless as he was in the face of the enemy, there was but one idea now driving him forward: redemption, something to be earned, as avowed by Pope Urban II and the Church, through the penance of this crusade, even if it meant sacrificing himself.

"Shit!" swore Orla, awakening Guillaume from his thoughts. "After coming all this way, look yonder, dammit! We'll never break into that rock. What is there to do?"

"Ah, do not lose heart," affirmed Tristan.

"Heh?" snorted Crowbones, pointing the stub of his left arm toward Antioch. "Unless we wake up with wings on our backs one fine morning, we'll not in a thousand years get over those walls! I begin to think the old beggar on the bridge was not harping, dammit, but was warning us!"

"We may not have to get over the walls," said Tristan. "Guillaume and I have spoken a good deal with Taticius along this leg of the road, and he has suggested by-passing Antioch altogether, as was done once before when the Byzantines faced this same dilemma."

"What?" questioned Letellier. "But Antioch stands squarely in our path to Jerusalem. We dare not leave our rear flank exposed to the Turks."

"Ja," agreed Hroc, "only to be caught in a vice from north and south."

"J-ja, a v-vice," muttered Guthroth, his expression glum.

"There is much detail to it," replied Tristan, "but what Taticius proposes makes far more sense than siege."

Puzzled, the others looked to Guillaume for affirmation, but Guillaume's eyes were half-closed and his lips were moving as in self-conversation, or prayer.

Recognizing this, Tristan gestured to the others, pulling their attention from Guillaume. "I will explain after we set camp," he told them, nudging his brother across the shoulder before setting off at a canter. "Come along then, Guillaume," he whispered, "and leave your burdens to God."

CHAPTER SIX

THE CRUSADERS PITCH CAMP

In terms of defensive posture, Antioch was strategically located, capitalizing heavily on two defensive advantages provided by regional landscape. First, the city stood at the base of two craggy mountains, Mount Staurin and Mount Silpius, rendering attack from the east impossible. There were six gates total—three along the northern wall, and one on each of the south, east, and west sides—but only a single hidden entry on the entire eastern perimeter, the Iron Gate, and its narrow, mountainous path prohibited maneuverable deployment of large troop numbers, making it impossible to mass assault troops near the rear walls of Antioch. Secondly, the Orontes River hemmed in the city from the west, creating certain natural obstacles to attack.

Reinforcing these natural barriers, the entire city was enclosed within a massive defensive wall over nine kilometers in length, two meters thick, and ten meters in height, punctuated with 400 towers. Further fortifying the city, an imposing eastern citadel sat perched 500 meters up, constructed near the summit of Mount Silpius. As documented by Raymond of Aguilers, chaplain of Raymond of Toulouse: "This city extends two miles in length and is so protected with walls, towers and defenses that it may dread neither the attack of machine nor the assault of man even if all mankind gathered to besiege it."

Nevertheless, as the unified crusader force arrived, its tentacles began to spread, separating into national groups focusing on the northwestern quarter of Antioch. Being the first to arrive, Bohemud staked his camp before the first, most important, and probably most perilous gate: the Saint Paul Gate. He instructed Tancred and his troops to camp behind him in reserve, as he did Guillaume and his Tuscan Knights. This decision to plant himself before the Saint Paul Gate did not hinge on gallantry alone. Bohemud was thinking of quick access and first entry into the city; both of which would heavily determine the distribution of spoils and possible title to the city.

Moving counter-clockwise from Bohemud's northeastern position, the Northern Franks of Robert of Normandy, Robert of Flanders, Stephen of Blois, and Hugh of Vermandois pitched camp, but not before a gate. Rather, they situated themselves between the Saint Paul Gate and the next gate, the Dog Gate, claimed by Raymond of Toulouse, Adhémar of Le Puy, and the Southern Franks, known as Provençals. Neither the Northern Frankish princes nor Adhémar of Le Puy held intentions of claiming territory or cities. But Raymond of Toulouse, like Bohemud, had already set sights on acquiring

Antioch. Godfrey of Bouillon, possessing similar aims, camped his Germans before the third gate, the Gate of the Duke, while Taticius and his small Byzantine force were ordered to camp well behind the crusaders, presumably to serve as reserves, but in truth, to keep him at a distance.

This left the two southern gates, the Bridge Gate and the Saint George Gate, uncovered, as well as the inaccessible Iron Gate along the mountainous eastern perimeter. Antioch was simply too massive for complete encirclement, and attempting to block more gates would have spread the crusaders dangerously thin. As a means of countering this shortfall, the Council of Princes placed a thinly manned 'false camp' near the Bridge Gate and another near the Saint George Gate as a ploy, giving the impression of larger forces positioned there to guard the two southernmost gates.

Bohemud had arrived with the crusader vanguard on Tuesday, October 20th, followed by the arrival of the remainder of the army the next day. Most of the troops, not being privy to the Council of Princes, expected an immediate entry into battle and failed to realize that a final decision about Antioch had not yet been determined by the leadership.

In truth, there were actually several proposed strategies floating about the various camps, the first being 'direct assault.' On catching sight of the enormity of Antioch, and in light of the challenging geography, it became evident that direct assault would be far too perilous, if even possible at all.

The second strategy centered around 'attrition siege,' a form of medieval warfare that had become prevalent in Western Europe. It was a tedious, drawn-out process of warfare for both aggressor and defender hinging less on actual fighting than on grinding down enemy logistics, resources, and morale. For aggressors, the aim was to isolate the besieged city from outside supply and reinforcement in expectation of starvation, loss of will, or disease to eventually force capitulation. For defenders, the counter-tactic was to outlast the enemy, hoping they had weak lines of supply, or to wait for reinforcements, thereby trapping the attacking force between two defending armies.

Cruelty and ruthlessness were inherent characteristics of attrition siege, as was brutality. Consequently, many efforts were made to terrify and horrify the enemy from both sides. Prisoners were mutilated in public view, bodies were hung for display from ramparts, corpses of dead troops and diseased animals were catapulted over walls, and other unspeakable atrocities were committed to weaken the will of the enemy. In the case of the First Holy Crusade, the barbaric Tafurs, under the command of their Beggar King, Tafur, had already established the bestial practice of ritualistically roasting and cannibalizing enemy body parts in plain view of the enemy purely for purposes of terrorizing them.

The third possibility for handling Antioch was a strategy known as 'distant investment.' This was a novel approach, and in actuality had been discussed by an exclusive segment of the Christian army, to include Taticius and the

Byzantines, Bishop Tristan de Saint-Germain, and Guillaume de Saint-Germain. Infinitely cautious in design, distant investment avoided both direct assault and attrition siege. It involved establishing strong, permanent defenses at a distance to contain and harass the enemy, thereby allowing the main army to simply by-pass a dangerous city, averting costly confrontation and saving precious time.

With three different strategic approaches circulating within the leadership, Bishop Adhémar deemed it critical to convene the Council of Princes to decide on a final disposition for Antioch as soon as the crusaders established positions, pitched defensive lines, and settled into camps. This was followed by an odd period of lull as crusaders and Antiochians observed each other, initially, from a cautious but suspicious distance.

Yaghi Siyan had not yet deciphered crusader intent and wished not to inflame the circumstances. Subsequently, while alien entry into his gates remained prohibited, he did allow Antiochians to come and go at will, and even allowed crusaders to approach the walls of the city as long as they presented no threat. Bohemud had approached the walls on several occasions, exchanging both greetings and barbs with guards stationed along the walls.

Yaghi Siyan's seemingly loose approach raised virulent objections from his city commandant, General Ahmet, but time had often proven to be the old emir's friend. Siyan rarely moved too quickly, refusing to fall into the deadly trap of haste that often lured the 'quick-minded' to doom.

"Ah, but settle down, Ahmet," Siyan clucked again and again in fruitless attempts to soothe his general. "No need to overly alarm nor hobble our Christian population. I've allowed you to expel or imprison the worst of our dissidents, so let's continue to take a gentle hand with the other Christians while we wait to see what unfolds. Besides, this buys time for my sons as they make embassy in Duqaq and Aleppo."

Like General Ahmet, the crusaders themselves were thrown off by Siyan's disconnected approach, which bred their own interpretation of what was occurring. As documented by one crusader scribe: "The hostile Turks within Antioch were so frightened that for almost fifteen days they did not harass any of our men. Soon we were ensconced in the neighborhood, where we found vineyards everywhere, pits filled with grain, apple trees heavy with fruit for tasty eating, as well as many other healthy foods. Having wives in Antioch, the Armenians and Syrians would leave the city under pretense of flight and would come to our camps every day. They slyly investigated us, our resources, and our strength and then reported on all they had seen to the accursed Antiochians."

To be certain, Yaghi Siyan had slipped spies among those circulating through the gates. But the crusaders were playing a similar game, gleaning whatever possible from those expelled from the city as well as from sympathetic Armenian visitors. Regardless, the ensuing two-week period proved to be a pleasant time for the crusaders. Raymond of Aguilers fondly wrote many years later: "Those who stayed in camp enjoyed the high life so that they ate only the best cuts, rump and shoulder, scorned brisket, and thought nothing of grain and wine. In these good times, only watchmen along the walls reminded us of our enemies concealed within Antioch."

CHAPTER SEVEN

ANOTHER ARRIVAL

In hot pursuit of Mahmoud Malik since the Persian renegade's attack against his realm, Lord Abdul Azim of Eastern Asia Minor led his force of 1,000 ghazis against Malik through Asia Minor and into Armenia. There he was surprised to learn that Malik's flight back to the protection of Kilij Arslan's sultanate of Rüm had been cut off by an invading Christian army that had defeated Kilij Arslan. Malik, therefore, changed direction and made a run south.

Lord Azim, continuing his chase of Malik, adjusted his course and made Syria a day and a half behind Malik, but then all trace of the Persian butcher disappeared. Receiving word that the Christian army had blocked Antioch north and south, Azim assumed the Persian and his 700 renegades had slipped into Antioch seeking refuge.

"We'll camp near Yaghi Siyan's hidden outpost of Harim to the east, but keep our presence unknown to both Christians and Antioch," said Lord Azim to the man he trusted most in life, an aging scout named Kareem. It was he who had saved Azim from being murdered as a boy when Azim's entire family was assassinated by an incoming Seljuk branch intent on taking Syria from earlier Seljuks establishing realms there.

Kareem nodded, knowing Yaghi Siyan's predecessors had thieved the Azim family kingdom within the Antioch region. "Ah, so we come onto the old slave turned master, Yaghi Siyan," sneered Kareem. "Seems his cat whiskers are caught in a bit of a pincer all of a sudden."

"Allah's justice swinging back to repay the tribe that murdered my family," spat Azim. "Although I've nothing for either Christians or invaders, I've also no heart for thieves and assassins!"

Abdul Azim, Seljuk by birth, had been raised a devout Muslim by his Sunni fundamentalist parents, both of whom had converted to Islam, as had most other Seljuks migrating into and taking over both Byzantine Asia Minor and the Fatimid Arabian empire to the south. Since childhood, Azim's father, strict but fair, had taught him to respect others unless disrespected, give unless taken from, and extend generosity until abused for it. Simply put, young Abdul learned the value of consideration and charity at a young age, but would never fall victim to either; refusing to allow kindness to become his downfall.

His father was a general beneath the fierce Seljuk Kahn, Tugrul Bey, who in 1055 attacked and conquered the Arab caliphate of Baghdad, marking the end of Arabian rule and spiritual dominion in that part of the Muslim world. As a reward for exemplary military service, Abdul's father was awarded a vast track of territory in Syria. Abdul, therefore, enjoyed a privileged upbringing.

By early adolescence the family's fortunes shifted and he was forced to join his father's side in war, which had now become constant due to incursions by feuding Turks, revolts by Syrians and Armenians, and uprisings by opposing Shia Muslims. In the end, through subterfuge, Abdul Azim's entire family was slain and their wealth stripped. Abdul survived through the brave and bold efforts of faithful family servant, Kareem. After fleeing Syria, Kareem led Abdul north to join Sultan Alp Arslan's war against Emperor Romanos IV Diogenes and the Byzantine Empire. The horrid reversal of fortune suffered by his parents taught Abdul humility as well as about the bitter plight of the defeated. It developed in him an inclination for mercy toward the conquered.

Being ambitious and exceptionally adept at military strategy, young Abdul came to the attention of Alp Arslan, Malik Shah, and other Seljuk sultans during the Greek wars, proving himself at the Battle of Manzikert and ensuing wars throughout Cilician Armenia and further west. For these efforts, he was awarded a small realm fifty miles southeast of Manzikert.

In the year 1079, having established a reputation as a capable diplomat, Azim was placed at the head of a Seljuk delegation sent to Rome to negotiate with Pope Gregory VII concerning Turkish molestation of Christian pilgrims traveling to Jerusalem. This embassy, for Abdul, became a distasteful experience. Pope Gregory and his Vatican delegation had treated the visiting Turks with contempt and condescension, and yet it was the Christians themselves who were requesting concessions. The only individual Abdul had taken a liking to during the entire visit was a young Christian boy of thirteen assisting as interpreter for the Vatican. This particular boy possessed frightening intelligence and perception, and an infinite curiosity. Furthermore, he possessed a phenomenal knowledge of Arab and Persian tongues, in addition to the culture of Islamic peoples.

Despite shabby treatment at the hands of the Vatican, Abdul had learned much about the West during his visit to Rome, and after returning east he continued to rise within the Seljuk world as both politician and general. By the year 1085, his holdings south of Manzikert had magnified twenty-fold, establishing Azim as a sultan of major wealth and military power.

But at age fifty, Abdul Azim found himself confronted once again by a nemesis he had first encountered during the Battle of Manzikert, the rapacious Mahmoud Malik. They had both served Alp Arslan's invasion force as younger men, but came to despise each other. Abdul Azim viewed the Byzantine wars as a spiritual Islamic victory over heathen Byzantines, while Malik saw it purely as an opportunity for plunder and bloodletting.

The two actually met prior to Manzikert, and immediately began to butt heads over strategy and how to handle defeated Byzantines. Whereas Malik favored rape, butchery, or slaving for profit, Abdul Azim advised that subjugation be tempered with tolerance. In the end, the troops of Malik and Azim had actually clashed, trading blood in the aftermath of Manzikert over treatment of the vanquished. From that moment, each had declared the other an enemy for all eternity.

It was with adamant resolve that Abdul Azim sought retribution for Malik's recent incursion into his sultanate to plunder, steal horses, and kidnap Greek children for enslavement. Azim had long felt that other sultans and emirs should have brought Malik to justice, but constant infighting among them had only encouraged Malik's criminality; the services of Malik's vicious mercenary army had bought him much forgiveness. That's why Abdul Azim had pursued Malik all the way into Syria, intent on severing the head of the Persian snake, putting an end to his atrocities.

"Kareem, how well do you remember the Armenian tongue?" asked Lord Azim after settling his army on the eastern side of Mount Staurin for cover in a discreet nook of an area surrounded by foothills.

"Better than most Armenians," replied Kareem.

"And could you—No, do you think you could pass for an Armenian should I send you into the camp of these Christians along the Orontes?"

"Better than most Armenians," replied Kareem.

"Go then, posing as a local shepherd or traveling tradesman or such, and learn about the Christians; why they've come, their numbers, their leadership. Take your time, stay a while. Cultivate an acquaintance here and there among the lower ranks. That," he held his finger high, "Kareem, is where you shall find truth."

"Best then that I take a few donkeys, Sire. Gestures and gifts open doors."

"Ah, yes, Kareem, you sly fox," nodded Azim, slipping an appreciative grin the old scout's direction. "Another question then: How well could you pose as Syrian?"

"Better than most Syrians," replied Kareem, making Azim laugh. "Allah gave me little but a bag of tricks, which I've learned to ply like an old wizard."

"Ah, and so you have!" replied Azim, laughing and slapping his leg. "See then if you can approach Antioch, since you are such a wizard, Kareem. With your wiles, maybe slip in posing as a Syrian, perhaps in flight from the Christians. Find out for certain whether Malik is hiding there as I believe. Learn, too, whatever you can about Yaghi Siyan's state of affairs, whether he stands strong or leans toward surrender. Such shall be your mission while I wait out Malik here. Keep me apprised of things, and about every two weeks report back to me."

"With Allah's blessing, it shall be done, Master." Bowing, Kareem left Azim's tent to gather donkeys. Loading satchels with trinkets, he strapped them to the beasts' backs. "Beware you fools of this earth," he hummed to himself, "old Kareem is about to pick your heads!"

CHAPTER EIGHT

THE LEATHER POUCH

Having pitched tents and settled near Bohemud's camp across from Antioch's Saint Paul Gate, Guillaume's Tuscan troops were making the most of the lull following their arrival to Antioch. Sleeping late and relaxing more than at any time since leaving Nicaea, the Danes took full advantage of this unexpected standstill. Other than filing weapons, currying horses, and tending to camp, the four had spent a good amount of time hunting, foraging, and feasting.

Bishop Tristan de Saint-Germain had begun the crusade alongside Bishop Adhémar of Le Puy and Raymond of Toulouse, but since the fiery dispute with Adhémar in the olive orchard back at Camp Pelekanum, Tristan had abandoned Adhémar's camp in favor of his brother's camp. Whereas the two high bishops had managed to remain distantly cordial to each other since that ugly fracture, there remained a distant emotional gulf between the two.

Scule, the dwarf monk from Cluny, had begun the crusade on his own. Happening to discover his old Cluny classmate, Martin Letellier, upon arrival in Constantinople, he then joined Letellier's camp during most of the march to Antioch. Since taking nine-year-old orphaned Christos Laskaris from the road in Armenia, he and the boy had both moved into Guillaume's camp.

Of those within the Tuscan camp during this short period of peace and plenty, it was Guillaume alone who remained restless. Not understanding it, the Danes nevertheless sensed a slow deterioration crystalizing within Guillaume's spirit since early in the crusade. It was futile, of course, to address such a thing because Guillaume was like Tristan in that neither allowed others to breach their inner walls. As their mother, Asta, had done, the two brothers erected fortifications around their hearts, defending them as patriots fervently defend their homeland. Guillaume attempted to disguise outward signs of restiveness, but its lingering existence was evident in the dullness of his eyes, as on the tenth day in camp when Martin Letellier stopped by to visit him from the camp of the Northern Franks.

"Ever since setting eyes on Antioch's fortifications, Robert of Normandy and the other Northern princes have ruled out direct assault," Letellier told Guillaume. "So, attrition siege it shall be, apparently. But saints of Heaven, I'm not looking forward to it! And to think we're so close to Jerusalem just to get stymied up to our necks here."

"We'll see," nodded Guillaume. "Taticius and Tristan believe there's another way, and I agree. We'll be presenting it tomorrow morning to the Council of Princes."

"Ah yes, the Council of Princes," clucked Letellier, taking on a look of antic- ipation. "I've been looking forward to my first meeting with them." He had not begun the campaign as a member, but after insistence from Robert of Normandy based on Letellier's courage, loyalty, and wealth, Letellier had recently been approved by the other princes. "Tell us, Guillaume," he asked, "how is it with them? Should I speak straight or take a winding path?"

"It's like a gathering of hens, I suppose; one clucking louder than the other, insistent about knowing more, or emphasizing their position back home on the continental hierarchy, or throwing about the weight of family heraldry. They may have shown a decent amount of unity during our final approach to Antioch, but disagreement tends to outweigh agreement."

Guillaume was little interested in the Council, actually. His attempt to engage and explain failed to deceive his boyhood classmate. Letellier smelled something amiss. His friend's tone carried an unfamiliar vacancy. Although Guillaume had been but four years old when the two first met, he was even then ever vibrant and astir; his startling eyes exuding expectancy, tugging at the hearts of others by instilling anticipation and the promise of irresistible prospects. Those attributes were but a moot point now.

Nonetheless, Letellier went about his days as though all was as it should be. Having never been one to poke into the private affairs of others, intimate talk was, for him, a source of discomfort. "Ha! And just look there at the Danes," he said, moving into lighter channels. The Danes were seated about a campfire, devouring haunches of wild boar. "A ravening pack of wolves if ever I've seen one!"

"Aye," agreed Guillaume.

As he said this, Tristan and Scule approached the fire with young Christos Laskaris in tow.

"Hold there, you Danes! This is outrageous, I say," scolded Scule, lacking actual indignation. "Am I to assume the lot of you Nordic savages failed to cite your prayers before wolfing down your feast?"

"N-no," muttered Guthroth, lifting his char-smeared mouth but briefly. "I pr-prayed."

"Of course, me, too," agreed Hroc.

Orla and Crowbones exchanged glances. Shrugging, they crossed themselves, bowing their heads, and began mumbling, sounding remotely religious for a few seconds, then resumed inhaling boar with loud smacks and grunts.

In mockery, Tristan threw his hands in the air. "Ah, but you've been caught, you two!" he brayed, like Scule, jokingly.

"Yes, caught!" snorted Scule, as Christos peeked over the dwarf's dimin- utive stature, certain his mentor was actually angry at the two men who combined were six times Scule's own size. "What kind of converts are you two?!" Scule poked.

But Orla and Crowbones were lost to gnawing, oblivious that Scule was still addressing them.

Instead, it was Hroc who spoke, "Uncle Tristan, at the Iron Bridge Uncle Crowbones grew anxious about the old man hounding us as we crossed, insisting his presence was a bad omen, but that's the superstition of paganism, is it not? The old beggar was there by happenstance, I say. Yet Uncle Crowbones continues to fret, ignoring what Guthroth and I told him. Perhaps your word, being a high Vatican bishop, might carry more weight. Maybe you could take a few minutes to enlighten him?"

"Hold there, Hroc!" objected Orla. "Dammit, Son, leave Crowbones to his thoughts. And God's spine, show him respect. He, like me, gets confused at times trying to sort out our new faith with the old beliefs we were raised on. They don't match up, you know. Besides, omens do exist, by damn, as told by our ancestors, and it's these ancients sending omens to help us!"

Crowbones had, in fact, been riding a see-saw of confusion since converting to Catholicism as he and Orla had promised on being spared from the massacre of Nicodemia by the last-minute rescue of Emperor Alexius' navy. But that conversion had actually been a matter of honoring a vow to Hroc and Guthroth, not of belief. Even then, clinging to certain tenets of the old faith, Crowbones and Orla had been playing at an odd dance of acknowledging Christian rituals and preaching, and at the same time privately nursing reservations about their actual legitimacy. But as evangelism is wont to do, its mysticism over time had begun to creep into Crowbones' ideation.

This in itself was a bit contradictory because it was Ivar Crowbones, more than Orla Bloodaxe, who had been finely attuned to the practices of the Nordic paganism taught to him by his Finnish grandmother. Nonetheless, unlike as with Orla, for Crowbones, certain aspects of the new faith offered potential and validity. But at the present it was creating confusion within Crowbones' inner skirmish between the two faiths; the main issue being their blood-certain, sanctimonious, final Christian stance in the commandment: "Thou shalt not hold false gods before me." The Catholic Church allowed absolutely no margin, no forgiveness, no compromise.

"Even Christianity is riddled with omens!" remarked Orla, his tone signaling ire. "But ha! Christians call them 'signs' and 'miracles' instead of omens. In the end it's all the same shit, I say!"

"But there is a difference. Tell them, Uncle Tristan!" insisted Hroc. Since being baptized a year earlier Hroc had embraced Christianity with a full heart, to the point of piety, and it disturbed him greatly that his father and eldest uncle could in any fashion, to this day, cling to darkness.

"Well, we must be careful," replied Tristan, not really wishing to delve into the semantics of theological thinking and dispute in this particular setting. He well appreciated Hroc's ardor, yet understood Crowbones' perplexity. Picking his words carefully, he said, "Omens, signs, just a matter of vocabulary in the end. In truth, it is neither the definition nor the difference between 'omen' and 'sign' that breeds complexity but man's interpretation of the words that ignites dispute and invites, at times, hostility between men because of their differences of belief. Aye, therein lies the problem. Best then to dwell strictly on God, not vocabulary and semantics."

Failing to understand what Tristan meant, both Orla and Hroc took Tristan's words as agreement. Nodding, they returned to their boar meat.

But Crowbones' expression fell sullen in deep confusion; pricked, first by Hroc's words, then by Tristan's. "See here!" he objected, misunderstanding Tristan's point. "I took the water, I accepted the teachings, and I do the best I can with my new god. But unlike you, Hroc, and you, Guthroth, it's hard for me to swallow everything I'm told! Virgin birth, raising the dead, turning water to wine? What the hell? I wish to believe those things, but how are they any different than what Christians decry as 'pagan' myths? What's the difference between Heaven and Valhalla? Angels and Valkyries? Is it unforgivable to wonder, at times, or get confused, or challenge teachings?"

Hroc remained silent, realizing he had stirred a hornet nest.

Scowling, Crowbones turned his hard look from Hroc onto Tristan. "And you, Boy, your church rules require that as a Catholic holy man, you're not to have a woman, yet you do. I've no problem with that, as you well know, but what difference lies in me questioning Church doctrine or you challenging Church law?"

Such complexities confused Crowbones, a man who lived in a world of black and white, right and wrong. His question, although sincere with no intention of offending, just fishing for an answer, spilled out and, lacking that rising lilt characteristic of a question, caught Tristan by surprise, giving him pause. Interpreting Crowbones' remark as an affront, he went quiet, and in this he did not stand alone. A wave of discomfort quietly washed over everyone listening.

"Crowbones! A p-poor thing to s-say!" grumbled Guthroth, setting his meat aside. "S-say no m-more."

Scule stiffened, as did Christos and Hroc. Tristan, too, had lost his tongue. Not since Tristan's birth had Crowbones ever once crossed words with him, which left him reeling a bit from within over Crowbones' analogy. More pointedly, his question was, in truth, on point.

"Ah, shit," complained Orla, "it was just a damned question asked around a campfire! Loki's ass, no point in anyone getting their hackles up."

Warranted or not, Tristan was wounded. Whereas he had launched a vociferous attack against Bishop Adhémar back at Camp Pelekanum over the topic of Mala, any such intimation coming from beloved Ivar Crowbones in the midst of the men he loved most on this earth was hurtful. Dropping his head, he walked away.

"Lort! Er d-du glad n-nu, Crowbones?" growled Guthroth, shaking his head.

"No, I'm not glad," fired Crowbones, his ears reddening. "It was a question, that's all. And a reasonable one, I say." Looking to his brother, he added, "Huh, Orla?"

Orla was gazing into the embers of the campfire. "Ja, a reasonable question," he said, not looking up. "But dammit to hell, no need to drag Boy into this dispute with Hroc over religion. Ja, Hroc, see what you started?"

"I'm sorry. I shouldn't have said anything in the first place, Uncle Crowbones," said Hroc, his face turning contrite. "It's just that I was thinking about your soul. There's no forgiveness in Christianity for acknowledging other gods or accepting heathen superstitions. None. But then, that's your affair, Uncle Crowbones, not mine, and your soul. Ja, I should've just kept my mouth shut. I'll not bring up such things again."

"J-ja," grumbled Guthroth. "It w-was a p-poor time, Hroc, and a p-poor subject."

Close as Guthroth and Hroc were, Guthroth's words cut him to the quick, but less than Guthroth's expression as he spoke them.

"Dammit, jeg var forket!" said Crowbones, standing. "Ja, I, too, should have kept my mouth shut. There was no need to put Boy on the spot, good as he is and has always been!" Shaking his head, he raised his hands skyward. "De gamle måder er døde! It's time to decide then, so hear me! For me, this very day, the old ways are dead. No more talk of omens, then, nor Nordic superstitions." Shaking his head with affirmation, he added, "And to prove it, I should make a gesture to my new god, lest I be forever punished." Reaching to his throat, he tugged at the small leather pouch tied about his neck, snapping in one motion the leather thong that had since boyhood held the pouch of desiccated raven bones around his throat. "My grandmother's bird bones, rolled many times and read for many years to foretell things to come . . ." he said, holding the pouch high. "Færdig!" he declared, flinging the pouch into the fire.

No one around the fire was prepared for this, least of all Orla. Vaulting to his feet, he knelt into the fire grasping to retrieve the pouch. Wailing as though some sacred relic had been openly defiled and damnation was about to drop, he probed into the white-hot embers, but the leather pouch had already curled, shriveling into ruin, and the tiny raven bones themselves dispersed into ash.

Pulling his blistered hand from the fire, Orla stiffened, staring at Crowbones with disbelief, and started to speak, but his tongue caught, so he remained crouching there, appearing as he had just been struck across the forehead. Finally, his shoulders raising to his ears, he gasped, "Hvad har du gjort, Ivar? What the hell have you done?!"

CHAPTER NINE

FIRST FRACTURE: ATTRITION SIEGE OR DISTANT INVESTMENT?

When Bishop Adhémar arose that morning to recite his prayers, his heart was full. Up to this point, he had faithfully served as the good shepherd, acting as Pope Urban's direct hand and voice in the Holy Crusade. By the grace of God, the Christian army had been spared from catastrophe at Nicaea and Dorylaeum, and during the insufferable ordeal of traversing the desolation of Anatolia, it finally stood before Antioch, the final obstacle standing along the road to the Holy City of Jerusalem.

"Almighty Father," he prayed, ending his Pater Noster in Latin, the only tongue The Lord's Prayer was uttered in the year 1098, "I thank You for the guiding grace and full blessings You have bestowed on these saintly crusaders serving as Your instrument against the heathen host, Amen."

Leaving his tent, he sat alone at the command table to await the crusader princes, knowing their arrival was more than an hour away. *Such a morning,* he thought, gazing about camp, *full of promise as we prepare to set the final compass of this holy quest.*

The sweet smell of smoldering hardwood from distant campfires hung low in the branches, wafting lazily in aromatic currents as sporadic bursts of breeze gusted in from the mountains and the Orontes River. Through the sparse cluster of trees drifted incoherent voices of men in other camps, chattering, breaking from time to time into laughter, or rising in complaint. Horses were heard, too, stamping their hooves, snorting, communicating bestial sentiments to one another or to the men tending to them. Above, the sun shone brightly, warming the western plains of Antioch, reflecting off the Orontes as it wound around the western flank of the massive city. Beautifully set, bathed in pastoral tranquility and perfection, the surrounding landscape seemed a distant impossibility from the drums of war and battalions of men from opposing sides brandishing instruments of murder and mayhem, going at each other with murderous intent like wild beasts clashing in lethal confrontation.

As expected, the morning unfolded as gradually Christian princes from France, Italy, and Germany began assembling at Adhémar's table, arriving in twos and threes, exchanging greetings and friendly jibes, taking their places on campstools. The tone was friendly and the air light with levity. Having endured many hardships during the march, the good will of cohesion had begun to reassert itself, and swell. As such, the princes viewed the morning meeting as a cordial and final formality than an arena for dispute like many previous gatherings.

Bishop Adhémar opened with a prayer, followed by a warm greeting during which he waxed eloquently about faith, fraternity, and the fruits of the army's recent spate of collaboration. Next, he extended an impromptu olive branch to Tristan. "Bishop Saint-Germain," he said, "would you, as Pope's Counsel and First Scribe to the Holy Crusade, offer a prayer for these courageous men of God gathered here this morning?"

Bowing to acknowledge Adhémar's unsolicited gesture, Tristan recited a prayer during which neither war nor the march was mentioned. Instead, his prayer emphasized chivalrous humility and the plight of innocents caught in raging currents beyond their control. This inference about honorable treatment of enemy civilians was unmistakable, which crawled under the skin of many in attendance. Something else caught the attention of those listening, Bishop Saint-Germain's subdued tone. Unlike others at the table, he had refrained from all pretense of fraternal chatter and casual exchange. Only Guillaume and Martin Letellier understood. Tristan had not slept the night before, stung by what he misinterpreted as cross words uttered by a man he held dear, Ivar Crowbones. But such, then, is the burden carried by those possessing phenomenal perception; an acute advantage that can, at times, actually turn against a person, morphing into oversensitivity and overthinking.

As discussion opened, it was the minor lords who claimed the floor first; not to offer up strategy but to lodge inquiries about Antioch: the population, the geography, and the ratio of Christians, Muslims, Armenians, and Turks within the fortress. Since none in the company had been to Antioch nor knew anything about either the city nor Syria, it was Tristan providing the answers. He had not previously been there either, but his extensive studies allowed him to answer at least a few questions, though neither adequately nor accurately as concerned the most recent political and military circumstances impacting the immediate region. While addressing these inquiries, he noticed, up to this point, none of the primary princes had spoken one word. Specifically, Raymond of Toulouse, Bohemud, and Godfrey of Bouillon had all three remained silent, a highly unusual occurrence.

After twenty minutes of such questioning by the minor nobles, without anyone bringing forward one iota of actual military strategy, Tristan seized the initiative. "I fully realize that the tide of thought present here this morning is washing toward setting attrition siege to the city," he said, looking from prince to prince. "Direct siege is out of the question, I'm certain we all agree, due to the size and fortifications alone of Antioch. But there is another path involving far less bloodshed. I ask, then, that you keep an open mind and give consideration to what I'm about to propose."

This comment surprised all at the table save Taticius, Guillaume, and Martin Letellier. Taticius, of course, had originally outlined the plan to Tristan, and

Guillaume had informed Letellier of the plan during their conversation the day before. Listening, Council members offered no challenges, but many took on the appearance of skepticism.

"Speak up then," said Raymond of Toulouse, appearing bemused.

"As related and described by Taticius, based on an earlier Byzantine strategy implemented against Antioch," said Tristan, "I should like to propose that we consider a policy of distant investment."

"Taticius?" grumbled several voices about the table. Other than taking possession of captured cities that once belonged to Byzantium, Taticius had played few other roles during the campaign. Accordingly, certain resentments against him had arisen within crusader ranks. Indeed, many of the princes thought the crusaders were doing the fighting, while the Byzantines were simply sweeping up the prizes.

Disregarding this undercurrent of complaint, Tristan spoke undeterred, "To begin, we can set up a fortified position to the north of Antioch at the old Byzantine stronghold of Baghrās."

"Baghrās?" questioned Hugh of Vermandois. "But the old Byzantine fortress there lies in ruins."

"Far easier to resurrect it than to sink into the tar pit of attrition siege here at Antioch," countered Tristan. "Then, from Baghrās, we can patrol and monitor the entire region."

"But what of the Turkish army inside Antioch?" asked Godfrey. "We can't just ignore them."

"From our position in Baghrās," Tristan went on to say, "we can harass and break Antioch's lines of communication and supply along the entire western plain, holding them in check and averting direct battle, enabling the main army to move forward against Jerusalem.

"And don't forget that Emperor Alexius has promised to send Byzantine troops now that we've reached Antioch. Also, we are expecting even more reinforcements from Europe and the Pope, not to mention that a Genoese resupply fleet will soon be arriving at the nearby port of Saint Simeon."

"I see," nodded Robert of Normandy, "and it makes sense. I like it." This caught the attention of the table because it was well known that the Northern French princes were a tight bunch, rarely disagreeing amongst themselves. If Robert of Normandy approved distant investment, then Robert of Flanders, Stephen of Blois, and Hugh of Vermandois were most likely to follow.

Disturbed, Raymond of Toulouse objected, "Not wise to turn your back to the enemy. I've been at war since a young man, and if ever I've come across an enemy not to be trusted, it's these damned Muslims. After years of fighting them in Spain, I learned to never, ever allow Muslims access to the rear flank! They—"

"You were fighting Moors in Spain, not Turks," interrupted Tristan. "The Moors have been engaged in war for decades against us and are well versed in our tactics, but not the Turks, and especially not the Antiochian Turks."

"Moors, Turks, they're all the same breed of rat!" growled Godfrey, a scowl beginning to take root. "No, I say. If we leave Antioch, the Turks'll come at us from behind. No question about it!"

"The defensive forces at Baghrās would contain such an attack," offered Guillaume, speaking for the first time. "And just as well, should Antioch be foolish enough to attack Baghrās, then we simply reverse the main army, crushing the Turks with superior numbers."

"And what if that doesn't work?" grumbled Raymond, looking about for affirmation. "No, too risky I say!"

Bohemud, listening carefully, clearly understood the advantages of distant investment, but such talk obstructed his own private ambitions. He began sensing the prize of Antioch eluding him, sliding beyond reach. "I say attrition siege is the most logical tactic to take," he declared willfully. "It will take time and blood, yes, but we can most certainly choke Antioch to submission, overcome the Turkish garrison within, and guarantee safe passage south to the Holy Land. I know that—"

"Dammit!" objected Taticius, to the surprise of others, slamming his palm against the table and rising. Taticius was stoic by nature, and had only once during the entire march been lost to impatience. "What the hell's the matter with you, Bohemud?" he barked, jamming a finger toward him. "And you, Raymond, and you, Godfrey? Distant investment is an obvious choice here; far safer and offers an immediate attack on Jerusalem. It's as simple as the nose on your damned faces!"

This unfortunately, and despite Taticius' earnestness, was absolutely the wrong choice of words. Taticius' nose had been brutally severed at the Battle of Manzikert and in its place he had since worn a replacement nose of tin fabrication, strapped to his head, giving him a devilish look, as ascertained by many Christian crusaders. And as a eunuch, his high-pitched voice likewise offended many, stirring ridicule behind his back. These offenses were suddenly outweighed by the fact that Taticius had bluntly called out Bohemud, the most short-fused and violent of all the Western princes.

"Never interrupt or point your goddamn finger at me again!" bellowed Bohemud, spittle flying from his mouth. Pointing at Taticius' face, he followed with, "And don't be talking about our noses, you tin-faced fright of a half-man!"

An earlier incident had broken out involving Taticius' appearance and feminine voice in Nicaea, as incited by Baldwin of Boulogne, Godfrey's brother. During that episode, to the surprise of all, Taticius had swiftly pulled his sword, spun it about and slammed it across the table in a stunning display of speed and dexterity, threatening to kill the next man who dared to belittle him. Unsettled by Taticius' lightning reaction and unexpected skill with a blade, the crusaders present that day all backed away, seeing Taticius, afraid of no man, was lethally dangerous as well.

Recalling this incident, those seated near Taticius backed off their camp stools, knowing what was likely to ensue. Bohemud's insult about Taticius' disfigured face, coupled with his barb about the brave soldier's castration, was far, far beyond tolerance. Those sitting near Bohemud also moved back a bit, knowing that once ignited, Bohemud's volatile temper swiftly turned deadly.

As expected, before others could blink, Taticius shot a hand to his scabbard, withdrew his sword, and raised it, cocked for a lethal blow so quickly that others failed even to see Taticius' phenomenal hand-speed. Bohemud, rising as he was from a seated position, was a half-step behind Taticius and was just beginning to pull his own sword, too late to counter Taticius.

Dumbstruck, the table fell silent, too taken and too late to intercede. It was now but a matter of Taticius dropping his blade.

From nowhere an outstretched hand grasped Taticius' up-raised forearm. "Hold there, Taticius!" shouted Guillaume, bracing the Byzantine's arm from dropping. "And you, too, Bohemud!"

A flicker of uncertainty passed as others, eyes glued to the two combatants, held their breath. Burning with hate, Taticius spat at Bohemud but slid his sword into its scabbard, gaze fixed upon the man, seething. Bohemud, not as quick at the draw—had never actually managed to unsheathe his blade—removed his hand from its pommel and sat down, the veins of his neck visibly pulsing.

Breathing easier, the attending princes thought the incident over. Guillaume, however, was not done. Looking hard at Bohemud, he said, "Bohemud, you have grievously insulted an ally who just happens to be a good man, despite what some here may believe, and that shames me, as it should yourself. Perhaps you might wish to retract such vile words."

This was, by no means, a question.

Apprehension resurfaced, again because of Bohemud's fearsome temper and inclination toward eruption. No other man at the table would have dared tell Bohemud to do something as Guillaume had just done, causing a second confrontation; this time involving Guillaume and Bohemud.

While others watched mutely, Bohemud rolled his shoulders, fore-signaling an outburst. Snorting, trying to decided which direction to take, he became motionless, his eyes went black as anthracite, and he muttered unintelligibly to those in his presence.

As things were, and regardless of what had just transpired, Bohemud owed the greatest debt possible that one man can owe to another, to none other than Guillaume de Saint-Germain. During the deadly ambush of Dorylaeum, Bohemud had been thrown from his horse and swarmed by a pack of advancing Turks. At great risk, and in a seemingly hopeless effort, Guillaume jumped from his mount, flung himself into the fray, and pulled bloodied Bohemud to safety.

Remaining motionless, Bohemud returned Guillaume's iron-willed gaze one for one. "Yes, a gesture poorly made to an ally, Guillaume," he said aloud for all to hear. "Taticius, one proper man should not address another in such fashion. My pardon."

This satisfied all at the table except Tancred. "Uncle Bohemud," he complained, "no need to apologize to this damn Byzantine! He carries no weight here!"

"Enough, Tancred!" growled Bohemud, grasping his nephew by the shoulder. "Hold your tongue, dammit!"

"Aye, Tancred, enough," echoed Guillaume, issuing a look of disdain in his direction. He'd disfavored the insolent man since their departure from Constantinople.

Appearing to have dismissed any further remnants of anger, Bohemud placed both hands on the table. "Let's get back to the task at hand," he said flippantly.

Bishop Adhémar was taken aback by the fiery flare-up; the imprint of alarm etched onto his expression. Sighing heavily, he gathered himself, indicating the floor had reopened for further discussion. His initial hopes for a benign, amiable meeting had turned against him. And of more importance, the choice of attrition siege versus distant investment had not been settled, and feelings obviously still ran virulent from proponents of both approaches. Taking care to move forward with firmness tempered by caution, Adhémar directed the discussion on the topic. Nonetheless, disagreement and tempers arose again, albeit not to the previous level.

An hour later, the discussion remained deadlocked and disputes came to a climax.

Frustrated, absolutely rejecting distant investment, Raymond of Toulouse took to his feet, summoning an air of pontifical righteousness. Reaching into his tunic, he pulled out his defunct, dried-up eyeball, holding it up to his empty socket for all to consider. "As certain as each of you sees this grave sacrifice I hold here in my fingers, a sacrifice I made during a time of excruciating suffering for God in Heaven, then be equally certain that I shall never turn my back to the heathen Turk! Go then, those of you who must, and set your defenses at Baghrās. Go then, the rest of you, and make your way straight to Jerusalem. But I shall begin making preparations for my army to set attrition siege to Antioch!"

This aroused both camps seated at the table, precipitating objections from one and cheers from the other.

"Damnation!" groaned Robert of Normandy, disgusted. "You have the greatest army in our midst, Raymond. But I thought to be here for discussion, not to be pushed aside by threats of grandiosity!"

"Aye!" agreed Robert of Flanders. "Does our opinion not count for anything? Bishop Saint-Germain's and Taticius' proposal appears to be the wiser choice!"

"Indeed!" claimed Stephen of Blois, joined by Guillaume, Martin Letellier, Hugh of Vermandois, and several others.

This stirred a response from Bohemud. "I stand with Raymond of Toulouse, and shall stand my ground here at Antioch until the Turks either surrender or are ground to dust!"

Following suit, Tancred stood. "Siege, or die! We Normans of Southern Italy will make our stand in Antioch before marching south!"

Tristan, listening, dropped his head in discouragement. Without the might of Raymond of Toulouse and Bohemud of Taranto, there would be no chance of advancing against Jerusalem. Instead, the march was imminently destined to become mired in a bloody bath of attrition before the walls of Antioch. Oh, but God, he thought, wilting within, you have brought us so close to Jerusalem, yet we sink here in the blistering sands of Syria!

Then Godfrey of Bouillon stood. "We Germans shall hold here at Antioch as well, and share in the title and plunder of this damned city as our prize!"

As he said this a pall fell over the table, even amongst those favoring attrition siege. Godfrey's declaration was the first instance of a primary prince openly voicing to the Council or before Bishop Adhémar the actual seizure of former Byzantine territory for self-gain. Whereas lesser princes had strayed, like Baldwin taking Edessa and Tancred claiming Mamistra, this was actually the great Godfrey of Bouillon boldly staking mercenary claim to what was, ostensibly, a spiritual quest in the name of God.

"Aye, so be it!" declared Raymond of Toulouse. "We shall claim Antioch as our own!"

Drawing back on his camp stool, Bishop Adhémar stared first at Godfrey, then at Raymond. "R-Raymond?" he queried, his voice turning tremulous and uncertain.

These bold pronouncements by Godfrey and Raymond, to Tristan, were like familiar knells of a thunderous, quaking cathedral bell; deafening into oblivion any and all prospects of uncertainty. Whereas, just moments earlier, his resolve having taken a knee to discouragement, this bold utterance by Godfrey tethered to Raymond's reinforcement instantly set him afire.

"Oh, but now the truth is dragged into light," Tristan declared, ascending to his feet, his voice taking on the tenor of a grief-stricken moan, "and your true hearts are exposed, splayed and naked for all to see! Oh, but is this not treason to the cause of God? What? Shall you really drag men by the tens of thousands to their graves fighting beneath your private banners just so you yourselves may seize title to Antioch?! Oh, vain princes, I say, pretending to fight in God's name and at the same time secretly calculating the filling of personal treasuries!"

With each pronouncement Tristan's tone rose, emoting rising passion. But his words were infuriating the major princes, and as they smoldered with rage, Guillaume grew concerned and leaned in to his brother. "Tristan, stop!" he hissed lowly to not be heard by others. "These are proud men here, and won't tolerate such talk. They'll turn on you. Quiet, I say!"

"I'll abide no more of Bishop Saint-Germain's accusatory blathering!" retorted Godfrey, his face glowing red. "I joined this quest to regain Jerusalem, but I'll not turn my goddamned back to Turks. It's a decision of strategy, not greed! Nor shall I be insulted by this . . ." he waved his hand, "this damned false monk who keeps a Romani harlot at his side, even having children with her, violating his sacred vows to the Church. Yes, there it is, Saint-Germain. I said it aloud!"

This attack emboldened Tancred. Shooting to his feet, shaking a fist at Tristan, he yelled full of vinegar and piss, "You carry no moral authority here, Saint-Germain! You've no right to accuse others of false intentions until you clean your own filthy nest, you pretender!"

This inflamed Guillaume, Letellier, and Taticius who bounded to their feet in defense of their friend, shouting down Godfrey and Tancred, echoing the very charges Tristan had lodged against the three princes. The Northern princes, too, grew incensed that Godfrey and Tancred would speak disrespectfully, irreverently to a high bishop who stood appointed as Pope Urban's First Scribe and Counsel.

Bohemud then stood, joining the fray, as Bishop Adhémar of Le Puy placed a palm to his forehead, dismayed. Within seconds, the entire assemblage fell into chaos as jostling and cursing broke out in a chorus of animus and friction.

In the midst of this, Tristan let loose a howl so loud as to rise above the pandemonium. "Oh, but speak Adhémar!!" he shouted. "Speak, I say, for Raymond and Bohemud and Godfrey do not lead this crusade! You are the voice of Pope Urban, appointed and anointed! What shall it be, Adhémar? Attrition siege or distant investment?!"

This frantic pronouncement stilled the table as all eyes fell onto the bewildered old bishop whose head had begun wagging helplessly, doddering in tiny, fitful spasms as often happens to the aged when confounded. Shrugging like a man lost, he motioned limply toward Raymond of Toulouse and Bohemud. His voice going thready, he muttered, "O-oh, but it would be f-futile to attack Jerusalem without the might of Raymond and Bohemud." Then his head and shoulders dropped as he added in a barely audible voice, "We must then set attrition siege to Antioch."

Satisfied, yet keeping their wits intact enough not to gloat, the proponents of attrition siege grunted agreement and shortly left the table grumbling to one another in disaggregated packs. They knew that to rub salt in the wound might alienate the opposition to the point of not fully cooperating with the siege itself. Meanwhile, the proponents of distant investment shook their heads, staring at each other incredulously over what had just occurred.

An odd, stilted silence descended over the table then, until Tristan's voice broke the air. "Oh, but shame on you, high bishop of Le Puy!" he said, wagging a finger at the target of his remark. "In the face of wealth and power, you have collapsed, knowing in your heart that many men shall now perish needlessly in the name of blind ambition peddled by others! You who accuse me of falling from the godly path. You who chastise me over false morality invented and mandated by Pope Gregory VII and his nest of radical reformist Benedictines, such as yourself! Oh, but shame, shame for losing courage when it most counts! God shall take count of this day, Adhémar!"

Tristan stalked from the table, followed by Guillaume, Letellier, and Taticius. However, the four Northern princes remained in place, lost to what had just transpired at the table, what had been nakedly and brutally voiced, and what dreadfully loomed ahead.

As they talked amongst each other in subdued voices, Adhémar's head dropped low on his chest, as deep within the wells of his sockets his eyes turned glassy, watering the least bit.

CHAPTER TEN

THE BLUE MAN

Every human enters this world equally naked, being one day rudely expelled from the sheltered haven of woman's womb. Newborns then gasp for air in a humble and helpless beginning, blinking and wailing in terror at entering the world. But then, having taken that first breath of air, all equity vanishes. From that seminal moment, each and every infant launches forward under circumstances predetermined, formed within an iniquitous mold cast down by genetics, family, and fortune. Whereas some are born blessed with the gifts of fine appearance, intelligence, and means, others arrive bearing burdensome crosses they must drag about the rest of their days.

Benito Fazio was of this latter group, his two curses being tiny stature and malformed larynx. He thought he was like other children, until the age of five when he realized those his age had grown twice his size. By age eight, that time when cruelty amongst children blossoms, he became the butt of scorn as girls shunned him and boys abused him.

It being impossibly problematic for 'normal' people to fathom the inner struggles of those suffering from abnormality, he became isolated, entirely lacking of playmates or friends. By adolescence, he was but half the size of peers, and the aberrant quality of his voice became quite pronounced, therefore cruelly ridiculed. Seeking refuge, he withdrew, further exacerbating an already lonely existence. Then in adolescence, he began to resent God. "God made all things," he concluded bitterly. "And, He has unjustly punished me by deforming me for no reason other than spite. I abhor God, for He is cruel!"

Overhearing her son talking to himself in this manner one day, his mother drew back, horrified. "Oh, but sacrilege!" she howled, then dragged him to the town cathedral, calling for their parish priest. "God gave you life, the most precious gift of all!" she chastened, slapping him across the back of his head. "Quickly give your confession to Father Manito and beg the Lord's forgiveness!"

After that day, and for as long as he lived at home, his mother made him kneel at her side each morning to recite a private prayer: "God in Heaven, Savior of all, please protect this boy for the rest of his years. And though you have burdened him with many troubles, look over him, keeping him safe no matter what else may arrive during his existence, I pray!"

As to her husband, their son was an embarrassment. Therefore, he refused to spend any time with the lad, often chasing him off with snide remarks or a kick in the breeches. "But what have I done to deserve such an abominable off-shoot?" he complained incessantly to family and friends. For these deeds, he was duly punished, according to random opinion. Shortly after Benito turned nine, his father was crushed beneath a team of runaway horses, bolting free, as the driver was hitching them to his wagon.

Neither son nor mother mourned the loss.

At age thirteen, the boy left home, becoming a street urchin, getting by as best as he could by depending on the pity of strangers offering a pittance here and there as he wandered the avenues. Eventually, he was forced to resort to thievery, hence the impetus for his eventual vocation; skulking about the dark underbelly of society earning coin by serving as an informant and surreptitious emissary for those of means.

But recently, having traveled to the East purely by happenstance, he suffered the misfortune of falling into the hands of Seljuk mercenaries intending to execute him. Yet fate intervened, allowing him a far better outcome than that of others captured with him and designated for the butcher block for being godless Christians.

Bound by rope, standing in line awaiting decapitation, he was forced to watch head after Christian head being lopped and hurled aside ahead of him. The executioner was actually a Persian general, he learned from another awaiting his turn. Executions were usually carried out by lesser men, but apparently this general had a peculiar and insatiable thirst for blood, as well as inflicting horror on others. Watching the bloody motions of the swinging ax, Benito trembled in terror, urinating in his breeches as the massive, bare-chested Persian signaled him to the block. Laughter erupted from the crowd as this occurred, and the executioner sneered, running a palm over his shaved, glistening crown. "Come forward, little mouse!" he growled.

As Benito stumbled forward, his heart thumping wildly against the walls of his chest, his thoughts turned to his mother. Shivering, he thought to hear her ghostly voice reciting her daily morning prayer for him.

"Oh, but such a damned wasted effort you made, Mother. There is no God!" he howled, his mind bursting with resentment and regret mixed in equal measure.

Hearing his cry, elfishly pitched and aberrant, Turkish guards standing close by broke into guffawing, pointing, and poking each other with amusement.

"Ha, he sounds like a tiny, squealing piglet!" shouted one.

"Ho! Malik, spare him for just a bit longer! We wish to be entertained!" shouted another.

"I won't, damn you," barked the executioner, "for this little troll's time is up!"

"No! Let us hear some more of his banshee squealing!" came loud cries.

Amongst the gruesomeness of the day's murderous activity, the sight and sound of the tiny man was thoroughly delightful to those watching. One of them, evidently a man of authority, shouted at the executioner, causing him to take on a look of dissatisfaction.

Quickly sensing an unlikely but remote possibility of salvation, and being deceitful as he was from years of street survival, Benito's panic subsided just long enough for his mind to devise a scheme of sorts. Refuting religion entirely, he nonetheless realized it was potent medicine for others, regardless of culture or race. Raising both hands skyward, taking on a look of celestial ecstasy brought on by seizure, he began shouting, "Allah! Allah! Spare me from death I pray. Allah, I'll ask for nothing else, just spare me!"

Not understanding Italian, the Muslim crowd did manage to clearly understand that the little man was shouting 'Allah,' beseeching him to spare his life. And simultaneously, it appeared that Allah might actually be 'touching' him, as evidenced by the seizures taking over the little man's body.

This caught the attention of two Turkish imams standing nearby, prompting them to rush toward the butcher block. As Islamic holy men, they suspected they were witnessing a miracle in the form of divine intervention. Instantly, the imams surrounded the tiny Christian captive, encircling him with their arms, launching into fervent prayer. Frightened, spotting the shifting mood of the crowd, Benito groped at the Koran one of the imams was holding and began kissing it over and over, shouting, "Allah! Allah!" This further aroused the crowd as the din of applause and prayer grew louder and louder.

Then the man of authority who had earlier stopped the Persian executioner shouted out again, "I'll buy the little fellow sounding like a bleating goat, and I'll give a good price!" he cried, jingling a pouch of coins over his head. "And for good measure, I'll convert him to Islam before reselling him!"

Shaking his head, the executioner set his axe aside. "Fine then," he snorted, "I'll take your money. But I feel like a thief! Who'd buy this little pile of shit!"

Not understanding what was being said, Benito did understand at least that he would be walking away from the butcher block with his head intact. Moments later, as shackles were bound to his ankles and hands, he realized he'd been sold into slavery.

But I'll at least live! thought Benito, slipping with pretension into the spiritual flow of celebration that had broken out around him, prompted by his own trickery. Better to be a living slave than a headless corpse!

In the midst of his play-acting, though, a cold finger reached down from nowhere, touching his heart, as he again heard his mother, 'God in Heaven, Savior of all,' the ghost voice echoed, 'please protect this boy for the rest of his years. And though you have burdened him with many troubles, look over him, keeping him safe no matter what else may arrive during his existence, I pray!'

Thunderstruck, Benito, at that instant, was jolted by comprehension. There IS a Christian God, and He has spared me at the blackest hour in reply to my mother's prayer! My being saved had nothing to do with Allah, for I made it all up. No, it was the hand of God that reached down to save me!

That's when Benito, pretending to convert to Islam to save himself, rediscovered his Christian faith.

This enlightenment incurred in him an underlying sense of guilt and remorse for denying God without thought, and having earlier closed his ears to the catechism of the Catholic Church. As things stood, despite the church upbringing fostered in him in his youth, he actually remembered very little about Roman Catholicism; had completely walked away from it and his mother years before. That aside, he reverently vowed to learn, and with an open heart.

Whereas it was true that Benito had narrowly escaped certain execution, somehow landing beneath the improbable but protective wing of Yaghi Siyan, it would be incorrect to presume that he felt content, safe, or secure. To the contrary, he clearly understood that Yaghi Siyan was a man of immense power, therefore highly susceptible to unforeseen flights of mood and mind. And, despite his elevated position at the hands of the old emir, he was no more than a slave; his existence hinging entirely on the wish and whim of Yaghi Siyan, while others of the Antiochian court despised him.

Masking these fears, Benito lived day to day quaking within a state of nervous exhaustion, much like those tiny lapdogs incessantly jumping about, happy-faced, trembling with perpetual anxiety. In truth, he had but one aim: escaping back to Italy.

To feed this hope, he turned to God. I must become a better person, he decided, and serve my Lord. But because I never paid attention back then, I don't really know how.

Ever resourceful, one evening he secretly removed his face paint and dressed in the garb of a Muslim girl, donning an enveloping burqa to disguise his body and hiding his face behind the cover of a full hijab, concealing all but his eyes. Slipping from the palace, he made his way to the residence of the Greek Orthodox patriarch of Antioch, John VII the Oxite. "I am Ben-fazi of Emir Yaghi Siyan's court," he said, removing his hijab. "They call me the blue man."

Taken aback with fright and suspicion, John the Oxite cried out for his servants until, fortunately, Ben-fazi was able to restore calm. Explaining his plight, Ben-fazi related his past to the patriarch, including Italy, his capture, near execution, and how he ended up in the court of Yaghi Siyan.

"Oh, but truly," agreed John the Oxite, "you are alive but by God's will!"

"Though not Catholic but Greek Orthodox, Patriarch, you are Christian," replied Ben-fazi. "Because I denied God early on, I solemnly wish to recover the teachings of Christ, the commandments, and the sacraments, for I owe God a great debt. I know the Catholic and Greek Orthodox churches split apart many years ago. But both being Christian, I have to believe they remain similar in most things. Will you please teach me?"

"Yes, yes, my son, of course," nodded the elderly patriarch.

"Be mindful though, I come here at great peril, hence the disguise. So, you, too, must keep my secret. Agreed?"

"Oh, to be certain!" exclaimed John the Oxite. "I'll instruct my servants do the same, and allow you to enter on hearing the following code: knock two times at my back door, pause, then knock three times, pause, and knock one last time. They'll recognize it's you and allow entry."

In absorbing the teachings of Patriarch John the Oxite, coupled with his own presumptions about godliness, Ben-fazi, for the first time, began to realize there existed people far less fortunate than even himself. Oh, but such a blind fool I've been, dwelling only on my own deformities! he lamented. There are those who've been brutally mutilated or slain, such as nearly happened to me, and there are others wasting away of disease or hunger. I, at least, am intact and have at least a feather of hope!

Looking to perform good deeds, the large prison of Antioch gained his attention; an antiquated structure burgeoning with unfortunate souls who had in one fashion or another run afoul of Seljuk, Islamic, or Antiochian law. Conditions within were horrendous, as testified to by the first ritual undertaken each morning, Turkish guards loaded carts with those who had succumbed during the previous night. Seeking to gain God's favor, Ben-fazi selflessly decided to lever his weight with Yaghi Siyan to acquire extra rations for the prisoners, a great many of whom were Christians of Armenian, Arab, or Syrian lineage.

His arrival once a week irked the Seljuk guards tremendously, but they only complained among themselves, well aware that the little man's position in court could spell punishment for anyone belittling him. When appearing, painted blue and accompanied by a wagon spilling with old bread and soured wine, Ben-fazi was not the least bit timid about flaunting his position to the guards; he resented them even more than they resented him.

Nevertheless, he made one good friend among the jailers, a kindly Armenian named Boros, a former chief jailer of the prison before the Turkish takeover. Boros was ill-treated by the Seljuk guards and consequently appreciated the consideration shown to him and the prisoners by Ben-fazi. "Ah, but you're a good man!" Boros would exclaim each week as Ben-fazi and the wagon appeared. "God is taking account, you know, of all you do for the wretched and unjustly confined!"

One particular morning, as Ben-fazi arrived, Boros was talking to a man Ben-fazi recognized, Firuz the armor-maker. Firuz and Boros were good friends, though Firuz cared little for Ben-fazi, especially since his children had begun being summoned to court.

"Ah, here he comes with goods for the Christian prisoners," remarked Boros. "A good sort, that little fellow!"

Firuz, knowing that Boros and Ben-fazi had become close, said nothing. In turn, Ben-fazi greeted Boros but gave no acknowledgement of Firuz, prompting Firuz to walk away.

"You two don't care for each other, do you?" asked Boros with a huff. "A shame. I like you both."

As he said this, General Ahmet appeared from around a corner, steeped in conversation with Mahmoud Malik, the recently arrived Persian. Spotting them, Ben-fazi walked behind the wagon to conceal himself, his short stature being lower than the wagon sideboards.

"And what the hell is this stupid charade Yaghi Siyan plays in court?" Malik was grumbling. "Is he completely touched, or just partly so?!"

Hearing this, Ben-fazi supposed that General Ahmet would object. Instead, the general agreed, chuckling, "Ha! Who knows? Siyan lives in his own world, and it's damn sure not the same one you and I inhabit!"

"And who's that little blue bastard seated beside his throne? What in thunder's that all about? The little shit reminds me of a brightly colored canary propped on a perch."

"Oh, Ben-fazi!" laughed Ahmet. But as he was about to speak, his eyes happened to catch a bizarre set of shoes planted behind the far-front wagon wheel; slippers, gold and yellow with upturned points at the toe, each being garnished with a small set of jingling bells. Lowering his voice, he gestured at Malik to change direction. "Hold your tongue about the blue man, Malik, for he's just there behind the wagon."

"Hold my tongue? Over that little pot of piss?"

"Keep it down!" warned Ahmet. "And another thing, Malik, best you start tempering that lizard tongue of yours. You came within a whisker of meeting your end in court this morning."

Malik simply snorted in defiance.

"You'd best walk lightly here," cautioned Ahmet. "Yaghi Siyan isn't quite as he appears. The old cat's got fangs, even as he smiles." As a military man, and with a threat as thick as flies, Ahmet was glad the Persian had arrived, albeit unexpectedly. Seven hundred ghazis would boost Antioch's chances if needed. "I'm glad you showed up," said Ahmet, "but remember this, the moment you entered the Iron Gate, you stepped into another world."

"Oh? And how's that?"

"Well, things changed when Yaghi Siyan took the throne. He's always been strange, granted, but when he took the scepter, those many things he repressed as a slave and counselor came into the open. We in court lost all firm ground of the past and now live by whim. Yaghi Siyan's whim! And as long as you're here, so shall you. The old man let you walk out of court this morning with your head attached for one reason alone, that you might yet prove useful. But don't push your luck, and don't mock the blue man, either. I made that mistake early on and, in the process, forfeited my favored position. Others, though, have lost far more—ears, noses, hands and feet."

As their voices faded beyond earshot, Ben-fazi's eyes followed Malik until he and Ahmet disappeared into the crowd.

Taking notice, Boros grunted, "That big fellow there, he scares the shit out of me, too. A real bastard, he is. When he first arrived through the Iron Gate, he was dragging about thirty prisoners in tow; has them stashed in the back of the prison, the old abandoned section, young Christian girls plundered from up north. Greek, I think. And whenever the Persian's nature gets up, he and that horny-ass lieutenant of his show up down here and rut those poor girls like a herd of sheep. Chrissakes! Anyway, the Persian's bribed the Turkish guards handsomely; told 'em to hold the girls for safekeeping but not let anyone know. But I know, of course."

"You've not mentioned this to Ahmet?" asked Ben-fazi, surprised.

"God, no, Ahmet's taken a liking to the Persian," said Boros, drawing back. "I'm only telling you, Ben-fazi. You're my sole friend around here, other than Firuz. But say nothing about any of this! That evil Persian would cut my tongue out!"

"I understand," said Ben-fazi, envisioning in his mind perversions being wreaked on the poor Greek girls. "That aside, I've a bit of news for you, Boros. At my request, Master Yaghi has approved an extra wagon of bread and other such leftover fare this morning. It's still being loaded behind the palace kitchen and shall arrive shortly."

"Oh, but you've got a good, solid heart!" Boros complimented enthusiastically, his face brightening. "God's taking count, you know, of all you do for the forgotten!"

Ben-fazi nodded, although his face showed little contentment. "I hope so, Boros," he said, "for I've much to make up for."

CHAPTER ELEVEN

FIRUZ

The grinding millstone of life's trials, much like the drop gradually wearing away the stone, slowly and painstakingly erodes hope, turning the future for some into a dark corridor winding ceaselessly ahead, lacking all avenue of escape. Gazing down this corridor, unable to turn aside or retreat, the human heart falters. Hope, after all, is what has enabled humanity to crawl from the chasms of primeval darkness toward the light. When hope is extinguished, existence becomes little more than a one-way conduit flushing toward discouragement and perdition.

This is, in essence, what had become of the Armenian armor maker, Firuz, husband of a beautiful but younger Armenian bride, Adelina, and father of two strikingly beautiful children, Karine and Garik. His early years were characterized by periods of blossoming promise, despite his father being but a journeyman blacksmith. Firuz advanced his smithy skills, along with the family name, to prosperous heights, specializing in the manufacture of fine armor breastplates, in particular. By age thirty, his business was thriving, his pockets were full, and he had his pick of any Armenian Christian woman within all of Antioch. As such, he made the most of his stature, living high and bedding one hopeful bride-to-be after another.

At thirty-five, Firuz settled on the raven-haired, eighteen-year-old beauty, Adelina. Of humble stock, with little financial promise to offer, she possessed irresistible sensual allure, a heavy bosom, which she was not afraid to flaunt, the most pleasing of possible figures, and an insatiable hunger for sex. For Firuz, this was enough . . . at first.

To his surprise, he discovered that the highly desirable Adelina, raised in poverty, had a taste for the finer things, and expectations to match. Firuz was generous enough by his very nature, happily providing all she could ever need. Yet, Adelina was forever nurturing within her garden of ambition some inexplicable, insatiable seed of 'wanting more'; having everything was never enough for her. Compounding this particular flaw, she fell into the habit of constant nagging, always pushing Firuz to rise even higher.

When the Turks arrived to subjugate Antioch, Firuz was certain his Armenian fortunes would tumble, but as luck would have it, the reverse occurred. Seljuk demand for high quality armor catapulted Firuz to an even higher stature. Adelina, keenly aware of this turn, grew annoyingly insistent that her husband 'cultivate' these newfound connections. In particular, she pushed him into gaining favor with Emir Yaghi Siyan who had taken notice of Firuz's exceptional craftsmanship.

These mercenary overtures by Adelina disturbed Firuz to a degree, leading him to complain to his brother and friends that, "She'd have me groveling to the Turks on hands and knees if I allowed it! Chrissakes, it's never enough."

But lo and behold, her prompting bore fruit and Yaghi Siyan appointed Firuz as commander of one of the many towers securing the city's defensive perimeter and was given command of the Tower of the Two Sisters located next to the Saint George Gate at the southwest corner of Antioch.

"Oh, but such an honor to be the first and only Armenian trusted to such a position!" Adelina clucked. "And well worth converting to Islam, my dear, despite objections you hold against me!"

It might seem that Firuz would rebel at being driven forward as a gelded ox dumbly minding a woman's stick, but Adelina's looks, youth, and adventurous passion on her back and knees managed to steer Firuz's unrest away from completely troubled waters.

Then arrived what Firuz hoped would be the rejuvenation of his gradually flagging marriage; first a daughter, Karine, then a son, Garik. Firuz shortly became the most devoted of fathers, spending time with his children, doting on them to no end; this being done, of course, beneath the meticulous gaze of Adelina. Firuz did not even mind her constant brow beating. Karine and Garik were beautiful beyond compare, garnering attention wherever they went. As such, Firuz loved them more than anything . . . in the beginning.

Karine, at birth, took immediate and full possession of his heart, and in doing so, he showered her with maudlin affection, attention, and gifts. As she developed, unlike most children, she grew oddly averse to being touched or held. By age three, when other children begin to babble openly, Karine stopped communicating. Instead, she stared, often failing to show any indication of understanding or caring what was being said or who said it. Such frigidity from his cherished daughter wounded Firuz, causing him to begrudgingly wonder whether she might grow out of this or whether this was to be her persona forever.

"Stop obsessing about nothing!" chided Adelina whenever he brought these concerns to light. "She's just a child, let her be. If she doesn't wish to be touched, then stop touching her. If she has no wish to talk, then stop jabbering at her day and night. It only agitates her."

As human hope remains eternal, Firuz's spirits were lifted by the birth several years later of Garik. "Ah, a fine, strapping boy!" exclaimed Firuz, going giddy on first spotting the boy's shriveled penis at the instant of birth. "Someone to carry forward my name and trade!"

Early on, to his dismay, it became evident that the boy suffered abnormally from anxiety. Garik cried too often, and grew frightened by the least commotion. And contrary to Firuz's expectations, Garik was extremely hesitant to explore or question. Unlike Karine, he insisted on being constantly held, but only by his mother or Karine. In turn, Karine became his shield, protecting and smothering him even more than their mother, who, after a time, lost interest in them both.

Confounded and buried in disappointment that his children had become impossible and far from pleasant, Firuz began to stew. Rather than becoming sources of joy, both Karine and Garik became festering sores of puzzlement and resentment, causing further disunion with Adelina who endlessly rationalized Karine's glacial façade yet excused Garik's dread of everything. Mostly, she had little interest in her husband's harping, and subsequently, despite Firuz's growing financial windfall and recent appointment by Yaghi Siyan to the Tower of the Two Sisters, his family evolved into a floundering disappointment that had begun to negate his other successes.

In addition, another issue pricked incessantly at Firuz's discontent. It involved the young commander of the tower adjacent to the Tower of the Two Sisters, a certain Colonel Talab. On returning home from his tower one evening, Firuz discovered the young officer having tea alone with Adelina. It might have seemed innocuous enough at first since Colonel Talab was first cousin to Adelina's wealthy Turkish neighbor and friend, a woman named Arzu. Firuz had seen Talab visiting the residence of Arzu a number of times before, and had once even found Talab and Arzu together visiting Adelina one afternoon at home. But finding this young rooster in the house alone with Adelina, lacking the company of Arzu, was beyond inappropriate to Firuz.

Questioned about it, she blithely passed it off as nothing. "There you go again being ridiculous!" she huffed. "Yes, Talab stopped by, but just for a minute. And really, no need to worry about the man! He's Arzu's favorite cousin and, as I learned today, a distant relative of Yaghi Siyan. Besides, he's simply the sociable type, and a dear, really. Never suggest again to me the idea of impropriety! I'm a Christian woman and deserve no such accusations!"

But suspicion is a slow poison. Colonel Talab was young, handsome, and had a reputation with women. Talk among the rampart guards was that Talab's prized compass was his 'over-sized' penis. This, coupled with Adelina's youthful beauty and sexuality, only served to intensify Firuz's growing displeasure with things in general.

One afternoon, shortly after the arrival of the crusaders outside Antioch, Firuz spotted Colonel Talab a good distance down the rampart at the tower adjacent to his own; apparently laughing, absorbing his guards in an old bawdy tale, no doubt. Irritated, Firuz resettled his gaze on the Orontes River, where to the far north crusader camps ranged for miles in massive clusters beyond the western walls of the fortressed city. As other Antiochians, Firuz wondered why they'd come, especially from places as far away as Italy, Germany, and France.

Lost to such musings, Firuz happened to spot three crusader knights crossing the Orontes near the distant Bridge Gate. Pointing and exchanging talk as they ambled along the wall, the riders neared his position and spotted him watching from the Tower of the Two Sisters. "Ho there!" shouted a voice. "How far is Jerusalem from here, my man?"

Firuz ignored the question, peering down at the man shouting the question.

"Oh, but simply a question!" the voice came again, chiding Firuz. "You there! Did you not hear me?" Leaning forward in his saddle, taking a closer look, the fellow egged on, "But say there, by damn, you don't seem as dark as these other guards we've seen manning the wall. How is that?"

"I'm Armenian, not Turkish!" shouted Firuz, more from boredom than interest.

"Armenian? Guarding the wall?" queried the knight, drawing closer to the wall so that he appeared directly below Firuz. "But then, you must be Christian, too, I wager?"

"Muslim. Recently converted."

"Well, I'll just be damned!" shouted the knight. "Chrissakes! All the Armenians that I've met along the road are Christian. Greek Orthodox, actually, not the true faith of Catholicism."

"Why have you come?" asked Firuz, ignoring the remark.

The knight, in turn ignoring Firuz's question, replied, "Impressive city, this. But as an Armenian, even though converted, I suppose you've no love of the Turks, am I right? After all, they're foreign occupiers! And not the least bit civil to those they vanquish, I'm told."

"They've not mistreated me," said Firuz. "I'm content enough."

But the knight was watching Firuz closely and thought he spotted something. "'Content enough,' you say?" he chuckled. "But I see trouble on your brow, my good man! Or do I simply imagine things?"

"You imagine things."

"Well then, perhaps I'm simply mistaken. In any case, my friends and I shall be on our way. But tell, sir, what's your name?"

"I'm called Firuz. But in return, be fair. What's yours?"

"I'm from Italy!" he grinned, gesturing west. "They call me Bohemud. Prince Bohemud of Taranto, in Southern Italy!"

"Never heard of you."

"What? Never heard of me?" protested Bohemud, feigning surprise. "Impossible. I'm told the very mention of my name makes Muslims quake and flee, shitting their breeches!"

"Prince Bohemud?" simpered Firuz, detecting a hint of jest in the knight's voice. "No. Never heard the name. But then, as I said, I'm Armenian, not Turk. And as you see, I'm neither quaking nor fleeing."

"The question remains then, since we can't see that high," sniggered Bohemud, "are you shitting your breeches?"

This, dismissing his earlier mood, made Firuz laugh.

"Ah, but a reminder then," shouted Bohemud, "you are still actually Christian, not Muslim!"

"Did you not hear me when I said I converted?"

"Once a Christian, forever a Christian!" replied Bohemud, looking to the other two knights who quickly agreed. "See there! For whatever reason you converted, your heart remains Christian whether you like it or not, Firoz!"

"Fi-ruz. My name's Fi-ruz, not Firoz."

"Oh, my pardon," snickered Bohemud, having made the error intentionally. "Well then, it's been pleasant talking to you, Armenian, but we've got to be on our way. And whether you've heard the name Bohemud or not, remember it, for you'll be hearing it a lot in the days to come. And should your Christian past reconquer this Muslim shit you've adopted, call for me."

"Call for you? But to what earthly purpose?"

"Because I could use a good Armenian or two when I take this city." Here he snaked his hand into a saddle bag and withdrew a pouch, jingling it. Peeling his lips back in that grin of a possum, he added, "And as those who know me profess, I pay handsomely!"

Turning his horse, he motioned to the riders at his side and all three ambled away as slowly as they had come.

As dusk dropped and Firuz remained at the wall, the sieging camps began to take on a different, threatening aura. Campfires were flickering for miles and miles along the Antioch side of the Orontes, glimmering like vast constellation of flickering specks fading into infinity. It was a daunting sight, that endless galaxy of military campfires, but Firuz was not unduly concerned.

This enemy was far from the root of that untenable desolation that had been coming after him for months, no years. That rope had been provided by Adelina, Karine, and Garik, and recently joined by Colonel Talab, along with Yaghi Siyan who had taken a sudden but suspect interest in his and Adelina's two children.

CHAPTER TWELVE

A REVELATION

After the rancorous Council of Princes meeting, the Tuscan camp began to swell with umbrage as Tristan expressed indignation, hurling accusations of spiritual corruption and greed at the primary leadership of the crusade while denouncing the morale weakness of its anointed leader, Bishop Adhémar of Le Puy. "Oh, that a man of God, supposedly the voice of the Pope himself during this crusade, would go weak in the face of serpentine ambition!" he complained, pacing from one spot to the next.

"It's done," insisted Guillaume, following Tristan about with Martin Letellier in a failing effort to settle him. Guillaume was as infuriated as his brother about the decision to lay attrition siege to Antioch, but accepted that once a tide had turned for shore, there was no stopping it. "We that are left, have to make it work, Brother. Either that, or fail entirely, pack up, and head home. That's not what you want, is it?"

"Aye," agreed Letellier. "Don't you dream, Tristan, of liberating Jerusalem from the forces of Islam? Unduly forced into siege here at Antioch, we shall end by making our way to the Holy Land. That's why we came, isn't it?"

From a distance the Danes were listening, having hoped distant investment would carry the day at the morning's gathering of princes; that the alternative of attrition siege was laden with risk. "Aye, it's soon to begin then," muttered Orla, looking at Crowbones.

But Crowbones was watching Tristan with regret, and had been ever since he'd returned from the Council meeting. Crowbones, knowing how sensitive Tristan could be, was hoping to patch up the exchange that had taken place the day before, but this was not the time. Tristan was stewing with anger, consumed by far more important thoughts.

"As Uncle Tristan says," shrugged Hroc, "siege makes no sense. But without Raymond of Toulouse, Bohemud, and Godfrey, there's no prayer of advancing against Jerusalem. It would be useless."

Guthroth the Quiet, nodding thoughtfully, placed his hand onto Hroc's shoulder as his eyes moved onto those of Orla and Crowbones. "W-we must l-look to G-God as w-we did during the G-Gamekeeper's Revolt, our fl-flight from England, the G-German Wars, and the m-massacre at Civetot and N-Nicodemia. H-He will see us th-through this."

At this, the longest single sentence the others had ever heard Guthroth struggle through, Orla could not help but chortle a bit. "Damn you, Guthroth!

Another speech like that and you'll be rousting Kuku Peter from the pulpit! What do you say, men? Is Guthroth turning into a preacher?"

Hroc said nothing, but a glimmer of pride took possession of his smile as Orla broke into laughter, seeing Guthroth's face crack the tiniest trace of a grin.

"Ho there!" came Scule's voice as the dwarf monk entered camp, followed by his new shadow, Christos, and another man. "Talk's spreading like wildfire," he announced. "I hear we're about to set siege to Antioch! I also heard bad blood broke out among the princes this morning, and violence nearly followed."

"Yes, unfortunately," said Letellier, "things got ugly, but not nearly as ugly as they will be once the blades come out and we bog down here in Antioch."

"I've just come from Bohemud's camp beyond the trees with my friend here, François Beltrane," said Scule. "The talk is fiery there, and it's pointed directly against Tristan. Such profanities I've never heard and aimed against a high cleric! If not for Rainald Porchet vehemently defending Tristan, I fear they may have even come this direction, swarming your camp!"

"Ah, my friend, Rainald Porchet," said Tristan. "Yes, a pious Christian for certain, and never one to back down from either his beliefs or the truth. If every crusader possessed his heart and virtue, then we would really represent the Army of God. As things are, I'm not sure what we represent, or whom."

"Aye, Porchet aside, the talk was fiery for certain over there," nodded Beltrane, suspecting one of the large Danes by the fire appeared to be eyeing him. Orla. "Do I know you?" asked Beltrane, eyebrows knit together.

Shaking his head, Orla said nothing, yet acted troubled.

"The talk in Bohemud's camp was hateful because I stood firm in the face of avarice and scheming," said Tristan, his bile beginning to simmer. "The Holy Crusade has been pirated, Scule, snatched from the Vatican, as well as from all men of good intent like yourself, Guillaume, Letellier, and Rainald Porchet."

As Tristan spoke, Letellier caught a telling glance from Scule, a look of apprehension. "They were calling Tristan a-a traitor," said Scule, looking to the ground, visibly distraught, "and shouting that he may have to be dealt with."

"The talk grew poisonous at the Council meeting, from both sides," said Letellier, his own face beginning to match Scule's. "There'll be some bridges to be mended. I assume the same piss and vinegar in Bohemud's camp is being sprayed in those of Raymond and Godfrey as well."

"Probably," agreed Guillaume, a bit discouraged, placing a hand to his brother's shoulder. He already knew that Tristan would neither falter nor bend in the face of such wrong crushing such right. "I tried to warn you to temper your words, Tristan, but you tossed me aside, swept away by your own anger. I'm in good stead with Bohemud, though, so, I'll take your part and soften the rift."

"You'll do no such thing!" fired Tristan, his face coloring as he set Guillaume's hand aside. "You and Letellier do what you must to stop this hemorrhage dividing the great army, but leave my name free of it. I've nothing to apologize for other than speaking the truth."

"Be reasonable," said Letellier. "It's done. The decision's been made and we have to move forward with it. We can't halt the current, but must join it, I say."

"Agreed, we must join the fight rather than hamper it," nodded Guillaume, his tone restrained yet certain.

"Bah!" groaned Tristan, pacing to a nearby stump, taking a position on it, letting loose a string of muttering.

"There's other news, too," said Scule, addressing all but looking at Tristan. "Tristan, I thought it might be of interest to you as it concerns two names I've heard you mention during the march."

Sighing with disinterest, Tristan attempted to disassemble the look of exasperation locked onto every feature. "Speak then, Scule," he said. "What could possibly be of interest to me at this point other than the lunacy of going out of our way to bathe in gore and blood here at Antioch?"

"It seems there's an old path up the mountains that leads toward the back, eastern part of Antioch," began Scule, "discovered by my friend Beltrane, here."

Beltrane nodded, distracted over Orla, standing to the side. He'd been watching Beltrane closely ever since he arrived in the Tuscan camp. "I'm from Normandy," said Beltrane, "distantly related to Bohemud's Hauteville lineage there. As such, I'm captain of Bohemud's scouting platoons. Before the rest of you arrived in Antioch, my scouting party advanced to Mount Staurin east of the Iron Bridge. We spotted a large force of heavily armed Turks working their way up a narrow rise. A tough looking lot dressed mostly in black, carrying black banners." Pointing to Christos, Beltrane added, "We suspected they were from Antioch, using some secret path to the back of the city, but as I was relating all this to Scule, the young boy there said differently."

"Christos claims they're not from Antioch," said Scule, "but from Asia Minor. He recognized their black banners."

Christos peered from behind Scule, his head two palms higher than the dwarf's. Knotting his fingers, he came forward tepidly, uncertain whether he should actually look at Bishop Saint-Germain directly. "It was the army of Mahmoud Malik, Butcher of Medina," Christos said, his bravery growing. "He burned our little town of Despina, killed my parents, and dragged off my sisters, burning everything in his path and raiding east of Manzikert."

"East of Manzikert?" asked Tristan, his curiosity pricked enough to set aside the events of the Council meeting.

"Y-yes, Bishop. He was raiding the sultanate of our Seljuk master, Lord Abdul Azim. Lord Azim put him to the run and has chased him this direction. He's still chasing him, I think. Just before my grandmother died in Armenia, we saw Malik's army battling a crusader army in a deep valley. After the battle, I was burying my grandmother under crusader shields when the beggar, Vaso, and I were chased from the field by the black banners. That's when Master Scule found me along the road."

Though Christos' story sounded disconnected, the mention of Mahmoud Malik and Lord Abdul Azim coming from the boy's mouth surprised Tristan. "They're both here!? In Antioch!?"

"Yes." Christos nodded slowly, not wishing to misspeak. "The Turks that Master Beltrane accidentally came across are led by Mahmoud Malik, and I'm certain that Lord Abdul Azim is but shortly behind him, in chase."

Taking pause, Tristan fell into introspection as confusion and puzzlement arrived at the same moment. He couldn't put a finger to it, but he suspected the unforeseen appearance of both men would, in one fashion or another, impact the struggle for Antioch. But how?

"What is it, Tristan?" asked Guillaume, noticing a spot of flush appearing above his brother's brow; the same discoloration that had arrived since childhood whenever he fell into disquiet.

"I'm not sure," said Tristan, dropping deeper into himself as he got up and shuffled away. The boy's words about Mahmoud Malik disturbed him, as when unknown footsteps are first detected emerging from the dark. Yet countering that uneasiness, the possibility of confronting Lord Abdul Azim caused a certain surge of anticipation. It was a confusing mélange of past fondness made complicated, possibly even impossible, by the crusade. Oh, but I could have never guessed back then in Rome, he thought, that Lord Azim and I should end on opposite ends of a struggle to the death.

CHAPTER THIRTEEN

AN EARLY MISSION

As Tristan vanished into his tent, Orla dropped his gaze from Beltrane, shaking his head with perceptible displeasure. This did not go unnoticed by the French scout. From the first footstep in the Tuscan camp, Beltrane had felt unwelcome by the large Dane. This perplexed him, having seen Orla several times during the long march but had never had occasion for either introduction or interplay.

Miffed with the Dane's impoliteness, Beltrane's interest piqued. "It seems something's bothering you there, big man," he addressed Orla directly. "Me, I'd guess. Tell, have I caused you injury, or is that simply your natural look?"

Orla spat to the side.

Shrugging, Beltrane looked over at his friend, Scule, mining for a possible explanation for the Dane's cold reception.

Responding in kind, Scule acknowledged equal uncertainty. To him, since Beltrane's arrival, Orla had dropped into an odd mood.

An uncomfortable silence ensued, broken only by the deep baritone of Orla. "Beltrane," he said, gesturing toward him, "if I'm not mistaken, you were one of Bohemud's advance scouts back in Dorylaeum, and now you're his lead scout?"

"Dorylaeum?" queried Beltrane. "Yes, I was there. But what's that to you?"

Looking to the other Danes, Orla said, "You and your bunch nearly got us butchered with your report that Kilij Arslan's Muslim army was nowhere to be found, then they attacked us by the tens of thousands as we crossed the river. Remember that?"

Turning a shade red, Beltrane could not deny the charge. "I remember," he confessed, his shoulders dropping a fraction. "Aye. It was a mistake. We were wrong that day. But know this, I insisted we search further into the hills the day before the attack, suspecting trouble, but I wasn't leading the foray, nor was I Bohemud's head scout at the time. The head scout was another fellow then, and he made us turn back, adamant there was but a small enemy force camped in the hills and ravines ahead. Because of that misjudgment, Bohemud removed him after Dorylaeum and put me in his place."

Taking his friend's side, Scule broke into the conversation, "You know scouting's tricky work, Orla, and uncertain at best. Beltrane here is a good man, and a damn fine scout, and I don't feel he deserves to be chastised for the mistake of a superior."

"It was a mistake that nearly cost us our lives," growled Orla, unmoved. "Only because of the last-minute arrival of the trailing half of our army did we survive slaughter."

Beltrane took offense to Orla's statement, accurate as it was, especially since he had already explained to Orla that he was not in charge that day. "I'll not argue the point, dammit!" he shouted between clenched teeth, his eyes drawing down with controlled resentment. "Aye, it was a mistake, as I said, and a damned big one at that. And true, we could have all been slaughtered, but we weren't, by the grace of God and a bit of luck." His face tightening, Beltrane's tone became rigid. "But you there, then, big man, you must be staking claim as the perfect soldier. No flaws, no misjudgments? Let me congratulate you then, seeing as half of any war is about falling into traps, guessing wrong, and miscalculating things as shit unravels!"

Orla had grown red-faced, near eruption, and it appeared, forgetting Beltrane's much smaller stature, the two were on the cusp of exchanging blows.

Feeling Beltrane had been unjustly affronted, but understanding Orla's position about Dorylaeum, Scule stepped between them. "But what's this?!" he squealed with his high-pitched voice. "Stop it, I say! You're both friends of mine, and I'll not watch this meaningless shit escalate into fist-a-cuffs!" Crouching, he waggled his fists about like fluttering birds. "If you wish to fight, then come on, I'm waiting on the both of you, by God!"

Scule, since birth, was extraordinarily strong and quick with his fists, but squaring off as he was, bobbing his head beneath the hulking shadow of Orla and throwing fake punches in Beltrane's direction, presented too comical a picture for those watching. Orla stepped back, amused by the absurdity of it all, and Beltrane and the others began to snicker.

"Odin's ass!" brayed Orla, shrinking back with false fear. "I'll not be pounded by a snip of a monk in front of my own family!"

Scule straightened, dropping his fists.

Beltrane loosened his stance, saying, "Aye, this is foolish. We're allies here, all of us," then dropped into reflection. "Before you of the main army arrived at Antioch, I was leading a scouting party east of the Iron Bridge, as I explained earlier, and happened across the Muslims of the black banners going up the mountain. Being outnumbered, we turned back. I suspected the path they were taking might give rear access to the city, so I'm leading a scouting party back up the trail tomorrow morning. I'll be sending another party to the south beyond the unguarded gates of Antioch in hopes of finding an unknown path up Mount Silpius from a southern approach." Here Beltrane stopped as a look of engagement slipped onto his face.

"And?" prodded Orla. "What's that to us?"

"Should you think that we, as Bohemud's scouts, are inadequate, then perhaps you'd wish to accompany us in the morning?"

"A fine proposal, and quite reasonable, I say!" volunteered Scule, hoping the offer might mend the crossing of words between two acquaintances for whom he held equal affection.

"Beltrane," huffed Orla, "is that a challenge?"

"No, an invitation."

Having criticized the scouting effort back in Dorylaeum, and knowing the other Danes held similar sentiments about that near debacle, Orla turn to Crowbones. "What do you think, Ivar? Should we go?"

"Hell, I suppose," replied Crowbones, his eagerness appearing lukewarm. "You and I could accompany Beltrane's bunch, I guess, and let Hroc and Guthroth follow the party probing south, but only if they wish."

"Agreed," said Hroc quickly, regarding Guthroth who was already nodding consent. "It's been nice sitting around day by day, but it's beginning to grow tiresome. Besides, I'd like to take a look around, find out what we've gotten ourselves into here in Syria."

"Very well then, Beltrane," agreed Orla, "we'll meet you in the morning then, and see what we can find."

"That's settled," Beltrane proclaimed, straightening his stance. "Bohemud's already assigned me scouts for each of the two missions, but he'll not object to adding two more men to each party. There'll be forks along the paths, and offshoots, so extra eyes won't hurt. I'm intending on splitting up anyway to cover more ground. I'll ask Bohemud to assign your son and the quiet fellow there to the scouts going south. And Orla, you and your brother can ride with me and the others scouting to the north."

As the scout finished, Orla started, a bit abashed, "Beltrane . . ." then paused, "if it was your head scout that gave the bad order back in Dorylaeum and not yourself, then I mean you no offense. I ask your pardon. I've been in that situation myself a time or two."

This meant a great deal to Beltrane, causing his expression to lighten. "All offense withdrawn, then," he said, then did an about-face to leave, but looked back. "And it'll be good to have you Danes at our side tomorrow. You're damn good men, I've heard, to have along in a tussle."

CHAPTER FOURTEEN

OH, BUT VANITY . . .

On the grand stage of humanity, most history-altering days are heralded with glorious fanfare or ritual; salient battles announced by the fury of thundering drums, coronations touted by the blare of trumpets, royal weddings announced by the reverberating toll of deeply resonating cathedral bells. Watching and listening with heart-thumping expectation, whether spurred by dread or joy, a waiting world braces for inevitable change; anxiously preparing for what is about to unfold.

Truly, the great days of great men stir attention. But within the microcosm of those trekking through life in anonymity, there is no thunder of drums, no blast of trumpets, nor tolling bells forewarning change. Rather, arriving with the silent guile of the slithering serpent, such days for men of lower rank quietly slip in, unnoticed, to unexpectedly uncoil, striking with the speed of light.

And so it was on the morning of November 5, 1097, when Ivar Crowbones arose with Orla Bloodaxe to accompany the Norman scout Beltrane and company to reconnoiter the northern approach to Mount Staurin.

Hoping to fully survey the same precipitous trail leading to the back of Antioch from the mountains that he had come onto earlier, Beltrane instructed those accompanying him that day to ride light. "You Danes meet me and the other scouts in the heart of Bohemud's camp just before daybreak," Beltrane advised. "From there we'll break into two parties; one taking the northern approach, the others the southern trail. We'll be gone three to five days at the least, but dress and pack light for mobility and quick flight should we be intercepted. Swords only. Helmets are fine, but no armor, chain mail, or shields to load you down. Many of the areas we'll be scouting rise straight up. It'll be hard enough for the horses without dragging up a ton of other shit."

As the Danes gathered that morning, Hroc and Guthroth were in high spirits.

"Though the food and game have, up to this point, been good," remarked Hroc, "they're beginning to run out. While we're out and about, maybe we'll come across some new foraging sources. That'd be good, eh?"

"J-ja," agreed Guthroth.

Orla, having actually played catalyst in involving the Danes in Beltrane's scouting mission, was a bit less enthusiastic by morning; age had begun to punish his war-worn bones, as it had with Crowbones. Nonetheless, he saddled his mount, refusing to show indication of such.

Crowbones was the last to mount. Struggling a bit due to the absence of his severed left limb, Orla watched him with fraternal consideration. It had been twenty years since Crowbones had lost his arm in England to the Gamekeeper's Revolt, so long ago that Orla scarcely remembered him with both arms intact. Nevertheless, Crowbones had remained ever the same fierce warrior, engendering in Orla much admiration and pride. But watching his brother struggle at the saddle gave Orla pause this particular morning. Crowbones' effort at mounting the horse was little different than other times since the march began, yet Orla fancied that Crowbones had been laboring a bit more of late. Ah, but it's no different than with me, I'd suppose, thought Orla, age has begun to nest and it's finally showing its face. Aye, perhaps that's why Ivar didn't catch fire yesterday about tagging along with Beltrane on this mission. This, in turn, caused Orla to feel reticent about having prodded Beltrane about Dorylaeum, then later accepting his challenge to join the scouting mission. Me and my big mouth! But refusing a challenge to men like Orla was insupportable, and he let the thought pass.

As the Danes made Bohemud's camp, Guillaume was already there, having risen earlier than the others to meet with Bohemud for an early morning strategy session since the assault on Antioch was close to launch, and final tactics were being solidified. "Hold there!" he shouted, motioning for the Danes to pull aside.

What's this? wondered Orla, whose surprise was short-lived. Just then, he spotted the ever-hated Desmond DuLac, Tafur, and Geoffrey Burrel standing in the distance next to Beltrane. "What the hell are they doing here?" Orla snorted.

"Easy, Orla," urged Guillaume, keeping his voice low. "I've just learned that DuLac and Burrel have been chosen by Bohemud to accompany Beltrane along with you and Crowbones on today's scouting foray. On hearing this, I advised him to remove DuLac and Burrel, but Bohemud refused, insisting they're part of his regular scouting force now."

"What? Damn them to Hell, I sure wasn't planning on this kind of shit when I volunteered! And God's spine, Bohemud's well aware of the bad blood between us and DuLac. Everyone knows that's what the trial by champions between Hroc and Pierre Gustave was all about back in Dorylaeum!"

He had no sooner mentioned Pierre Gustave's name when Pierre Gustave himself appeared on horseback. Gesturing to Hroc, who had defeated him in the trial by champions but spared him by taking a foot instead, Gustave pulled aside. Having originally joined the crusade beneath the banner of Desmond DuLac and serving as one of his personal bodyguards, Pierre and his twin brother, Luc Gustave, had distanced themselves from DuLac after the trial by champions. Pierre, in fact, had even forgiven Hroc the missing foot; thankful that Hroc had shown mercy at the end of their deadly duel. "Hail, Hroc!" he shouted, motioning with his fist, offering a gesture of deference.

Hroc waved back, no longer holding any animosity toward Pierre Gustave and glad that God had struck him with the grace of mercy at the climax of the duel.

But since that fight, Orla had refused to trust neither of the Gustave brothers, alienation of DuLac or not. "Dammit," he rasped, "don't tell me Pierre Gustave's coming, too?"

"Aye," confirmed Guillaume. "But on learning of all this, I've pulled you Danes from the mission. It's a bad mix. No good can possibly come of it."

"You've pulled us from the mission?" said Hroc, his elation for the trip instantly dropping into disappointment. "But Uncle Guthroth and I are anxious to go." He cocked his head in his uncle's direction. "Father, you and Uncle Crowbones return to camp. Lord Guillaume's right, you riding with DuLac and Burrel is like mixing poison. You'd be fine with Pierre Gustave, I'm certain, but not with the other two."

"The hell you say!" barked Orla, boring holes through both Guillaume and Hroc, his eyes slipping to a squint. "But there's bigger horseshit here! Why won't Bohemud simply pull DuLac and Burrel for the day?"

"I'll not pull regular scouts in favor of temporary scouts," said Bohemud, entering the circle. "Orla, you got yourself invited somehow, and DuLac and Burrel had nothing to do with it. Chrissakes, think how they feel about this unexpected confusion. In any case, why don't you and your brother just ride back to the Tuscan camp and call it a day. Sit back and enjoy the time off. You both deserve it. As for Hroc and Guthroth, I'm happy to send them along with the southern probe as they're two of the best horsemen of the entire army. And yes, I appreciate your intent, Orla, but as we can all see here, it's inadvertently gone to shit. Beltrane and the others will do fine without you. Besides, you and Crowbones are getting a bit long in the tooth for an outing up a damned mountainside anyway."

Already afire, Orla took this unintended slight by Bohemud as a deliberate and pointed affront. "By damn, Bohemud!" he bellowed, pulling at his reins angrily, causing his horse to stamp with irritation. "My brother and I can ride any bastard of your entire army straight into the ground! And I'll not back out because of DuLac or Burrel. As vowed to my son back in Dorylaeum, and even though I still hate DuLac to the marrow, I've set aside my black blood with him! So, we shall ride with Beltrane, me and my brother!"

Bohemud looked to Guillaume for resolution, but Guillaume's eyes were set directly on Orla. "Your word, Orla," grimaced Guillaume, battling against his better judgment, "for there shall be no tolerance for violating it from Bohemud or any of the other princes. Even I, myself, could not rightfully intervene! Make no move against DuLac, or you're done. Understand?"

"Ja, jeg forstår! My word," snorted Orla, his eyes turning to coals as he glared over at DuLac.

DuLac was every bit as inflamed as Orla. Minutes earlier he'd discovered that Orla and Crowbones would be accompanying the foray up Mount Staurin, due to Beltrane's insistence. Having feared the Danes since their rebellion against him in England, DuLac knew a scouting mission presented ample opportunity for assassination, especially with Orla and Crowbones riding together. Stubbornness and pride ruling, he refused to back out of Beltrane's sortie, just as Orla had, as a matter of manliness. In the end, he would have to count on the weight of the Council of Princes who tolerated absolutely no infighting or treachery in the midst of warring against heathen Muslims. Hell, he counseled internally, surely Orla wouldn't sacrifice himself simply to get to me, nor would Crowbones . . . would he?

Mounted alongside DuLac, Geoffrey Burrel appeared to be rather enjoying this quandary that had arisen from nowhere. And beside Burrel, on foot, the barbarous Tafur appeared to be absorbing circumstances with a touch of satisfaction. Tafur, having no horse and not a scout, would be remaining in camp. But watching things unfold, he felt certain the stage was being set for drama, which was fine with him. Tafur despised the Danes so much that he, DuLac, and Burrel had conspired together about exacting retribution against both the Saint-Germain brothers and the Danes, but Tafur held no regard for DuLac either. DuLac was a nobleman, and Tafur had despised both nobility and clergy since childhood. Then, he mused, let things happen as they may during this little outing, and we'll just see who returns.

As for Hroc and Guthroth, both held enough confidence in Orla's Dorylaeum vow that his conduct during the scouting mission was not cause for concern. Orla had always been true to his word. They did, however, harbor certain doubts about DuLac and Burrel. Still, whatever folly transpired, those two would be swiftly overcome by Orla and Crowbones should there be trouble.

"All will be well," said Hroc, looking at Guthroth with assurance.

Guthroth merely nodded, never taking his eyes off the enemy threesome across the way. We shall see. But then, black blood runs thick and deep, especially as concerns Desmond DuLac and our Saint-Germain faction.

That morning, from the beginning, had begun with unanticipated complexity overrunning simplicity, and the past overshadowing the future. As such, the true engine driving decisions that morning was not forbearance, but purely vanity, a virtue oddly enough ascribed to and saddled onto women. Yet in truth, it is men who actually wear that badge with far greater haughtiness, while virulently denying it.

By way of analysis, it was this very trait that had bred Orla's initial ill reception of Beltrane. In turn, Beltrane's pride led him to rebuke Orla, which softened with time, but in the end led to challenging Orla to join the scouting mission. Taking then a double turn, arrogance would not allow Orla to decline Beltrane's challenge.

But that was not the end of it. Oh, no. Pride grew yet another head and ignited again in the camp of Bohemud when, against all counsel, Orla refused to withdraw from the mission for two reasons: his refusal to defer to DuLac by withdrawing from the mission, and Bohemud's inference that Orla and Crowbones had passed their physical prime.

DuLac, in turn, also fell victim by refusing to defer to Orla and Crowbones, whom he hated beyond measure. He could have easily volunteered to withdraw from the scouting mission, but to do so might have appeared to be a sign of weakness, which for him was intolerable.

Bohemud, of course, had the authority to put a halt to everything as the camp commander, but his self-importance forced him to believe mightily in the weight of his own threats that Orla and Crowbones had best behave. Therefore, he did nothing.

Guillaume, as a knight, could choose who went and who stayed, but deferred to Orla, not wishing to further injure his ego, and refused to order him and Crowbones to return to the Tuscan camp. Being a man who never backed down from anything, on this particular morning he did, to preserve the honor of the man he respected, admired, and loved as blood of his own family, and blood of his own heart. Forcing Orla to lose face, for Guillaume, was unacceptable.

In the end, then, the wheel of 'manly vanity' managed to run a full course among an entire troupe of extremely masculine men. Such is the true nature of males who've been driven by narcissism, a female foible supposedly, into forming opinions, making decisions and judgments, and giving rise to mistakes that need never happen.

CHAPTER FIFTEEN

SEEDS OF DISCONTENT

On the same morning that Bohemud sent out his scouting parties, Firuz stopped by his armor-making operation before reporting to the Tower of the Two Sisters, as was his custom. He wanted to check on the progress of two apprentices in training. When he arrived, to Firuz's displeasure, the two young apprentices were heavily engaged in conversation with a young Turkish nobleman rather than stoking fires for the ten breast-plates scheduled to be fabricated that day. On closer inspection, however, the apprentices were acting disturbed, or at the least, confused.

"What's this?" asked Firuz, addressing the nobleman. "You're keeping my lads from their work."

"Ah, Master Firuz, good to see you this morning!" excitedly replied the young Turk.

"Do I know you?" asked Firuz, sensing trouble.

"No, but you shall soon know me well, Master Firuz."

"Huh?"

"I happen to be the nephew of Emir Siyan's third and favorite, I should add, concubine. It seems you've recently been honored by a position on the ramparts by my uncle." Here he paused, grinning sheepishly. "Well, Emir Siyan's not my real uncle, actually, but that's what he's asked me to call him of late."

"I see. But what can I do for you this morning? Why are you here?"

"Well, I was hoping you might show me around a bit and introduce me to our ironsmiths."

Thinking he failed to hear the man correctly, Firuz went silent. "Our iron-smiths?" he asked indignantly, chortling a bit.

"Yes. You see, my Uncle, or rather Emir Siyan is planning on me taking over your operation here. Well, not necessarily permanently. But he said that—"

"What! What the hell did you say!?"

Confused, the young nobleman shrugged apologetically. "Did Emir Siyan not convey this plan to you? I thought—"

"Hell no! He hasn't conveyed any such thing! What in thunder are you talking about then?"

"I see," said the young man, retreating a step. "Perhaps I should leave then and—"

"Dammit," insisted Firuz, grabbing him by the shoulder, "tell me what you're talking about or I'll throttle you a good one! And I don't give a shit who you call your uncle!"

Frightened, the young man cowered a bit, shielding his face as he blurted, "We're surrounded and there's a good chance war is coming, Master Firuz! Emir Siyan told me your position on the ramparts is far more important than you making armor! So, he's turning things over to me."

"You're full of shit, you little bastard!" roared Firuz. "By damn, do you even have any damned training in iron work?"

"Yes, yes, of course I do!" he yelped, warding off the blows Firuz had begun to administer. "Stop! Stop I say, or I'll tell my uncle, and then you'll be sorry, you lout!"

Chasing the interloper from the stables, Firuz flung himself on a stool, incensed. "Ah, I see," he grumbled aloud, "the old bastard's been playing me all along. He intends to pilfer my trade and hand it over to placate one of his whores! Just like that!" He snapped his finger.

His temper aflame, he shared this news with his wife later that night, but Adelina merely dismissed his concerns. "Oh, but the young fellow did say temporarily, didn't he?" she asked.

"I-I think—I was just so damn mad I can't exactly remember what he said!"

"Well, there you go again, Firuz," she chastised, "erupting into fits, thinking the worst before getting the full facts! But while you settle down, I'll simply check with Colonel Talab. As I told you the other day, he's directly related to Yaghi Siyan, not related through one of the little bitches in Siyan's harem."

Though Firuz did not favor Talab in the least, Adelina's words placated him for the moment. "Very well," he muttered, "you might be right. See what you can learn from Talab, then."

Upon the rising of the following sun, Firuz felt as if in a fog. His mistreatment of the nobleman and possible repercussions had caused him to not sleep during the night. "I'm going to by-pass going to my shop this morning," he called to Adelina. "Besides, it's market day, isn't it?"

"Yes, dear, but why do you ask?" She'd stopped what she was doing, hearing the question.

"I think maybe I'll walk with the children as they head to market. My tower's along the way. It'll at least give me a few minutes to talk to them. Shit, I scarcely even see them anymore! They barely have anything to do with me unless I force it."

Garik and Karine both overheard this exchange, and neither was pleased by it.

"B-but I don't want to walk with father!" objected Garik.

"Shh," said Karine, putting a finger to her lips. "He'll hear you, Garik. Say nothing!"

"Ah, a lovely morning it is, eh children?" asked Firuz, locating them in the back of the house where Karine was slipping around trying to find a hiding place for Garik and herself, but too late. "Come along," he insisted, "I'll walk you to market as far as my tower, from there you two can run along and finish your market chores. How does that sound?"

Neither child replied, nor even offered acknowledgment that he had spoken. "Did you not hear me?" snapped Firuz, pressing for response.

"Yes, Father," replied Karine, curtly.

As they headed down the street, Firuz tried to encourage an exchange about what was on Adelina's market list for the day, but the two children trudged ahead in cathedral silence, staring straight ahead until their father made the Tower of Two Sisters. "Very well, I'll see you two later," said Firuz, sighing with irritation.

Again, neither replied. Instead, Karine quickened her pace away from him, pulling Garik along in tow. Tuesday and Friday market were Karine's favorite times of the week. Having shed themselves of their father, she had become impatient to begin perusing the endless stalls of wares on display in the Traders' Quarter, that designated section of the Antioch market reserved for caravans arriving from the Far East via the Silk Road. Staving off Garik's insistent whining about returning to the shelter of home, Karine delighted in spending hours combing through infinite offerings of distant and exotic perfumes, fine fabrics made in faraway lands, delicately embroidered tapestries, jewelry, jade figurines, and goldwares filling an entire three block area.

Having canvassed the Traders' Quarter, her routine for the remainder of market morning would be to laboriously drag Garik through the adjacent Antioch Quarter, bursting with regional tradesmen, craftsmen, and retailers. Not as fascinating as the Traders' Quarter, the prices were affordable and the local wares possessed a flair of their own, melding the confluence of Syrian, Armenian, and Turkish cultures into a distinctly Antiochian fashion.

Once satisfying her interest there, it was her custom to end the adventure within the Basket Quarter to complete her bi-weekly chore of filling hers and Garik's baskets with spices, produce, and meats for family consumption. She did not consider this task so much a chore as an opportunity to be 'out.' She found much pleasure in examining burgeoning stall tables spilling with fat grapes and berries, swollen melons, rich eggplants, greens, and other vegetables interspersed between butchers' tables where hung splayed hares, broken necked geese and swans hanging from hooks, slabs of beef, lamb and goat, and staples such as rice, wheat, other grains, and tea of every assortment imaginable. Of special interest stood countless butchers' stalls with flat-iron grills and griddles aflame, sizzling and smoking, wafting everywhere the rich aroma of marinated tenderloins, roasting cutlets, rib flanks, and spiced vegetables.

But today, Karine's routine was cut short. By the end of her and Garik's first hour within the Traders' Quarter, on spotting a jade wrist band that caught her eye, she fished into her pocket to retrieve her coin purse, only to discover it was absent. In her haste to hide from their father, she had left it at home.

"Oh, no!" she sighed, disheartened, staring longingly at the jade band she had thought to purchase. "We have to go back to the house, Garik. We've no money and we haven't even made it to the Antioch or Basket Quarter!" Yanking her younger brother by the arm, she turned for home.

"I don't want to come back!" insisted Garik. "I'll just stay home in my room and you can come back by yourself!"

"No, Garik. Mother won't allow it. She insists that market is our chore. You know that."

Garik slumped, already knowing that his pleas to remain home would go unheeded. Their mother had burdened them with this market chore twice a week for as long as he could walk, knowing full well the market frightened him. He didn't like being out in the streets among strangers or getting lost in streaming masses of people coming and going. Such exposure terrified him and the only way he managed was by clinging to Karine and trying, albeit uselessly, to hurry her along.

The market, being located in the southwestern quadrant of Antioch, was within view of the Tower of the Two Sisters where their father took his daily position. Happening to peer down from the tower as his children were making their way home, Firuz grew puzzled. Aware of Karine's penchant for lingering all morning at the market, this early departure pricked his curiosity. Looking closely, he perceived that Karine appeared perturbed. "Karine!" he shouted, leaning over the wall. "What's wrong?" The distance was too great and his voice did not carry, so his children remained undeterred, hearing nothing. Suspecting something amiss, Firuz gestured to a Turkish subordinate manning the wall, saying, "I'll be back shortly."

Running down the ramparts, he closed the distance between his children and himself, calling out to them just as they stepped into the house. They failed to hear him again, not because of distance this time, but because Karine and Garik had just then been distracted by something else. On opening the front door, they detected noise coming from the back of the house. It was an odd, troubled noise, similar to the low moaning issued by the elderly when severely ill, which unnerved Garik.

"Karine!" he whispered, cringing, moving closer, clasping her hand tighter.

More curious than unnerved, Karine's ears went vertical as she tried to better identify the traces of pleading that converged into moaning. Cocking an ear, an intermittent, detectable rhythm of lamentation filled the air. It sounded like it was coming from their mother. Thinking her injured, Karine loosened her grip on Garik and made her way toward the back of the house to her parents' room.

The door was open.

Then Karine heard her mother cry an unabashed release, "Talab! Oh, Talab!"

Leaning against the doorway, Karine's eyes flared to bursting as a tiny gasp escaped her throat, wriggling its way out in flutters, similar to a small bird struggling against a wire snare.

There before her, in the room, Adelina and Colonel Talab were thrashing about on the bed completely naked! Her mother was positioned on her knees and elbows with her rump elevated while Talab was just behind her on his knees, his hands tightly gripping Adelina's waist. It appeared he was violently . . . assaulting her rump? Both were moaning, lost to their senses, yet within their cries issued the timbre of supplication mingled with savagery and pleasure.

Repelled but entranced, Karine put her finger to her lips right when Garik reached her side. "Shhh," she motioned with her forefinger.

Catching sight of the two thrashing on the bed, Garik grew debilitated, certain his mother was being attacked from behind by Talab who appeared to have gone mad, his eyes upturned with rapture, his panting erupting into guttural, nearly bestial outbursts. "Mother!" he wailed. "Oh, Mother!"

Rudely jolted from their ecstasy, Adelina and Talab simultaneously went rigid, then clumsily separated as two dogs in heat interrupted by a furious master.

"Garik! Karine?" Adelina rasped, fumbling to cover her bare, pendulous breasts as Talab shoved her away, struggling to cover his genitals.

"Mother?" Karine's eyebrows rounded out her face, the corners of her lips arcing upward, not exactly into a smile but a leer, or smirk.

An instant later Karine was roughly pushed aside as her father burst into the room, bellowing with rage, attacking Talab with furious fists while simultaneously lunging out to strike his wife. "Talab, you bastard!" Firuz screamed, eyes hot as coals. "Oh, Adelina, you filthy whore! I'll kill you both, goddamn you!!"

Shielding his face from Firuz's frenetic attack, Talab broke free for an open window, hurling himself naked through it onto the street, in the midst of passing neighbors. Startled at first, they fell silent, several huddling in hushed exchanges, which morphed into snickering and pointing.

Humiliated and terrified thinking Firuz would follow him out the window, Talab cupped his oversized testicles and dashed down the street, snatching anything he could to cover his nakedness. Talab may have been a colonel of the elite Antioch Turkish Guard, but he was no fighter, merely a handsome, philandering dandy who had risen in Antioch through family doting, name, and wealth.

Unable to bury a fist into Talab, Firuz took out his anger and frustration on Adelina, straddling her, bashing her face. Garik, meanwhile, had launched into a mercurial fit, pleading for Karine to intercede. But Karine's feet remained nailed in place as she watched the beating, fascinated. As her father's fist exploded into Adelina's nose, bursting it into a flattened fountain of blood, Karine put a hand to her mouth, wondering what might occur next, how this might end.

Firuz, a lost man, had left this world; his entire psyche blind with bitterness, possessed by that single-minded rage of a bear having mauled an already incapacitated prey. Intent on squeezing the last breath from his wife's throat, he neither heard nor saw an entire company of Turkish Guard led by Ben-fazi enter the room. Nor did he feel them drag him from the bed, take him to the floor, and pin him in place; froth, spittle, and sweat pouring from his face, covered in Adelina's blood.

Within a half-minute of being forcibly bound, Firuz's vision began to clear as the constellation of white spots exploding in his pupils began to dissipate and the ringing in his ears deadened.

"What's this!" Firuz yawped, trying to break free. "Has that bastard, Talab, sent for you to actually spare my goddamned wife?! Or are you here on behalf of that other bastard Turk trying to steal my shop?!"

"Talab?" Ben-fazi shouted. "What's Talab got to do with anything here?"

His fog clearing, Firuz realized that Ben-fazi and the Turkish guards were not there to arrest him for assaulting either Talab or the man who had appeared at his shop a day earlier, but for another purpose of which Firuz could not fathom. Ben-fazi, of all people, had never before graced his door. "So," muttered Firuz suspiciously, "why are you here?"

"For your children," replied Ben-fazi, pointing to Karine and Garik.

"My-my children?" stammered Firuz, his resistance slackening as he glared at the little blue man.

"Yes. Emir Siyan has requested them."

"Another damn visit to court?" snapped Firuz. "And so damn soon?!"

At this, Ben-fazi shook his head slowly as his expression diminished into empathy. Crossing his arms, he explained, "No visit, Firuz, Emir Siyan has sent me to fetch them permanently."

"Huh?" coughed Firuz.

"Emir Siyan wants them to reside at the palace with him." As he said this, Ben-fazi's eyes again relayed a flicker of compassion, but it vanished quickly as, correcting himself, he took on the officiousness of declaring a royal decree. "This is not a request, Firuz, and Yaghi Siyan will abide neither objection nor interference. You know that."

Adelina, battered and bleeding on the bed, heard this exchange and was mortified. Moaning, she raised her arms out toward her children standing near the door. "Garik!" she wailed. "No, don't take my sweet son! You can have Karine, but not Garik!"

This caused Garik's bawling to escalate into delirium. "M-Mother! Mother!" he sobbed, trying to break through the ring of guards.

"Be still," commanded Karine calmly, catching him by the nape of his neck, reeling him back gently. Her eyes, then going vacant, rested on Ben-fazi. "Yes, Master Fazi," she said, "take us from this house as Master Yaghi wishes. Garik may, at times, cling to Mother, but I am unhappy here. And actually, Garik is as well. I shall certainly miss neither my mother nor my father. I think the palace will suit me, and I will ensure it suits Garik as well."

Listening, Firuz deflated. Head spinning, he could find no words adequate to vent his confusion.

Adelina lay there naked and bloody, hair a rat's nest, weeping and snuffling, too broken to rise from the bed.

Gesturing for the guards to follow, Ben-fazi turned to Firuz. "I am not your enemy. I will do my best for the children; protect and care for them as much as I am allowed. But just so you know, your fears may well be misdirected, Firuz. Yaghi Siyan is beyond the age of erections and fornication. He, instead, collects beautiful things, unusual things. You see, your children are beautiful, just as I am unusual."

At that Ben-fazi left, followed by the guards, Karine, and Garik.

On that Tuesday morning, the already threadbare existence of Firuz the Armenian armor-maker went from questionable to completely undone. Having overcome much difficulty from the day he took his first breath, earning prosperity and respect the hard way, the tide had turned against him completely, crushing him beneath the weight of happenstance. The Turks had come, imposing their will, might, and faith on Syria. Yaghi Siyan was about to thieve his thriving armor-making trade and award it to a young nobody, honoring Firuz with a position he never wanted as Captain of the Tower of the Two Sisters. And now the old bastard was even stealing his children, such as they were.

And as a final punishment, Firuz had been turned into a cuckold, having lost his wife to the seduction of Colonel Talab. This alone guaranteed eternal humiliation within the Armenian, Syrian, and Turkish communities, and especially from subordinate Turkish guards manning the Tower of the Two Sisters under his command.

But men possessing little power possess little recourse. Thus, as Adelina lay weeping and wounded just feet away, Firuz but sat motionless in an impotent stupor, surrendering to despair.

CHAPTER SIXTEEN

THE BRIDGE . . . THE BEGGAR

As Beltrane led his party from Bohemud's camp, DuLac kicked his mount in the flanks, giving Orla and Crowbones a passing sneer as he ran his horse to the head of the column, positioning close to Beltrane. "You two stick to the back with Gustave," he growled at Orla, "since you're late being assigned to this scouting squad."

Geoffrey Burrel followed DuLac's maneuver, spurring his horse as well, joining Beltrane up front. Saying not a word, his passing face betrayed a touch of conceded satisfaction.

"Bastard! All the better to keep my eyes on your foul French ass, DuLac!" retorted Orla, his eyes turning to slits.

"Ah, but let it go, Orla," counseled Crowbones, shaking his head. "We've a long day ahead of us. No point in jousting all the way up the mountain."

Remaining silent, Orla glowered ahead at DuLac's back. In turn, DuLac refused to even acknowledge the Danes' presence.

It turned into a quiet ride from Bohemud's camp to the Iron Bridge, albeit strained by the dark history between DuLac and the two Danes. The self-induced silence was broken only by the clatter of hooves against rocky terrain and, on occasion, a perfunctory exchange between Beltrane and DuLac, muttering thoughts about what might lay ahead once they began scaling the heights. DuLac, of course, was much tempted to spill his ire concerning the Danes to Beltrane, but knew instinctively that Beltrane would be little interested. Unaware of details between DuLac and the Danes, he had in camp that morning expressed appreciation for the Danes' fighting skills. Bah, muttered DuLac in his head, Beltrane could give a shit about my hatred for those bastards! Seems he's already taken a damned liking to Orla!

Nearing the Iron Bridge, Orla looked over at his brother, baffled. "Crowbones, does this not boil your blood, riding so close to that snake up there, and him with his back to us? Such an easy damned mark he'd be, yet he remains haughty as ever. I'd like to bash his skull to fragments, wouldn't you?"

"Ja, lort, det er vanskelit," nodded Crowbones, slipping into Danish. "It's not easy, him within such close reach like this. But then the reach is farther than it appears, I'd say. Besides, after the trial by champions, we owe it to Hroc to leave things alone. Sure, I despise DuLac with every fiber of my being, but Hroc holds far more weight to me than all of DuLac's sins combined. It's because of Hroc that I tolerate DuLac's existence. You must do the same. Then, too, there's the full weight of the Council of Princes against us should we touch DuLac, remember?"

Not understanding Danish, but having heard 'trial by champions,' Pierre Gustave advanced from his rear position, coming alongside Orla. "If you're talking about me, I should like to know what's being said," he said, his voice lacking all suggestion of defensiveness. "Just curious, that's all."

"No, not really talking about you; talking about DuLac," replied Orla with sharpness, harboring, even now, vast resentment against the big Norman from his days of serving as bodyguard for DuLac, as well as from the trial by champions when Pierre Gustave came within a thin whisker of killing his son. "If I was talking about you, I'd let you know, don't you think, Gustave?"

Feeling the chill, Pierre Gustave said, "Hroc could have killed me in Dorylaeum, Orla, but he didn't. Honorable. Do you think a man forgets such a thing? And I may be hindered sorely by my missing foot, but I'm happy to be alive and proud to be riding alongside you and Crowbones."

Orla said nothing, prompting Crowbones to intervene. "Gustave, forgive my brother's cold shoulder. He holds a hard line at times, and has a long memory. But you should know something about him. He lost his wife in England because of DuLac, then his first-born son, Knud, in Tuscany to the Germans years ago during the Investiture War. Hroc is all he has left, and you nearly got the best of him in Dorylaeum but for a blink of fate. Such is battle. But know this, I am with you on the matter. Dorylaeum's done. More importantly, you and your brother washed your hands of DuLac afterwards." Looking over, Crowbones addressed his brother, "Come on, Orla, give Gustave a crumb of credit at least. He deserves it, I think."

Turning in his saddle, Orla gave Gustave a brief consideration. "Ja, then," he said, "you're a decent man, I suppose. You just fell in with bad company."

This was enough for Gustave. Giving a nod of satisfaction, he returned to the rear of the column.

As they neared the Iron Bridge, they spotted the figures of two men, both of later years; one had crossed the bridge and was approaching them on horseback with three donkeys in tow, the other being the old beggar, perched on a boulder just adjacent to the bridge entrance.

"Ho, you fellows there!" the rider said in Armenian. "Could you tell me exactly where the Christian army is camped?"

None speaking Armenian, Beltrane at least thought to recognize the man's utterance of 'K'ristonya banaky,' having heard it many times among Armenians from Antioch visiting or staying in the crusaders' camps. "The Christian army?" asked Beltrane. "Aye," he said pointing back, taking the man for a trader, "just follow this road from the Iron Bridge around Mt. Staurin and south. From there, it's everywhere."

Not speaking French but comprehending that he was on the right path, the man acknowledged Beltrane with a grateful salute. "Shnorhakalut!" he said, nudging his horse forward as his three donkeys followed, braying, objecting to the heavy weight of trinkets, hardware, and other goods overloading their backs.

"No matter what that fellow's selling, he'll find takers amongst our many men," remarked Beltrane, continuing toward the bridge.

Reaching the edge of the bridge, the old beggar jumped from his perch. As before, he was naked save a ragged loincloth scantily covering his bony frame, and he again launched into howling and cursing, waving his hand in wide arcs as casting over them the net of an ancient Armenian curse. "Aiee! Fools! Yes, run back from whence you came!" he screeched in Armenian, thinking perhaps the men were returning west. "The Turks own this land! And can't be beat by the grizzly lot of you Western barbarians!"

Then, as before, on spotting one-armed Crowbones, the beggar stooped and tucked one hand beneath his arm-pit to resemble a broken-winged bird, fluttering the bent elbow, rotating it in tiny circles and cawing plaintively, as if injured.

This struck Crowbones. Of all the birds the old fool could have mimicked, he had chosen Crowbones' very namesake, a crow.

"Dammit, you crazy bastard!" bellowed Orla, infuriated even more than he was during the first run-in with the beggar. "Move aside, you old pile of shit!"

Incensed, Orla pulled his sword. Since the day Crowbones' arm had been severed decades earlier in England, no man had ever once dared belittle his brother's remaining knob of a stub. To do so would have invited blind fury and bloodletting from both Orla and Crowbones. Yet, twice now, this shriveled, half-naked remains of a man dared mock Crowbones' injury. "I'll not tolerate this!" he shouted, spittle flying from his mouth.

"Oh, but let him be!" called Crowbones, gesturing Orla back. "He's mad as a March hare, can't you see? He has no idea what he's even doing! He's harmless, I say, and—"

Before Crowbones could finish, Orla reined his horse into the old man, spinning him into the dust. Collecting himself, the beggar wobbled to his feet, dazed, his eyes rolling about like eggs slung into a bowl. When his vision cleared, his eyes settled not on his attacker but on Crowbones. Immediately, his entire countenance changed and he began to quake intermittently. He cocked a trembling finger at Crowbones, ignoring Orla and the others, moaning, "Oh, but soldier, you are dead atop that horse. Poor man, you just don't yet know it!"

None understood a word the old man was muttering in Armenian, but they all saw him transfigure from the bellicose raving madman into a trough of despair, resembling one stricken by sorrow. DuLac and Burrel laughed, passing it all off as an act of insanity. Flicking their reins, they nudged their mounts onto the bridge, following Beltrane.

Orla, eyes afire, sheathed his blade with one hand, issuing an obscene gesture with the other before moving onto the bridge. Gustave followed, leaving Crowbones alone in his place. For the old man, it mattered not; everything on this earth had vanished, dwindling singularly to the one-armed rider saddled before him.

Then came one of those rare moments that defied nature, explanation, or logic; an occurrence, owing to humanity's ceaseless rush toward science and enlightenment, which is generally relegated to 'a trick of imagination.' His eyes glued to Crowbones, the old beggar issued another distressful moan, his eyes rolling back in their sockets until nothing showed but the whites. There he stood, stiff as stone, his entire essence hurtling from this world into another, to drift aimlessly into that vaporous realm of necromancy and superstition set aside for those of demented minds or possessed souls.

Entranced, eyes melting to glaze, Crowbones watched, believing to perceive that same dark, odious world into which the beggar had launched.

Standing before each other, motionless as statues, for what seemed an eternity, but in reality took but a fraction of time, the beggar's head lolled forward awkwardly as the pupils of his eyes settled again onto Crowbones, whose own eyes had never left the beggar since his own transcendence into the nether world. Staring mutely at each other, there arose between the two a queer and bitter communion, as each man, probing deeply, felt the other.

Both nearly collapsed then, wilting in unison as two dry leaves bursting afire. Then as quickly as it had descended, the spell shattered. The two acknowledged each other with a series of blinks, tilting their heads as on signal, having communed over something furtive and obscure, defined as 'ethereal' or 'intimate.'

Depleted, no longer able to endure the old man's piteous gaze, Crowbones turned away, thinking to join the others already traversing the Iron Bridge. As the horse completed its pivot, he was overcome with an onrush of cold tremors washing through his chest, closing in fast and palpitating hard. He felt himself dropping; involuntarily lost to ancient Nordic instincts bred in him as a small boy deep within the abandoned forests of Finland, during long winter stays with his aged Finnish grandmother. It had been there that she had apprenticed him in pagan magic, relating tales of the raven, teaching him the mythic mysteries of its desiccated bones long after actual bird-life had fled.

Shuddering, he felt an icy hand reach down as his grandmother's weathered face began knitting itself together so clearly, he thought to smell her dead breath streaming through his nostrils. "Grandmother?" he whispered, hearing for a flickering instant the gravel of her ancient voice rasping half-intelligibly about 'the unforgiving hand reserved for those who would dare forsake Nordic magic.'

Unnerved, shaking her ghostly image aside, Crowbones fell to shivering, like having just pulled himself from a frozen lake. Trembling, he crossed himself. "In nomine patris, et filii et spiritus sancti," he whispered, making certain that those beyond the bridge were not watching. "I ask You, my Christian God, to walk with me this day. My pagan past, through the shadow of this old beggar, is unearthing itself, rebelling against my taking of the water and belief in a single God."

CHAPTER SEVENTEEN

TO THE MOUNTAIN

Overcome by what seemed an endless journey put into motion by the surreal cerebral communion with the Armenian beggar, Crowbones spurred his horse, catching up to Orla just as Beltrane led them off the road, turning east into the foot of Mount Staurin.

"Orla," asked Crowbones, "do you remember our Finnish grandmother?"

"Tuulikki of the Hidden Forest?" Orla recollected. "Yes, but why do you ask? You were far closer to her than I was."

"Ja, for certain. But Orla . . ."

"What, then?" insisted Orla when Crowbones did not finish.

"Tuulikki came to me, just now on the bridge. I think the old beggar conjured her up."

Shaking his head, Orla said amused, "Ha, if anything conjured the old bitch, it was you throwing her raven bones in the fire! Ass of Odin, Ivar, I'm mystified why you'd do such a thing, especially as much as you loved old Tuulikki! And even more because I know how much the bones meant to you. Dammit, couldn't you have simply packed them away? You know, if nothing else, as a keepsake? You didn't have to burn them!"

"I did pack them away upon reading them right after the Battle of Nicaea. Remember?"

"Ja, I remember it was there you said the bones prophesized that 'some of us would never see Jerusalem,' yet we're nearly there, Ivar. And, the only one we've lost has been Jurgen Handel, the assassin monk. Not a single soul have we lost from our Saint-Germain-en-Laye bunch. So, what the hell? I begged you a dozen times to pull them from your pouch for a reading during that insufferable trek through Anatolia, at Dorylaeum before Hroc's duel during the Trial by Champions, as we made our way through the Cilician Gates, and at Mamistra and Tarsus, but you refused every time, which is another thing I've never understood."

"It was time, Orla—to set them aside, I mean."

"Oh, horseshit, Crowbones! Why was it time? Has our new God and Church frightened you to the point of rejecting everything from the old ways? Unlike Guthroth and Hroc, you've choked on as much of this Christian gristle as I have! Yeah, we took a vow to be baptized, you and me, back at Nicodemia when we were trapped in the old Byzantine fortress and thought our end had arrived. And dammit, we kept that vow, and took the water as promised. But that doesn't mean I actually believe in it! Nor you, or at least I thought. Ja, what's going on with you, Ivar? What's this all about? First you put the bones aside, then you burn the bones, now you claim you saw Tuulikki back at the bridge. And what's this shit with the old beggar back there who's made a habit of ridiculing your lost arm?"

"I don't know," mumbled Crowbones, exasperation filling his face. "But then . . . Shit, I haven't known for a long time. Aye, going all the way back to ever since we left Saint-Germain-en-Laye when Asta married DuLac."

This comment surprised Orla, even though he had noticed that a vacuous, unwanted strain of malaise had been haunting Crowbones. Having surfaced slowly at first, by tiny degrees, it had of late become increasingly evident, its roots so deeply planted as to be suffocating his brother.

But deciding that Crowbones, more than anything, needed an ear, Orla said, "Well, explain yourself then, Ivar. You're the best man I've ever known; steady, even-handed. Shit, I wish I was more like you, actually. Alright, go on, talk to me."

Even had Orla reacted differently, Crowbones would have bared his thoughts anyway. Things had been piling up for years, in that head of his, and he had spoken to no one about it. But it was time. He felt a crushing weight had just been yoked across his shoulders at the Iron Bridge with the old beggar, and that weight could only be lightened by divesting himself of his most private concerns, something he had rarely done.

"We wasted too many years fighting for DuLac in England when his castle was attacked," he began. "We took out Saxons, Scotts, the Irish. Anyone who opposed or attacked DuLac, we killed, though DuLac himself was a breathing plague. Oh, but how many did we send to the grave for him? Men simply wishing to rid themselves of a raving beast, and we killed them."

"No, not exactly. Those attacking us in England were brigands and raiders, Ivar. And there were murdering rebels in the lot, too, don't forget." Orla adjusted his horse to stay on course.

"Perhaps, but most just wanted to be out from under DuLac's boot. But I'd already begun to weary of killing before DuLac, at the Battle of Hastings. Such butchery we saw, and committed; many good men on both sides put to axe, blade, and bow. And again, how many Saxons did we slaughter there in the names of William the Bastard and Roger de Saint-Germain? Ja, two more raving beasts every bit as wicked as DuLac. We've spent our entire lives murdering for fools and rats. And that, Orla, makes us complicit. We, in the end, are the true fools, then."

Orla was mute.

"Remember, Orla? After escaping England, we started killing Germans for the popes," recalled Crowbones. "And look at us! Again, for another pope, in this damn crusade, we're killing Muslims, a race we don't know, in a place we don't belong. For what?" Here Crowbones spit to the side in disgust. "I'm tired of killing, Orla. And I'm getting old, just like you. Have you not drunk enough blood to be weary of it? Will your thirst never slacken?"

"It's all I know," Orla said with a shake of his head. "It's all you know, Ivar. We were forced to fight beside our father and uncles by age ten to save our clan. Then later, we fought for employment, to feed our families. And we were damned good at it! And still are, by God!"

"Orla, I'm sixty years old, and you, sixty-four. Most men never make it half that far, especially in war."

"Shit, Ivar, what's your point, here? I plan to fight until I can no longer hold a sword, or stand."

"Not me. I'm tired, Orla. I wish to-to go home."

Orla's face drew in a bit. "Home? But just where might that be, Ivar? We have no home."

"I'd wish to return to Denmark, Orla. Maybe board an old Viking Gokstad long ship, dragon head carved over the stern, sail bursting in the cold open wind. Ja, and sail north, spend my final years in the homeland, the place of our birth. You lost your wife, and son, Knud, but you still have Hroc, at least. Me, after losing my wife and daughter during the escape from England, I've had nothing but fighting and war. I'm weary, Orla."

This wounded Orla deeply. "No!" he objected, his blood rising. "Ivar, that's not true. You have me, Brother. And Guthroth and Hroc. And Tristan and Guillaume. Ja, we are your home. We are together, and shall forever remain! Denmark is but some foggy dream, Ivar; a distant memory of childhood, dammit! You're just being a fool! A dreamer!"

Lowering his gaze, Crowbones shook his head. "Orla, just listen to yourself. You're shouting at me for simply telling you my truth. Jeg er ked af jeg abnede mit hjerte! Say nothing else. I already regret telling you any of this today. I should have never opened my damned heart, but I thought you might understand. Jeg var forket! I was wrong. Forget everything I've said, then. To Hell with it! And to Hell with you, too!"

CHAPTER EIGHTEEN

THE ASCENT

DuLac, riding beside Beltrane and Burrel, cocked his ear back to what he interpreted as bickering between Orla and Crowbones as the scouting party began its ascent up Mount Staurin. "Ha," he snarked to Burrel, "sounds like a crack opening in the great wall of Denmark back there, eh?"

"I guess," replied Burrel, apparently not too interested.

Hearing this hushed exchange between DuLac and Burrel, Beltrane grimaced. He had been stuck with these two by Bohemud since crossing into Syria, but cared for neither. Beltrane, born of mid-level nobility, had been raised by devout Catholic parents who imbued in him elements of virtue and humility. To him, the combined traits of DuLac and Burrel were despicable, which made him question why they had enlisted in the crusade to begin with. But then, Beltrane was naïve about those using the Church to meet private ends rather than as a path to salvation. Unlike many crusaders, the scarlet cross emblazoned across his tunic meant something to him. Everything, actually.

The base of Mount Staurin, lacking signs of a visible trail, began to rise gradually at first, offering little resistance. Beltrane led them aimlessly through several massive boulder outcrops, then, arriving at a rather inconspicuous point, gestured to an oddly shaped rock formation, distinct from all others. "There," said Beltrane, "the trail begins just yonder. It's hidden, and deliberately. But hold tight to your saddles for the trail goes vertical from this point."

On making the trail, if it could be called that, the rocks began to rise and close in, forcing them to advance single file; twisting, angling upward at a rather precipitous incline, going nearly perpendicular in spots. Before long, the horses began to struggle as snouts took on foam and haunches began to lather.

"Damnation, is it like this all the way to the top?" hollered Orla.

"Never made it beyond the next bend," yelled back Beltrane, "which is where we slipped onto the tail end of the Turks with black banners! But some good news, too. Halfway up, the trail supposedly widens; almost like a damned avenue, actually. A lot of excavation's been completed up there over the centuries. Probably to facilitate troop movement from the midpoint to the top where there's bound to be a rear entry into the city. Like I said, the first part of the trail's disguised so's not to be spotted from either the Iron Bridge or the north road. One hell of a clever strategic set-up, I'd say."

"Ugghh," grunted Orla, "how would you know that if you've never been that far up, Beltrane?"

"Armenian rumors, Orla. And for the most part, what we've heard from them has been pretty solid."

"Well, widened or not, up the final leg," said Orla, "it'd be damn impossible to send an attack force of any size through what we've covered. As well, the Turks could easily bottleneck an attack at the very point the trail opens, them massing on the open side while we'd be forced to come at them in small numbers from the narrow end. So, Beltrane, a fool's errand we're on then. What the shit! Little point in going any further. Even if there is a gate up here, our army'd have a tough time just getting there, and even if they did make it that far, they'd never be able to mass enough forces for a full assault."

Having begrudgingly left things alone all morning, DuLac sensed an opening and simply could not resist poking at it. "Ha!" he snorted with belittlement. "Giving out already, are you, Orla? Just about what I expected from you gutless Danes. As Bohemud said this morning, you and old Crowbones have gotten a bit long in tooth, eh? Yeah, you two old bastards should've just stayed back with the camp followers . . . and the women."

"Shut your trap, DuLac," snapped Orla, giving his horse a swift kick, "before I ride my horse right up that filthy French ass of yours!" Agitated, the horse neighed with contention, jumping forward in a single bound, its raised legs mounting the ass-end of DuLac's horse.

This caught DuLac by surprise, nearly throwing him from his horse as the animal in reaction bucked forward, then sideways, with no room to maneuver. "Orla, you bastard!" he shouted. "By damn, Beltrane, take note of this, would you? You'll be my witness on returning to camp. Bohemud'll have Orla's ass on a lance by day's end."

"Shut up, DuLac," replied Beltrane sharply. "You started it with that yapping mouth of yours."

"I'll be your witness!" barked Burrel.

"Knock it off," ordered Beltrane.

At this, tempers cooled and DuLac and Orla fell into grumbling to themselves. Beltrane, resigned to the fact he had a possible situation with his own men and what lay ahead, led the file further up the mountain. Arriving at a turn on the western slope of Mount Staurin, the scouting party became aware of distant voices. "Dammit, look there!" bellowed Beltrane, pointing over the ledge. "It's Bohemud's camp, and within archers range from where we sit. When I came up last time, our camps had not been set, nor did I make it this far."

"Over there," said Pierre Gustave, pointing to remnants of an ash pile tucked within the rocks. "The Turks have been here; likely spying on Bohemud's camp blocking the Saint Paul Gate. Christ, if they wanted, they could post a few hundred archers up here and hold a damn duck-shoot. We'd best report this to Bohemud, maybe have him secure this spot before the Turks come back to it."

"For certain," assented Beltrane, motioning up the trail. "But come on.

Somewhere ahead, as I recall being told, the path settles onto a tiny plateau, widening, allowing four or five riders to advance abreast."

Following his lead for another ten minutes, the party came to the place Beltrane had described. "We'll rest our horses here before continuing," he instructed, cantering onto the plateau. "Though the ride from this point should be easier, our mounts are spent. They—"

Before finishing his thought, from around the bend ahead appeared a full troop of Muslim riders, two dozen at least, heavily armed. In the lead rode a massive man, his head shaved and gleaming in the sun. Mahmoud Malik had this same morning decided to foray down Staurin to survey the crusader camps and hopefully discover a path of escape from Antioch for his entire mercenary force.

Stunned, both packs of riders froze in the saddle. For a moment it was as if some highly skilled sculptor had chiseled in stone the perfect embodiment of opposing warriors caught in a chance encounter; their expressions of paralysis and bewilderment captured and carved with masterful precision; eyes agog, jaws open.

Then, as if a match had been lit, a systematic eruption spewed forth as both sides surged blindly forward, smashing blindly into each other, spurred by warrior instinct, fueled by murderous intent.

CHAPTER NINETEEN

THE SOUTHERN PROBE

To the south of the crusader encampment, Bohemud's other scouting party was being led by a capable Norman named Foulon, devout of faith but equally inclined toward jest and laughter. Subsequently, unlike the northern probe scouting Mt. Staurin, the six riders of the southern probe engaged in friendly chatter, something Hroc truly enjoyed. Guthroth remained silent, as was his custom, but took a quick liking to Foulon and his companion scouts; one he knew to be Foulon's brother, a more jocular fellow than Foulon himself.

After leading the party beyond the southernmost crusader camp, that of Godfrey of Bouillon and his Germans blocking the Gate of the Duke, the party came across a single Armenian fellow, past his prime, riding a horse and leading three donkeys in tow toward what appeared to them, the fortified bridge. "Oh, but beware, old fellow," warned Foulon, who had actually learned a bit of the tongue from an Armenian whore back in France where, before declaring for God and the crusade, he'd owned a brothel. "Those Turks may come dashing over that bridge when least expected, and those swift bastards'll have your ass on a lance before even you can jump in the river!"

"Oh, I'm not going near that bridge," the old man shook his head, "I know it leads straight to the Bridge Gate. And from what I've been told in your camp, the Bridge Gate is the Turks' favored way out of Antioch to attack you fellows."

"So then, you've spent time in our camp?"

"Certainly, along with the other herd of Armenians who fled Antioch and the Turks when you arrived."

"Ah, then you already know the area."

"Huh, like the back of my hand!" He jutted his chin out and held up a hand, swiveling it back and forth.

"Very well then," said Foulon, satisfied, "you already know then to avoid the fortified bridge yonder."

"Yes, yes, certainly," laughed the man, waving his arm in a wide arc salutation as he went about his way.

But when Foulon's group vanished from sight, the man headed straight for the fortified bridge, changing a few articles of garb before coming in view of guards. "Ho there," he shouted, "let me across! I'm a poor Syrian Muslim whose farm up north has been burned along with my family! My own wife and daughter were set afire after being raped and tied to a stake together by these bastard Christians who've unwelcomely infected our lands!"

Having already taken in a stream of frightened Syrian Muslim refugees over the past month, the guards let him through, neglecting to ask how the old fellow had managed to escape such a horror, along with a horse and three donkeys. Leading his animals over the bridge and making the distance to the Bridge Gate, he repeated his tale of woe.

"Yes, yes, come in old fellow," shouted the gate keeper, "for the Christians are thick as flies out there. Some even eat their prisoners we've been told by those fleeing to our city from the north!"

"Aye, I've seen it with my own eyes!" lied Kareem.

Meanwhile, Foulon's party came onto the crusaders whose purpose it was to man two false camps intended to trick the Turks into believing the southern quadrant of Antioch was populated by a sizeable Christian army.

Making contact with the captain of each camp, Foulon asked, "Have the heathens tried to come out of the two southern gates yet?"

"No," replied the first.

"Seems our ploy is holding."

The second captain agreed, "No sign of them daring to make a move. They must think we're thick in numbers down on this end, just as we really are on the north end."

Riding but a short distance beyond the false camps, Foulon stopped his party at a fork in the road. "In order to cover more terrain," he said, "it's here that we'll split into three separate directions. My brother and I will take the fork west to the port of Saint Simeon to check on Captain Charton and the fleet from Genoa we've been waiting on."

"Charton's at Saint Simeon?" asked Hroc, who had befriended Charton during the arduous march through Anatolia but had not seen him since crossing into Syria.

"Yes," answered Foulon. "As soon as our army made camp at Antioch, Raymond of Toulouse sent him and his contingent there to await the ships la Gran Signorina had summoned from Italy to resupply and shore up our attack on Jerusalem. When she arrives, Charton will accompany her and thirteen ships' worth of goods she's mustered."

Turning, Foulon then pointed to the other two scouts. "Gautreaux," he said, "from here I want you and DuBuisson to travel due east around the Saint George Gate vicinity to the base of Mount Silpius. Search for any hidden trails that might lead up the mountain from the side or the back of Mount Silpius."

"And what of Guthroth and myself?" asked Hroc.

"I'd like you and Guthroth to continue south for another ten kilometers, then veer south-easterly another forty or fifty kilometers. But stay off the road once you get ten kilometers from here since we don't know what or who's there. No sizeable towns in that direction we know of, but Bohemud suspects there could be uncharted Seljuk strongholds tucked away which could come into play during the siege."

"But that's sixty kilometers in all," said Hroc, "and well, well beyond our theatre of siege."

Guthroth nodded agreement. "J-ja, a g-good distance in unknown t-terri-tory. We shall l-look. B-but know this, Foulon, we will take c-care and t-take our t-time."

"Yes, yes, by all means," agreed Foulon. "And since you two will be longer than the rest of us, we won't be expecting you back for four or five days. We'll already be in camp by then, so we'll see you when you make it back." Turning his horse west, Foulon gestured for his brother to follow him toward Saint Simeon.

Gautreaux and DuBuisson then left the road, moving across open country toward Mount Silpius, and Hroc and Guthroth traveled the road south as instructed.

"Nothing but sand, then more sand," chortled Hroc hours later, breaking the long silence that had fallen between him and Guthroth as their horses ambled down the road; the relentless heat something they would never get used to. He silently prayed they had enough water in their botas to get them back. They would definitely have to ration.

Sweat pouring from his brow and trickling down through his red, now graying beard, Guthroth, not one for conversation anyway, grew especially mute when scouting. Besides being on high alert, he had time to ponder. Hroc was aware of this and was not bothered by it. In acceptance, he, too, slipped back into silence as they rode, the sun to their backs, casting long shadows ahead of them in a slow, delib-erate cadence counted out by footfalls of steel-shod hooves plodding over hot sand.

As dusk arrived, they spotted a sparse growth of Lebanese firs about sixty yards from the road and made camp, having encountered no one along the way since the Saint Simeon fork other than a slight herd of goats being driven by a Syrian shepherd and a young boy.

"We'll c-camp in this c-cover," said Guthroth, dismounting, tying his reins to a fir branch in preparation of pulling his saddle.

Right as the words escaped his lips, a sound drifted towards them with the breeze.

Moving deeper into the firs, Guthroth and Hroc calmed their horses as the animals, too, detected the noise and had begun to react.

"Just dark enough that I can't quite see that far," said Hroc. "You?"

His eyes focused down the road, Guthroth raised his shoulders. "Riders c-coming," he said, his voice low. "Three or f-four, maybe."

"Riders?" asked Hroc, moving his hand to his scabbard. "Turkish ghazis if it's a group on horseback. What do you think, take them by surprise? They've no idea we're here and wouldn't know what hit them."

"No," replied Guthroth. "Let them p-pass."

Remaining unclear, figures and shadows emerged from the road. Guthroth and Hroc, fully expecting them to pass, grew surprised when the ensemble arrived parallel to the fir grove and halted. Unexpectedly, a voice rang out softly singing lyrics.

"For fanden!" rasped Guthroth, pulling his sword. "They're c-coming our w-way!"

Separating, positioning themselves to attack from opposite directions, Guthroth and Hroc crouched low in the firs, intent on making their move the very second the lead horse made it into the firs. But just before lunging forward, Guthroth put up his hand and shouted in a whisper, "Hold there, Hroc!"

Terrified, the man who had been singing cried out, certain he had fallen into a nest of robbers. Turning his mount, a mule, not a horse, he tried to flee, but two other mules were tethered behind his own and they refused to move. Gawking dumbly at Hroc and Guthroth, the two beasts were more curious than afraid about men appearing from thin air, ears twitching.

Stepping out, Hroc confronted the lone man on the mule. "Who are you and what are you doing here!?"

"Aiee! Spare me!" the man shrieked in Armenian, feeling he had but moments left. "Take my animals, pots, and baskets! They're yours!"

"Shh!!" motioned Guthroth, sizing up the fellow and his donkey train laden neck-to-tail with clay pots and baskets of every size and fashion.

"You're crusaders?" wheezed the man, settling a bit on discerning the two men's dress was neither Syrian nor Turkish but Western, though not Byzantine. "Ah, I've heard you were coming but didn't know you'd arrived."

Guthroth and Hroc did not speak Armenian, but did recognize that the little man had begun to speak Greek, of which they also did not speak but were familiar enough with that they were able to identify the tongue. Sensing no threat from the traveler, they sheathed their swords.

Seeing that the two men did not understand Greek either, the man made an effort in rather broken French, "Français? Vous parlez Français?"

This gained a nod from Guthroth.

"Yes, we speak French," interceded Hroc. "But again, who are you?"

"I'm Arnag, a wandering merchant," the man said, continuing in French. "My mother was Byzantine, traveled and educated. My father was an Armenian trader, well-traveled."

"You're Christian, then?" asked Hroc.

"Yes, when I have to be. Muslim, too, when necessary. It's good to be many things in Syria. You never know who's going to stop you these days."

"You're familiar with the area south of Antioch then, as a merchant?" asked Hroc.

"Aye" nodded Arnag, "all the way to Jerusalem, and even beyond to Egypt where the Fatimid Dynasty rules."

"We're scouts for the Christian army," said Hroc, pointing to Guthroth. "Do you swear the Turks do not hold your allegiance?"

"Certainly not," replied Arnag, spitting into the sand. "They're interlopers to this land."

"We are, too," replied Hroc wryly, his expression softening. "Then, Arnag, you'd not be against helping us a bit?"

Until this point Guthroth had said nothing, just edged closer. "Are th-there Seljuk fortresses between h-here and Hama?" he asked. "Our maps sh-show n-nothing."

"The city of Hama?" echoed Arnag. "Yes, there are two between here and there; not fortresses, though, merely outposts. Thinly manned. Their purpose, actually, is to keep an eye for invasion from the Realm of the Assassins further south. But these outposts would pose no threat to you if truly your army is as huge as rumors say." His brows furrowed with that. "Your bigger interest, I might suppose, might be the Oasis of Sparrows, midway between here and Hama, thirty kilometers southeast of here."

"Oasis of Sparrows?" Hroc was caught unaware. "No such place is marked on our charts, nor have we heard mention of it."

"Though out of the way, it's one of several sparse sources of water between Antioch and Hama," said Arnag. "As such, it's visited from time to time by Yaghi Siyan's outlying ghazis to supply their outposts. Then, too, once in a rare while, other Turks pass through; small scouting parties nosing about from the Realm of Assassins, or even a few from the north. The oasis could be of interest to your army should they march south."

"We'll not be marching southeast of Antioch," said Hroc, "or straying far from the coast. Once we take Antioch, we'll be heading due south to Jerusalem. But tell, Arnag, the oasis you describe, is it walled as a fortress?"

"No. Only the palace is walled, and weakly."

"P-palace?" Guthroth's eyes opened wide.

"Yes." Arnag shifted in his saddle. "The oasis has been owned by the same wealthy Arabic bloodline for over two centuries, the Daba clan. They've survived in peace over generations because of their oasis' outlying location, and by cooperating nicely with whoever carries the hammer. But there's no male bloodline left, except the old man, and he's far too old to reproduce. They call him Papa Daba, a good man, actually. He rules the oasis with his three daughters."

"Daughters?" echoed Hroc, shocked.

"Yes, old Daba has no sons, nor even a single son-in-law. His eldest daughter's name is Haya, and it's she, actually, who runs things. Papa Daba has become decrepit and can barely see, so he leaves things to Haya. Oh, and she's a clever one, too! Speaks four or five languages, and as may be of interest to you, she happens to be Christian."

"Christian?" This evidently pleased Hroc.

"Indeed. When she was a child, an old French Benedictine monk happened onto the oasis after his pilgrimage to Jerusalem. But he'd gone lame and was offered a stay of respite by Papa Daba. Poor old monk never made it back to France; spent the rest of his days preaching at the oasis. He gained some converts, too, one of them being young Haya. She and the old monk became inseparable until his dying day."

"Then she speaks French?" asked Hroc.

"Indeed. And I'll say this, too. At age forty-four, she's not one bit unpleasant to look at!"

"Hmmm, we shall t-take a look," grunted Guthroth.

"Ha! At Haya?" sniggered Arnag.

"N-no," scowled Guthroth, seeing no humor in Arnag's quip, "at the Oasis of th-the Sp-Sparrows."

"Huh?" Hroc's head snapped to his uncle, surprised. "But it's inconsequential to our purposes, no military threat to speak of, and well east of both Antioch and our course to Jerusalem."

"We shall l-look," repeated Guthroth.

"Very well," acceded Hroc, shelving puzzlement. He knew Guthroth rarely made decisions unless directed by purpose, spoken or not.

"B-but, Arnag," warned Guthroth, "b-best you n-not go to Antioch. Turn b-back."

"Eh?"

"W-war is s-soon to begin, and f-foraging is g-going bare."

Arnag, his brows arcing, considered the statement for a moment. "Oh, but I was hoping to do good business there, with your army being so big, I mean. No?"

Guthroth shook his head 'no.' "Your mules and wares w-will b-be taken."

"I see," muttered the trader, visibly disappointed. For some reason there was just something about this fellow that conveyed truth. "Shit! Too bad." He frowned, his voice going slack. "But come then," he said, dismounting and pulling out tin cups and an ingenious little fire pot fueled by dried mule dung he kept stored in saddlebags. "Let's at least share the cover of the firs tonight, and enjoy some tea."

A lively conversation ensued then, carried mostly by Hroc and Arnag as they sipped tea and exchanged pleasant chatter into the evening.

To Hroc's surprise, as Arnag's description and history of the Oasis of Sparrows deepened, Guthroth opened up a series of questions, after which he said, "Arnag, since y-you are t-turning back, we w-would like to pay y-you to lead us to th-the oasis."

"Indeed?" Arnag smiled broadly, his face swelling with satisfaction. "Yes, of course I'll take you there. And I'll even introduce you to old man Daba himself. He actually enjoys visitors. But beware, his daughter, Haya, is not as receptive. Ha! She's a strong woman, you know, and tells others how things will be, including her father."

CHAPTER TWENTY

A BLOODLETTING

In that dark, brutal era when men made war face-to-face, driven to kill one another within arm's reach, staring into the eyes of the man to be slaughtered or that would slaughter, hesitation meant death. As Hroc and Guthroth were making their way south of the Saint Simeon fork, the northern scouting party had attained the plateau halfway up Mount Staurin, only to unexpectedly encounter Mahmoud Malik, the renegade Persian, and two dozen of his ghazis. As mad dogs baring fangs, hurtling themselves thoughtlessly into death or survival regardless of odds or outcome, the two opposing sides spurred forward in a barbarous charge of finality.

Malik and Beltrane smashed into each other first, each driving half a ton of surging horseflesh into the other. Colliding, hooves sprang airborne, tangling as the two horses neighed angrily, gnashing at each other's neck and snout with bared teeth. Bracing himself to his saddle, Malik swung his curved saber with murderous efficiency, quickly out-muscling the bold but hapless Beltrane. Seconds later, Beltrane's severed head tumbled to the ground, his crumbling torso shortly following.

Orla and Crowbones, despite the inequity of numbers, bolted their mounts into the oncoming crush of charging Turks, but DuLac and Burrel were in their path. DuLac, having sized up the numbers, had already fallen into panic. A blink later, his cowardly instincts kicked in and he swung his horse about to flee, colliding into Burrel's horse, knocking the beast back into Orla. In an instant, with the momentum of DuLac's horse crashing forward, the full weight of both his and Burrel's horses careened into Orla's mount, snapping its front legs.

Feeling his horse collapsing beneath him, Orla tried to leap from the saddle, but his right boot caught in the stirrup. Snared, he went down with his horse, his right leg getting buried beneath the struggling injured stallion and rocky soil. Pinned, he fell victim to the horse's thrashing; his trapped leg being ground to raw meat.

Glancing up helplessly, his eyes instantaneously met those of DuLac in passing, whipping his horse to escape. In that flicker of exchange, such hatred and venom arose as to make both believe that time had come to an abrupt halt; generations of mutual hatred erupting in light of the present realization of what was occurring. DuLac had turned yellow once again and spun about, attempting to flee. Both assumed how things would end. The coward would live another day to lie about the circumstances of his survival, and the stalwart warrior would perish, his story going untold.

Crowbones, meanwhile, broke past the fleeing DuLac, directly into the onrushing goliath with the shaved head who had dispatched Beltrane. The two met in a jarring collision of rearing, biting horses; their riders' sword and sabre breaking the air in a vicious bout of parrying that could have, at any instant, gone either way. One-armed Crowbones, understandably, was at an immediate disadvantage. Missing his left limb, he showed neither fear nor doubt, clinging to his mount with just his legs. Swirling around and around in horse-driven circles, Crowbones and Malik tangled back and forth as, from the perimeter of their titanic clash, other Turks began to close in.

Seeing this, Pierre Gustave spurred forward, protecting Crowbones' flank with heroic but suicidal ferocity. Yet his doomed effort shortly fell to shambles as more Turks began attacking him, coming from several directions. Knocked from his horse, Gustave struggled to rise but was immediately trampled by four horses as their riders deliberately drove over him in short but repetitive onslaughts, crushing his skull and shattering every bone in his body. Iron-clad hooves drove downward like pile-drivers, mangling his body beyond all recognition of having once been human.

From the ground, firmly pinned, Orla watched the decimation of Gustave's corpse for a moment, then realizing Crowbones' plight, shouted encouragement to him, "Fight, Ivar! Hold your ground!"

Burrel, to his credit, and counter to a lifetime of connivance and voracity, did not join DuLac in flight. Unexpectedly, and for once in his existence, a shred of selflessness arose from nowhere. He determined he would stay with Crowbones and Gustave, not that he cared for either, but because they were being set upon by dark heathens of an inferior race, which, to Burrel, was reprehensible. Moments later, Burrel lay dead; his single gram of courage costing him everything as he slumped from his terrified horse, pierced by eight arrows after having his arm severed and his frame sliced in-two like lopped fruit from his right shoulder angling down to his upper belly.

Seeing this, Orla's heart dropped. With Beltrane, Gustave, and Burrel dead, and DuLac already in flight, Crowbones had no chance of surviving other than breaking loose, turning about, and following DuLac's path. This, by the grace of God, Crowbones might have actually managed, but he knew Orla was aground and refused to abandon him. Gathering every fiber of muscle and will he could summon, Crowbones charged again at Malik as six Turks converged on him from every direction, sabers swinging.

Seeing the end had arrived, Orla screamed to his brother, "Run, Ivar! Goddammit, run!"

Crowbones heard the plea, but facing the murderous fury of Malik's saber and ensconced by swarming ghazis, he remained. "I'll not leave you Orla! You're my broth—"

Before the second syllable, Malik swept across with his razor-edged sabre, lopping Crowbones' good arm off in a single, clean sweep. So sharp was Malik's saber that Crowbones felt but a quick sting at first, yet actually witnessed his lone arm dropping from his shoulder to the side, its fingers still clinging to his sword.

Horrified, he blinked, slowly, dispassionately, like a frog blinks when watching the hungry serpent slithering toward him in undulating arcs atop the pond surface. Then the agony struck. Howling, Crowbones shook his limbless shoulders back and forth in a grisly dance of horror, taking on the appearance of an eel-like creature, head raised and eyes asunder, writhing for air. Blood spraying from his shoulder-bone in a gush of scarlet, he tumbled from his saddle, writhing to and fro as blinding pain flooded his eyes with a bitter mix of salty tears and disbelief. Rolling to his belly, he felt the snap of his spine as Malik's agitated stallion struck down with angry hooves, stamping out the threat thrashing about at its feet.

Orla, pinned just feet away, watched numbly, then keened in agony, "Ivar!"

Overcome with abject horror and disbelief, Orla grew disoriented as the sky above turned kaleidoscope and his vision exploded into white. Then came a thunderous throbbing, arising between his temples, drowning out all other sound.

Falling limp, Orla blacked out.

Turning his attention from the de-limbed Christian at the foot of his horse, Malik surveyed the scene before him. It appeared that all the other Christians were dead, as well as a dozen plus of his own men. His ghazis had prevailed, but the small enemy force had been far more ferocious than anticipated, extracting a grievous toll of their own before surrendering their lives.

Turning an ear down the bend, Malik strained, detecting the clattering and scattering of rock of two horses being driven down the mountainside at full tilt.

The first horse belonged to DuLac, who was more terrified of the Turk pursuing him than of the sharp bends and precipitous drops in his path. The Turk, having chased DuLac halfway down the descent but gained little on him, came to a stop and nimbly slipped his saber into his belt. In one fluid motion he grasped the compound bow slung over his back, simultaneously picking an arrow from the quiver slung over his shoulder. Standing stiffly in his stirrups, he leaned forward, drew back, and fired.

The arrow struck DuLac's bone at the tip of his left shoulder blade, deflecting into the flesh of his left upper-arm. Grasping at his shoulder, reflexively leaning away from the wound, DuLac slipped from his saddle and tumbled over the edge of a jagged precipice. Instinctively, and with unexpected resignation, he knew his end had arrived and issued neither wail nor scream. This is how it ends, all for nothing, he realized in a blazing instant, then his mind went blank and the rocky crag reached up to greet him.

Dismounting to peer over the ledge, the Turk heard nothing, nor could he spot the crusader's corpse. As it happened, DuLac had fallen but eighteen feet, struck a lower edge angling back toward the mountain, then tumbled back into a rocky recess carved into the mountainside by time, wind, and weather, and had been surreptitiously hidden from view.

Satisfied that the Christian he shot had careened down the entire drop of the steep precipice and that his brains had been splattered to mash, the Turk mounted and made his way back up Mount Staurin. "I've killed the one that ran," he told Malik on reaching the plateau. "Shall we continue down the slope to spy on the crusaders as first planned?"

Malik shook his head 'no.' Seasoned in quick skirmishes and unexpected confrontations, he had begun to suspect that this small cadre of crusaders had likely been riding point for a much larger force; one perhaps to arrive shortly. Holding the plateau would be easy enough, should this be the case, as his remaining riders could stave off a much larger force by simply controlling the open plateau, keeping the enemy bottled in the narrows, exactly as Orla had explained to Beltrane during the ascent.

Rather than tempt fate, Malik decided to disengage in favor of returning to the Iron Gate and advising General Ahmet to heavily man this spot where the plateau narrowed to a meager trail. Besides, Malik had it in mind to lead his full renegade force of 700 ghazis away from Antioch altogether as soon as opportunity prevailed. Rather than getting stuck fighting the crusaders for Yaghi Siyan's offer of a pittance, Malik hoped to abandon the city to seek profitable employment beneath the banners of Duqaq of Damascus, Ridwan of Aleppo, or even the great Mesopotamian, Kerbogha, atabeg of Mosul. But to do so, he would have to garner information about the placement of massive crusader encampments to avoid ambush or capture during his escape.

Waving his saber toward the peak of Mount Staurin, he circled his surviving men. "Quickly, back up the rise!"

"And what of the wounded Christian on the ground there?" asked Malik's lieutenant, a man named Hasan. "Do we put him out of his misery?"

"No," replied Malik, his eyes going cold. "He'll not be going anywhere. He has no arms, and it appears his back is cracked. We'll leave him to suffer. Yes, he has time to ponder his mistake of coming East, while bleeding out beneath the smile of our Islamic sun."

CHAPTER TWENTY-ONE

IN THE STILLNESS

As Malik's troupe vanished up Mount Staurin, Orla's horse began entering the throes of death. Lying crippled on one side, prisoner to it, Orla's right leg beneath the saddle, the animal's head and neck began to thrash about in a doomed effort to regain footing. Neighing loudly, confused by its demise, the beast's frustration grew, as did its thrashing. In combination, its hysterical braying and futile motions jolted Orla back to consciousness.

Groaning, Orla thought himself dead at first, then to be awakening from a nightmare. The struggle of the horse hammered Orla back to reality, crushing his trapped leg and sending excruciating pangs running from his boot to his upper thigh. In desperation, Orla, too, began to wrestle against his injury, just as the horse.

Struggling, he perceived that each time the horse thrashed his head and neck upward, the beast's motion allowed him to inch his leg from beneath the saddle a fraction, but only for an instant. Pondering this dilemma, he decided he needed the horse to struggle more.

Pulling his dagger, Orla stretched forward, with all his might, and plunged the blade partially into the beast's neck. Blood erupted fountain-like from the wound, but as hoped, the laceration shocked the horse into bolting its crippled frame upward violently. Summoning everything he could muster, Orla shoved against the saddle with one hand, while clawing forward with the other. In a miracle of timing, he cleared his thigh and most of his shin. When the horse relapsed, only Orla's foot remained pinned, but with some wiggling, he was able to pull it free. Spent, he gasped for breath, flopping to his side. That is when he heard the mournful caterwauling of his brother but a short distance away. "I-var?" he shouted, aghast. "Ivar?!"

Crowbones, half conscious, was stunned to hear his brother's voice; the torment eating at his severed shoulder and his life's blood leaving him set aside. "Orla?" he then rasped, overcome. "But I thought you . . . dead."

The last thing Orla remembered before passing out was the severing of Crowbones' arm by the huge heathen. The shock of it had overwhelmed Orla, causing him to collapse into blackness. "I thought you d-dead, too, Ivar," he replied hoarsely, laboring his way up to a seated position to catch sight of his brother.

On gaining his rump, Orla ran his fingers down his injured leg to check for splintering. Raw flesh and shredded lower tunic and pant leg, but the leg was not broken. Gouged, bleeding, and severely bruised, he wasn't willing to attempt standing. Scuttling forward, as would a legless man, placing weight on his palms to scoot forward in tiny hops, he made his way to Crowbones, who was gushing profusely to the beat of his heart but had somehow rolled flat on his back.

Due to the sheer brutality and ferocity of face-to-face combat, dismemberment during battle was not uncommon, nor was surviving if application of pressure and bandages was quickly provided by self or others. Rather, the greater risk arrived later, in the form of infection and gangrene. But Crowbones, completely armless, had been rendered incapable of tending to his wound. By the same token, he assumed nobody existed who could assist him and reconciled to the fact that in his particular case, he would be crossing over to the other side very soon.

"C-can you stand, Ivar?" asked Orla, becoming nauseous by the sight of his mutilated brother; sickened even more by his plight.

"No," gasped Crowbones. "Lost too much blood. Can't move. I think my spine's been . . . broken. I'm dying."

"No!" snapped Orla. "You're still breathing, by damn! I'll get you off this mountain. I swear it!"

Crooking his head, Crowbones spotted the condition of Orla's leg. "Shit . . . you can't even stand," he winced. "But at least you can crawl. I can't even do that. Ja, det er f-formig, Orla. Crawl out of here. Me . . . I'm d-done."

This ugly admission spurred Orla to action. He began placing pressure on his hurt leg in an attempt to stand. Grappling, he made it to his feet, but when he tried to take a step, he nearly crumpled to the ground. "Dammit!" he said between clinched teeth. Refusing to give up, he advanced his injured leg a short step, then dragged his good leg forward to hold balance. "Oh, but damn that hurts," he groaned. "Ivar, I can walk, barely. As such, I'll drag you back down the mountain. Ja, you're going to live, I say!"

Staring up into the bright, hot, torturing sun, Crowbones closed his eyes and grunted, envisioning that horrid possibility. "With neither arm? Oh, the very thing . . . you have so long feared . . . and me, too. Please, Orla . . . don't move me. My back!"

"Dammit, I'm going to carry you off this goddamned mountain if it kills me, Ivar! Hold still while I try to stop your bleeding!" His mind raced and his hands fumbled in an attempt to staunch the flow. "Odin's ass! You're hemorrhaging like a split bucket!"

Crowbones had already lost nearly a third of his blood and was entering a critical state of exsanguination, deadly enough to spell his end, as forty percent blood loss or more is fatal. Then, too, seeing the grievous state of his own dismemberment and the blood-soaked earth surrounding him, he had begun to panic. This, of course, caused his heart rate to spike in his body's reflexive effort to speed oxygen to its tissues, making him breathe harder and his blood pressure to soar, accelerating his demise.

"Stay calm," pleaded Orla, his heart thumping as violently as that of his brother. "You've survived this once before, Ivar, you'll make it again!"

But Crowbones was edging toward that final, most injurious stage, the onset of hypovolemic shock. The strain on his circulatory system was becoming too great to overcome, and his heart was barely able to maintain blood pressure and circulation.

Leaning over him, Orla saw that Crowbones had paled, and in touching him felt that his skin had taken on a chill. More critically, blood continued to pulse currents, albeit with less force, from where his shoulder joint had been. Running his palms along the ground, Orla scooped them full of hot sand and grit, pressing the raspy mix into the open meat of Crowbones' wound, then half-turned his brother onto his uninjured side in an attempt to raise the wound to a higher position than Crowbones' heart. In reaction, Crowbones' upper body rebelled, stung to the marrow by the movement and the coarseness of the packing.

"Stop squirming!" commanded Orla gruffly, ramming another dose of sand and grit.

"Aiee! Let me be, goddamn you!" bellowed Crowbones, his head jerking side to side.

"You're going to live, Ivar!" shouted Orla, feeling his brother's horror in the pit of his own belly. Grabbing Crowbones by the nape of the neck to hold him in place, he shoved handfuls of sand into the gaping wound. Blood trickled on, until finally, after several applications, it began to pancake. Seeing this, they both rested for a time, giving the grit ample opportunity to slow the bleeding to a molasses-like seep.

Surveying the corpses scattered over the tiny plateau, Orla shook his head. "Beltrane was killed right off," he told Crowbones. "And credit to Pierre Gustave. Ja, that big Norman bastard tried to save you, Ivar. Even that son-of-a-bitch Burrell stood his ground and put up a hell of a fight."

"At least, in the end, DuLac finally got his, too," sighed Crowbones, a speck of bitter satisfaction slipping into his eye.

Orla did not reply, but when Crowbones repeated himself, Orla admitted, "No, Ivar, that bastard took to the wind. He's down the mountain by now, heading back to camp, I'd suppose."

"What?!" groaned Crowbones, eyes wide, filling with despair.

"Ja. He got away."

Slipping back into silence, they stayed in place a few moments longer, breathing heavily, until Orla broke the silence, "The Turks'll be back sooner than later. We've got to get off this plateau."

"Orla, don't move me!" begged Crowbones, alarmed. "I mean it, dammit!"

Disregarding the plea, Orla went to a knee, scooped his hand beneath his brother's neck and waist, and hoisted him up in his arms, making it only to one knee. Crowbones went berserk, launching into as much of a fit as his spinal injury allowed, but Orla clung to him with vice-like finality. Tethered to one another, the two teetered for a time in shared misery and anguish. Exhaling through his nostrils to calm himself, Orla, a giant of a Dane, found his balance, then hoisted again. Somehow, he gained his feet, albeit unsteadily.

Again, Crowbones screamed in agony, "Oh, but put me down! Let me die in peace, damn you! Take out your dagger . . . and put an end to this! I'm begging you, Orla!"

Orla understood, and ever so clearly. Disregarding all common sense, pain, and emotion, he struggled mightily to take a step forward, burdened by the full dead weight of his massive brother. Though the torment of that tiny movement made him swoon, it gave Orla hope, having advanced a foot, maybe more.

For the next hour, Orla sacrificed himself to Herculean efforts and Crowbones implored for mercy from the tip of Orla's dagger. Orla strove desperately to remain resolute, but try as he might, on hearing Crowbones' incessant pleas and knowing that his own efforts were injuring his brother beyond repair, his emotion burst forth. Orla convulsed irrepressibly, unable to control his lament through this excruciating struggle. Refusing to accept the inevitable, his determined rivulets of anguish flooded forth, mixing into the salt of Crowbones' own doleful tears of agony and horror.

CHAPTER TWENTY-TWO

WITHIN THE WALLS OF ANTIOCH

By nightfall the clarity of what had occurred that afternoon midway up Mount Staurin had been twisted beyond recognition within the walls of Antioch. Malik, on regaining the Iron Gate, still covered in the detritus of battle, sought General Ahmet to give report. "I took a small force out this morning to spy on the crusader camps for you," he said, disguising any intent of seeking a future avenue of escape from Antioch. "Just on reaching the choke-point where the road narrows, we came onto a large force of crusaders ascending the rise, seeking a rear point of attack against your city! Only because we were able to hold the choke-point against their larger numbers, and although I lost a good number of my own men, we were able to repulse the attack and turn the enemy back down the mountain. But be warned, they'll be back, trying to figure out how to get beyond the narrows. Best set a permanent defensive force to protect the plateau."

Alarmed, Ahmet absorbed Malik's words with full credence. "Immediately," he agreed, "and I'll report such to Emir Siyan as this indicates, finally, an open act of treachery. An armed force slipping up Mount Staurin leaves no doubt about Christian intentions. They mean to take us."

"As I warned earlier, Ahmet," said Malik, licking his lip with satisfaction, "Yaghi Siyan refuted my counsel in favor of hoping the crusaders were but passing through. No. They're here to claim the riches of Antioch."

Gathering his generals and reporting to the palace, Ahmet conveyed Malik's report to Yaghi Siyan. "It's time to move against the Christians!" he insisted, as his commanders clamored the same. "We've no choice, Master!" Pausing, his expression filled with hope. "The carrier pigeons, Emir Siyan, have you heard from either Shams ad-Daulah or Muhammad about their mission for reinforcements from Duqaq in Damascus or Ridwan in Aleppo?"

"No, not a word from either of my sons. No pigeons have returned from either kingdom."

"We can't wait any longer, Master," said Ahmet. "Whether Duqaq or Ridwan show or not, we've got to take the initiative."

"I understand," replied Siyan, becoming solemn. "War has arrived, it appears, and there's no time to tarry, Ahmet, even should we have to go it alone, in the beginning, at least."

"Then," sighed Ahmet, "you still expect reinforcements to arrive?"

"Certainly."

Seated adjacent to Siyan, Ben-fazi had been listening to the exchange carefully. Although his peculiar captivity beneath the boot of Yaghi Siyan had been unexpectedly generous, he'd begun wondering whether a crusader victory might not liberate him from this strange land that had swallowed him whole after the massacre of the Peasants' Crusade. Ah, he thought wistfully, I appear to be safe beneath the wing of Yaghi Siyan at the moment. Yet I should like to return to Italy, my people, and the taste of freedom once more before leaving this world behind.

"Alert the troops then, Ahmet," ordered Siyan. "Execute a series of surprise sorties; begin probing the crusader flanks. Large as their army may be, there will be weaknesses, there always are. Find them! Send a force out the Iron Gate to establish camp near the foot of Mount Staurin to begin laying archer fire into the northernmost crusader camp, the one commanded by the Italian-Norman called Bohemud."

"And what of the Persian, Malik?" asked Ahmet. "Are we to expect him to fight as well?"

"Yes. He's trapped here. Should he and his troops wish to eat and remain sheltered within our walls, he has no choice. No, don't ask him to fight, make him fight."

"Yes, Master!" snapped Ahmet, issuing a stiff salute, signaling his commanders to make ready for war. "In the name of Allah, we shall repel these snakes and send them back to their pagan lands and false idols!"

"Indeed," nodded Yaghi Siyan. "That we shall most certainly do, Ahmet, for they'll never be able to break into our walls."

CHAPTER TWENTY-THREE

FLIGHT OF THE RAVEN

Through unswerving perseverance and rabid loyalty, Orla made it off the plateau, around a bend, and into a covering formation of jagged rock. Dizzy, blinded by tears and sweat, he paused. Feeling this, Crowbones breathed easy, thinking Orla would now put him down and pull his dagger as needed, hopefully. But the thought fled when Orla began to advance.

"What's this?!" objected Crowbones.

"We're still too close, dammit. I've got to get you further down the trail and into better cover. The Turks could show up any time!" Having said this, Orla strained, engaging every muscle. "Dammit, but you're a fat-ass, heavy as rock!" he grumbled involuntarily, neither barb nor humor intended.

"You're the fat-ass, Orla!" snapped Crowbones. "And the hard head . . . and damn you . . . the big-mouth, too!"

These final words cut Orla with the precision of a razor. Although Crowbones had meant nothing specific by his last retort, Orla well realized that their entire involvement in this doomed mission was a result of his own words. Had he kept his mouth shut the morning Beltrane showed up in the Tuscan camp, the wheel of destiny would not have rolled them up Mount Staurin in the first place. Just as Crowbones' words opened yet another heart wound, Orla faltered. Guilt. Undeniable guilt gnawed at his soul. Silence ensued.

Time ticked on with every step; Crowbones growing weaker and weaker. Orla carried his brother off the trail, nestling him within the pocket of a stony formation.

"We'll be safe here," he heaved, swiping his brow with a forearm as he gazed skyward. Dusk had begun its descent, transforming the sky into a grey shroud; only a sliver of sun remained, its upper arc afire but darkening as it slipped beneath the crest of a distant peak. A welcomed respite from the merciless sun, the on-coming night brought with it a cool breeze. Crowbones' breathing had grown increasingly sporadic, his pulse barely drumming, coming in shallow bursts, less frequently, and he'd not opened his eyes in a good while. Lying motionless, his lips had taken on a bluish tint, and like his pallid face, resembled those ghostly aspects of the already deceased. He rested in comfort knowing Orla was at his side. "You're a fool, Brother," rasped Crowbones, almost inaudibly, his eyes remaining closed. "Go. Leave. My blood is done. The pain is gone. I feel nothing. There is nothing left to do but for you to give me peace."

"I'll not put the dagger to you, dammit!" Orla squalled, wiping snot and tears from his face. "I'll put it to my own goddamned throat before I put it to yours! Do you hear me?"

Crowbones said nothing; he'd heard nothing. Instead, his breathing softened as if in sleep.

"Ivar!" shouted Orla, knowing that would spell Crowbones' end. "Ja, I'm a fool, maybe," he said, to keep his brother engaged and alert, "but I'm your fool, Brother." Then, stumbling for words, he grunted, "Ha! You know, I was but four when you came into this world." Here he paused, choking with emotion before continuing. "Ja, and since that time and through all things, we've never been apart, right, Ivar?"

"We shall part ways . . . soon," murmured Crowbones, licking at his cracked, parched lips. "But you know . . . I hope this Heaven the Christians talk of . . . shall accept me."

Orla grunted in protest. "But you're not going to die, Ivar."

"Oh, Orla . . . my full-of-shit big brother, I've but a short time . . ."

"You said Heaven, Ivar," blurted Orla, his speech quickening to keep Crowbones' attention, "but what of Valhalla and the Valkyries leading you to the Hall of the Slain in Glaðsheimr, where Odin awaits with the chosen heroes at Ásgarðr, the einherjar?"

Crowbones squinted his eyes, gasping with each breath, each word; his energy spent. "No . . . when I b-burned the bird bones . . . I made my choice. Valhalla . . . slipped away into the mist."

"A mistake that was, Ivar! Why in all hell would you forsake the bones after all this time? Ja, dammit, why?"

"Because I lied to you . . . in N-Nicaea," said Crowbones, opening his eyes fully to those of Orla, seeing in them the reflection of his own dying face.

"You lied to me in Nicaea?" echoed Orla, confused. "About what?"

"It was there . . . I last rolled the bones, after we . . ." he took a shallow breath, "put Kilij Arslan to rout . . . and the Nicaeans surrendered. You were watching me do it, Orla. I told you the bones said . . . 'some of us would never see Jerusalem.' Remember?"

Orla nodded. "And I asked you to roll them again, but you refused. And?"

"It was a lie . . . what I told you. The bones actually foretold that . . . none of us would ever set eyes on Jerusalem. But I kept that from you . . . and the others."

Hearing this, Orla recoiled. "No!" He coughed and swallowed the little spit he had left, unable to at first accept what had been said. Orla, of all the Danes, had always maintained the greatest faith in the raven bones of old Tuulikki, their sorceress grandmother, even though he had spent very little time with her. There had always been something terrifying about her, yet solidly prophetic. "None of us shall lay eyes on Jerusalem?" he repeated.

"Ja, none within our Saint-Germain faction. Not me, not you . . . not Guthroth, nor Hroc." His voice was getting weaker and weaker by the moment.

"But then, Guillaume? Tristan?"

"Even though . . . I refused to roll the bones again in front of you . . . I rolled them again in secret . . . later that night. And that next night . . . two times more."

"And?"

"Same prophecy," rasped Crowbones, his mouth dry as sand. "None of us . . . shall lay eyes on Jerusalem . . . not even Tristan or Guillaume. That's when . . . I put the bones away, Orla. I could not . . . bear to think . . . all of us would be slain. I began . . . to think of the new God . . . hoping He might see things differently." Crowbones paused then, to clear his parched throat. "But Orla, have you any water? My throat . . ."

Pulling a bota from his belt, Orla trickled a fine stream through his fingers, dribbling the water slowly down Crowbones' gullet. "There, take it in, Ivar. You'll feel better."

"Turn back, Orla. Don't you see? Leave this hell of sand and stone . . . Make the others go with you . . . back to Italy!" He wanted desperately to prove the bones wrong, to change their fates.

"But—"

"Ah-hrg," strained Crowbones, breathing deeply, feeling death's cold claws reaching at him from the blackness. "Orla . . . tell Guthroth and Hroc . . . they were in my heart here at the end. Such a good lad . . . Hroc. And no finer warrior or friend . . . on this earth . . . than Guthroth . . . though he can't talk."

"Aye, a good one, that Guthroth," muttered Orla, his tone going vacant.

"Guillaume and Boy, too." Crowbones wrestled through his last words, his throat taking on gravel; the rattle of death cocking itself. "I spoke sharply to Tristan . . ." a stray tear rolled from the corner of his eye, "that day . . . by the fire, and shouldn't have. Beg my forgiveness. Swear it!"

"Ja, ja! My word, Ivar," vowed Orla, his throat lumping, his forehead filled to bursting with hurt. He wished to say something, anything meaningful or significant, but his throat was too full, his heart too laden with emotion. When he tried to utter that first word of farewell, it caught somewhere between pronouncement and a sob. Then tears came, in rivers, as his head slumped into his lap, both palms slipped over his eyes, and he shuddered, rocking and keening, "Oh, but Ivar!! I—"

There came a rattle from Crowbones' throat as he tried to reply, then a second, slighter than the first. This was followed by a third, barely audible. A moment later, Ivar Crowbones passed from this world into the next.

CHAPTER TWENTY-FOUR

THE LONG DESCENT

When faced with improbability, stark adversity, or even possible annihilation, the human heart's propensity to unearth hope is boundless. It is hope, after all, that has dragged humanity from the darkness of prehistory toward the light. To be certain, yes, there are those struck by innate weakness, lacking perseverance, courage, or fight in the face of doom. But to counter such lapses of human spirit, God gave rise to a chosen breed of stalwarts for whom even the impossible itself cannot trump the granite of their inner strength. One of those extraordinary men was Orla Bloodaxe, the Norman-Dane.

Saddled with the crushing death of his beloved brother and given the crippling condition of his leg, it would seem inevitable that instinct and logic would coalesce, entreating Orla to save himself by abandoning the mountain. Leaving the body of his slain brother tucked within a hidden death-nest, he could make his way down Mount Staurin. Leg mangled and bota nearly empty, in flight he stood at least a speck of a chance of survival. To remain guaranteed his end.

Sitting there, the darkness within and without consuming him, legs sprawled, back against a boulder, Orla held Crowbones' mute head propped in his lap. His mind a fog, Orla calculated his odds of making the descent alone. Scant, he decided. He then envisioned leaving Crowbones in this place, to the elements and the scavengers. No, horrid, never, he thought. Then he envisioned carrying Crowbones down the mountain. Impossible, his mind chastised, his eyes scrunched, lamenting tears seeping from their corners.

Discouragement darkening his face, he was drawn to his brother's eyes as the last bit of daylight vanished. Rather than possessing the dull lethargy of death, they were oddly clear, reflecting that sky-blue sheen inherent of the Nordic race. This pricked a memory in Orla, and his heart raced back in time. There Crowbones came into view as a stout, bold young man, then as a child, then as an infant on the day of birth. Orla saw himself, too, nervously accepting his new baby brother being laid in his outstretched arms. Having just turned four, he stood on shaky legs, gawking with unbridled fascination at the newborn. Bloody, wailing in terror, blinking at the bright candlelight, struggling for breath, the infant's arm flailed and reached forward, his tiny hand grasping one of Orla's boyish fingers. Just a child himself, having never experienced a birth before, Orla was convinced his brother's motion was intentional and took it as an omen that the two would be locked together, until the end of their days. Glowing with pride and adoration, he had stared into the newborn's clear blue eyes and murmured aloud, "My baby brother!"

As suddenly as this apparition appeared, it vanished, reeling Orla back into the cold wash of reality, staring into the now glazed-over blue eyes of his baby brother with honor and determination. "I'll get you off this mountain, Ivar," he vowed, running his fingers through Crowbones' thick mane of greyish-red hair. "Even should it kill me."

Thus began the greatest struggle, both emotionally and physically, of Orla Bloodaxe's life. Lifting his deceased brother, teetering upward in unsteady increments, he found his feet. Then came a slow but calculated step, one that nearly took him down again. Anchoring himself, he shored-up his resolve for another with the other foot. Swooning, his vision erupted into a constellation of white spots, throbbing and blinking in a wild, blinding dance of obstruction.

"Arg!!" he moaned and gasped for breath. Succumbing to the stabbing pain in his right leg, he collapsed, resting Crowbones' back across his left knee, then squeezed his eyes closed in torment. Damnation, such pain! He gnashed his teeth and winced.

Within that same instant he was overcome by the abject realization that his intended quest was as impossible as bringing Crowbones back from the dead. A hulk of a man, as muscular as Thor of old, Orla was not stronger than fate. Descending the mountain was, in the end, to be his final gesture of fraternal loyalty, but one steeped in sheer futility. It was a good thought, groused Orla, clearing his vision, staring into the dark, only able to see the first few feet down the twisting trail. But I must go it alone. Ivar would wish it that way!

Regaining his breath, Orla further braced Crowbones against his knee rather than setting him aground. Glancing down, he happened to catch his reflection in his brother's eyes—but no, not of himself.

"Ivar?" he whispered, startled, drawing back. Orla and Crowbones had since birth shared a strong resemblance, even causing confusion amongst others from time to time, but now it was Orla who knelt there transfixed in perplexity. A ghostly chill skittered up the length of his spine, settling in his neck and shoulders as he peered deeper and repeated, "Ivar?"

Blinking, he broke the spell, cursing the night, Syria, and Islam, and stood once again, clutching Crowbones to his chest. He placed one foot feebly before the other, rested a moment, then repeated the motion with the other foot. I'll go forward, he thought. I have to go forward, even in the dark!

Advancing but a hundred yards, Orla came to the very spot where DuLac had fallen over the precipice.

From below, DuLac heard movement and the grunt of one straining, as wounded perhaps. Being trapped as he was below the ledge, with no hope of escape and his left arm useless, he disregarded all risk, calling out in desperation. Being captured or slain would be better than slowly dying of thirst, infection from the still bleeding arrow wound, or going mad. "Ho, there!" he shouted. "Down here! Throw a rope!"

Stunned, Orla stopped in his tracks, gazed about, thinking the voice had come from inside his head. But when the voice came again, he recognized it. "DuLac?" he whispered, then demanded, "DuLac? Is that you, dammit!"

DuLac, in turn, immediately recognized the voice of the man he most despised on this earth, and wilted against the side of the precipice, concealing his presence. As soon as his back struck the rock wall behind him, though, the reality of his predicament again overcame all trepidation. "Orla! Orla, down here! Throw me a rope or anything else you might have up there!"

Setting Crowbones gently aside, Orla peered over the ledge and spotted DuLac signaling for assistance. "Oh, you goddamned bastard!" he seethed, spittle forming around his mouth. "You cowardly piece of shit!" Grabbing a rock, he flung it down at DuLac with all his might, but missed. Grabbing another and flinging with all he had, he forced DuLac to retreat into the concave impression that centuries of wind had carved into the face of the mountain. "You can rot in Hell before I lend you a hand!" Orla screamed, his voice shredding with fury as he pawed about for rocks, shoving and sliding them over the side in heaps, hoping that DuLac would be forced from his hole.

"Leave me then, you goddamned pagan!" DuLac spat, realizing that Orla would throw himself over the ledge before deigning to help. "Aye, to Hell with you and all the other Danes, by God!" DuLac realized his fate was sealed. Back to rock, he slid down, all fight leaving him.

Livid that he could not reach DuLac, yet satisfied that the hated Frenchman would meet his end alone, stranded on the edge of a cliff, Orla moved from the ledge to recover his brother's body. "Oh, but Ivar," he said, lifting him into his arms, "though not by our own hands, that bastard DuLac has finally gained his hard-earned reward! Aye, and so shall the vultures!"

CHAPTER TWENTY-FIVE

WAR

It took all night, at a torturous snail's pace, for Orla to make the foot of Mount Staurin with Crowbones held tightly in his grip. Nonetheless, his vision deceiving him, his deteriorated limbs failing, he refused to give in. Groggily placing one foot before the other until finally, in the distance, he made out the skeletal frame of the iron bridge by dawn. Staggering forward in a fog, his dead brother slung across his shoulder, Orla thought he saw two figures on donkeys approaching. But dehydrated and disoriented, he decided it was a mirage. The figures were moving in slow motion, and he heard no voices, nor clattering of hooves against the barren, rocky road.

"It's but my mind playing tricks on me," he whispered. "I was but hoping someone was there."

Moments later, disheartened, his knees buckled and he collapsed backward, Crowbones landing by his side. Just as before, the old bridge beggar appeared from thin air, making a run at him.

Staring up dumbly, Orla heard the deranged old degenerate gabbling and jabbering, struggling to pull Crowbones' corpse aside. Next, Orla felt the soothing mercy of water against his lips. The old man was streaming river water into Orla's gullet from a small clay bowl, the only possession the beggar owned.

Orla then sensed the shadow of two men stooping over him, exchanging surprise, blurting a series of questions. Although Orla could not discern what they were saying at first, the timbre of one of the voices became unmistakable. Peter the Hermit?

"What's this?!" Peter loudly exclaimed. "You all mangled up, and Crowbones dead?"

"He can't hear you. He's in shock," said the other man, Peter Bartholomew, the Hermit's obsequious sidekick since saving the Hermit from dying of thirst during the terrible trek across the barren wastelands of Anatolia.

A French peasant existing on the fringe of invisibility, Bartholomew had gained, for the first time in his miserable existence, a modicum of recognition through his new association with Peter the Hermit. He'd even begun to fancy himself being touched by the Hermit's own self-acclaimed divinity, mimicking the Hermit's rabid preaching. But unlike Peter the Hermit, he was not, in fact, a monk.

"Get up, man, get up!" the Hermit harped, pulling at Orla as though he was not the least bit injured. "The war's begun without you, by God, and you're needed! The heathens've come out the gates, overwhelmed our two false camps, and attacked our two southern camps! And they're spilling arrows down from a vantage point near the bottom of Mount Staurin right into Bohemud's camp, killing at least a score just an hour ago!"

"M-my brother," stammered Orla, "he's—We were ambushed atop—"

"Aye, I see he's dead," interrupted the Hermit, waving his palm over Crowbones in a sign of the cross, "and we'll give him a proper burial, certainly. But let's get you both back to camp lest the Turks show up."

"But what are you two doing here?" Orla asked, sitting up on the hardened sand, staring from one face to another.

"Making ourselves useful," replied Bartholomew. "Just taking a gander to check whether the Turks had crossed the bridge to attack Bohemud's north flank from the Iron Bridge. But quickly, get on my donkey and we'll load your brother on the Hermit's."

This was easier said than done. It took the Hermit, Bartholomew, and the old beggar, all three, to hoist Orla onto the donkey. And once settled there, the poor beast nearly gave way. Positioning Crowbones on the other donkey was beyond difficult. But with considerable effort, they managed to tie the armless Dane belly down across the donkey's back.

"We're on our way then," declared the Hermit, dismissing the beggar who sadly watched them until they disappeared over the bridge and among the tents.

"Orla, they've been awaiting word from your scouting party, you know, as well as from the one they sent south."

"S-south?" muttered Orla. "No word from them either?"

"No," frowned the Hermit, shaking his head. "And since the Turks have now swarmed out the gates, our men of the southern scouting probe are cut off, maybe even captured or killed."

"But my son, Hroc, and Guthroth," Orla mumbled, filling with despair as all went black. Having suffered through such a long, dreadful ordeal, unconsciousness finally overcame him and he collapsed forward onto the ass, barely staying atop.

"God will direct their path," said the Hermit with certainty, "and it'll be good fortune either way. They'll either make their way back to us, or they'll make their way to God."

"Aye," echoed Bartholomew. "God will direct their path, and it'll be good fortune either way, by damn!"

CHAPTER TWENTY-SIX

THE OASIS OF SPARROWS: PAPA DABA AND HAYA

Upon rising, Arnag led Guthroth and Hroc off the road into open country to avoid the first of two Turkish outposts he had mentioned the previous night. "We'll cut a diagonal, southeast," he said, "and slip our way to the Oasis of Sparrows across open desert."

As he said this, Guthroth's eyes flickered, which did not go unnoticed by Hroc. Then, too, Guthroth had said earlier to move slowly and take extra precautions, yet he urged Arnag to quicken the pace. Hroc remained silent, knowing that reconnoitering to the southeast would be fruitless in the scheme of capturing both Antioch and Jerusalem. He had long since learned that arguing with Guthroth, once his mind had been set, was like dislodging a mountain.

A day later, having traveled over especially barren and desolate terrain, they came onto a rocky rise.

"The oasis lies just beyond the other side," directed Arnag, "tucked in a small valley. Best perhaps you two remain here in the rocks, let me go in alone should there be Turks passing through by chance."

Guthroth, nodding agreement, made the rise and dismounted, as did Hroc. Peering down the slope, Hroc whistled, surprised that such a lush landscape could appear like a dream from an endless sea of sand and stone. The oasis was larger than expected; verdant with olive, date, and palm trees surrounding an ample lagoon fed by springs bursting forth from three different rock formations whose bottom appeared as it had long ago been lined with paver stones. People were scattered in disparate clusters watering camels and donkeys, filling pitchers and buckets, going about other business, or resting beneath the shade of rich over-head growth. Some paused from time to time, pointing, appearing amused by the dozen children squealing and splashing each other in the waist-high water.

To the side of the lagoon stood a small village from which people streamed back and forth, lost to daily chores and regimen. And just beyond the thicket surrounding the village, rising above a four-meter wall, stood the capitol and upper decks of the 'palace' described by Arnag. The edifice was massive, structured in polished marble and granite with many spires, appearing regal within the environment of the oasis, yet out of character standing astride this particular span of abandoned desert.

"P-Peaceful. Un-touched," said Guthroth, following Arnag's progress down the slope.

"I see no ghazis," reported Hroc, raking his eyes over every inch of the oasis.

"Ja," agreed Guthroth. "But th-then, l-little to attract th-them here to n-nowhere."

Waiting there for nearly an hour, Hroc began to feel uneasy. "He should've been back by now," he said, looking at Guthroth for agreement.

He got none. Instead, Guthroth shook his head. "P-patience, Hroc. He has to check th-things first, th-then explain who w-we are. Arnag w-won't betray us."

Not believing a word, Hroc squinted back down the hill, hoping to catch sight of Arnag—not a sign. "How do you know that? He could be enlisting help to overtake us. You know, to steal our weapons and horses or such."

"N-no," yawned Guthroth, laying his head back in the sand, stretching out under the tree's shade, seeking respite from the unforgiving heat. "I t-talked to him last night and w-watched his eyes. He's a g-good one, th-that Arnag."

Five minutes later, Arnag showed, making Hroc wonder about his uncle's intuition.

"Come, the old man welcomes you," Arnag said jovially, circling his arm, motioning them to follow down the rise. "After our conversation, seems he and his daughter, Haya, have become a bit curious. They'd heard rumors about a great Christian army entering Syria from a caravan passing through weeks ago, but passed them off as exaggeration; certain no army could be as big as related by the traders. I told them you were part of that army, but simply scouting around with no ill intentions. They bid you come forward."

As the two massive men in unusual clothing and weapons neared the lagoon, they caught the attention of those milling about, yet their arrival appeared to cause little alarm, possibly because of Arnag, a familiar visitor to the oasis. Several villagers called him out by name, exchanging greetings in Arabic.

Leaving their mounts with two attendants, they passed through the gate to the palace, Hroc remained wary, his weapons at the ready, yet Guthroth appeared unbothered.

"Relax, Hroc," chortled Arnag. "You're in good stead here, I promise."

Arnag led them past a dozen guards manning the palace entrance, through a spacious foyer, and into a room that could be best described as a throne room lacking all air of exquisite décor or pretentions of grandeur. An old man wearing a palm frond crown sat awaiting them. Directly behind him stood a tall, lithe woman of grave countenance whose eyes bore in on Hroc and Guthroth with single focus, assessing their figures and unfamiliar military garb, including gambesons and Norman helmets. She appeared to take special interest in the armaments hanging from their belts. Hroc carried bludgeon and sword, and Guthroth his hammer, sword, and dagger. Behind her stood two younger women who, unlike the first, wore head-coverings and veils, exposing only their eyes; even their brows were hidden. Hroc and Guthroth both surmised these were the two younger Muslim daughters Arnag had described.

"I am Haya," declared the bare-headed woman in French, as the old man strained to make out the visitors; his vision failing for years and on the verge of blindness, "and this is my father. He is Emir here at the Oasis of Sparrows, but takes his title loosely as seen by the crown he wears. Rather, unlike other emirs, he is less concerned about his title than about his responsibilities, which are keeping this oasis open to all and safeguarding those who live here. You may call him, simply, Papa Daba." She then bowed her head slightly in her father's honor.

"I welcome you," rasped Daba, straining to be heard. "But tell, what of this army you bring? Why are you here? Where did you come from?"

At this, Haya leaned into her father's ear and whispered an exchange in his tongue, "These men do not speak Arabic, Father. I will be your voice. And before more questions, allow them to introduce themselves at least." Then she stood back up, rigid and formal.

"Y-yes, certainly," grunted Daba, smiling sheepishly at being corrected. Haya, even as a young girl, had been rather imperious, and as a woman, even more. Having no sons or male heirs, he saw having a strong daughter as a blessing, not a bother.

Switching to French, Haya offered the first hint of a smile, thin as it was. "We know Arnag well," she said, her tone flat, "but what are your names?" She arched one eyebrow.

Her expression was such that Hroc felt chastised for disrespect and impoliteness. "I am Hroc Five-hands," he offered quickly, "and I am—"

"Five-hands," interrupted Haya, her voice not rising as in question.

Hroc saw something shift in her face, sensed disdain perhaps, not amusement, and felt compelled to clarify. "Yes, because as a child I was into everything. We are Normans, kind of, but we've retained our Danish roots; Viking ancestry, actually."

From there Hroc launched into a brief history of the origins of the Danish Guard. Haya listened carefully, her eyes settled directly on those of Hroc, but he suspected her attention was elsewhere, as to the side, where Guthroth stood, who to this point had said nothing. Since entering the hall and first sight of Haya, Guthroth had cast his eyes downward, refusing to make eye contact with her or speak; concerned with how his speech impediment would make him look to her.

Midway through Hroc's history of the Danish Guard, Haya pursed her lips and interrupted, "This is odd, I find." Staring directly at Guthroth, she spoke to Hroc, "You, Hroc Five-hands, are the younger man, yet you claim this man is your uncle. In our culture, it is the older man, especially if a relative, who speaks for the younger. Does your uncle not have a tongue?"

Stung by this suggestion, Guthroth stepped forward, his knees giving the tiniest bit. "I am Gu-Goot-Guthroth, and I-I . . ." he blurted, staring directly at Haya. Falling silent without finishing, his face flushed as he lowered his eyes again and took a step back, thinking he had made an utter fool of himself, precisely what he was hoping not to do.

Though Haya said nothing, it was evident she was surprised, or at the least puzzled.

Seeing this, Hroc interceded, gingerly, "My uncle's full name is Guthroth the Quiet. He speaks little because he prefers to."

"Oh, he prefers to," replied Haya, sensing deceit as shown by the hint of ambiguity entering her huge almond eyes. It was not the look of one smelling fish, but the same one that had surfaced when hearing Hroc's name.

"I d-don't sp-speak," declared Guthroth, a mammoth of a man who raised his gaze but halfway, "be-because I c-can't speak very w-well. It sh-shames me."

Eyes wide, mouth agape, Hroc stared at his uncle, shocked. He had never once heard this man he loved and respected openly address his own speech defect; an underlying truth no one had ever dared to discuss or point out, especially Guthroth.

"I w-wish I did n-not carry this curse," stated Guthroth ruefully, his face flaring red in embarrassment and shame. "B-but then, God has gi-given me other g-gifts."

"Ha!" clucked Haya. "And indeed, Gudrock, I believe you." She nodded, her solemnity retreating a fraction for the first time since greeting the visitors.

"Guth-roth," Hroc corrected, uncertain whether she had misunderstood or was being sarcastic.

"G-Guthroth," interceded an insistent voice, correcting Hroc's exaggerated pronunciation of his name. "I am G-Guthroth, H-Haya."

Craning forward, putting a single finger to her mouth, Haya studied Guthroth intently. Straightening, she indicated her approval with a tip of her head. "Yes, Guthroth," she said, nearly smiling, "I believe you. You do look like a man with other gifts. Odd, but I sensed that very thing as you entered the hall, and again as you stood silently, lost to a world that others don't know exists. You were thinking, weren't you? Thinking hard."

Guthroth did not answer, but his face lightened, slowly at first, then broadened, sensing acceptance and understanding.

"I know that, Guthroth the Quiet," sympathized Haya, "because I, too, spend time in a world that no one knows exists."

Hearing this, Guthroth's eyes glistened, bolstered by what he interpreted as sheer sincerity in Haya's voice, then even more by the welcoming sheen slipping onto her smooth caramel face.

Despite his anchored heart and ferocity in war, this stern figure of a woman had managed to intimidate him from the moment he set eyes on her. This in itself was further astounding because Guthroth had pursued, by choice and by nature, a preference of male company, military camps, and war. Not that Guthroth had ever held women in low regard, as testified to by his respect and devotion for Asta of the Danes, no, he simply had never been 'struck' by a woman. As such, he had never experienced the slightest heart-pull from any female, including those flirting with him, nor even camp whores tempting him with open displays of their wares. He had always considered the former to be ridiculous, and the latter to be filthy.

"Arnag," instructed Haya in Arabic, "you know where the dining hall is to be found. Tell the servants to prepare a feast, and show our guests where they may make ready. My father and I wish to better acquaint ourselves with our visitors." Gently grasping her father by the arm, she assisted him to his feet. "Come along, Father, I will enlighten you about our guests. There is much to be learned."

Upon seating themselves, according to Haya, servants scuttled about the dining hall bringing in platter after platter of fruit, smoked meats, and a plethora of delicacies unfamiliar to Hroc and Guthroth. Naturally, the two became immersed in conversation with Haya and Papa Daba, along with Arnag. The two younger sisters said little for the most part, but their coy silence could not conceal an obvious interest in Hroc. Like Guthroth, Hroc's existence had been sparse of females, which made him feel awkward as he grew conscious of their glances and twittering; apparently entailing exchanged comments between themselves about him. As a result, Hroc found himself talking less to Haya and Daba so he could have a miscellaneous conversation with Arnag and keep an eye on them. Not that he was interested in either sister, but they were making him feel uncomfortable, and he wanted them to know he was watching them. To what purpose, Hroc had no idea, other than being drowned in self-consciousness; something he had rarely ever experienced and did not much care for.

To further astound Hroc, Guthroth's tongue loosened as he spoke to Papa Daba, and even more when addressing Haya. He had never witnessed this in Guthroth, ever, nor even imagined it possible. Guthroth had lived reserved in quiet shame brought on by his speech impediment ever since he'd known him. Astonishingly, stone-serious as he was by nature, Guthroth had even begun to smile from time to time during these exchanges, his face taking on a new and unfamiliar color. As did Haya, who had initially struck Hroc as stiff and emotionless.

Through it all, Papa Daba sat content as an old purring cat. Indeed, this stuttering visitor had struck a happy chord in his daughter, who in truth, did incline toward sobriety.

The impromptu feast lasted over three hours with little indication of ending until Haya finally stood and said, "Ah, but afternoon has fled and darkness approaches, Arnag, and it is too late to travel. I ask that you and our other two visitors remain overnight in the guest quarters and not depart until later in the morning."

But it was Guthroth who replied, "Th-thank you, Lady H-Haya. As y-you request, it sh-shall be done."

The next morning, Haya and Daba greeted their visitors with tea and a light meal followed by hours of conversation before seeing them to the gate and onto their horses. "Be safe in your travels. A storm awaits you both, and perhaps even us here at the Oasis of Sparrows," said Haya, her tone and expression laced with a trace of lingering. "But then, should God allow, you would pass our way again?"

"Aye," nodded Papa Daba, a look of satisfaction filling his worn expression.

"Allah has always blessed us with visitors, many of whom return, each bringing gifts. Sometimes they even bring hope." There, a visible twinkle was seen in his eyes.

Hroc, puzzled by both of these cryptic farewells, expected that Guthroth would reply, due to his unanticipated loquacity of the day before. But Guthroth said nothing; simply tipped his head, lowering his eyes onto Haya. His smile and color of the day before had disappeared, as had Haya's. To Hroc, everything that had transpired between the two the day before and during this very morning had vanished into the blowing desert wind.

Having abandoned Arnag, who wished to remain at the oasis to peddle his wares, it was not until an hour down the road that Guthroth spoke his first words. "Hroc," he said, staring ahead, "wh-what we s-saw th-there . . ." then he went silent.

"Ja?" prodded Hroc.

Directing his eyes onto Hroc, while moving his head back and forth with firm negative affirmation, Guthroth's voice went low, "We sh-shall say n-nothing of the Oasis of Sparrows to the cr-crusader princes," he commanded. "V-vow it."

Hroc was about to object, or at the least question Guthroth's declaration, but before he could speak Guthroth cut him off.

"V-vow it!" he insisted. "Th-there is p-peace and happiness th-here. Our ar-army would tr-trample it! B-Bohemud and R-Raymond are bastards, and Godfrey, t-too."

Hroc caught the urgency of Guthroth's tone and spotted an unfamiliar determination in his eyes. "Ja, then," agreed Hroc, nodding slowly, his gaze not shifting from his uncle, "we shall say nothing about the Oasis of Sparrows except to our family within the Tuscan camp, and vow them all to secrecy."

"Ja," said Guthroth, "only Tristan, Guillaume, Orla, and Crowbones."

CHAPTER TWENTY-SEVEN

SAINT SIMEON: MALA, THE ROMANI

It is an undeniable reality that, despite the destruction and horrors of war, war itself generates unimaginable amounts of wealth in many forms and on many fronts; in the process creating a genre of entrepreneurs known as 'war profiteers.' Not that this was Mala's intention by any means, but the Holy Crusade had created a boom market well exceeding the already successful nature of her established trading empire.

As la Gran Signorina of Genoa, and possessing of one of the most competitive and productive fleets of the entire Mediterranean, the Holy Crusade could not help but further fill her treasury, as well as that of hundreds of others steeped in high commerce, if for no other reason than the sheer scope of the war, the number of people involved, the amount of travel it induced, and the vast quantities of supplies and necessities it required.

This boom for Mala was not restricted to trade in Europe alone. Her financial scope of operation was international, including commerce in North Africa, Byzantium, and the Middle East. Much of her business involved Islamic nations and principalities; trading with Muslim entities regardless of the Pope's holy war against Islam. Her arena was business, not politics, nor religion. And despite being Catholic herself, Mala held no particular loyalty to the Vatican nor to the Church hierarchy. They, more than anything or anyone, were the very forces who had from the beginning created obstacles keeping her and Tristan apart. Consequently, Mala had little interest in the crusade, other than the safe-keeping of Tristan de Saint-Germain, whom she had loved since childhood.

At Tristan's request, she organized the assembly of a thirteen-ship fleet out of Genoa for purposes of resupplying the Army of God in Antioch in preparation for its push to Jerusalem. Having had her agents organize this fleet in Italy ten months earlier to amass arms, horses, food supplies, and recruits, la Gran Signorina of Genoa instructed them to sail for Constantinople where she would board ship and accompany them to Saint Simeon off the coast of Syria, arriving in early to mid-November.

Tristan and Mala's relationship, since its early stages, had been a tempestuous and illicit ordeal that had caused them both severe outbreaks of loneliness and separation, trust and uncertainty. In equal doses came reunion and heartbreak, including the devastating death of their infant son who fell victim to the turbulence of their illicit affair by freezing to death in the Alps. Tristan's undying love for her had taken a severe toll on him as well. Different in nature, more in spirituality and dogma, it resulted in the breaking of his vows and sanctification through self-flagellation for three days that nearly killed him. Then there was a nagging crisis of faith in the laws and motives of the Catholic Church, and a deep inner struggle entangled with the elements of God, Church law, love for Mala, and loyalty to his father figure, Odo de Lagery, who was presently serving as Pope Urban II.

Lamenting deemed futile, the future had to reign. It was the 17th of November 1097, and as she stood at the rail of the fleet's flagship, the Duxia de Falaise, all obstacles of the past seemed to have finally evaporated. The wind lifted her loosely braided, exquisite ebony locks from her left shoulder as her thoughts settled on the sheer joy that would wholly consume Tristan on setting eyes for the first time on their two-month-old son, Christophe de Saint-Germain.

Holding the infant to her bosom, protecting him from the spray as she looked out to sea, she envisioned the future encounter with abandonment. Mala was completely content thinking the crusade was nearing its end and Tristan would finally resolve his troubled relationship with the Church; possibly denying his vows, rebuking Odo de Lagery, and forging a new existence with her and Christophe.

Any such life would have to be established far from Europe and the Church. With Tristan's high position, his abandoning the Church would be an anathema. He would be hunted down, excommunicated, and punished; meaning imprisonment or possibly even execution. For that very reason, Mala had earlier sent a message of inquiry to Lord Abdul Azim, a powerful Muslim friend and trading partner, concerning the possibility of establishing asylum within his realm. Unfortunately, she had yet to receive a reply from Azim; unaware that he had been in hot pursuit of Mahmoud Malik or that both men were, this very day, within an arm's reach. More critically, she was not privy to the Council of Princes' decision to lay siege to Antioch rather than muster at Saint Simeon to await the last shipment of supplies before advancing on Jerusalem.

As the Duxia de Falaise anchored and the gangplank lowered, Mala gathered her elegant skirts and carried a sleeping, tiny Christophe, swaddled in a light-weight blanket against the incessant winds from the sea, onto the dock. Greeted initially by three officers, she then witnessed a jubilant score of crusaders cheering the fleet's arrival a determined distance behind them.

"Gran Signorina! I am Captain Charton, and I welcome you," said the man who appeared to be in charge, bowing slightly with arm extended, palm open. "We've been hoping and praying to see your ships for weeks!"

"And I am Captain Foulon," said one of the other men, bowing in reverence, "and this ugly bloke here is my brother, though he resembles me not in the least! We just arrived yesterday from scouting the road to Saint Simeon."

Offering a toothless grin, Foulon's brother extended a welcome, chiming, "Aye, and we came to check on Charton's bunch as well. But God's spine, Signorina, your arrival is both welcome and timely. Foraging has gone bleak round Antioch!"

"God's timing, not mine," firmly replied Mala, peering about, thinking to spot Tristan, Guillaume, and the Danes within the assembled crowd. Searching faces, horses, and other sundry modes of transportation, no evidence of the massive Christian army came into view. "But . . ." she started, confusion washing through her face, "I thought the entire crusader force to be here in Saint Simeon awaiting my fleet in preparation for the march on Jerusalem?"

"Ah, no, Signorina," said Charton, unsure of how she would take it. "The army has entrenched itself around Antioch and will shortly open attrition siege there."

Aghast, Mala said nothing, just simply stared ahead, her mind flitting with uncertainty and options.

"After capturing Antioch," interceded Foulon, "we shall march against Jerusalem, as decided by the Council of—"

"Bishop de Saint-Germain," she interrupted, her expression going dark, "he, too, is in Antioch?"

"Aye, awaiting your arrival," said Foulon proudly. "He wished to accompany us here to greet you, of course, but Bishop Adhémar objected."

"Oh?" Mala's visage instantly took on a flush of heat. "And to what earthly purpose?"

"As we had no idea exactly when your fleet might arrive," said Foulon, "Bishop Adhémar felt that Bishop Saint-Germain's presence would be better served in camp, as did the major princes. But no harm done. All is well now that you've dropped anchor. And believe me, the arrival of your fleet will bring great cheer to our camps. Antioch, with its massive fortifications, is soon to become a bloody affair."

Mentioning blood did not falter Foulon's tone, no, not at all. It carried confidence. He, like other crusaders, felt that once the siege actually began, the Christians would prevail within months. But having been on the road and away from Antioch, Foulon had no inkling that Yaghi Siyan had already unleashed his forces against the unsuspecting crusaders, inflicting a heavy toll.

"I shall require a coach, immediately," said Mala, her voice going cold, "and an escort to Antioch."

"But Signorina," objected Charton, "my orders are to unload the boats upon your arrival, a task that will take two full days at least, then proceed to Antioch with me and my troops serving as guard detail for both you and the supplies."

"Absolutely not," insisted Mala, her brow rising with evident agitation. At that same moment, baby Christophe began to squirm and fuss. Mala nuzzled her cheek against his, cooing a bit, though the fire in her eyes did not dissipate, nor did her dark gaze ever leave Charton. "This child is impatient to meet his father," she said, "and has no wish to delay any further. Nor do I."

"But—"

"Oh, but Charton," interceded Foulon, feeling his friend's discomfort, "there's no problem here! My brother and I can accompany la Gran Signorina to Antioch. Simply send a small guard contingent along with us and things'll be fine, I say. The road is clear. My brother and I just traveled it yesterday. Besides, we're all extremely indebted to la Signorina's generosity. She took it upon herself to finance much of this fleet from her personal treasury! The least we can do is extend a small gesture."

"Those were not my orders," insisted Charton. "Bishop Adhémar instructed me to—"

Her eyes contracting, Mala rolled her shoulders with indignity. "That old jackass of a bishop, Adhémar, may well be your master, Captain Charton, but he is most certainly not mine. Move aside then, and I shall follow Captain Foulon and his brother to Antioch immediately. Step in my path, though, and every man aboard my vessels will join in posting you to the mast of the Duxia de Falaise! Comprenez-vous?"

Scalded, Charton offered a weak nod of assent. "Yes, of course," he said. "But allow me time to at least assign a small guard detail to safeguard your travel! I beg you, Signorina."

"Certainly," agreed Mala, her tone softening. "And Captain Charton, I do thank you for your consideration. I shouldn't have become so curt. I was anticipating but a brief stay here in Saint Simeon for the great army to resupply, then march directly to Jerusalem and bring this campaign to its end. It appears things have changed, something that does not bode well in my estimation. But that shall be my burden, not yours. In any case, you were but doing as commanded. Please forgive me my shortness, Captain."

"I understand," lied Charton, having no idea what Gordian knot lay concealed within the obscurity of her words 'does not bode well in my estimation' or about 'that shall be my burden, not yours.' Setting those thoughts aside, Charton bowed, kissed her hand, and issued his farewell. "Antioch is but thirty kilometers from here, my Lady. May the journey be short, and may you arrive safely!"

CHAPTER TWENTY-EIGHT

BLOOD ON THE PLAINS

In ordering a pre-emptive attack out of Antioch, Yaghi Siyan caught the Christians by complete surprise. General Ahmet sallied forth from the Bridge Gate, while Mahmoud Malik and a hundred of his ghazis were ordered by Siyan to attack out of the southernmost entrance, the Saint George Gate. Due to the sheer size of the crusader army, these two forays constituted a gambit. Siyan may have been aware that the greater bulk of the Christian forces were concentrated before the three northern gates, but he had no idea how many had made bivouac further south, rendering his stratagem with certain risks.

To the Turks' surprise, the southern path lay wide open save two small enemy encampments whose purpose had been to deceive Siyan into believing that his two southern gates were blockaded by two large crusader forces. Ahmet quickly overcame and slaughtered the unfortunate crusaders covering the Bridge Gate. Malik did the same to those crusaders camped beyond the Saint George Gate with the only difference being that Malik had his victims stripped, castrated alive, then beheaded.

Ahmet's brigade then attacked the southern flank of Godfrey of Bouillon's camp, wreaking havoc with deadly compound bows while riding full tilt. At the same time, Malik's force rode south to the fork leading to Saint Simeon, falling by chance onto Foulon's two scouts, Gautreaux and DuBuisson, who were on their way back to camp. As with his earlier captives, Malik ordered the two stripped, castrated alive, and beheaded. "Now hang them upside down from that tree so all passing can see their pale white hides!" he ordered his men.

"Yes, Sire!" replied Hasan. "But where to from here? Do we reconnoiter with General Ahmet to the north as Siyan ordered?"

"No," said Malik, pointing to the road leading west from the fork. "I suspect Ahmet may well have his hands full, and I've no wish to further stir a hornet nest!"

Malik's main objective remained escaping Antioch, and he would have, in fact, taken flight on exiting the Saint George Gate, but wily Yaghi Siyan had suspected as much and only allowed Malik to take but a hundred of his 700 renegade ghazis on the day's sortie. Desertion was not an option for his devious guest, especially in light of learning more about him from Ben-fazi. The Persian could not be trusted.

"West?" asked Hasan, stumped by Malik's counter-command.

"The coast is less than half a day's ride from this fork, and I'm told the port of Saint Simeon sits just at the end of this road. We'll leave a dozen men here at the fork to keep watch while the rest of us raid the port. It might well provide a bounty of plunder!"

"But what of General Ahmet? Will Siyan not be furious that you ignored his command to reinforce his general in favor of plunder?"

"What's he to do, Hasan? What if the old cat's got my leg by a claw! I've got him by the toe. Never forget, Siyan is snared and needs us. I'll claim we encountered crusaders on the march from Saint Simeon; that they engaged us and we were forced to investigate the port for further enemy activity rather than turning north toward Ahmet."

"Ah, a clever ruse, that," complimented Hasan.

"I'll delude the old bastard for a time, at least into thinking we're with him until I figure out how to spring our entire force from Antioch. Then we'll be on our way. My bigger concern, Hasan, is Abdul Azim. He's out there, just to the north."

"Aye, and with blood on his mind," nodded Hasan, "calculating where we could be and how to get at us." Dropping into reflection, his eyes narrowed to a squint. "You know, Sire," he said slowly, "we are far beyond the gates of Antioch, and no one knows we are here. We could make a run for Jerusalem, could we not?"

"I've considered it," scowled Malik, "but without my full force, I bare myself to the Christians, as well as to Azim. If we run for Jerusalem, Azim is sure to follow and I'd not have a prayer without my full troop. Then again, with a mere hundred horses rather than 700, my bartering hammer as a mercenary commander dwindles greatly."

"Ah then, you still hope to find employment with Ridwan of Aleppo or Duqaq of Damascus?"

"Most certainly. With the defeat of Kilij Arslan by the Christians my opportunities in Asia Minor have evaporated. But this war in Syria revives new prospects. It's going to last a good while, Hasan, and there's much to be gained, but only for those who seize it. Unfortunately, this old bastard, Siyan, offers but scraps. Ugh! Nothing but rations and a damned roof! So, any riches to be had shall have to be mined beyond Antioch, beginning with Saint Simeon."

"As you say," bowed Hasan, turning in his saddle, gesturing to the pack of blood-soaked riders circulating about the tree that had been chosen for a scaffold. "Ah, it appears the two Christians have been strung," he said. "On to Saint Simeon!"

CHAPTER TWENTY-NINE

THE COUNCIL OF PRINCES

Stung by Yaghi Siyan's bold maneuver, the crusader camps quickly mobilized, bristling with arms and activity as Bohemud called an immediate assembly of the Council of Princes.

"Damn that Turcoman's sly old ass!" he swore as the meeting convened. "He's caught us flat-footed!"

Nodding, Godfrey of Bouillon slammed a fist against the tabletop. "And dammit," he snorted, "my camp took the brunt of it!"

"Horseshit!" insisted Tancred, Bohemud's fiery nephew. "We've been dodging archer fire in our Norman camp from the side of Mt. Staurin all day, and the corpses are piling up!"

"But my camp holds the southernmost position," fired Godfrey, "and the Muslims swarmed in full bore between us and Raymond's camp!"

"Aye, they came out the Bridge Gate," agreed Raymond of Toulouse. His and Adhémar's camps were located between Godfrey's and Bohemud's positions, therefore they suffered much of the day's havoc, along with Godfrey. "Therein lies our obstacle," he pointed out. "We've got to do a better job of securing the Bridge Gate or the Turks will come and go, attacking at will, especially with the Saint George Gate completely open."

"And they're using those two gates to resupply Antioch as well," added Robert of Normandy.

"Well shit, Raymond," scowled Bohemud, "we simply don't have enough manpower to cover those last two gates, which is why our two false camps were so easily overrun."

"Alright," asked Robert of Flanders, "what's to be done?"

Not aiming his words at Robert of Flanders, but others, Tristan took to his feet. "I'll tell you what's to be done," he said. "Abandon this hopeless siege, just as Taticius and I advised from the start!"

"Ah, hellfire!" sniffed Raymond. "Don't start that 'I told you so' shit!' Shut up, Saint-Germain! We're here, and here we stay until Antioch falls."

As he said this, a chortle arose derisively from across the table; Taticius, arms crossed, face beaming with mockery.

"And wipe that smirk off your face, you Byzantine oaf!" ranted Raymond. "Your damned emperor has done nothing to this point but sit on his Greek ass. And just where are the troops he's been promising since Nicaea, dammit?!"

"I've no comment," replied Taticius coldly. "You've ignored and belittled every counsel Bishop Saint-Germain and I have offered since entering Syria. Hence, I shall now hold my tongue other than to say, simply: we warned you that distant investment was far wiser than attrition siege. But you Latin wizards of strategy chose otherwise! Now prepare to wallow in your own folly! This little bit we've bled today is but the beginning, damn you, and—"

"It is not too late to disengage," interceded Tristan, looking to Adhémar.

This, tied to the tart words of Taticius, caused a stir at the table. Within minutes the alliances of the week before reignited. The major princes, Raymond, Bohemud, and Godfrey, refused to acknowledge the possibility of disengagement, and in defiance, Tristan, Taticius, Guillaume, and Letellier refused to abandon the position of distant investment. Robert of Normandy, Stephen of Blois, Robert of Flanders, and Hugh of Vermandois remained the only parties willing to consider both options. After an hour of vitriolic exchange, tempers peaked as emotion again started to overcome order and bad blood began to overrun sanity.

"Saint-Germain, I'd expect Taticius here to throw obstacles in our path," shouted Raymond, "but you? Hell, man, you preached this war! You swung the Pope in its favor, I was told! Dammit then, get aboard or get your ass out, I say!"

The impertinent nature of Raymond's biting attack surprised others, offending many. A hush descended over the table. But two ticks of a clock later, Raymond's allies broke into loud support of his stark words, shouting and pounding their chests.

"Aye, if you're not with us, Saint-Germain, then get the hell out!" barked Godfrey.

"Expel him from the crusade!" chanted Tancred, shaking a fist, taking to his feet. "Expel him from the crusade, I say!"

Several others took up the chant.

"Hold there!" declared Tristan, retaining his calm, although his posture had turned rigid, pointing at Adhémar. "And to you, Bishop, I pose a question. Is there no room here at this table, during this supposed quest in God's name, for differences of opinion? And oh, but are only the loudest voices to carry the day simply because they carry the heaviest purses? If that is the case, Adhémar, then simply say it! I and some others here should like to hear it from your own voice."

Staring back at Tristan, his neck going crimson, Adhémar set his jaw, but said nothing.

"And on hearing it," Tristan continued, rising nearly to his toes, "I shall record word for word what issued from your own tongue, then take those words back to the Holy Father, Pope Urban who chose you, Adhémar, to be his voice on this campaign, and the final judge, as well!"

Drowning in discomfort, Adhémar sensed all eyes watching; felt as caught in a vice with both sides closing. Lost to a long silence, he coughed a bit before finally saying, "As before, I shall support the stand of the major princes. Not because of their purses, but because of their combined experience in warfare and strategy.

But as to Bishop Saint-Germain leaving or being expelled from this crusade . . ." here he paused, moving his gaze from one major prince to the next, certainty settling over his face, replacing earlier confusion. "No!" he declared, wagging a finger. "You men there, I shall neither hear nor abide by any suggestion that he be sent from this crusade. He is the Pope's First Counsel as well as the Pope's First Scribe! Despite questions and points of disagreement from time to time, the Bishop has remained true to this endeavor. Just this week he had wished to await the Genoa fleet in Saint Simeon, but agreed, at my request, to remain here in camp with you men since we were uncertain when the fleet might arrive. Agreeing that a possible long absence from the front could be detrimental to your spirits, he stayed. Such is his commitment to you and to God's cause!"

In citing the fleet, Adhémar had avoided mention of la Gran Signorina, though everyone in camp was aware she had mobilized the support effort through her connections in Genoa. Moreover, the entire Council of Princes had been made aware of Tristan's and Mala's history, and that she had recently given birth to his son in Constantinople. This in itself had precipitated certain fractures within the Council as concerned Bishop Saint-Germain's credibility as a high clergyman representing the Vatican. Oddly, or perhaps not, it was the most conniving princes who reacted most unfavorably to Bishop Saint-Germain's breaking of religious vows, especially since this divisive feud over the disposition of Antioch started. Of all, Adhémar was the most critical of Tristan's relationship with Mala the Romani, yet his sentiments were rooted neither in pretension nor conniving but was fueled purely by earnest concern for Saint-Germain's soul, which had, according to Adhémar, been lost to sins of the flesh with Mala.

Adhémar had just finished speaking when commotion broke at camp's edge. Peter the Hermit and Peter Bartholomew had returned from the Iron Bridge with the severely injured Orla and the body of Crowbones strapped across a donkey's back.

"Bohemud, bad news!" shouted the Hermit. "Your scouting party was butchered on the mountain! They're all dead save Orla Bloodaxe here, who's half dead, poor soul! And yet he was able to carry his brother down for a proper burial!" Spotting Tristan, the Hermit shouted. "Yo there, lad, come quickly and offer your final words over Crowbones. I know you held him dear, and he, you!"

Tristan felt his wind leave him and his knees buckle. Guillaume propped him up, whispering, "Steady, Brother." He, too, surged with shock, but had since birth lacked the fragilities of Tristan's extraordinary sensibilities. As a lifetime warrior coarsened by battle, he understood better that all men-of-arms were victim to mortality, even those close to the heart.

Not moving toward Crowbones as asked by the Hermit, Tristan's face went ashen and a tiny rivulet then slipped down his cheeks to the corner of his mouth; its salt carrying the taste of grief across his lips onto his tongue. "Oh, but God in Heaven!" he heaved, feeling the walls of his heart closing in as his voice broke. "Must you have taken this dear man, our beloved Crowbones, from our midst?"

"Steady," whispered Guillaume, grasping Tristan's arm. "God's will, Tristan. Remember, all is as God wills it."

"N-no," stammered Tristan, his voice dropping so low that only his brother could hear, "not God's will. He did not engineer this war. It was us. We did it on our own. And I, Guillaume, sparked the fire."

Taking Crowbones' body back to the Tuscan camp with Orla, Tristan, and Guillaume set up an altar made of planks. Setting Crowbones on it, Tristan, Guillaume, Scule, Christos, and the Tuscan troops prayed for three days and nights, stopping only to eat. Even refusing calls to battle or any other calls to leave camp, the entire Tuscan camp became one long prayerful funeral service honoring Ivar Crowbones.

At the end of the third night, Orla, exhausted and unable to walk, said, "I should like to dispose of Ivar's body in a Nordic ritual by fire. Lay him in a flat-boat stacked with hardwood and lumber scraps, set it afire, and push it out to sea at Saint Simeon. One of the last things Ivar said was that 'he was tired and wished he could see the old country.' That's impossible, of course, but the least I could do is give him a Nordic farewell by fire."

Hearing this, Tristan and Guillaume both revolted. "He may have been born pagan," said Guillaume with heat, "but he died Christian, Orla, surrendering his last breath to God while fighting heathens! He became bathed in grace the day he flung his grandmother's pagan pouch of bird bones into the fire, by God, and embraced eternal salvation in doing so!"

Tristan stiffly reinforced Guillaume. "No, Orla," he asserted, "the early Church retained the Jewish practice of bodily burial, rejecting the common pagan Roman practice of cremation. God has created each person in His image and likeness, therefore the body is good and should be returned to the earth at death, Genesis 3:19. Remember, our Lord was buried in a tomb, then rose in glory on Easter morning. That is when Christians began to bury their dead both out of respect for the body and in anticipation of the resurrection at the Last Judgment. As Saint Paul wrote, 'The Lord Himself will come down from Heaven at the word of command, at the sound of the archangel's voice and God's trumpet, and those who have died in Christ will rise first.' Orla, Crowbones must be buried, not cremated!"

"Remember, too," insisted Guillaume, "how the godless treated and mocked our martyrs, burning them at the stake and scattering their ashes as a sign of contempt for the Christian belief in resurrection! No, Crowbones must be buried facing East, so when Christ returns to this earth your brother may stand up in his grave and see the light of the Lord emanating from Jerusalem!"

Orla held great misgivings, but too injured to stand against both Guillaume and Tristan, and too confused to defy them, he conceded to placing Crowbones in the earth. Nonetheless, on the night before his brother's burial, he secretly had himself carried to Crowbones' body, cut a lock of his hair, and then was taken to the Orontes where he had arranged to have a flat-boat put in place.

Placing the lock of hair in the boat, Orla set the boat afire and shoved it adrift on the Orontes. "Sleep in peace, Ivar," he declared, saluting his brother as flames licked the night sky. "And may you never see another drop of blood, nor day of war!"

CHAPTER THIRTY

TUSCAN DISASTER DEEPENS

Guthroth and Hroc, having no idea that Yaghi Siyan had gone on the attack, ambled their way from the Oasis of Sparrows back to the fork leading to Saint Simeon, intent on rejoining the Tuscan camp.

As they neared the fork, Guthroth's eyes flared and he pulled back on his reins, bridling his horse to a halt. "L-look there," he said, pointing toward a scraggy grove just off the path.

"Cru-crusaders?" stammered Hroc, struck by the pale-skin of the two stripped, headless corpses strung by ankles from one of the trees.

"J-ja," muttered Guthroth, raking his eyes across the terrain. "B-but there—"

The howl of a pack of ghazis, baying like hounds converging on prey, streaming out from behind a short rise just beyond the trees, cut off his sentence. They had spotted the two riders approaching in the distance, suspecting them to be Christian.

An instant later a shower of arrows whistled past Guthroth and Hroc, barely missing them. Kicking their horses in the flanks, both bolted back across the open desert. But escape, as they suspected, was unlikely. The Turks had taken them by ambush and were already nearly on top of them. Bravely, Guthroth and Hroc slunk low in their saddles, grasping for sword and hammer from their belts, having accepted the futility of hand weapons against archers firing from behind, galloping in full pursuit.

Feeling the hot breath of enemy stallions in his wake, Guthroth spun his horse about, jerking the reins hard, turning the beast on spot. Whinnying with fury, rising on hind feet, the beast struck out savagely with heavily laden hooves. This maneuver unfolded so quickly that the closest Turk's saddle loosened, sliding rider and saddle beneath the bucking stallion. Confused, growing increasingly aggressive by the moment, the Turk's horse stamped and kicked wildly, trampling its rider to death. Simultaneously, the next closest Turk collided into the first ghazi's mount and was thrown from his horse. Within a blink, Guthroth rode over him, reached out with his hammer and split the ghazi's head open like a ripe melon.

Hroc, as taught by Guthroth years earlier, orchestrated a similar maneuver with his own horse, taking one Turk from his horse, just before slashing another with his blade. But from the distance an arrow whistled past Hroc, just missing him but striking Guthroth in the right side just as he had raised his hammer to bludgeon another attacker. Groaning, Guthroth dropped his weapon, doubling over as in slow motion. A blink later, another arrow whistled in, striking him just inches from the first wound. "Arhgh!" he groaned, his vision blurring.

Seeing this, Hroc shouted out in helpless defiance, his wits vanishing with his fleeting breath. Then, grasping Guthroth's reins, he made a mad dash toward a rise in the dunes, praying for miraculous though improbable intervention.

Unbelievably, it came. Shocked by the violent turnabout inflicted by the two Christians, the Turks lost their nerve, even though one of the Christians had been seriously wounded. The Turk whose head had been opened by Guthroth was the youngest brother to two of the other riders. Shocked, both discontinued the chase to recover their brother's body.

It was not until another half mile of retreat that Hroc realized the Turks were no longer following. Breathing heavily, he stopped, dismounted, and hurried to Guthroth.

"I-I'm finished," groaned Guthroth, his tone dull, dispassionate. "G-go, Hroc, fl-flee."

"They're gone," said Hroc, his heart surging with confusion. Guthroth had been the better part of Hroc's existence since the Danes' flight from England, when Hroc was but a child. Guthroth had taken time with him, been patient, taught him to ride, hunt, and fight, even more than Orla. "We're safe now," said Hroc, offering solace and hope in a single breath.

Head slumping awkwardly onto his horse's mane, Guthroth's eyes opened, then blinked three times in rapid succession. "I'm hurt too b-bad, Hroc," he rasped. "R-run b-back to the oasis, Hroc." Weakly, he issued a weary sign of resignation, as to do any more was impossible. He had lost so much blood he could no longer feel even his fleeting heartbeat. "J-ja, and God b-be w-with you."

At this, a frail look of surrender filled his eyes as a muffled moan issued from his throat, and his eyes grew vacant.

"Breathe!" shouted Hroc. "Oh, but Guthroth, breathe I say! You'll not end this way! God won't have it!"

Numbed, Hroc remained standing there beside Guthroth and his horse for several minutes, insistent that he still felt the tiniest of breath issuing from Guthroth's nostrils. "I'll get you back to the oasis with me," he muttered, mounting his horse, turning southeast. "For it was there, Guthroth, that I saw you crack your door."

Within hours of Hroc's and Guthroth's encounter at the Saint Simeon fork, the Foulon brothers, Mala, baby Christophe, and twenty knights arranged by Captain Charton had traveled ten kilometers east from port.

Though steeped in silence, Mala's heart was full, imagining Tristan's heartfelt reaction to seeing their son for the first time. Oh, but he shall be struck dumb! Moments later, that conclusion changed. No, he shall dance and cry out with pride and joy! she determined, laughing aloud. And oh, after all this time of uncertainty, separations, reunions, fighting the Church, and fighting ourselves our struggles will finally be done! Tristan and I shall revel in eternal happiness, and with tiny Christophe, we shall end our years in well-deserved peace.

But even as she assured herself, ahead of her procession a spire of dust arose in the distance.

"Eh, but what's that, do you suppose?" Foulon asked his brother.

Unconcerned, his brother replied, "Don't know. Could be our other scouts have finished their look about and decided to ride our way?"

"No," squinted Foulon, "too much dust being kicked up for that. Crusader wagons, maybe, or possibly a Syrian caravan headed to Saint Simeon."

But the approaching dust was neither crusaders nor caravan, and before Foulon's brigade could even mount a defense or retreat, a hundred ghazis washed forward in a thundering assault. The Foulon brothers were the first to be murdered, surrounded by a score of Turks hacking at them from all sides. As other knights moved forward to defend them and the coach, they, too, were overcome.

"Decapitate the corpses and sack the heads!" shouted Malik, dispatching the last Christian from behind just as the man had turned his horse in a fruitless attempt to flee back toward Saint Simeon.

Surveying the Christian dead, Hasan noticed that a good number of them had assembled around the coach, purporting to defend it to the death. "Must be a Christian dignitary inside. Pull the bastard out!" he barked to three ghazis who had anticipated his command and dismounted, shouting for anyone inside the coach to surrender.

But no movement came from within.

Shouting louder, the ghazis flung the door open, peering inside with weapons raised. Then followed one of those odd moments heralding the unexpected; all three men froze, their eyes widening as witnessing the extraordinary.

Seeing this, Hasan dismounted. "Well," he said, shouldering them aside, "what's taken ahold of your damned tongues?" Muted, he, too, fell silent.

Sitting there within the coach, holding an infant to her bosom, sat the most stunningly beautiful woman he could have ever thought to encounter, and in a war zone. Then, too, he expected that the sheer trauma and brutality of the attack would have created hysteria in any passenger, especially a woman, but this woman sat motionless, staring back at him.

Mesmerized, Hasan blinked, as if to reassure himself that what he was looking at was indeed, real. Gathering his breath, he shouted, "Master Malik! I think you'd best come see what we've found here in the coach!"

"Riches, I hope!" answered Malik, anticipating through Hasan's tone that good news was soon to follow.

"Aye, Komutan, of the highest degree! Come quick!"

The effect of feminine beauty on men, even coarse, violent men, is palpable. The effect of ultimate feminine beauty on men, however, is absolute. Setting his eyes on Mala the Romani, Malik's jaw tightened, then his heart skipped a beat, violently gripped by an attack of uncontrollable obsession, spiking into an insatiable need to possess this woman in entirety—body, mind, and spirit. Sheer lust stood squarely at the forefront, infecting him. But beyond the gross swelling of his loins, there was something more, something stronger. This, in itself, was peculiar. To Malik, women were worthless, sexual vessels to be used, abused, and forced into unnatural acts of sodomy and bestiality, anything to satisfy his rapacious pleasures and physical satisfaction, both of which were inexhaustible.

But within those piercing anthracite eyes staring back at him, not with fear as much as with loathing, he sensed something beyond his ability to comprehend. I shall have her in every way a man can possess a woman, he vowed, his dark eyes meeting hers in an unspoken struggle of wills, and she shall belong to me for as long as she and I shall breathe.

Though Mala's face betrayed no emotion, her heart was thumping wildly, racing from one terrifying supposition to another as Malik's gaze lowered to baby Christophe bundled in her arms. Mala knew she was in trouble. This man's serpentine expression exuded evil and perversity in equal measure, worse than even the most depraved of drunken men slathering and lusting after her as a young street dancer in younger years. Most distressing, though, her son had now been thrust along with her beneath this beast's shadow. With all stacked against her, she refused to cower.

This only spurred Malik on. In his mind, he was already playing at crushing her will—physically, sexually, emotionally. Slamming the coach door shut, he shouted to Hasan, pointing east. "Back to Antioch!" he commanded.

"Antioch?" Hasan questioned him, surprised. "But Komutan, what of plundering Saint Simeon?"

"Another time!" declared Malik, his jaw set in great anticipation. "I've just acquired a prize Saint Simeon could never hope to offer!"

CHAPTER THIRTY-ONE

AN UNFORESEEN BRIDGE

When Guthroth awoke, blackness welcomed him. He felt nothing, which led him to believe he was dead. Then he began to feel minuscular twinges in the muscle of a forearm and in the tips of fingers, signaling that he was alive, even if barely so. Then the black void enveloping him erupted, jounced by lightning, creating a luminous, glaring field of vision starker than the most bedazzling snow slope of a Nordic mountain reflecting the radiance of a hot sun. A terrified Guthroth concluded that he had gone blind. Panic stricken, he groped about hoping to feel . . . to feel . . . anything.

Writhing, the field of auroral blankness confronting him began to soften by degrees, then a vaporous, ethereal figure hovered directly over him, cloaked in a hooded robe so pallid as to blend seamlessly into the halo of white surrounding her.

"H-Haya?" he sputtered, blinking rapidly to clear his vision.

"Yes," came a voice, but it was a man's voice. "Haya and me," said Hroc. "I got you here alive by the mercy of God alone, but it's Haya here who has tended to you day and night. She's yet to leave your side since two nights back."

"She strained lamb's blood and water down your throat to replenish your own lost blood, urging her God and yours to spare you," clucked a third voice, in Arabic, though neither Guthroth nor Hroc understood what Papa Daba had just said. "It seems you shall live after all, having tipped a foot into the realm of the dead. Haya claims your God must still have purpose for you. Me, I say 'twas Allah bestowing you a second chance. But the question remains, to what end?"

"Father, they understand nothing of what you're saying," said Haya, gesturing at him as one dismissing the babble of a child.

"H-Haya?" muttered Guthroth again, absorbing the warmth of her hand covering his as she stooped over him, caressing his hair with her other.

"I did not expect to see you again so soon," Haya cooed, her face betraying but the tiniest vestige of affection, "though I hoped it. Then, seeing what had happened to you, I prayed to our Lord that He would bring you back, though all here already thought you dead . . . except me. I felt God's mercy surfacing as you lay there fighting to live."

This warmed Guthroth and he offered a feeble acknowledgement, but just like with Haya, his unchanging expression relayed little emotion. Yet, it was there. And within Haya's own somber expression, Guthroth guessed that she was feeling a similar precipitance toward an obscure yet palpable communion.

As Providence alone would have it, Haya and Guthroth were of corresponding vein, both sparing words, each possessing a veritable hoard of secretive perception and thought; born deeply anchored within themselves, but reticent, rarely allowing the boiling caldron constantly bubbling within to emote. It was the most extraordinary of circumstances that dared unsaddle either's composure; both facing the world before them with a singular level of consideration, acting and reacting with definitive purpose.

Frivolity had little place in neither's head, nor did idle chatter. In Guthroth's case, his sparsity of the spoken word had been attributed by others strictly to the speech impediment he inherited at birth and the resultant beatings as a child from his father who thought him thick-headed. But what remained unknown to others, and possibly to Guthroth himself, was that God imbued Guthroth at birth with the admirable traits of silence and reserve. Just as God had deceived Guthroth, Guthroth had, in turn, quietly deceived the world.

As to Haya, her attributes had been chalked up to receiving the gifts of extraordinary self-discipline, accompanied by dignity and maturity, albeit touched with a peculiar degree of what could be described as 'frigid indifference' as related to circumstance and people. So, unlike Guthroth, Haya commanded an authority that Guthroth lacked.

During their first encounter of just days before, the two had struck an unspoken, fortuitous connection, unlikely and unanticipated as it was. Yet neither had in any manner intimated such, the message had translated itself in the language of gazes; Guthroth's being furtive, Haya's forthright. In this manner, two kindred hearts had quietly bridged an improbable gulf of distance, culture, race, and future.

But such is the indecipherable depth of human receptivity, one person to another, even when words remain absent. In such cases as this, communication arrives on silent winds, conscience to conscience and inner voice to inner voice, in a transaction unperceived by most.

"You must remain with me. To recover, I mean, Guthroth," said Haya. "Unless, of course, you wish to be buried in the hot sand along the road back to Antioch. Do you understand?"

"Y-yes," replied Guthroth, offering the slightest nod. "G-God w-wills it, I be-believe."

"Aye," chimed in Hroc, "you certainly won't be riding for a time, nor even walking. But me, I'd best get back and tell everyone what's occurred at the Saint Simeon fork and that the Turks have come out from behind their walls."

Raising a hand toward him, Guthroth's expression contracted, conveying urgency. "R-re-remember, Hroc. Say n-nothing, nothing of the Oasis of Sp-Sparrows, save to our own b-bunch. N-not a w-word t-to anyone else."

"I swear it," replied Hroc, right hand on his heart.

"Good. Th-then God sp-speed, Hroc. R-ride safe."

CHAPTER THIRTY-TWO

THE PRISON CELL

Returning to Antioch, Malik's troop streamed into the Bridge Gate at full gallop. Malik directed the coach toward the prison, dismounted, and shouted for Hasan to extract their captive from the coach and bring her inside. Brushing Boros the Armenian jailor aside in favor of the Turkish guards, Malik instructed them to find an isolated cell located away from the others.

"There are none," replied the guard captain. "They all stand side by side, separated only by bars. There remains but a single empty cell, adjacent to the young Greek girls you brought with you here to Antioch."

"Then dammit," growled Malik, impatient to get at his captive, "put this woman and child in it! Show the way!"

Leading Malik and Hasan down a long corridor lined on one side with cells filled to bursting with prisoners, separated by gender, the guards stopped at the last cell within the structure.

"Here," said a guard, unlocking it and entering. As he did this, the young girls in the adjacent cell scurried away, huddling in a far corner. Most were adolescent or younger, all bearing bruises and cuts inflicted during repeated bouts of individual and gang rape committed by Malik, Hasan, and at times, favored ghazis being rewarded for one thing or another.

Hasan shoved Mala inside, forcing baby Christophe from her grip and handing him to Malik. Taking but a brief look at the infant, Malik tossed him unceremoniously onto a pile of straw bunched to the side as a bed of sorts. Startled by the impact, Christophe began to squall, crying at the top of his lungs, his little face trembling uncontrollably as all four limbs launched into frenetic motion.

"Christophe!" Mala gasped, striking out in rabid fury, clawing Hasan's face with her nails.

"Ahghh!" cried Hasan, as blood effused from three scarlet streaks she'd tracked across his cheek. "Damn you, bitch!"

Laughing, Malik knocked Mala aside, his massive bear-paw sending her reeling against the stone wall at the rear of the cell. "Ha, Hasan! She's already made short work of you, I see! Take off then, and be gone. She requires a real stallion, I think!"

Infuriated, Hasan shot Mala a hot glance before turning his eyes back to Malik. "But Komutan," he objected, palms up, "I was hoping to . . . well, you know!"

"What?! Ah no, Hasan. You'll not be filling her with your slimy seed. She's mine, all mine! Now get the hell out and take the guards with you."

"Could I not just watch then?" insisted Hasan, intent on at least seeing the beautiful captive stripped naked and violated.

"Out, I said!" commanded Malik, retrieving Mala from the floor by one arm, flinging her onto the pile of straw next to a distraught Christophe. "Hasan, I don't need you salivating like some drooling dog howling for scraps while I take my pleasure rutting this woman front and back, by damn!"

Hasan pointed to the huddle of girls clinging to each other in the next cell, their eyes frozen on Malik and Hasan who had hungrily entered their cell too many times during the night. Terrified, they knew what was shortly to happen to the new prisoner. "And what about them?" insisted Hasan. "They'll be watching, you know! What harm then, if I stay?"

"Ha, I want them to watch," snorted Malik. "But I'll have no other man hungering over this prize, or getting at her crack!" Loosening his belt, he dropped his breeches, exposing massive genitals. Sneering, he grasped his swollen penis, flagging it at Mala lying at his feet. "Now get out, Hasan, or I'll run this big pole of mine up your ass!"

Scalded, Hasan turned, taking the guards with him. Malik listened through the child's screams for the echo of bootsteps to dissipate down the corridor. Then, standing astride Mala who had reached for Christophe and was shielding him in her arms, Malik locked eyes with her, his baritone timbre sending chills down her spine. "This will be very simple, woman. Set the child aside, or I shall grab him by the feet and splatter that soft little head of his against the bars. Do you understand?"

"Yes," replied Mala without hesitation, setting Christophe aside in the hay, praying for his protection and their deliverance. Please, God, keep him quiet. Send Your angels to protect him, and give me the strength to survive this.

"Good," grunted Malik, his tongue flicking his lower lip with anticipation, taking on that glassy gaze of the predator sizing up helpless prey. "Now strip for me, and lay back. Then spread your legs. You've already got my nature up and I'm impatient to get between your thighs and start plying that sweet, delicate flesh of yours." At this, Malik laughed aloud, gazing scornfully into the adjacent cage where several of the young girls stood staring as others turned away, masking their eyes and ears against what would follow.

Saying nothing, Mala complied with Malik's command. Unbuttoning her dress, letting the upper portion fall to her waist, she exposed the perfection of porcelain amber skin and the sculpted curves of large, perfectly upturned breasts peaking in large areolas and dark, taut nipples, framed in ebony curls about her shoulders and down her back.

Malik's breath caught, as pricked by a thorn. This woman's shape was prodigious, far beyond anything he'd ever seen. Wholly devastated by her feminine bounty, he scrambled to his knees, quickly pulling her skirt up over her waist, prying her thighs apart, digging his fingers into her vagina, opening it wide to accommodate his manhood, so fully swollen as to cause Malik searing discomfort.

But Mala's seductive allure had dulled the sharp edges of his normally wily senses, and he failed to sense anything awry. Unlike previous victims of his violent rapes, and there had been many, this woman's eyes were not filled with dread but with calculation. Pulling him in, even grasping and pulling at his penis with both hands as to urge him on, she flicked her tongue into his ear. This sent shock waves through Malik and he pushed up on his hands, staring deep into her eyes to closely watch and absorb what was about to become her sudden change of expression and outcry at the moment of penetration.

Staring back at him, her eyes offered what Malik interpreted as a glint, inferring 'Yes, I'm ready for you.' Then with every ounce of spiritual strength, she prayed, God help me! and tightened her left grip on his penis while releasing her right hand from it. Fumbling about her waist, she quickly located the disheveled cuff of her right sleeve and the dagger she always kept hidden there. In one brisk motion, she extracted and struck up, then down across his face, and over his chest and belly, ending just behind his throbbing member. This was the very same dagger with which at age fourteen she had killed Tristan's errant classmate, red-headed LeBrun, who had raped her aunt and sliced her mother's face beyond recognition. That was the day she vowed to never be caught helpless, and about the sweet blood of retribution. Since that first bloodletting, her faithful dagger had remained hidden up her sleeve within easy reach, no matter where she was, the company at hand, or the circumstances surrounding her.

Unaware at first of what had just occurred, Malik groaned aloud, thinking she had clawed him like Hasan and that his manhood was indeed aflame. Then came the blood, spewing fountain-like from a single body-length slash that now pursed open like yawning lips from above his right eyebrow, across his eye and nose, down the run of his cheek to the tip of his chin, then down his entire torso. A flicker later, he was blinded as blood gushed from both eye sockets; his face having been dissected into diagonal halves. Then came the searing pain from his groin, forcing him to lurch aside. In doing so, he struck out with the fury of a wounded beast, striking Mala full force across the flat of her nose, smashing it to a bloody pulp, spurting blood like a font. But Malik's side movement allowed space for her to wriggle out from beneath him, his disconnected penis in her grip. Swearing, Malik struggled to his feet, hampered by breeches tangled about his ankles, exposing his missing cock, which was erupting blood and semen.

Neither could see at this point, but Malik struck out, flailing, seeking his prey. Staggering clumsily about, he bellowed at the top of his lungs, now intent on killing this woman that had dared defy him. Lumbering around in circles like a blind bear, his fist caught her again, across a cheek this time, crushing it, causing her to drop his limp, spurting member in the straw.

"Christophe!" she wailed, stumbling about for her infant who was bawling in protest, hoping to remove him from Malik's path but unable to locate him.

Hearing her voice, Malik lunged her direction, catching her again, across an eye, as in the adjacent cell girls shouted, "Back up! Go to the right! Fall to the floor!" in an attempt to direct her away from danger. But instead, in the small cell, she kept charging forward, blindly lunging out with her dagger, once slicing Malik's arm, once raking the dagger across the side of his neck.

Hearing what sounded like the outbreak of a riot, Turkish guards scrambled to the end of the prison corridor to be greeted by Malik's hideous, repulsive state, as well as that of the captive.

"Pull him out! Get him out before that bitch kills him!" shouted the guard captain.

It took five men to take control of Malik who raged blind, spurting blood. Dragging him from the cell and down the corridor, the guards forced him to the ground in an effort to restrain him, covering his face and neck but could not take their eyes off his truncated, bloodied crotch.

"I'll kill you, you damned whore!" he shrieked hoarsely, his voice no longer even remotely human as he thrashed and wrestled against those holding him. "I'll peel your skin from head to toe, damn you! And open you from your crack to your head! But first, I'll skin your baby alive and make you watch!"

A guard slammed the cell door shut, making her jump. Coated in blood, Mala searched the dank cell in a fog, groping for her son; his incessant wailing her homing beacon. Finding him, she let the dagger fall to the floor, and pulled his thrashing body to her bloody nakedness. She could hear Malik's bestial wailing in the distance, and quaked in her spirit that once on the mend, he would be back. And when he returned, it would be her end, as well as that of baby Christophe.

Struck by that singular horror, what he would do to Christophe, she quaked and the dam broke; tears arriving for the first time of that entire horrid day, mingling with the crimson flow. Paralyzed with shock, she began to pray, choking between woeful sobs, trying to collect enough air to breathe.

"Oh, but God in Heaven!" she bawled uncontrollably. "If ever I have needed You, come save this son! You took away my firstborn, and I cannot possibly survive such hurt yet another time!"

Leaning her bare back into the bars of the adjacent cell, she let herself slide to the stone floor in a heap, lost somewhere between consciousness and dream-like numbness, clutching her son desperately to her bloody chest. "Oh, but Christophe, I have failed you this day, just as I failed your tiny brother in the Alps," she whispered, sputtering blood, her mind slipping back in time. "And oh, but Tristan, I've failed you as well, my love. We thought God to be with us, but it was Duxia who foresaw our end. Yes, old Duxia de Falaise, the ravaged wretch that I dearly loved. She warned me time and again, but I turned her words away. 'The hammer of God will block your path,' she'd said."

Mala fell quiet then, chin to chest, her long dark tresses cascading around them both, and closed her eyes as Christophe latched onto her left breast, his caterwauling muted upon finding comfort. In the darkness, though, she thought to hear soft footsteps approaching from behind. Someone pulled her hair aside, then a damp rag and a gentle touch began cautiously dabbing at her face.

"Be still. Don't be afraid of us," whispered a girlish voice as a hand reached between the bars. "My sister and I shall tend to you, at least until the Persian returns. And even then, we shall both pray for you and the baby. God directs all, you know."

"Yes," whispered a second voice. "All is in His hands."

The five guards who carried Malik from the prison fought mightily to keep him under control on the way to the infirmary for medical attention.

Over his right brow, the knife blade had cut deeply, leaving a gaping furrow through the raised skin of it. From there the blade had cleaved across his nose, cutting to the bone, then caught the left corner of his mouth, causing his upper lip to split wide at the bottom. The gaping gash traversed Malik's lower cheek, splitting it wide open to the gums, then down the entire left run of his neck, just missing his jugular. The gaping wound of his missing, mutilated genitalia had been haphazardly packed with whatever material they could find to quench the flow.

Entering the military infirmary, no one was there.

"Dammit!" swore the guard captain. "What do we do now?"

"Close the wound; put pressure on it!" one of the others cried, jerking his head toward the youngest of the guards. "Here, we'll hold him down while you do it. Hurry!"

The four holding him, laid him to the floor, restraining his arms and legs with every ounce of strength they had; one even digging his fingers into the gaping wound running the length of Malik's forearm.

Having never seen so much blood, the young guard stared at his trembling hands. Already scarlet from carrying Malik, being covered in another man's blood was making him nauseous. "I feel sick! I feel sick!" he wailed, turning his eyes away.

"Damn you, pull his face together; close up his cheek!" screamed the captain through gritted teeth. "Then we have to pack his crotch before he bleeds out!"

On his knees, by Malik's head, he peered down at the split cheek, then flattened his palms against Malik's face flesh, one on each side of the cut. But seeing Malik's bleeding gums in the opening, vomit spewed violently from the guard's mouth, dousing Malik and the others; the force of it so fast that he himself was not soiled by it.

"Damn you!" shouted the other guards in unison, turning their faces, wiping them against their shoulders and upper arms in an effort to not release the raving Malik. But as they did, the young man retched again, his puke mixing inexorably with blood, forming a repugnant mix that began to nauseate the others.

"Take his arm, you piece of shit!" Roughly trading places with the young man, the captain took over, pressing Malik's cheek closed as hard as he could. When he did, the flow ebbed from the closure . . . for an instant. "There, I've got it!" he exclaimed prematurely. The raised flesh of Malik's eyebrow erupted, saturating those in the line of fire.

As all this transpired, Malik bucked and kicked like a dying bull intent on decimating anything and anyone in his path. Finally, one of the guards found the wherewithal to reposition, holding Malik down with a knee, strip off his shirt, and wrap it around Malik's entire head like a tourniquet, tightening firmly. Pinning him, the combined weight of all the men was enough to eventually subdue Malik's movement, but not his voice; baying and groaning with such abandon, like a wounded wildebeest.

Spent from loss of blood and struggling against the combined weight of the giant guards, Malik's movement weakened, then stilled, save for occasional twitching attacking his shoulders and legs. From beneath the shirt/bandage, the guards heard labored, heavy breathing and gurgling broken by barely audible mewling as made by one struggling against a bad dream. His neck and arm wept with every heartbeat; his mutilated genitalia oozed milky semen and coagulating blood.

Exhausted, the guards looked at one another, trying to regulate their own breathing; all thinking, Well, who's going to tend to his missing dick?

"Damn," said one of them, "this bastard's as strong as Hannibal's elephants!"

"Think he'll live?" asked another, trying to skirt the obvious.

The captain nodded in the affirmative. "Yeah, but we have to tend to his . . . his . . ." He motioned toward Malik's lower half. "What are you waiting for? You, you there," he pointed to the nearest soldier, "get more rags and pack him hard. The infirmarian will have to stitch him up when he gets back."

Staring at the loosely bandaged head, he added, "Aye, his face will never be the same. And every time that bastard sees his reflection, he'll find a monster staring back at him. But when he finds out about that . . ." he cocked his thumb at Malik's crotch, "Mercy of Allah, I'd not want to be the woman who did this!" He wiped his hands against his breeches but the blood had already begun to congeal, mottling between his fingers and beneath his nails. "The Persian lost a lot of blood tonight, and he'll want it back one way or another."

CHAPTER THIRTY-THREE

BY GOD'S DESIGN?

As Guthroth healed beneath the watchful eye of Haya, time began to slip into new channels for him. He had felt the grim approach of death pulling at him through wounds that would have killed most men. That experience alone was so succinct as to deceive him into thinking he had already joined the dead. On regaining consciousness, escaping from his tomb of eternal darkness, he had thought himself blind, something even more terrifying than being dead. Yet, surviving the trauma of these bleak experiences was not what had set him on a path of new direction.

It was something else entirely.

From the beginning, Guthroth's existence had been unusual, veering off track at the juncture of birth. His mother had endured an extremely difficult pregnancy, and died during labor, bringing him into this world. This was a crushing blow to Guthroth's father. By the time Guthroth was able to communicate, his father began pounding into his son's head, "Had you never been conceived, your mother would be here with me, alive and well!" Obsessed and bitter, his father, during these diatribes, failed to see the burden of hurt being carried by his son. Of course, it is equally possible the father did see the pain he inflicted, and relished it. He possessed questionable character to begin with, according to all whom Guthroth spoke with later.

Guthroth's direction toward anomaly deepened by age two-and-a-half when he began to speak, or more accurately, when he began 'attempting' to speak. For one reason or another, he could not properly form words with what his people referred to as 'flow.' His tongue would get caught in cycles of sporadic repetition. In other words, he stuttered. Frustrated by this, he would try harder to speak correctly, which aggravated the situation, subsequently entrenching itself. Even young children learn to spot stares and smug sniggering, especially when being the target. In response, by age five, he stopped talking unless absolutely necessary, which is when he was given the moniker 'Guthroth the Quiet.' Prior to that he had simply been Guthroth.

Being an impatient dolt as well as a drunk, Guthroth's father began to ridicule him both at home and in public. "Ha, there, just listen to that thick-headed little shit that caused my wife to die!" he ranted. "He's as dumb as a damn door knocker and an embarrassment to me as a father. Hell, I wish he'd never seen the light of day!"

From verbal insults, Guthroth's father graduated to slapping and kicking the boy by age seven, punching him by ten. Understandably, over time, identifying his stuttering as the source of his troubles, he spoke less and less, especially around his father. His last year before leaving home at thirteen, to join older cousins Orla and Crowbones in the Danish Guard, Guthroth had not said a single word to his father, choosing instead to ignore him completely or walk away. No longer fearing his father, the young man had begun to fight back viciously, hence deterring much violence.

This being Guthroth's childhood, it impacted the young man's character and sensibilities. Others, and even Guthroth himself, attributed his reluctance to speak to beatings by his father, though, in truth, he was simply saddled with a handicap at birth. Alas, one of the many consequences to Guthroth's stuttering is that it became the impetus to a downward spiral leading from one disadvantage to another.

To begin with, by not talking early on, a child does not ask for much from others, and in turn receives less, which is a trait that Guthroth displayed his entire life. And not hearing a request or a demand, adults often fail to antici-pate needs. But there is more. By receiving less, one expects less, and therefore complains less, gradually becoming invisible, and most definitely misunder-stood. As time elapsed, this descending cycle didn't just 'happen' to Guthroth, it gained control over every aspect of his existence as he moved through adoles-cence into manhood.

Under such trying circumstances, an individual takes one of two paths, either developing into a mouse, or digging within to prospect for inner strength and confidence in self over others. Guthroth took the second track. Far from causing him to fold, Guthroth's silence gave rise to advantages missed by others. He began to think and contemplate, analyze and dissect circumstances, refute panic, and stand by his own judgment over that of others. Stuttering essentially became the bedrock from which Guthroth developed into an extraordinary man, regardless of what others failed to recognize in him.

In the end, Guthroth became content with the hand he'd been dealt; not to say that he was happy, or fulfilled, or that it held special significance. Being as he was, rather than seeking self-realization or pursuing private ambitions, he placed himself in service to others, such as Asta, Orla, Crowbones, the Danish Guard, and most recently, the Church. As a soldier, his service had generally entailed violence and war, two endeavors in which he had become deadly. Lethal and cold in battle, he was not 'brutal' by either character or will. Actually, he was thoughtful, kind, and uncommonly attuned to the circumstances and plights of others.

Having had no mother growing up, other than his wet nurse, nor sisters, grandmothers, or aunts, and furthermore lacking all experiential interaction with women, he concluded early on in his development that females, in general, kept him on edge and made him nervous . . . except Asta of the Norman Danes, the only woman who had not. When Guthroth joined the Danish Guard, Asta was a newborn, and the Danish Guard had just been formed by Asta's father,

Guntar the Mace, for the sole purpose of protecting and serving Asta for the remainder of her life.

Moving to the present, Guthroth found himself, at age fifty-five, a continent away from a place where 'home' had never rooted due to war, military service, and moving, severely wounded but recovering in the care of a lovely forty-two-year-old Syrian woman named Haya at the Oasis of Sparrows. Past his prime, having neither established nor pursued even a single rainbow of his own choosing, he lay there contemplating his future, though the hourglass had already streamed beyond his favor.

"Your wounds are coming along nicely," said Haya, rubbing expensive essential oil salve over them. "I suppose you'll be able to ride in another two weeks, perhaps, but you'll not be able to fight." Pausing, she looked at him. "You won't be able to fight for at least another two months, unless you wish to enter battle at half strength. Is that what you wish?"

"No," replied Guthroth. "A s-soldier at h-half strength is a d-dead soldier. And I w-wish to l-live."

"Guthroth, I wish you to live as well. I am sure that within two months you shall be whole again, but then . . . that means you shall be leaving us." As she said this, her countenance saddened in affirmation, yet no trace of satisfaction could be detected, knowing his survival depended on God's grace and the gifts and talents He had given her.

Saying nothing, Guthroth's eyes settled on hers, holding there for a time. Gone were the furtive glances of a week earlier. From Haya he derived comfort, and felt at ease. But there was a foreign emotion fermenting within him, like a seed germinating beneath the warm spring earth, not yet seeing light but reaching for it. Had Guthroth, in any fashion, understood women or love, he might have known what was stirring. But having never experienced either, he understood neither.

Besides, love for Guthroth was not love as others know it; being the way he was, it couldn't be. He felt no need to possess Haya, there was no inferno burning within his breast, nor lustful passion nagging his loins. Rather, it was comfort, the kind that he had never found in another human.

As to Haya, an odd thing, she, like Guthroth, had never dabbled in attraction to another nor had she even shared her bed. But unlike Guthroth, the opposite gender did not unsettle her. Instead, she felt she 'knew' men, taking them for what they were, unimpressive creatures forever on the hunt to possess what does not belong to them. But Guthroth was a different breed of man, and she had liked him from the beginning. But that initial 'liking' had miraculously developed into something more substantial, and she recognized what it was . . . Guthroth did not.

The two had fallen in love.

* * *

On leaving the Oasis of Sparrows, Hroc cut across open dessert, avoiding all paths and roadways the Turks could be patrolling. He was especially careful on approaching the fork to Saint Simeon where he and Guthroth had been ambushed. However, upon arrival, he found the area void of activity and the two crusaders that had been hanging from the tree had been removed.

Nearing the Orontes, Hroc made his way back to the Tuscan camp, having received a wave of access from the sentries, and entered near the main tents. Orla spotted him first. Being his father, he had held his own private intuition, telling him Hroc would be safe beneath the hand of Guthroth, but upon seeing him, he jumped from the log before the fire, heart racing, thinking to see a ghost. "God's spine!" he whooped, half hopping/half running toward Hroc, nearly knocking him from his mount. Then angst tightened his chest and he grabbed his son, asking, "But where's Guthroth? Was he slain?"

"Not slain, Father, but wounded severely," replied Hroc.

"But where is he?" insisted Orla, searching his son's face for an answer.

"Fifty or sixty kilometers from here," said Hroc, "under medical care at a place called the Oasis of Sparrows."

"In Muslim hands?" asked Orla, heart racing, thinking of Guthroth captured.

"Yes, Muslims, but Syrian Muslims, except for the woman, Haya, who rules the place. She's Christian, by chance."

"Huh?" grunted Orla. But before allowing Hroc to answer, his face suddenly drooped and his eyes saddened. "Bad news, Hroc. Crowbones is gone."

"Gone? Did he leave?"

"No. He's dead, Son. Slain atop Mount Staurin during the northern scouting probe."

Slumping, Hroc went pale. "Uncle Crowbones dead? Mercy of God! Oh, not possible!"

"Yes," said Orla. "Dead, never to return to us except in memories. We buried him just behind the camp. You may wish to say a few words over his gravesite."

"Buried him!?" Hroc was most definitely surprised. "Good. A Christian burial then, at least."

"Ja, but I cut a lock of his hair and put it aboard a small boat, setting it afire, then pushed it onto the Orontes as a salute to the old world. At the end, Ivar talked about Denmark and wishing he could have ended there."

Hroc nodded, not contesting his father's final pagan ritual for Crowbones. "A good thing, meaningful, what you did," he lied, covering his disturbance over the paganistic vent of what his father had done. "Ja, I'm sure Uncle Crowbones appreciates what you did, Father, for he lives, you know. Ja, his spirit lives with God now."

As he said this, Tristan and Guillaume appeared.

"Oh! Hroc!" cried Tristan. "Merciful Heaven, we thought you and Guthroth both dead!"

"Aye," agreed Guillaume, slapping him on the forearm as he dismounted, "but God's mercy is eternal and everlasting. You're here, safe and in one piece, by God!"

Hroc explained Guthroth's circumstances to Tristan and Guillaume, as well as the discovery of the Oasis of Sparrows, enforcing the pact he made with his uncle to keep it all a secret. "We shan't be seeing Guthroth for a good while," he concluded, "he nearly met his end. But he's in good hands and will fully recover in time. But tell, what's been happening here? The Turks have come out of their shell, as Guthroth and I discovered returning to camp ten days ago. Have they attacked here as well?"

"Several times," said Tristan, filling Hroc in on all that transpired during his absence.

Hroc's head dropped. "More terrible news then, added to that of Uncle Crowbones." Pulling his prayer beads from his gambeson, he gave Tristan an earnest look. "Uncle Tristan," he said, "I shall pray every day and every night. Don't despair."

"Oh, but I do, Hroc," lamented Tristan, "yet I pray fervently. Since you have come back to us, and Guthroth still lives as well, my hope is at least renewed. Perhaps all shall be well in the end."

"It shall end as God wills it, Brother," said Guillaume, crossing himself. "In the end, all ends as He wills it. As to us, we're but specks in the wind."

CHAPTER THIRTY-FOUR

AND THUS IT BEGAN . . .

It took Charton, his contingent of 200, and the new recruits from Genoa two full days to unload the ships, then reload wagons and mules with the trove of arms, lumber for catapults and ballistas, and dry goods. Extra horses were also included in the cargo, but the number was not great.

Four hours after departing Saint Simeon, Charton's company had come across the mutilated remains of the Foulon brothers' guard detail that had departed just days earlier at the insistence of la Gran Signorina, and then the dangling remains of two headless crusaders at the fork. There was no sign of the coach, nor of a woman or child.

"Poor bastards," remarked Charton. "Bad enough what happened to these two soldiers of God on the day they died, but the crows have been desecrating them ever since. Cut them down, what's left of them, anyway. We'll take them all back to camp and offer a proper burial."

On making the Christian encampments, Charton had shared the grisly revelation of the Foulon brothers, la Gran Signorina, and the two crusaders, exponentially increasing the ire of the men already stung by Yaghi Siyan's surprise attacks. In particular, the Tuscan camp.

Rainald Porchet, a first-hand witness of the carnage in Saint Simeon along-side Charton, personally delivered the horrific news to Tristan. "It wounds me to inform you of this loss, Bishop Saint-Germain. But being one of the few in camp that truly understands your circumstances, I thought it best for me to be the one to address it. In any case, my prayers and condolences, Bishop. I know la Signorina means the world to you, as does your son. With much prayer, they will be found."

"Thank you, Rainald," choked Tristan, stunned beyond words to learn that Mala and Christophe were missing. Oh, such is the price for holding here at Antioch! he lamented, slipping into bouts of prayerful weeping sporadically interspersed with cursing the crusade.

"Though I don't understand it," said Porchet despondently, "it must have surely been God's will. But then, it could be but a trial of your will and hope. Be strong, Bishop. There is nothing else to be done."

"No, Porchet, there is something to be done," said Tristan, gathering himself. Turning, he left Porchet where he stood and made haste for the camp of Adhémar and Raymond. Arriving in a fury, and spotting the old bishop standing in the midst of several princes, Tristan lost control. "Oh, but damn you, Adhémar!"

he railed, accosting him with balled fists even as he stood talking to Raymond, Bohemud, Godfrey, and Tancred. "It was your spineless deference to these rich princes that brought this on, you gutless coward!"

Dismayed, the four princes reacted swiftly to Tristan's attack, all in turn attacking him, precipitating a swift counter-assault as Guillaume, Letellier, and Scule jumped into the fray, having followed Tristan from the Tuscan camp, knowing that anger had gotten the best of him on hearing from Porchet. As the fisticuffs intensified, flailing fists and boots escalated to drawn swords.

Shocked, seeing that irreparable blood had begun to flow, Adhémar, after gaining his footing, erupted into a shrill diatribe that rang above the brawl, startling all. "Stop it, damn you!" he cried. "Goddammit! Stop this madness immediately lest I pass a sentence of eternal damnation on every one of your wretched souls!"

Having never heard the old religious curse, nor, unimaginably, him take the Lord's name in vain, the wild mêlée came to a halt as breathless, disbelieving, disheveled, and bloody crusaders stood in place.

Turning cerise at his own utterance, Adhémar crossed himself, looking skyward. "Forgive me, Father. I beg you!" he stammered. "We have descended into insanity here and I beg Your intervention!"

Tristan, having been knocked to the ground with bloodied lip, glared up at the old bishop, his eyes hot as coals. "Intervention? Aye!" he shouted. "Get on your horses and find my wife and child, you useless bastards! You owe Mala an entire fleet, damn you! You wanted to stay here in Antioch like imbeciles? Well then, now go charge the goddamned walls and get my family back!"

Struck by the fact that his probing attack was followed by neither counter tactics nor signs of immediate close siege, Yaghi Siyan set in motion a strategy of cautious harassment. As recorded by one Latin eyewitness: "After the Turks had found out about us, they began to emerge gradually and to attack, wherever they could lay ambush for us."

Wily as he was, Siyan's strategy unfurled in the form of a triple-threat. First his garrison took advantage of the Iron Gate on Mt. Staurin. From there he dispatched archers to the lower elevation of the mountain where they began raining missiles down with impunity into Bohemud's camp, the one blocking the northernmost Saint Paul Gate. These bombardments were intermittent and unpredictably timed, confounding those within Bohemud's camp, forcing them to be ever anxious and on guard.

Consequently, the Turks began making frequent use of the unblocked Bridge Gate, which allowed them to cross the Orontes River and access the plains west of Antioch. Strategically placed, their mounted archers easily ranged at will, attacking or ambushing crusader squads as they foraged across the river. Using the western plains to their advantage, Turkish mounted archers sallied back and forth, disrupting the entire run of the Orontes.

As with the archer barrages being fired from the stony outcrops of Mount Staurin, these swift cavalry attacks by the Turks from the western plains were impossible to predict and difficult to defend. Being lightly armed with bows and wearing no armor, the Turkish horsemens' phenomenal speed and agility allowed them to retreat quickly, dashing back across the fortified bridge leading to the safety of the Bridge Gate.

Camped closest to this gate, Godfrey of Bouillon and the Germans suffered the brunt of these raids. And on top of that, the Turks' hit and run tactics began to take a severe toll on crusader horses, a favored target.

The third aspect of Yaghi Siyan's strategy involved a small satellite fortress of Antioch named Harim, fifteen kilometers to the northeast of the city, perched along a ridge of rocky hills called the Jabal Talat. The crusaders had early on taken control of satellite outposts north and south of Antioch, but failed to explore east of Mount Staurin and Mount Silpius. Learning the crusaders were unaware of Harim, Yaghi Siyan sent forays from Harim to attack or ambush Christians traveling back and forth within the vicinity of the Iron Bridge, a critical crusader gateway to the north. Mystified by these attacks, the crusaders incorrectly suspected these raids to be originating from the Iron Gate on top of Mount Staurin.

By mid-November, Yaghi Siyan's maneuvering, exacerbated by the depletion of crusader foraging capacity, began to inflict pressure on the entire Christian army. Brimming with frustration and amid growing concern, the Council of Princes met.

"If we're to succeed with attrition siege," complained Raymond of Toulouse, "then we must cut Turkish mobility! Christ alive, they come and go as they please. We've got to take better control of the Bridge Gate, by God!"

"Not likely," sniffed Godfrey of Bouillon. "They storm out, cross their heavily fortified bridge across the Orontes, attack us, then run back across the bridge while their bridge defenders lay down heavy archer cover from the towers, not to mention the barrage being fired from the city's ramparts just in range of the river and the bridge."

"Well then," frowned Stephen of Blois, "if we're to keep them from running into the safety of the Duke Gate, we've no choice but to attack their bridge, impeding them from getting back in the gate."

"Shit," scoffed Godfrey, "we'd get clustered up like a herd of sheep to slaughter trying to attack and cross that damned bridge. Chrissakes, we'd become a Muslim pincushion!"

"True," frowned Adhémar, "but Raymond is correct. We must block them from crossing the Orontes coming out of the city from the Bridge Gate and running the western plains. I see no alternative but to take our chances and prepare a direct assault on their bridge leading to the Bridge Gate."

"Suicide," said Robert of Flanders. "A loss of good men, not to mention horses, of which we're running damn short."

"Well, what the hell do you expect us to do then?" belched Tancred. "Sit on our asses while the Turks keep twisting the noose?"

Having opposed sieging Antioch from the beginning, Tristan, Guillaume, Letellier, and Taticius had said nothing since arriving.

"Well, dammit," grunted Bohemud, aiming his dark gaze primarily at Tristan and Taticius. "None of you have anything to say here, today?"

"Yes, I have something to say," replied Tristan crossly. "Find my family and get them back!"

"Dammit," growled Raymond, "we're sorry about that situation, Bishop, but we've no idea where they are, really, or even if they're still alive."

"Aye, all because of your own greed, along with a few others. Don't you see? The blindness of ambition has—"

"Stop," whispered Guillaume, who empathized Tristan's bitterness but also recognized the glacial hearts of those opposing him. "You're but making yourself a target!"

"And what about you, Taticius?" muttered Bohemud, egging him on. Their bad blood extended back for decades due to Bohemud's earlier military campaigns against the Byzantine Empire.

"Go to Hell, Bohemud, and count your dead!" snorted Taticius. "You know where I stand. I haven't moved!"

"Grrr!" sneered Tancred, looking first at Bohemud, then pointing at Taticius. "Uncle, why bother asking the 'Byzantine freak' for counsel? He, like Emperor Alexius, is as useless as tits on a gelded bull!" His face twisting like a root, he crossed his arms, looking away.

This insult, couched in the fact that Taticius at some point in the past had been castrated, bordered on heinous. Smelling a disastrous repeat of the earlier meeting, Adhémar had to intervene. "This is no time for infighting, men!" he interjected brusquely. "We need solutions and agreement! We are allies, not enemies! And Tancred, another comment like that, and I'll have you leave the table."

This brought silence, punctuated intermittently by barely audible spates of grumbling and perturbed side-glances.

In the midst of this silence, Martin Letellier stood. "Might I simply suggest," he said, humble of tone, "that we build our own bridge?"

"What?" grunted Raymond and Bohemud in unison.

"What?" chimed in Adhémar.

"It'd take too long," said Godfrey, dismissing Letellier. "We'd be arrow fodder while digging foundations on both sides, framing, and laying planks. Christ! That'd cost a thousand men if not double, triple that number!"

"But then," countered Letellier, "we don't really need foundations or framing, do we?"

This caught the table's attention as all eyes cranked toward Letellier.

He braved on, "Once when we were assaulting a castle during the Normandy uprisings, my battalion ran into a similar problem. Our solution? We fashioned an impromptu bridge made of boats. No digging, no framing, no days and weeks of mining operations as open targets. The bridge was strapped together in a single day, planked on the next, and we charged across on the third."

As if light had suddenly pierced darkness, Letellier's plan caught fire.

"Say," nodded Raymond, "why not construct flat-boats with the newly arrived lumber from Genoa?"

"A flotilla," said Stephen of Blois, "and line them up across the river!"

"Of course," Hugh of Vermandois added, "and shield our engineers while laying down our own archer fire in defense!"

"Along with barrages from the catapults and ballistas our engineers are constructing with the new lumber!" shouted Robert of Flanders.

Thus was seeded the Christian army's counter offensive to Yaghi Siyan's newly opened aggression. Construction began immediately. The so-called Bridge of Boats project across the Orontes down from the Gate of the Duke developed into a chaotic ramshackle operation. But after a week of fabricating makeshift flat-boats, crusaders began placing them. First, selecting a location on their side of the river beyond archer range from both Antioch's rampart walls and the fortified bridge leading to the Duke Gate, engineers anchored the lead boat against the river bank, in safety. As they began linking other boats one-by-one with rope, cleats, and spikes, enemy arrows drew nearer until, halfway across the river, the arrow shower grew deadly. Those working in the water made limited targets of themselves, their heads and shoulders bobbing sporadically to enemy fire, but those hapless souls laboring atop the boats began to suffer heavy losses, a tragedy they had sadly expected. Persevering, by nightfall of that same day, the crusaders had managed to line the boats from bank to bank, albeit precariously in spots.

The following day was spent laying and spiking planks across the tops of the tethered boats, which quickly became even more perilous than the labor of the first day. Clumsily working aboard the bobbling platform of boats, engineers depended on the efforts of others to provide shield-cover, but alas they still attained heavy losses. Far from being done by nightfall, the engineers worked on through the night, fumbling in the dark, operating by torchlight, feel, and instinct. As the sun broke, new engineers took their place until the setting of the sun. In the end, it took two days and a night to plank the Bridge of Boats to the opposite bank.

That morning Bohemud pulled a man from his own ranks to test the structure, a young Norman known simply as Riquiqui, owing to his skinny frame and lack of height and weight, which would allow a horse to swiftly gallop the needed distance. Filling the nervous youngster's gambeson with extra padding and draping a specially fashioned chain-mail cape over his regular mail-armor to protect his back, Bohemud declared, "What an honor, lad! Perhaps, in fact, the grandest you'll ever experience! When you look back on this day as an old man, you'll relate this tale to saucer-eyed grandchildren, by God, and relive it proudly a thousand times in your dreams!"

"Indeed, sir!" trembled Riquiqui, suspecting he would now never have either wife nor offspring; that he would not make it back across the boats.

"Go! Ride like hell straight across," instructed Bohemud, "then turn and ride like hell straight back! And don't dally, boy! We just need to see whether the damned thing holds up or not!"

Staring across the water at fortress ramparts spilling with enemy archers who had been perforating engineers for days on reaching the Bridge of Boats' center, Riquiqui uttered, "I've said my prayers, Master Bohemud. Will you say some for me as well?" At that, hastily making the sign of the cross, he kicked his horse's flanks, baying, "Yee-Ho!" as from behind thousands of crusaders began to cheer, raucously clanging sword against shield.

Tucking low in the saddle and craning his neck upward to keep an eye to the ramparts, Riquiqui sped across the top of the boats beneath a sky suddenly darkened by thousands of arrows thudding ahead of him, sticking the boats and slishing into the Orontes. Nearing the middle of the boat-bridge, he found himself in the midst of this deadly deluge. "Oh, Maman!" he wailed, envisioning his mother stuck alone in the hovel of a shanty at the failing farm in France he had abandoned to join the fight for God. "My end is but seconds away! Be well, I pray!"

But miracle of miracles, he reached the far the end of the bridge. Quaking, he turned his horse, certain his luck could not hold. But it did . . . until halfway back across. Just before clearing the midpoint, his horse stumbled, pierced in the back, flanks, and neck by a score of arrows just missing their actual mark, the rider. Squealing and mewling with confusion, not understanding death, the horse crumpled to its front knees, flinging Riquiqui over its mane and across a length of planks into the water.

"I can't swim!" he cried, the weight of chain-mail taking him down.

Without thinking, a dozen knights, including Bohemud, selflessly jumped into the Orontes to save the diminutive hero. Wearing armor themselves, they began to sink like rocks. Seeing Bohemud go under, Guillaume dove in after him. Acting with equal heroism but with infinite caution, Letellier flung his helmet aside, wriggled out of his chain-mail tunic, and followed Guillaume into the water.

All of those in the river were struggling mightily against the current of the river and the downward pull of heavy boots and chain-mail. As panic set in along the bank, Scule bravely jumped in the water, not weighed by armor, just his monk's robe. Short in stature, he could swim very well, as testified back at Dorylaeum when he had rescued both Tristan and Letellier from the Thames River during an ambush set by Kilij Arslan.

Knowing none of this, unable to swim, and having not taken into account the fact that Scule was not weighed by chain-mail, gambeson, helmet and boots, Christos ran back and forth along the bank in a frenzy crying, "No! No, Scule! Come back!"

After much confusion and heaving in the currents, some men vanished beneath the surface; others struggled to the bank, dragging comrades along.

"Guillaume," gasped Bohemud, coughing water from his lungs, "you saved my Norman ass once again. But a fool's errand, boy! You yourself could have drowned!"

"Aye," Guillaume sputtered, face to the bank, closed eyes, gasping for breath.

By the time the ill-advised attempt to save Riquiqui drew to a close, seven knights had drowned, yet the entire Christian side of the river arose in jubilation. "The Bridge of Boats stands!" the crusaders whooped. "God wills it! The Bridge of Boats stands!"

In conclusion of this episode, the crusaders again pulled from the recently arrived lumber hoard, focusing their efforts on the lower heights of Mt. Staurin from which the Turks had been raining arrows down on Bohemud's camp near the Saint Paul Gate. Persevering through weeks of intense archer and ballista fire, the Christians began engineering along Staurin's lower slopes a fort, if indeed it could be called that. With much effort and many casualties, the fort was completed. Being dubbed "Malregard," the wooden structure, in essence, brought a halt to harrying archer attacks against Bohemud's camp from Turkish positions along the lower confines of Mt. Staurin and further secured the northern quadrant of the Antioch blockade.

Yet another Christian counter-measure attended to an outbreak of damaging enemy attacks arising around the Iron Bridge where, as recorded by a knight from the Loire Valley: "The Turks were daily killing many of our men who were going back and forth from our army."

Bohemud was appointed by the Council of Princes to 'fix' the problem. Having benefited most from the construction of Malregard, and because the Iron Bridge was located nearest his camp, the Council of Princes felt Bohemud was the obvious candidate. In response, Bohemud gathered Guillaume and a small reconnoitering party to investigate the environs of the Iron Bridge, expecting to locate the source of Muslim infiltration but not initiate a foray.

The Council of Princes had initially, and incorrectly, supposed the recent Turkish attacks near the Iron Bridge had emanated from Mt. Staurin. They now knew of the citadel and Iron Gate located atop Antioch's mountainous eastern wall. Because the crusaders had scouted but a short distance east of the Iron Bridge, they were as yet unaware of Yaghi Siyan's satellite outpost of Harim, the true source of Turkish attacks on the Iron Bridge.

Being an astute tactician, and realizing his manpower to be limited for this particular mission, Bohemud decided to side with caution. He divided his force by sending an advance element to probe the craggy Jabal Talat, hiding himself, Guillaume, and other knights in reserve. His intent was for the advance element to first draw the Turks out, then pretend to flee in what was actually a favorite Muslim tactic that had been adopted by Bohemud, the 'feigned retreat;' luring the Turks into ambush at the hands of crusader reserves.

Several knights were killed as the Turks surfaced just near Harim, but Bohemud's ploy worked brilliantly. In rabid pursuit of Bohemud's fleeing lead element, the unsuspecting Turks fell into the Norman prince's snare, establishing once again Bohemud's wiliness and guile as a commander.

The ambush was hotly contested, swaying back forth for nearly an hour. The crusader advantage of surprise did nothing to dispel the number of Turks. Assailing each other with the blind fury of one wolfpack attacking the encroachment of another, clashing horsemen hacked and hewed at each other in a lethal scrum, each side considering the other to be godless enemies. It was Guillaume, within the savage din, who especially came to the fore. Wielding his sword as driven by Gabriel the Archangel, he slayed one Turk after another, charging audaciously into their oncoming ranks with no regard whatsoever for his own safety.

When the bloodletting subsided, Bohemud sought Guillaume out. Appearing concerned, Bohemud said, "Good work today. But damnation, friend, one might think you to be carrying a death wish on those broad shoulders."

In the end, the Harim outpost had been neither attacked nor vanquished, but now the Christians, having been briefed of the satellite fort's existence, began taking measures to neutralize it.

CHAPTER THIRTY-FIVE

AH, BUT HAPPENSTANCE

Ben-fazi, riding alongside the ox-man, directed him to pull the wagon perpendicular to the prison entrance. "Some of that bread and fare in the wagon for the prisoners," said the man, his eyes cast downward apologetically, "might I take just a bit for my family? With the siege and all, we—"

"Yes, yes, certainly," assured Ben-fazi, knowing the man to be a Syrian Christian struggling to be a good husband, a good father raising five children, and a good son-in-law supporting his wife's debilitated parents and grandmother.

"Hey there, Ben-fazi, come quickly!" came a voice. It was Boros, standing next to another man dressed in Syrian garb. "I've something to tell you," the jailer said, eyeing the entrance to make sure the Turkish guards watching could not hear him. Although they despised the tiny blue man, the guards found diversion in watching him during his intermittent deliveries of palace scraps to the prison. In particular, they enjoyed mocking his mannerisms, trying to out-mimic among themselves the blue man's aberrantly high voice.

"What is it?" asked Ben-fazi as he slipped from the wagon, ignoring the three guards snickering in a huddle by the gate. Instead, his attention was focused on the man with Boros. He'd never seen him there before, nor anywhere else for that matter. "But, Boros, who is this?" he asked, acknowledging the stranger.

"A new friend I made this past week. He's Syrian, but a Christian. Learning that his wife and daughter were Muslim, the crusaders murdered them both when their army crossed into Syria. Poor fellow! In fear, he didn't know what to do but seek haven here in Antioch."

"He fled?" asked Ben-fazi. "And he's Christian?"

"Yes, I fled," said the man. "My name's Lukos, named after Saint Luke by my Syrian Christian parents. But the crusaders refused to believe I was Christian, being dark as we Syrians are. They know nothing of the region, the many faiths, the intermarriages! I escaped just moments before being executed, saved by a band of ghazis fleeing Artah across my farm." Making the sign of the cross, he muttered under his breath.

"I see," said Ben-fazi, turning back to Boros. "But Boros, you sounded urgent as I arrived. What's wrong?"

"No, not for me," said Boros, "but for someone else. As I was just telling Lukos here, a strange thing happened last night. The big Persian shows up well after dark from raiding the crusaders with a coach in tow. His men drug a woman out, holding a baby in her arms, and it's apparent what's going to happen to her just by seeing the look on the big man's face."

"Oh?"

"Yes, I told you about the girls he keeps penned up on the far side of this place, and what him and his number-two fellow do to them."

"I remember," said Ben-fazi, beyond disgusted.

"Well, they didn't let me back there, of course, when they took the woman back there, but half an hour later I hear all hell breaking loose. Next thing I know, they're dragging the big Persian out, all cut to Hell, bleeding like a stuck pig! Shit, his face looked to be split in two from brow to chest!"

"Huh?" Ben-fazi found it difficult to believe that any man could get close enough to Malik to cut him that badly. "Did a fight break out?" he asked. "Was it his lieutenant, the man Hasan?"

"No," replied Boros, sinking his head into his shoulders while slipping into that smile of one passing along the improbable. "It was the woman! Elegant as she was, demure as she was, she had a damn dagger in her garb. Chrissakes, can you believe that?"

Taken by the story, Ben-fazi knew things could not have ended well for the woman, whoever she was, nor, probably, for her child. "They killed her, I suppose?"

"No," said Boros with obvious contentment. "As I was telling Lukos, the big Persian beat her terribly, but she had a damn knife hidden on her. Slit him to ribbons from head to balls! When the guards came in, she was huddled in a bloody heap, her back to the bars, flashing that blade around like a damn Gypsy bitch! Guards were afraid to go near her! And I think she still has the damn dagger on her, of all things!"

Reflecting, Ben-fazi said, "Boros, I'd like to see her, this woman, before they come back and kill her, which they surely will."

"Ha! I thought you might, Ben-fazi," nodded Boros. "Follow me."

"I'd like to go, too," interjected Lukos. "I know a bit about doctoring from working on my mules. Maybe I could help the woman a bit."

"Yeah, maybe," agreed Boros. "Come along then."

As Boros led them past the Turkish guards, they made their scorn for Ben-fazi known through sneers; none dared say a word. The blue man's weight with Yaghi Siyan had become the stuff of stories in Antioch, as had the punishment meted out by the old man over his pet jester, or whatever he was.

Making their way down the stone corridor, reeking of piss and shit and filthy bodies, they encountered additional surly but silent Turkish guards. Glaring at them from time to time through his blue paint, for amusement not vindication, Ben-fazi gained satisfaction simply knowing he held a stick over these men. He had been treated similarly by others ever since he could remember, but these Turkish guards especially chaffed his sensibilities.

As the three walked the long hall with cells on both sides, prisoners called out for Ben-fazi, praising and thanking him. Boros had made sure to let them know who their benefactor was. "Kind sir, bless you!" "God is taking count of your generosity!" "Help us! Help us!" "Tell Yaghi Siyan to be merciful!" they shouted as one conglomeration.

Reaching the far end, the petition outcries stopped, as did the two Turkish guards following Boros. Handing Boros the key to the woman's cell, they turned and left.

"Eh? But what's that about?" asked Ben-fazi.

"They're not allowed any further, as ordered by Malik. Only me. I feed and water the girls, and the woman."

"But why you?" Ben-fazi asked, dumfounded.

"Because Malik's afraid the other guards might dally with them, you know, taste the honey, they're not allowed back here unless he's here. Neither is his man Hasan for that matter. Ha, no trust amongst thieves!"

As they approached the girls' cell, the girls fled to the far corner. The very sight of Ben-fazi frightened them, and they backed away holding onto one another, whispering back and forth. Two girls, one about twelve and the other slightly older, approached, pointing to Ben-fazi, ignoring Boros and Lukos. "A-are you a-a jester?" asked the older girl, her eyes squinting with curiosity, or wonder, perhaps, in the dim light.

"No," said Ben-fazi, taking no offense. He pitied her, all these girls, actually, knowing firsthand the heartlessness of men, and what they'd endured. "No, I'm not here to entertain you." Taking in the filth of her innocent face, the bruises and abrasions discoloring her cheeks and arms and legs, the ripped sackcloth tunic betraying signs of rape and abuse, half-exposing her still budding breasts, his eyes spoke volumes. "I'm here to take a look at the woman in the next cell."

"Oh," she sighed, her shoulders sagging with disappointment. "But what do they call you, then? I bet you have a funny name at least."

"They call me Ben-fazi, because that's what Yaghi Siyan calls me. He's the emir of Antioch, and my master. I, like you, am a slave, though the bars holding me are far different than yours. But then, what's your name?"

"My name is Agda," said the girl, pulling the younger girl forward. "And this is my sister, Berna."

"And how is it you fell into the hands of Mahmoud Malik?"

Her eyes lowering, Agda glanced toward her sister before answering. "We come from a tiny village called Despina, in the realm of Lord Abdul Azim. One morning, Malik's black banners showed up. He attacked and burned the village, killing everyone but the children. Most of the boys and girls he kept as slaves."

"But I see no boys here," said Ben-fazi, searching the shadows of the cell.

"Malik sold them while on the run from Lord Azim. They bring a better price for sex with old men and for castrating into eunuchs."

Ben-fazi fell quiet, surprised a girl so young would know about such things. Stepping up shyly, Berna spoke up, "There were five of us children in the family at first, but now it's just me and Agda. Everyone else, our other two sisters and our parents, were killed. We had a grandmother and a brother, as well, but they must have been killed, too, for we never saw them again."

"Oh . . ." sighed Ben-fazi, seeing in his mind the horror these girls had endured, and were still enduring.

"Such a terrible thing," whispered Lukos, shaking his head.

Turning, Agda pointed. "You said you've come to look at the woman lying there on the floor, the one they brought here last night. Have you come to take her away? Execute her?"

Ben-fazi shook his head. "No, just to take a look."

"She's hurt bad," said Agda. "My sister and I tried to help her through the bars last night, clean her up a bit, then she pulled on her dress, best she could, and tended to the baby."

"I think she has broken bones in her face," added Berna. "I don't know if she's going to live."

"Oh, she's not going to live," assured Agda, "because even if she gets over her injuries, she'll be murdered for what she did to Malik the Persian. Right, Ben-Fozu? Look over in that corner." She pointed. "Malik is missing something."

"Ben-fazi. My name is Ben-fazi," he reiterated, eyeing the dank corner of the cell, seeing what looked like an overly large, wilted sausage.

"Oh!" twittered Agda, the sensation of her own girlish laughter running through her like an unexpected current of warmth. Just like all the caged girls, she had not laughed in nearly a year. "If you go to her, Berna and I will meet you by the bars from this side. She might be less afraid that way, I think. She knows who we are, but you and the jailer might frighten her, otherwise."

"Aye," said Boros, "good idea."

"Clever girl," added Lukos.

Nodding, Ben-fazi agreed.

All were curious about the woman and what lay limp on the floor.

Boros opened the cell door and soon Ben-fazi was on his knees examining the prisoner. Not cheap clothes by any means. And a child? He stole a glance at the baby in the hay, wrapped in what looked like tattered cloth.

Through the bars, Agda offered a length of material she had torn from the bottom of her tunic. Taking it all in, Lukos shivered a moment, struck by the woman's condition. Then he took the rag that Agda had meant for Ben-fazi, casting all other thoughts aside, and began gently pressing it against the woman's face, concern consuming his own. "Oh, dear Lady," he murmured, surveying the damage that had been wrought on the woman before him. Her face was black and blue from bruising and her nose appeared broken, as well as one of her cheek bones. Crusted blood mottled and stained her once flawless skin, all the way down her chest to her exposed breasts. Unable to pull her arms through the sleeves of her dress, it rested bunched up about her waist, the knife hidden within the folds.

A frightful mess, yet Lukos and Ben-fazi both recognized exquisite form and undoubtedly striking beauty beneath the damage inflicted upon her. Her long raven strands fell richly about her shoulders, although mussed and stained with blood, dirt, and hay, and her dress was made of fine materials from foreign lands. Lukos held a length of her hair to the side and back to tend her wounds, shaking his head in pity.

"Had you seen her when they brought her in," commented Boros, watching Ben-fazi raise her head and Lukos dab at her wounds with the cloth, "you'd have said this was surely the most beautiful creature God has ever placed on this earth. Sadly, I don't know that she'll ever look like that again."

Unexpectedly the woman groaned, opening her eyes for the first time since the men had arrived. "M-my baby . . ." she rasped through swollen lips, panicking. "Christophe?" Her head popped up and wild eyes shot from one man to the other; her arms instinctively wrapped about herself, patting her sleeve to ensure the blade was where she'd put it.

As she said this, Lukos shivered as if a haint had run up his spine and his eyes narrowed, reaching for something he didn't quite comprehend. Then it hit him like a stone. This woman . . . she is Mâh of Genoa, Lord Azim's primary Western trading partner! But this he kept to himself.

"Lukos?" asked Boros. "Are you not well?"

"It's her wounds," Lukos lied. "Horrid."

"Yes, your baby," said Agda, pointing through the bars. "He's just there on the straw, lady. Berna and I have been keeping an eye to him all night. He fussed a bit after you laid him down, but went back to sleep. I think he may have soiled himself."

"Is he hurt?" asked Mala, peering towards the straw.

"No," replied Berna. "He was never touched."

"Oh, but thank the Lord," the mother heaved, just then realizing the man before her appeared to be blue? Confused, foggy, she blinked, eyeing him intently.

At this Ben-fazi consoled, "Don't be afraid. It's just paint, and I'm not here to hurt you. Stay calm, and I'll have Boros fetch your baby so you can hold and nurse him. And please let Lukos tend to you."

She had not even noticed Lukos. Instead, as Boros went for the child, her face went blank, as lost. But lost, she was not. Rather, she was trying to remember . . . just as Ben-fazi seemed to be. For her, that secret seemed locked within the voice of this odd little man painted blue. To Ben-fazi, it was tied to the woman's remarkable features. Returning from the past, she strained to see through the paint, but its impossibility blocked her.

"Here he is," said Boros, waking the infant and placing him on Mala's bosom, where he rooted and immediately latched on. This brought her to tears. She pulled her son in close and began to heave with joy, all modesty laid aside. "See there, he's just fine, no worries," he assured her, knowing the statement was absurd due to what stood ahead for both mother and child. Still, her contentment brought him a moment of satisfaction. "And oh, to be so handsome as this fortunate child!" Boros cooed. "He's blessed!"

But the mother was not looking at her baby. Her swollen eyes were glued to the blue man in an incongruent expression of confusion mixed with revelation. Then, as if a key turned and a long-locked door opened, her eyes flared with surprise. "Your voice!" she whispered, aghast. "Do I know you? Benito, is that you?" she cried. "Are you Benito Fazio?"

Hearing his real name, Ben-fazi gasped and his jaw dropped. Her voice, too, dry and crackly as it was, took on a subtle familiarity. Staring beyond the contusions, beyond the broken facial bones, he zeroed in on her dark, piercing eyes. "Oh-my-god!" he moaned, distressed beyond measure. "Signorina?" he wheezed. "Signorina Mala, the Romani of Genoa?"

Totally unexpected and shocking was this mutual recognition that both dissolved into sobbing and nodding as Boros, Lukos, Agda, and Berna watched, marveling, stupefied. The other girls simply huddled in awe and fear, not knowing what all this meant.

For Ben-fazi, so many things began overwhelming him at once that he lost control. To begin, this was the very first link to his previous life since his capture. He had been deprived of his language, his culture, his religion, his freedom, and his future. He felt like a castaway, clinging to a spar in a raging sea with no hope of survival, that had just caught a glimpse of his homeland. More significantly, since his time on earth began, every day had been excruciating and cruel due to the deformities of his size and his larynx, both conspiring to make him an eternal target of scorn. Signorina Mala was the first person to ever treat him with respect or allow him any form of self-esteem. Setting aside her great wealth, influence, and power, la Signorina had treated him humanely and professionally throughout his many years of employment with her, serving as her eyes and ears on the streets of Italy.

Benito had been but one of her many, many informants who were generously paid to give her an edge in commerce, investment, and private matters. And other than a young fellow named Innocenzo, who Ben-fazi presumed had been slain with others of the Peasant's Crusade, Signorina Mala was the only other person who had earned, been worthy, of his affection. And yet here she is, battered, bruised, inevitably bound for the butcher block along with her baby. As these twists swirled in his head, the harder he wept. Oh, but God above, how can such things be?

Contrary to the great influence Mala had brought to the world of Benito Fazio, he had never graced Mala with due respect, nor did she hold him nearly as dear. All such emotions were never entertained, yet she had always liked and appreciated him. As an informant, messenger, and look-out, he was among the best she had ever employed, being reliable and efficient as well as remarkably faithful to her. Benito had even tried to pry her loose from Tristan, not out of jealousy but out of genuine concern. As a result of misinformation, he had believed the young bishop to be neck-high in scandal and licentiousness. Then, too, she had always reserved a soft spot for Benito, understanding all too well the intolerance of others.

But now, at this moment, within the confines of her cell and under such impossible circumstances, discovering Benito there was a gleaming moment of respite and comfort. She had thought him slaughtered at Civetot, along with tens of thousands of others belonging to that ill-fated evangelistic expedition wrangled together by Peter the Hermit, the infamous Peasants' Crusade.

But there was more. Seeing that Benito was alive and apparently free, she sensed the possibility that he might be able to, one way or another, get word to Tristan of her ultimate fate and demise. As horrible as things were and would be, she could think of nothing more hurtful than Tristan never knowing what happened to her and baby Christophe. Benito's skills at secrecy and covertness were unparalleled, therefore he, better than anyone else, could figure out how to manage this final task for her. And this alone made her heart soar with joy, instigating a flood of tears.

"I'm going to die very soon," she confessed to Benito, pulling him near with her free hand, preparing to disclose her last wish, "and there is but one thing I want and need. I—"

"You're not going to die, Signorina," vowed Benito. "I swear," he put his hand to his heart, "you are not going to die!"

"And we others shall pray you live," added Lukos, drawing near to tears.

"Oh, but Benito, my dear little messenger and friend," Mala responded, her eyes dropping closed. "This is no time for happy talk or wishful thinking. I know my fate, and am resigned to it. Even had I succeeded in killing Mahmoud Malik, mine and Christophe's fate would be the same. And seeing my future with the Persian, I had to either kill him or be killed. I refuse to live as his whore for the rest of my days, and I refuse to live in slavery. And I—"

"You shall not die here. As long as I breathe . . ." interrupted Benito, shaking his head with certainty. "Give me a little time, Signorina, the day at least. There's no telling when Malik will be healed enough to come back for you. Sooner than later, I'd guess."

"Ah, ha!" said Boros, holding up the dissected penis. "As bad as he was cut up, he'll be a damn long while recovering! That I know after seeing the condition the poor bastard was in when they dragged him out of here!" Boros then began digging and scratching about beneath the straw. "Ah," he sighed shortly, withdrawing something.

"Good," replied Ben-fazi, shocked at what he saw. "But Boros, I will need your assistance one way or another."

"Yes, I thought so, Ben-fazi, but what to do with this damn thing?" asked Boros expectantly.

Lukos shrunk back a measure, suddenly aware that Boros was offering up what appeared to an open fist with a dismembered penis. "And I shall help, as well, should you need me," he gulped, thinking, This revelation will change the course of all future decisions. Devoid of face and manhood, Malik is forevermore vulnerable!

"Hide that under the straw for now," instructed Ben-fazi, ignoring Lukos. "It'll be dangerous, Boros. And no matter what the plan, if ever I get la Signorina and the baby out of here, suspicion will immediately fall your way as the only Christian and Armenian guarding the prisoners, even before it falls on me. Do you understand?"

Boros nodded.

"Very well then," said Benito, rising. "Pray, Signorina. If nothing else, pray."

"And we shall pray for her, too," said Agda, placing her arm around her sister.

"And we shall pray for you, too, little blue man," said Berna, innocently.

Turning to leave, Benito paused a moment, looking back at Mala once again. "And I am with you on one thing, Signorina," he told her. "Better to die than live the rest of one's days as a whore."

At that, the three men left the cell, each having been deeply touched by the woman. Ben-fazi because of his adoration for la Signorina; Boros because, even though he did not know her, she had won his heart by cutting the Persian; and Lukos because he knew how much this woman meant to his master, Lord Abdul Azim.

CHAPTER THIRTY-SIX

OH, BENITO!

Hurrying back to the palace to gather his thoughts, Ben-fazi learned the emir had been asking for him. "Yes, Master Yaghi?" he said, reporting dutifully.

"Where have you been, Ben-fazi? I've been calling for you all morning."

"The prison delivering scraps, Master."

Pulling at his beard, Siyan said, "Ah, about that . . . the very reason I was calling for you. As you know, Ben-fazi, several days ago I determined that the Persian was right about the Christian foreigners, then I came across other interesting news. No doubt, the Christians are here to take Antioch! That is why I played out my strategy and yesterday sent General Ahmet and Malik to strike the first blow. Furthermore, as you know, I've had a change of mood as concerns the city's Christian population. Not as much the Christian Arabs or Syrians, but the Armenians."

"Yes, Master, I know."

"With yesterday's attack on the crusaders, I began pulling Christian prisoners from our jail and executing them in full view of the public, to quell any thoughts of treason or rising up. And I believe you're aware of that as well?"

"Yes, Master Yaghi. But you remained benevolent by picking only men to execute," said Ben-fazi, extending his palms outward as one acknowledging graciousness.

"That changes this evening, Ben-fazi. I shall select twenty women to hang from my walls in plain sight of the crusaders. A chilling message to them as well as our own Christians."

Walking the prison corridor with Boros, Ben-fazi had taken a cursory count of females. There were scarcely twenty females, excluding Malik's hidden girls. Realizing this, Ben-fazi's heart stopped. I now have even less time than initially anticipated to help la Signorina.

"And at this very moment," Siyan said with a twinkle in his eye, "John the Oxite is already hanging by his feet from the wall, just by the Saint Paul Gate, in view of the foreign camp blocking that gate."

Hearing this, Ben-fazi felt the approach of a new apprehension. "John the Oxite?" he asked.

"Yes, and my guards are beating his feet with iron rods as I speak."

"But then, surely, you're not going to execute John the Oxite as well, are you?"

"No. He better serves my purpose by remaining alive. I'll have him removed from the wall after the flats of his feet turn to mush, and repeat the process each week for good measure, just as his feet begin to heal."

"But he's not a young man," said Ben-fazi, concern bleeding through his paint. "Exactly. His weekly suffering will weigh heavier on our Christians than a quick execution. But back to why I called you. Your delivery of extra food to the prison is to be halted. Immediately."

Though perturbed about John the Oxite and the scraps, Ben-fazi's mind lingered within the cell where he had vowed to devise the rescue of la Signorina. But Siyan's plan to execute twenty women by nightfall could well sabotage any effort made on her behalf. Mala could, this very evening, be chosen as a victim, meeting her end even before Malik recovered from his wounds.

His mind reeling, he began to think. Having learned over years of under-cover work that trickery was the primary pillar of deceit, he had also learned that when all else failed, truth might be levered as the last straw, though the risk be great. For a split second he considered simply revealing la Signorina's plight, especially since the old emir loathed Mahmoud Malik. But reality struck back at him, and he dismissed the idea. Yaghi Siyan did possess a merciful side, which surfaced at unexpected times, but when riled, he grew contrary and unpredict-able—no, impossible—not to mention dangerous. Knowing that Siyan's fangs were purposefully directed against Christians, not the Persians, and la Signorina was Christian, time was of the essence.

"But Ben-fazi," said Siyan, "I've neglected to tell you the best news. One of my birds finally arrived three days ago to reclaim his perch."

"One of your birds?"

"Indeed," replied Siyan, with a gleam in his eye. "As I told General Ahmet weeks ago, I released pigeons from here to their other nest in Damascus. After all that's happened, and after all this time, the first of them has returned with a message from Duqaq of Damascus. He's coming, Ben-fazi, to shore us up!"

Ben-fazi remained silent.

Siyan shook his finger at his little blue pet. "Remember, no further deliveries to the prison. None."

"As you say," he replied, disappointment hiding behind his paint.

"In fact," Siyan insisted, shooing Ben-fazi toward the door, "I want you to return immediately and retrieve what you just delivered. No gestures of kindness to any Christians, especially those behind bars!"

"Of course, Master Yaghi," bowed Ben-fazi, wheels turning rapidly in his mind.

"Oh, but I nearly forgot! One other thing, how are Firuz's children? Have you settled them into their private apartment?"

"Certainly, Master, exactly as requested. They're getting adjusted, and both hope you shall call for them soon."

"Ah, excellent," Siyan clucked. "I had intended to be with them on a regular basis, but this war situation has held me back, obviously."

Siyan's mention of the children sparked an idea in Ben-fazi, and even as he had been talking to him over the last minute, a plan had begun to formulate in his quick little mind. "Speaking of the children," he started, knowing how much the old emir adored them both, "the other day Karine addressed a request to me, concerning Garik. Sweet girl, always talking for her little brother, generous and thoughtful!"

"Request? Karine? But certainly, anything that girl wants. But what was the request?"

"Well, Master Yaghi, you know how terrified Garik is of his own shadow, and strangers? It seems that when the servants enter the room, he dissolves into fits of fear and anxiety."

"What?" shrieked Siyan. "He's even afraid of the servants? The ones feeding and clothing him?"

"Oh, according to Karine, he's especially frightened by the servants. She wished to know if, perhaps, they could be prohibited from entering the apartment?"

"But how will the children dress and eat?"

"They've always dressed and fed themselves, Master. And neither likes to be touched, as you know. And I have actually seen the servants agitate and cause great anxiety, not help them. Food and clothing can be left outside their door. And one other thing, Karine wishes to know if you would please install extra locks on the apartment door to ensure their privacy."

"Anything she wants," smiled Siyan. "And tell me, Ben-fazi, have you ever seen such a beautiful young girl in all your days as Karine? My greatest regret of all would be to not live long enough to see how she shall blossom as a grown woman! Oh, she will be unimaginable, eh, Ben-fazi?"

"Yes, Master. No doubt."

"Very well then, you take care of the details with the servants and the locks. But for now, quickly, back to the prison and fetch back my scraps from the Christians!"

"Immediately, Master Yaghi!"

But Ben-fazi did not. He hastened instead to the scribe's complex where official documents were put into writing and recorded before being sent out for intended purposes, whatever they might be. Scribbling words on a scroll and stamping it with Yaghi Siyan's official seal, Ben-fazi made no recording of it for documentation but covertly slipped it into the waistband of his trousers.

Scurrying outside, Ben-fazi summoned a coachman to take him to the prison where Boros and two guards happened to be manning the entrance. "You two guards!" he shouted, acting as officious as one could, being painted blue and wearing preposterous clothing. "Come read this, if indeed you oafs can read, and gather me the woman that was hauled in here last night, and her infant as well. Yaghi Siyan wants them both brought to the palace!"

The guards came forward, neither of them knowing how to read. Examining the order briefly, one looked to the other and said, "Don't know what it says, but that does look like the emir's stamp on the bottom."

"Here, I can read, dammit!" said Boros, grabbing the scroll. He had no idea what was transpiring but suspected Ben-fazi had, as promised, come up with a ruse to help the woman. "Aye, it says right here," he said, reading the order, "that Yaghi Siyan wishes her to be brought to his palace for interrogation concerning crusader presence at Saint Simeon . . . Says she'll be returned within 24 hours and—"

"Give me that!" barked the guard, snatching the scroll from Boros. "Lieutenant Abad!" he then shouted to a superior standing just within the entrance. "Come look! You can read."

"Of course," sniffed the man, sauntering over, though his reading level was that of a young child. "Ah, yes, this is from Emir Yaghi Siyan, right?" he said, directing his gaze toward Boros.

"Yes," said Boros. "He wants her brought to him for questioning, then will send her back when done."

"Right," snapped Ben-fazi, impatience seeping into his voice.

Running his eyes over the order again, moving his lips as if he was reading it, Abad looked at the other guards. "Yup," he said. "That's what it says all right, so I'd start hopping. You two get the key and accompany these fellows inside. But dammit, don't go beyond Malik's line or we all forfeit what he's paid us for hiding the girls at the ass end of this rock!"

The two guards balked, being amongst those whom Malik had gratuitously bribed to surreptitiously safeguard his young captive girls. "B-but the Persian," stammered one of them, "he'll be furious if we release her to Ben-fazi, even if it's for just a short time! He'll take it out of our flesh!"

Placing his fists to his hips, Ben-fazi feigned anger. "Then give me back the damn order! Shit, I'm not the one summoning her, it's Yaghi Siyan, you fool. I'll simply tell Yaghi Siyan you two refused his direct command! Give me your names. Now!"

Filling with apprehension, both guards went stiff. "Ah, shit on the Persian," said one, grabbing the other. Shortly they were accompanying Boros and Ben-fazi down the corridor as the starving prisoners again clamored over the little blue man. Nearing the cell where Malik had stashed his girls, the guards turned the key over to Boros. "We'll wait here while you get her," one of them said, pointing to an imaginary line at his feet.

As Boros slipped the key in the lock and opened the cell door, Mala watched, wide-eyed and confused, clinging tightly to a fussy, soiled Christophe. She'd since dressed herself and cleaned him best she could under the circumstances.

"Come along, we're taking you," said Ben-fazi hurriedly, motioning for Boros to help move her along. Batter and bruised, walking on her own was difficult.

Her heart thumping its way nearly out of her throat, she cast her eyes about as a mouse just escaped from the cat's fangs, knowing danger remained ever near. "Oh, Benito, my tiny friend," she whispered, "what have you done? You shall pay a dear price for this gambit, whatever it is!"

"Shh! Say nothing!" he directed as he and Boros ushered her down the corridor, outside, and into the coach as a huddle of guards watched, exchanging comments. "To the palace, the back approach!" Ben-fazi instructed, signaling the driver to make haste.

Twenty minutes later, they made the rear structures of the palace and Ben-fazi gave the driver directions to a nondescript entrance. Arriving, he helped Mala down a ceaseless network of corridors, and finally into a foyer leading to the private apartment sequestering Firuz's children. Garik happened to be napping on a cushion close to the door as they burst in and immediately grew afraid. "Ahgh!" he shouted. "Karine! Karine!"

"Hush! Hush!" shushed Ben-fazi, as Karine appeared from the next room.

"Be quiet, Garik," commanded Karine, quickly assessing the blue man's appearance in the apartment with a woman and a baby. It was evident to her their arrival was clandestine, and that the brutal condition of the woman's face indicated a horrific story. She had taken a bit of a liking to Ben-fazi, therefore neither alarm nor calling for help was among the many thoughts spilling through her head.

"Karine," implored Ben-fazi, "I need your help! I need your silence and your strength! Let me explain, and may Allah touch my words, and your heart!"

Saying nothing nor acknowledging either Ben-fazi nor the woman, Karine stared vacantly at the baby squirming within Mala's arms. Mesmerized, she felt an immediate attraction to the infant, wanting possession of it. Like her brother, the distressed infant appeared helpless and lost, and this stirred a distant longing in her abnormally indifferent heart. Garik was the one person who had ever been allowed in that sacred place. In reality, it may have actually not been him, but his frailty and dependence on her.

Receiving no response, Ben-fazi asked, "Karine? Did you hear me?"

"Let me hold the baby," she said, moving forward with outstretched hands.

CHAPTER THIRTY-SEVEN

THE TUSCAN CAMP

By late November, Turkish attacks and ensuing Christian countermeasures began to escalate. The Battle of Antioch had evolved into a probing game of cat and mouse, as was common of attrition siege, which operated at a far slower cadence, employing different tactics than close or direct siege.

Direct siege required attackers to assault walls in mass with ladders, wheeled towers, and battering rams, while defenders repulsed them by unleashing arrows, stones, pitch, hot oil, and molten metal. Less violent, attrition siege lacked suicidal clashes beneath heavily defended walls, but was equally visceral. One primary tactic of attrition siege was arousing 'terror' aimed at horrifying and disheartening the enemy through any means possible. Terror, therefore, became a staple in the fight for Antioch; the more brutal, the more effective.

Siyan had begun hanging executed Antioch Christians and captured crusaders from his walls, and dragging John the Oxite regularly for public punishment in sight of the crusaders. In addition, the Turks began hurling severed crusader heads and limbs gathered by raiding parties into enemy camps via ballista and catapult.

Being well-practiced themselves in attrition siege tactics, crusaders reciprocated by hurling bodies of captured Turks back into Antioch or holding executions in plain sight of the city. To further heighten the level of horror, the crusaders called on Tafur and his 'beggar army' to roast Turkish body parts and ritualistically devour them within sight of Antioch; a ruthless and inhuman practice they had begun during the battle of Nicaea against the Turks of Rüm at the beginning of the Holy Crusade. Having been ignored, disavowed, and set aside since Nicaea, Tafur regained importance within Antioch's unraveling war of attrition after being kept at arm's length by Adhémar and the Council of Princes who thought him barbaric yet believed his lowly roots were undeserving of anything but exploitation by higher men. Nonetheless, the peasant army that had adopted their leader's name by calling themselves 'the Tafurs' were, at this very instant, orchestrating horror on the stage of Antioch, delivering an undeniable message: "Because you refuse to surrender, once we breach your walls, there shall be no mercy, only sadistic retribution."

To their favor, the crusaders secured the road to Saint Simeon, a vital link to maritime resupply from Byzantine-held Cyprus as well as a portal to the entire Mediterranean as far as Western Europe. Having been exiled to Cyprus by the Turks, the Greek patriarch of Jerusalem began entering into communication with Bishop Adhémar, and together they drafted a letter of appeal to the West for additional troops and assistance.

The Council of Princes' resentment against Emperor Alexius did not deter Adhémar's overtures to Cyprus but encouraged détente with the emperor, causing him to approve the shipping of supplies to Saint Simeon. Furthering the Christian cause, the bigger port of Latakia, located sixty kilometers south of Saint Simeon, was secured as well. Latakia provided even better access to Cyprus.

By November's end, then, the fight for Antioch settled into a period of stalemate.

As these events unfolded, the shroud of misery that had settled over the Tuscan camp deepened. Tristan, Guillaume, and Orla, all three, found themselves floundering within despair.

On learning of Mala and baby Christophe, Tristan's world collapsed into a trough of anger and bitterness, much of it directed at the Council of Princes, the rest against God Himself. How could You be so merciless? Tristan raged. Is this yet more punishment You fling at me for simply loving another human being? Will there be no end to it for as long as we breathe, Mala and me?

After such bouts of accusatory heresy, Tristan would of course think, then inevitably turn red with shame, realizing it was heartbreak combined with apprehension, not God, causing his debilitating crisis of faith. This shame, then, would lead him to supplication. Oh, but God, let there be a chance, just a tiny chance even, that Mala and Christophe may be alive! I would sacrifice myself for them, Father! God, I beg, do not take yet another son from Mala, nor from me! Mea culpa, mea culpa, I am guilty, I am guilty. But do not make my baby nor this woman I love pay for my sins!

Guillaume felt his brother's anguish but was hobbled by his own, as well. Memories of Pelekanum kept resurfacing in his dreams, followed by scenes of him suffering the wrath of God, crying out from searing flames of eternal hellfire. Bohemud had alluded to a death wish at the ambush of Harim, and though he had been but half-serious, he was closer to the truth than he thought. Since Nicaea, Guillaume had fought battle after battle as one crazed, defying fear of death in favor of blind fate, helped along by throwing himself into imminent peril. If I die, so be it! This crusade takes the place of my penance. Prayer may help me, but should I be slain fighting in God's name, His forgiveness is assured, as vowed by the Holy Father, Pope Urban II.

This, of course, brings into question the unique effect of faith on one person as opposed to another. Undeniably, once infused into the human heart, the passion of true faith can become a sweeping, irreversible tide washing over all logic, all objection, and all obstacles. Accordingly, the term 'faith' was defined as: "confidence or trust in a person or thing; belief that is not based on proof; belief in God or in the doctrines or teachings of religion."

Trust, by way of example, is based purely on faith, not knowledge nor actual certainty. Loyalty, equally, is based on faith. Love, too, as is a plethora of other behaviors and emotions binding human hearts together, one to the other.

But faith entails the concept of 'degree;' some are tepid about faith, while others are profoundly steeped in it; labeled 'zealous' or 'touched by the spirit' or 'fanatic.' Given that the Catholic Church was the mightiest institution of the Dark Ages, and acknowledging that its many, many tentacles reached into every single aspect of European Medieval life, it consumed Guillaume and others driven by the dogma of Christian beliefs and Catholic doctrine. But Guillaume's degree of piety and devotion, extraordinary compared to others, could not be moved nor manipulated since he possessed an inordinately high degree of faith described flippantly as 'blind faith.' That religion had become the root and well-spring of politics, money, and power was inconceivable to Guillaume whose unconditional 'faith' refuted such notions.

Guillaume de Saint-Germain, as it happened, had become the most faithful, earnest, and altruistic of all in this insane crusade. And because of that, he chose, through his particular confluence of upbringing, Dark Ages influences, and religious interpretation, to adopt an extreme faith-driven existence with one purpose: eternal salvation. Even after totally accepting and embracing Catholicism, including the concept of God's forgiveness, the guilt of Guillaume's carnal transgressions against God at Pelekanum with Queen Irene had crawled into a corner of his soul, refusing to vacate. Consequently, Guillaume battled in misery a war within himself.

And finally, there was Orla; gradually healing, walking now, albeit with a limp. His other cuts and wounds had begun to close, at least, and he escaped infection despite being the victim of primitive medical attention. His spirit, however, was broken.

Hroc's timely return aside, the loss of Crowbones had been a crushing blow to Orla. Since birth the two had been inseparable, fighting together as one against other Vikings by early adolescence, followed then by an endless string of enemies, including the French, Flemish, other Normans, Saxons, and Germans in multiple wars stretching over the next half century. Now it was the Turks. Both having suffered loss of spouse and children, it was from one another that each had received solace and counsel. Fighting and bleeding side-by-side and back-to-back, it was to each other that Orla and Crowbones looked to for undying trust, support, protection, amenity, and fraternity. And now, atop Mount Staurin during an ill-fated foray, that bond had been shattered by Crowbones' passing.

How shall I fight without, Ivar at my side? he lamented from deep within where Crowbones had left a massive void. How shall I overcome this black, all-encompassing grief that follows me day and night? What shall become of me now that half my heart has been slain along with my beloved brother?

CHAPTER THIRTY-EIGHT

KAREEM, THE CHAMELEON

After surveilling both Antioch and crusader camps for nearly three weeks, Kareem returned to the Ruj Valley on foot to report to Lord Azim.

"But Kareem," asked Azim, watching his scout trudge into camp, "what has become of your horse and donkeys?"

"The crusaders took them from me as I returned to their camp after scouting Antioch," complained Kareem. "When I first arrived in their camp, food was plentiful and I had no problems with the Christians who were friendly. Unbelievably, during my two weeks in Antioch, things changed drastically. They began running low on food as well as on disposition, damn them. They butchered my poor donkeys into quarters, fighting over the meat like squabbling rats! My horse fared no better."

"I see," said Azim. Feeling bad that Kareem had been forced to cover such a long distance on foot, he handed him a cup of water and patted him once on the shoulder. "You were gone so long I began to fret! But tell, what did you learn?"

"I learned much!" Kareem downed the water and wiped his face with the back of his hand, then rested on a camp stool to gather his breath. "The crusader camp is enormous. Beyond belief, actually. I've never seen such a mass of men-at-arms and weaponry ever. And if you should ever get near enough, you'll say the same. But numerous as they are, there's little chance they'll be able to overcome Antioch's fortifications from what I saw while within the city. Antioch is simply too well fortified and spread out to attack directly."

"Ah, attrition siege then," said Azim. "They hope to wait them out."

"Yes, but good luck, I say. While the crusaders are running low on food, Antioch maintains storehouses spilling with grain, and the stables are packed with horses, cattle, and beasts of burden. As usual, the poor of the city are hungry, but the rest seem content as fat little termites holed up in their mound!"

"What about Malik? Is he there?"

"Oh, he's there alright," acknowledged Kareem, a smirk overcoming his expression. "I didn't see him, actually, but he's there. And you'll be happy to know that his face has been split in two like a sliced apple and . . ." with a twinkled in his eye, he uttered the last few words, "his manhood has been removed! I saw it with my own eyes."

"What!?" shouted Azim. "By whom?" Nothing could have shocked him more . . . or so he thought.

Kareem's gleam evaporated and a shadow swept his over face. "Your Western trading partner, the woman you've always fancied, Mâh of Genoa, the one they call la Gran Signorina in the West."

What Kareem said about Malik was shocking, but this . . . this . . . Taken aback, Azim launched into that state of wonder one gets upon arriving at the impossible, where the disconnected circles and delivers a blow to the head.

"Yes, I know," said Kareem, nodding. "Completely unexpected that she should be here in the midst of war. A small world, yes? She was delivering ships to the Christians. Remember that last message your courier delivered from her as we turned south in chase of Malik?"

"Yes. She was asking about political asylum in my kingdom, for her family. You and I were confused because she was not married, nor did she have children."

"She's still not married," said Kareem, "but she has a child, and a lover, apparently, which is why she came this direction. He's a high cleric within the Vatican representing the Pope!"

Astounded, Azim thought back on his embassy to the Vatican to meet with Pope Gregory VII and his cardinals. Ah, that visit left a bitter taste in him regarding Catholicism, the Vatican, the College of Cardinals, and Christianity in general. "But Pope Gregory prohibited Catholic holy men from consorting with women, or even marrying, Kareem. 'Celibacy' I think they call it. Yet you claim that Mâh of Genoa has had a child with a highly placed cleric in the Vatican?"

"Oh, but it gets interesting, Master!" said Kareem, shaking his head. "A moment ago, I said 'it's a small world.' Brace yourself, it gets smaller. Remember that extraordinary boy we met in Rome, serving as the Pope's interpreter?"

"Yes, yes, of course, but I fail to recall his name. I simply referred to him as 'Little Brother' because I developed an affection for him, and admiration as well. For such a young man, he possessed wisdom of the ages, out shining the entire papal delegation combined!"

"Well, that young boy, 'Little Brother,' that you introduced to hashish and took into your harem on our last night in Rome, is also here at Antioch."

"What!!?" exclaimed Azim, beyond confounded, mind reeling. The news gets better and better.

"Ah-hum, let me put it together for you, Sire. That young boy is now a man, a Catholic bishop named Tristan de Saint-Germain, who represents Pope Urban II in this war. But it gets deeper. He is the father of Mâh of Genoa's child, a newborn son."

"B-but—No, that can't be! As foolish as the rule is, it is a severe violation of Christian Church law for Catholic holy men to marry, lay with a woman, or even be tempted by sins of the flesh."

"Ha!" laughed Kareem, derision etching itself across his expression. "Tell me my dearest friend on this earth, how many Muslim imams have you known that violate every law of Allah's teachings on a daily basis? Picking the pockets of the poor, drowning in their own lies, arranging political webs of deceit, even dabbling in assassination and bloody revolt to advance themselves!? Or look at that snake, Mahmoud Malik. Everything he does, every rape, every murder and atrocity, is, according to him, by the direction of Allah. A Catholic holy man bedding a woman, then, is but a trifle, I think!"

"Yes, certainly. But you have to understand these Catholics, Kareem! Imbecilic as their rules may be, they adhere to them like venomous spiders defending their web, controlling their people with fear of punishment, death, and damnation."

"In any case, Mâh of Genoa slit Malik's face to ribbons and cut his penis off! But during the fracas, he beat Mala horrifically, yet the baby miraculously escaped injury, by the grace of Allah."

"But where is Mâh now?" asked Azim, most concerned.

"A little blue man, at great risk to himself, has sprung her from Siyan's prison to save her from being murdered by Malik. He's hidden her in the city. Where, I've no idea."

Kareem had lost Azim at the mention of a blue man. "A little blue man?" Azim froze, eyebrows arched, astonished.

Grinning, Kareem tilted his head into his palm. "It's quite a story, Master. I'll share more details later. At the moment, I'm hungry, thirsty, and exhausted. Do you suppose I could—?"

"Yes, most certainly," answered Azim, attempting to connect all the lines of his scout's report. "It is a small world indeed, Kareem. And with all of us set upon the same stage, we shall see how Allah moves us about."

CHAPTER THIRTY-NINE

HUNGER AND TROUBLE

When winter arrived in December, crusader bloodlust became secondary as hunger took command over battle. Even with help from Cyprus, which was in fact limited in the face of the huge army's numbers, and because foraging possibilities within range of Antioch had been depleted, the vast size of the Christian army, once its advantage, had become its biggest liability. Mathew of Edessa, a contemporary Armenian Christian, reported: "The princes of Cilicia sent whatever provisions were needed to the commander of the Franks. Likewise, the monks of the Black Mountains assisted them by sending provisions, and all the faithful acted benevolently towards the Franks. Nevertheless, because of the scarcity of food, mortality and affliction fell upon the Frankish army to such an extent that one of five perished while all the rest felt themselves abandoned and far from their homeland."

Further impeding the Army of God, the weather turned. The Latins had incorrectly assumed that rain would be sparse in Syria. Worse, they never imagined it might snow. Writing to his wife, Stephen of Blois lamented: "Before the city of Antioch, throughout the whole winter, we suffered for our Lord Christ from excessive cold and enormous torrents of rain. What some would say about the impossibility of bearing the heat of the sun throughout Syria is untrue, for the winter there is very similar to our winter in the west."

Such became the ordeal of weather, and especially hunger, that Christian morale began to plummet by mid-December. One Latin observer within the crusader camp chronicled: "The people of God began to run short on rations. With the severity of hunger growing daily, and the army dying of want, especially the humble people, wretched groans and laments assailed Adhémar and all the princes. So, they conferred about these problems and how the people could be nourished."

Recognizing that circumstances were becoming dire, the Council of Princes devised a plan to send a major foraging party led by Bohemud and Robert of Flanders further beyond the occupied countryside. By sending a large force, the princes felt that it could pillage and seize profoundly needed food and supplies from the untraveled territory with impunity. This, on the other hand, did create certain risk. Deploying such a large-scale operation might weaken the Christian hold on Antioch, especially should the Turks learn of this deployment and decide to mass an attack against those crusaders remaining at Antioch.

Following a subdued and lean celebration of the Birth of Jesus on December 25th of 1097, Bohemud and Robert of Flanders struck out with 400 knights and a far larger force of infantry. Guillaume, being a favorite of Bohemud, and fifty of his Golden Knights of Tuscany accompanied the expedition.

Traveling south of Antioch, the expeditionary force then cut east through the Ruj Valley and onto a fertile plateau known in Arabic as Jabal as-Summaq. This was further east than the Christians had ventured before, and had they not cut north twenty kilometers, they might have come across the Oasis of Sparrows. Instead, they remained far from it.

As the earth of Jabal as-Summaq was rich and had not yet been ravaged by foraging armies, the crusader haul was fruitful. They commandeered all they could from the area, amassing a sizeable train of food to take back to Antioch. On the night of December 30th, believing their mission to be done, Bohemud and Robert of Flanders camped near the town of Albara.

But in a grievous oversight caused by the confusing dynamics of double-command, possibly caused by haste and miscommunication, Bohemud and Robert of Flanders neglected to post scouts throughout the region while foraging. Consequently, they had no idea that a large Muslim force led by Duqaq of Damascus was but kilometers away, on the march to rescue Antioch. Shams ad-Daulah, one of two sons that Yaghi Siyan had dispatched earlier to seek outside assistance, had finally succeeded in convincing Duqaq that the invasion was truly a threat to the entire region, including Damascus. Alarmed, Duqaq mustered a large military force of just over 10,000, including his own formidable atabeg, General Tughtegin, and his ally, the Emir of Horns.

Had this Muslim army reached Antioch unhindered, there is an excellent chance they would have swung the battle, but fate intervened and the army of Duqaq of Damascus and the forces of Bohemud and Robert of Flanders crossed.

During the early hours of New Year's Eve, the crusaders camped and sleeping, totally unaware, Duqaq's army appeared before them from out of nowhere. It would have been impossible to tell who it shocked first and to what degree, Muslims or Christians. This actually leaned in favor of the crusaders. Due to the close proximity of the two unsuspecting armies, the encounter became a battle of Christian sword against Muslim saber, effectively eliminating the deadly toll often taken from a greater distance by the devastating Muslim compound bow.

Duqaq, surmising immediately that his force vastly outnumbered the crusaders, ordered a swift encirclement maneuver, which under normal circumstances would have worked, and the crusaders would have been shortly surrounded and slaughtered, but Duqaq's troops had never run into the likes of Bohemud and Robert Flanders, both being astute tacticians and brilliant commanders.

Without hesitation Robert of Flanders rallied his knights into a frontal, heavy cavalry charge straight into the advancing first line of Turks. The Damascus Turks were unfamiliar with Western heavy cavalry and armor, and as such, the shock of Flanders' attack repulsed and broke the Muslim advance, creating chaos and confusion among oncoming ghazis. As this battle raged, Bohemud held position. Then, just as Turkish flanks began to encircle the Christians, Bohemud led his knights and footmen in a vicious charge against the circling left flank of Turks, while Guillaume did the same against the circling right flank. Again, it was the heavy cavalry that shocked the Muslims, thwarting their effort to surround the enemy. And again, Guillaume proved he lacked all fear, plunging into thick ranks of oncoming Turks with sword ablaze, exhorting those behind him to follow.

Far outnumbered, the Christian heavy cavalry broke the Muslim line, supported by Christian infantry in its wake.

Seeing the Turkish front begin to scatter, Robert of Flanders and Bohemud both trumpeted a retreat of their knights. If the Turks restored order and reformed, their superior numbers alone would eventually overcome and crush the crusader heavy cavalry. But as the knights retreated, they left the slower-moving infantry and the entire foraging train exposed and at the mercy of the remaining Muslim troops.

Unbeknownst to both Christians and Duqaq's Muslims, they were being closely watched from a distant rise by a third army—that of Lord Abdul Azim—which had settled quietly into the Ruj Valley. Azims' scouts, on catching sight of Bohemud's and Robert of Flanders' advance south toward the Jabal as-Summaq, alerted Azim, who, in turn, prepared for war, thinking the Christians might be coming after him.

As Azim and two of his generals watched the bloody battle unfold and develop before their very eyes, one of the generals said, "Lord Azim, our Muslim brothers may need help. We could easily turn the tide of battle."

"These Muslims of Syria are not our brothers," replied Azim coldly. "Brothers would not slaughter family, as these Syrian Seljuks slaughtered mine. No, Allah shall decide this outcome today, not us!"

As battle dissipated into mutual retreat, random pockets of fighting remained as but a few stray packs of combatants remained in the fray. Then the field cleared, exposing scores and scores of dead men and horses, the wounded and maimed fumbling about the ground wailing for help, heaving their last breath, or gasping final prayers, whether Christian or Muslim.

Neither army had won anything. The crusaders had lost a good number of knights and horses, and because of the knights' hasty retreat, nearly their entire infantry was lost to slaughter or capture. Adding salt to the wound, the entire foraging train had been forfeited to the Muslims as well. In sum, the crusader expedition began well but ended in debacle. Weary and bloody, they headed back to Antioch empty-handed. Nonetheless, had it not been for exceptional generalship, the entire expeditionary force would have been butchered.

The Muslims knights suffered great casualties compared to those of the Christians, and their advance light cavalry had been crushed and chased from the field by this frightening, unfamiliar heavy cavalry that overwhelmed them. But the greatest blow was endured by Duqaq of Damascus himself. This small crusader force had fought ferociously and exacted copious amounts of Muslim blood, which rattled him greatly. Deciding it too perilous to continue the march to Antioch, he left Yaghi Siyan to his own fortunes and returned to Damascus with the hope that the great Christian army described by Shams ad-Daulah did not send its full force his direction. If indeed this small force he had just fought was any sign of Christian voracity in battle, then Damascus would be in trouble.

At the same time Bohemud and Robert of Flanders were under attack, the main crusader army remaining at Antioch became the target of a damaging attack, exactly as conjectured by certain princes during the Council of Princes meeting devising the foraging expedition. Whether through scouts or through Armenian Christian spies, Yaghi Siyan caught wind of the missing foraging expedition led by Bohemud and Robert of Flanders. He further learned that Robert of Normandy was on a mission to Latakia, and that Godfrey of Bouillon was ill.

Seizing opportunity, Siyan ordered an attack on December 29th, ordering a large cavalry force to rush out the Bridge Gate and charge both the Bridge of Boats and the Frankish camp of Raymond of Toulouse. Raymond counter-attacked, putting the Turks to flight. Aroused at seeing how quickly he had turned the enemy, he ordered his knights to catch them before getting back inside Antioch.

But this was a trap; the infamous 'feigned retreat' favored by Muslim cavalry.

By the time the Frankish pursuit began crossing the fortified bridge leading to the Bridge Gate, the Turks had already turned, reformed, and launched their counter-attack. Simultaneously, another ghazi force forded the stream further downstream in a shallow spot unknown to the Crusaders and circled around behind the Franks.

Within minutes, the Franks were outnumbered and outmaneuvered. The rout was on, then, as confusion befell the surprised crusaders. According to Raymond of Aguilers, chaplain to Raymond of Toulouse: "Frankish knights, who stopped to fight, found themselves grabbed by the fleeing crusader rabble, who snatched their arms, the manes and tails of their horses, and pulled them from their mounts. The Turks hurriedly and pitilessly chased and massacred the living and robbed the dead. In the running fight from their bridge to ours, the Turks killed up to fifteen knights and around twenty footmen. The standard bearer of the Bishop of Le Puy and the noble young man, Bernard of Béziers, lost their lives, and Adhémar's standard was taken."

Although the Christian casualty loss was not disastrous, the battle was a serious blow to Latin morale for two reasons. The first was the loss of Adhémar's banner depicting the Blessed Virgin Mary. This was deeply humiliating to the crusaders, symbolically equivalent of 'a defeat' because during this era, the battle banner was an extremely prized possession representing the character and integrity of the owner. In addition, it could be raised over cities to declare ownership or conquest, or used to signify a place of sanctuary for surrendered enemies to huddle beneath. Accordingly, in the weeks that followed, the Turks took special delight in taunting the Christian army by flying Adhémar's banner from Antioch's ramparts and walls.

The second blow to crusader morale was the chaos that had developed between Raymond's cavalry and infantry. The first breakdown was brought on by the growing shortage of that ever-valuable commodity—horses. Rather than adequately covering the footmen at the beginning of the battle, many knights dashed off to capture riderless horses, leaving footmen exposed in favor of securing horses to replace the many they'd lost. The next breakdown occurred at the bridge, as previously cited. Consequently, the infantry/cavalry lack of cohesion during the battle against Duqaq of Damascus and the same during the battle at the bridge both led to disaster.

As a consequence, both failures colluded to breed distrust between horseman and footmen. This consequently raised the question as to whether the two fighting groups could actually coalesce as a single effective fighting unit rather than as two disaggregated units, one causing the downfall of the other.

In the end, and as demonstrated by crusader military performance during these two battles marking December's end, it was evident that crusader leadership would have to begin reassessing certain aspects of their military strategy, especially the interaction of cavalry and infantry.

CHAPTER FORTY

AH, BUT SIN!

On New Year's Day, with the return of Bohemud and Robert of Flanders back from the plateau of Jabal as-Summaq and Robert of Normandy returning from Latakia, the Christian army was reunited, having narrowly survived two exacting challenges just days earlier. Unfortunately, languishing from lack of food and the extreme cold, the crusaders' plight deteriorated by the moment. Men died of starvation, disease, and in skirmishes. The survivors, left to stave off those same troubles, faced new ones, exacting their toll in other appalling ways.

To begin, because several gates to Antioch remained open and there were Muslim allies within Syria, the Turks appeared to be doing better in terms of acquiring supplies, primarily from the south and the east. As remarked by the crusader Anselm of Ribemont in a letter home: "The city is supplied to an incredible extent with grain, wine, oil, and all kinds of food." This was probably an exaggeration, but Antioch was, in fact, not in the same dire position of the Army of God.

But another problem now arose for the crusaders. On learning the crusaders' plight, local Armenians, Syrians, and Greeks ranged far and wide scouring food-stuffs, donkeys, and horses to sell to the strapped Christian army, at staggering prices. This market aside, crusaders perished, seeing most could in no way afford such inflated prices. To survive, crusaders began eating the shoots of bean seeds, herbs and weeds seasoned with salt, and even raw thistles that pricked the tongue due to being poorly cooked, and firewood of any kind had become scarce. Even when a rare carcass of horse, camel, donkey, dog, or rat could be scavenged, it, too, was eaten raw by those of means; the poorer crusaders had to settle for gnawing on bone and hide. The poorest of the poor even resorted to picking seeds and plant fibers out of animal manure.

Compounding these impossible hardships, even the heavens began to conspire against the crusaders as mysterious warnings lit the skies of Northern Syria in the form of a comet and an aurora. Many claimed to see 'an astonishing white light in the sky,' as well as something 'appearing to resemble a huge cross, whitish in color, advancing toward the East in a straight line.' Others insisted the earth quaked beneath their feet when such signs manifested themselves. Terrified by these unexplained celestial events, crusaders interpreted them as anomalous signs of God's displeasure with the Christian army.

For the first time since its beginning, actual fear began to infect the Holy Crusade as panic spread lizard-like through the ranks. Confused, men-of-arms began to wonder, If we are fighting a holy war in the name of God, why then is He allowing us to suffer and die?

The answer, as misery lingered, came from the clergy. After much conferring among themselves, the chaplain, Fulcher of Chartres, explained it with these words: "We believed that these misfortunes befell the Franks, and they, for so long, were not able to take the city, because of their sins. Not only dissipation, but also avarice, or pride, or rapaciousness corrupted them."

There it was, laid bare for all to hear. Sin. Bishop Tristan de Saint-Germain had earlier declared his own accusations against the Holy Crusade by pointing to similar digressions, in particular avarice and pride, not in terms of 'sin' but of vile intimate ambition. Nevertheless, his words went unacknowledged by other high clerics, even by Bishop Adhémar of Le Puy who heartily agreed with Fulcher of Chartres' identification of sin as the root and core of crusader misfortune. Nor did the major princes allow for any connection between Bishop Saint-Germain's earlier accusations as related to the recent clerical disclosure that 'sin was the problem.'

Sin being blamed, the unanimous solution, according to Adhémar and other high clerics, was the 'purification' of those sins. That is when they commenced preaching a 'return to righteousness' through austerity and Christian ritual, urging all to fast for three days, pray, give alms, and march in procession. Asking starving people to fast for three days may appear absurd, but the imposition of physical denial followed with intense liturgical ritual was a long-established staple of the Catholic Church.

Another phase of this purification formula centered on a tenet of medieval Christian dogma believing that women, fundamentally, were 'agents of sin.' This concept originated with Saint Augustine of Hippo (4th–5th century), who before turning to God had been an unadulterated womanizer. Upon finding God, Augustine concluded that his earlier philandering was not actually his fault, but the fault of the corrupt and dangerous women who had seduced him. Citing this teaching of Saint Augustine, crusader clergy made the following happen: "After holding council, the Franks drove out the women from the army, both married and unmarried, lest they, stained by the defilement of dissipation, displease the Lord."

For purposes of better understanding this particular purification process, First Crusade historian Albert of Aachen (born circ 1100, just after the First Crusade) provided a more general and comprehensive description: "All injustice and wickedness was to be cut out from the army; no one was to cheat a Christian brother; no one was to commit theft; no one was to take part in fornication or adultery. If anyone should disobey this order, they would be subject to the most severe penalties if caught, and thus God's people would be sanctified from filth and impurity."

Peter the Hermit, of course, openly embraced the new purification campaign, preaching it from camp to camp. Having always maintained an austere existence, having never committed sins of the flesh, and insisting that God spoke to him personally and directly, he launched into one fiery sermon after another, followed around by his sycophantic sidekick of the Anatolia rescue, Peter Bartholomew. From time to time the Hermit even allowed Bartholomew to add a few of his own words here and there, as long as they paralleled his views. Peter Bartholomew relished these opportunities, even beginning to see himself as 'touched' by the Hermit, and in turn 'touched' by God.

Guillaume, too, was set afire by the purification movement because he believed that sin was the wellspring of not just the recent ill fortunes of the crusade, but the wellspring of all evil, all punishment, and all loss of eternal salvation. Probably, this should have been of little concern to Guillaume. Of anyone within the entire Army of God, he had lived the most saintly, pure and virtuous, of anyone, except for those lost days at Pelekanum.

Nonetheless, the purification campaign became his revelation. I shall fast, as I have not been fasting but only been hungry, he thought. I have been so occupied with war that since Nicaea I have given alms neither to the less fortunate crusaders nor to the Church. I shall march in liturgical procession every time the bell is rung to march. And yes, I shall in penance continue fighting for God as before, but I shall now do these other things to help further cleanse my soul!

Of everyone in the combined crusader camps, it was Tristan who rebelled against purification, not because he doubted God, but because he doubted the newly announced 'word of God' as spoken by Adhémar of Le Puy, Fulcher of Chartres, Peter the Hermit, and other zealous proponents of purification. "We are not being punished by God, we are starving because the army is so huge and foraging has been laid bare!" he insisted. "Disease is decimating our numbers because we live like swine, urinating and defecating where we eat and sleep, taking in no sustenance. The foraging train was lost by Bohemud and Robert of Flanders through the foolishness of failing to post scouts and failing to coordinate knights and infantry, not because God has thundered punishment down on us from above! Nor are fornication and the presence of women the cause of our demise. Rather, the real cause is the stupidity and greed of a handful of princes bogging us down here in an attempt to stake special claim to Antioch!"

Giving voice to such statements, naturally, raised the ire of the purifiers, Adhémar in particular. "Oh, but Saint-Germain, stop voicing opposition to the cleansing of our camps!" he railed after summoning Tristan to his tent. "Can you not see that God is angry? That sin lies at the center of our hardships and woes? Can you not see that, as the Pope's man, there are those listening to your nonsensical explanations for what is happening to God's army? Quite simply, it is being damned by the Almighty, and shall only right itself by returning to purity!"

"Returning to purity?" scoffed Tristan. "Ha, but this horde of miscreants has never been pure! Not at the beginning of this fight, nor even back in Europe before the Pope's call to arms."

"And your call to arms, Saint-Germain! Or have you completely forgotten the passion you once held for stopping Islamic aggression?"

"Yes, yes. Mea culpa, I am guilty. But I could never have anticipated the twisted direction of the Peasants' Crusade then, nor their massacre of Jews in Worms and Mainz, nor their butchery of fellow Christians in Hungry, nor their rape of Constantinople!"

"The Peasants' Crusade be damned, as it actually was in the end," retorted Adhémar, "because even the Pope vilified it. It should have never happened. No, I'm not talking about Peter the Hermit's crusade, I'm talking about the real crusade, this crusade."

"Oh, but this crusade is even worse! It's not a horde of poor superstitious fools being led by a yet greater fool, but one being led by the high princes of Europe who are behaving like barbarians not dignitaries. Baldwin's thieving Edessa, Tancred Mamistra, others anything else they come across, and Raymond, Godfrey, and Bohemud are scheming amongst themselves as to who will take Antioch!"

His anger elevating, Adhémar raised his hands and arms over his head, shaking them as beating the air. "Damn you, Saint-Germain, your own brother who's not even a cleric sees the truth of purification! What has happened to you, man? Has the devil infected your soul? Have you lost your faith?"

At this, Tristan stepped back, his own anger falling aside as, and from nowhere, calm arrived, holding him in its grip. Dropping his tone, he shook his head. "Adhémar, oh Adhémar," he sighed. "Far from losing my faith, I believe, actually to have found it. Yes, in its stark reality, in its bare truth, and in its naked but Godly glory. After all these years of dancing to the fiddler and around the fringes of faith, dragging others into my own false jig, the clouds began to part as I began to see things as they really are. God truly is God, but man is merely man. And ignorant men are weak and easily manipulated. They blindly follow the Judas goats while they feast, then vanquish, and fill their treasuries . . . even you, it now appears. And if not for yourself, Adhémar, you do it for your friend Raymond of Toulouse and his shady cohorts."

Having never in his religious existence been chastised to this level with such naked accusations, the old bishop went pallid, seeing nothing but a field of red. "Oh, Saint-Germain, but I'm done with you!" he howled. "There are those calling for your expulsion from this sacred campaign, though I have defended you. But I'm through with you as of this very day, I say! And I don't give a rat's ass how goddamn close you are to Pope Urban, we are done, you and I! Forever!"

"Really now," chortled Tristan, issuing an 'ahem,' referring not to Adhémar's 'being done with him,' but to his outburst blaspheming God's name. "In truth, I believe God means nothing to you. You, like many of our blessed brethren, are only about appearances, rituals, and frightening people, aren't you, Adhémar!"

This was not a question, but a declaration.

"Uh?" coughed Adhémar, his expression freezing, as when people are struck by the realization that the man they have been talking to is not sane at all, but completely mad.

"Oh, Adhémar, but let us stop this dance of dunces," said Tristan wearily, his own voice a distant drone. Even in the torrid heat of this dispute, he had been unable to shake images of Mala and Christophe from his head. Oh, but Lord, I ask for your heavenly mercy, he had been thinking from the beginning. I beseech you, protect them, I pray!

"Dance of dunces?!" shouted Adhémar, his head aching, thrumming like a big drum. "Oh, I've tried with you, Saint-Germain, but you've refuted my efforts, you've refuted your vows, and you've refuted the Church. A fool I was, but I now see the problem. You deny God Himself! You bathe in heresy!"

"No," replied Tristan, a rueful smile overtaking him. "No, no, and no. But in closing, then I must go say my prayers, this purification horseshit you have dumped on the troops is a sham, Adhémar, and you know it, I know it, and God knows it. May He forgive you. And I say that not as a barb, Bishop, but mean it with all my heart. Because I feel sorry for you."

"What!" shouted Adhémar, going apoplectic. "You dare call God's command horseshit?!"

Walking away calmly, Tristan uttered not a sound.

As to the actual purification of the entire crusader army, it must be remembered that rhetoric flows easily from the tongue while compliance often stumbles. Due to the very nature of the purification campaign, needless to say, hordes of crusaders blatantly broke all the rules, ending up in chains, forcefully shaved, tied to the flogging post, or even branded with hot irons! As to married or unmarried crusaders sneaking off to the shunned 'women's camp,' and as to the women, married or unmarried caught fornicating with these errant crusaders, such couples were stripped, beaten with rods, and made to walk from camp to camp; paraded in front of prospective sinners, in hopes their wounds would deter them from committing such a wicked crime.

CHAPTER FORTY-ONE

TATICIUS

Draconian purification measures may have spiritually satisfied or uplifted to a degree, giving yet another knot to tie onto the end of their ropes, but hunger, cold, homesickness, and discouragement reigned throughout January. Understandably, with no noticeable change, the rate of desertion began to rise, which actually had been an issue throughout the crusade, occurring often as a trickle instead of a current. But in light of the circumstances, crusaders began to leave in packs. By way of deceit, groups would often depart camp under the auspices of foraging, never to return.

It was the poorer elements of the Christian army that had always suffered, even from the beginning. The march through Anatolia's drought, godforsaken terrain, and scorched earth retreat of Kilij Arslan was especially brutal on the crusaders, so it was among the poor that desertion first raised its head. But Anatolia had been a tolerable time in comparison to December of 1097 and January of 1098. Subsequently, not only the poor began to desert, those with means slipped off 200-300 at a time to Cyprus or back through Armenia, intent on making their way back to France, Germany, or Italy.

Among those running from Antioch in late January, raising camp-wide scandal, were two highly visible figures within the crusade: Lord William the Carpenter of Melun and Peter the Hermit. Stunned, the Council of Princes angrily sent Bohemud's nephew, Tancred, to hunt them down, which he succeeded in doing. Disgraced and riddled with shame, both deserters pleaded for mercy, and received it, but only because both were popular among crusader rank and file. William the Carpenter was made to lay on his belly overnight in Bohemud's tent like a piece of rubbish while Peter the Hermit was simply pardoned. Both were then made to swear an oath that they would persevere the entire campaign.

Taticius, the crusade's Byzantine guide and advisor, also left Antioch, though it is doubtful whether he actually deserted. He left the majority of his belongings behind, reporting that he was going back to Asia Minor to seek supplies and Byzantine reinforcements for the Antioch siege, as promised earlier by Emperor Alexius.

Before departing camp, Taticius stopped by the Tuscan camp to see Tristan and Guillaume whom he had befriended in Constantinople well before the campaign started. "I've heard you recently raised the unforgiving fury of Bishop Adhémar over purification," he said to Tristan. "Be wary, my friend, he stands firmly with your enemies on the Council of Princes. Best keep an eye over your shoulder, and maybe silence your objections, for a time at least."

"I shall," Tristan replied, embracing him, "keep an eye over my shoulder, I mean. But now is not the time for silence, Taticius." Stepping back, he then gave the Byzantine commander a long look of manly appreciation, respectively. Taticius was tall and muscular as an ox, his posture as erect as a shaft of wheat whether sitting or standing. He was handsome in a way, too, except for the bizarre tin fixture concealing his severed nose. Many crusaders considered the tin attachment hideous, devilish, even though it gave this already imposing figure of a man an ominous, formidable, almost frightening look. But then there was his voice. Notwithstanding, Taticius had the speed and agility of a cat, both bodily and with all assortments of weaponry, and he feared no one.

"Aye, we shall miss you," said Guillaume, slapping Taticius across the shoulders. "Travel in safety for you've a long journey, there and back."

Extending his hand in a farewell exchange to the two brothers, Taticius shook his head. "This siege is doomed at the moment," he said, "and we three know it. But perhaps, just perhaps, should I return with adequate reinforcements and supplies in time, the tide can be turned and you two can finally make you way to Jerusalem to complete the real objective of this crusade, Jerusalem. A happy day, that, when and if it ever comes to fruition."

"A happy day, certainly," agreed Guillaume. "And don't worry about Tristan, Taticius. I'll keep an eye to my brother's back. Rest assured, before I'd allow harm to come to him, they'd have to make their way through me."

"Ho," laughed Taticius, "and a hell of a task that'd be, I wager! But here, I must be on my way. Before leaving I simply wished to let you know, both of you, that I think much of you. Thank you for your friendship. All the others turned away. I know it hasn't been easy, but you've stood firm as rock. In any case, know I'm glad to be leaving for a while. I need a blast of fresh air after a year of bullshit with the Council."

"Agreed," smiled Tristan. "But hurry back. We need you here, Taticius, not only as a guide, but a voice of wisdom."

"I'll not dally," said Taticius, leaving, "and I'll be back sooner than you think!"

But that, unbeknownst to Tristan and Guillaume, and perhaps even Taticius, was the last time the Saint-Germain brothers would ever see him. Taticius never came back, even though, most likely, he intended to. Unforeseen circumstances would intervene.

Most of the crusader princes failed to see it that way. Even after having forgiven William the Carpenter and Peter the Hermit for desertion, as time elapsed and Taticius remained absent, the princes branded Taticius a traitor. As recorded by Raymond of Toulouse's chaplain: "Under the pretense of joining the army of Alexius, Taticius broke camp, abandoned his followers, and left with God's curse. By this dastardly deed, he brought eternal shame to himself and his men."

Surprisingly, as regards desertion, there is evidence that even Bohemud threatened to abandon the crusade. Raymond of Toulouse's chaplain, who held Taticius and Bohemud in equally low regard, later recorded cross words about Bohemud's prospective desertion: "Bohemud threatened to depart because of the suffering of his troops and his own poverty. We learnt afterwards that he made these statements because ambition drove him to covet Antioch, and noted that in order to maintain crusader unity, all the princes, with the exception of Raymond of Toulouse, offered Antioch to Bohemud in the event it was captured. So, with this pact, Bohemud and the other princes took an oath they would not abandon the siege of Antioch for seven years, unless it fell sooner."

CHAPTER FORTY-TWO

HOPE FADES

January proved to be the darkest days of the crusade since its inception, and hope became the sparsest of all commodities, even outdistancing starvation, disease, the weather, and the Turks. As vividly recorded by one of Bohemud's followers, enduring this bleak period, sheer desolation and despair infected the Christian camps: "We were thus left in direst need. The Turks were menacing us on the one hand and hunger tormented us on the other, and there was no one to help us or bring us aid. The rank and file, along with those very poor, fled to Cyprus, Asia Minor, or into the mountains. We dared not go down to the sea for fear of those brutes of Turks, and there was no road open to us anywhere."

In light of the crusade's deterioration, the Greek patriarch of Jerusalem exiled in Cyprus, Simeon, and Bishop Adhémar together sent another plea to Western Europe: "Come to fight in the Army of the Lord. Bring nothing with you except what may be of need to us. Let only the men come. Let the women, as yet, be left. From the home in which there are two, let the one more ready for battle come."

Adhémar went so far as to goad those who had taken a crusading vow but had not left Europe, even with the threat of 'excommunication.' A revealing sign of his desperation was his bending of the truth. Disregarding the real extent of crusader suffering in Antioch, he declared for all to hear that the Holy Land 'flowed with milk and honey' and 'the hardest part of the campaign was over.' What of virtue, truth, and the word of God?! When the trumpet of need begins to wail, apparently, he felt it was not against the commandments to falsely lure men to their death in the name of the Lord.

During the daily January skirmishes between Turks and crusaders, Godfrey's camp repulsed an especially vicious attack that had come, as had many before, through the Bridge Gate and over the fortified Turkish bridge. The Germans were ready, however, and, in the process of breaking up the attack, captured five prisoners. One in particular was finely dressed in exotically fashioned fabrics, wore a heavily bejeweled sash, and possessed finely crafted weapons that must have cost a small fortune. When the captives were brought before Godfrey, he ordered his men to have all of them dispatched on the spot save the well-dressed captive. "Spare this man for the moment," said Godfrey, having watched the man's reaction to the execution of fellow ghazis. He'd bawled as a child, and by the time the third head was severed, began to vomit uncontrollably, sending him into spasms of gagging.

"But why spare him?" asked Godfrey's captain. "He's a coward. Chrissakes, look there how frightened he is, not like these other dark, heartless bastards we run into!"

"I have been looking, Captain. Now you take a look. But a better look this time."

Impatient to have the heathen's head, the captain took a perfunctory look at the quaking Turk, scowling. To him the prisoner's demeanor had turned girlish and sickening. "Poor bastard's about to piss himself!" he remarked.

Godfrey explained, "This fellow carried himself in here with dignity, dressed as a prince, until heads began to drop. Don't you marvel at the elegance of his garb? And seeing the softness of his face and hands, I wager my balls he's lived an extremely pampered existence. Look, too, how immaculately he's coiffed, and how perfectly shaved his beard appears."

"Wonderful, he'll go to Hell immaculately coiffed!"

"Ha! Maybe!" Godfrey laughed, then his demeanor changed drastically. "Hurry! Go and fetch me one of those Armenians that can interpret this man's language. We must find out all we can about him."

The captain complied, having no earthly idea what was on Godfrey's mind.

A half an hour of questioning had passed before the young Turk divulged that he came from one of the wealthiest families in Antioch, as well as of all Syria. "And," he said, "yes, I am a Seljuk prince. I've been blessed in my upbringing and station, and I would most certainly wish to continue enjoying those blessing at any price."

"Any price?" asked Godfrey, smirking at the interpreter.

The Turk explained via the interpreter, "My father is extremely elderly and ill, not expected to live beyond winter. On his death, I shall inherit the entire family fortune. You see, this is not a good time for me to die!"

"Do you have other family?" asked Godfrey.

"Yes," came the reply, "a loving mother, two sisters, and two grandmothers. And they shall need me desperately once my father passes, don't you see?"

"Yes, of course," replied Godfrey, performing calculations in his head. "And I'm certain your family would be happy to pay handsomely for your release, no?"

As the interpreter relayed this question, the young Turk's face lit up such that Godfrey had no need for translation.

"One more question," said Godfrey, "ask him if he has any other relatives within Yaghi Siyan's army."

Another brief exchange with the prince, and the Armenian turned to Godfrey, saying, "Yes, one uncle's a general under Yaghi Siyan, General Ahmet, another commands the very battalion in which this young fellow serves, and a third uncle's a high officer in command of one of the rampart towers."

Dammit, I was right! gloated Godfrey, content that he alone had spotted the Turk's worth and was about to recoup much of the money the crusade had cost him.

At sunrise, Godfrey sent the Armenian interpreter to the Bridge Gate under banner of truce to contact the prince's relations. On learning what the Armenian had to say, the elderly father signaled to servants to shutter the windows and lock the door. He did not wish for the secret negotiations he was about to begin with Godfrey of Bouillon to become common knowledge. Taking a risk, he even kept this information from Yaghi Siyan, although he and Siyan had at one time been close acquaintances. As often happens, commercial rivalry and competing success had soured that once amicable relationship.

As a result, a series of clandestine exchanges with Godfrey initially demanding an exorbitant ransom, which with time the family agreed to pay. Had Godfrey closed the bargain at this moment, he would have become a rich man, but the hunger of greed is insatiable. The longer Godfrey dwelled on the trade, the more he began to see an even greater reward. He started to obsess about the prince's third uncle commanding one of the city towers. Should I be given access to a single tower? I could lead the charge over the walls and stake my banner to Antioch, claiming the lion's share of the city. And though I've already pledged the city to Bohemud, my banner carries more weight than paper!

The prince's family balked at Godfrey's new demand for access to a city tower, but did not rule it out of the question. But since the stakes were high, they counter-demanded time to consider. Meanwhile, the unexplained travels of the Armenian through the Bridge began to raise questions in certain quarters. Fate, fueled by Godfrey's greed, drove a spike into the conspiracy as Yaghi Siyan, uncovering the plot at the eleventh hour, swiftly ordered the execution of the prince's elderly father, who already nested in his death bed. To further secure Antioch, Siyan relieved the prince's third uncle from his command of a city tower and had him executed as well; the man having, in actuality, neither known nor even been informed of the plot. As to General Ahmet, Siyan took no action, convinced that Ahmet was not complicit in any of these underground negotiations with the Godfrey.

Infuriated, Godfrey decided it best to at least reveal to Raymond and Bohemud his ransom scheme, making no mention of the part involving trying to get access to the tower. In response, the Council of Princes began torturing the Turkish prince for three days. On the fourth day, the captive, barely clinging to life, was dragged before the walls of Antioch, displayed for all within to witness. His hands and feet bound, given no blindfold, in order that he and the women of his family could see each other, pleading for clemency, he was then kicked to his knees and instructed to lean forward, baring his neck. Wishing to drag things out for as long as possible, and making pure theater of the execution, the Christians took an inordinate amount of time getting to the final stage.

Following much cruel laughing and jeering by mobs of cheering crusaders belittling the prisoner's female relation's sobbing and begging atop the ramparts, an axe-man stepped from their midst. Huge in size, massive and muscled in girth, the shirtless but black-hooded German walked to the side of the prisoner with heavy steps, ensuring his approach was heard, carrying an enormous twenty-pound broadax attached to a four-foot oak handle.

Unexpectedly and slowly, as performing a ritual, he removed his hood. Then, glaring with hate at his Turkish audience, he thundered, "Oh, I remove this mask because I want you to know who I am! Aye, and remember this face, you black heathens! Look for me during your attacks! Seek me out, I say! I don't fear you godless savages! And when we breach Antioch, remember but one thing, I'll be coming after you, your children, your wives, and your imams!"

Those lining the ramparts understood not a word of what the German had bellowed, yet the horrid shadow of his presence alone conveyed much of his message.

Extending his thickly muscled arms, he raised the axe high over his shoulders, its blade hovering seven feet directly over his own head. As the iron razor dropped, a gasp issued from the walls followed by a sudden pall as the head separated from shoulders in a blink, tumbling to the sand. In that same instant, a roar arose from tens of thousands of crusader spectators standing in the distance, and at the same time, the city walls erupted into grievous screams, weeping, and mewling.

In the grand scheme of things, this spectacle was but a moment in time that accomplished absolutely nothing for the Christians other than providing an ever-needed but brief spate of retribution in exchange for their own months of suffering, anguish, and mounting hopelessness.

The execution aside, another snake raised its head. This initial secret negotiation with a Turkish presence within the walls exposed for the first time a hairline crack in the mighty city's defenses—betrayal from within.

CHAPTER FORTY-THREE

BENITO, MALA, KARINE

Hiding in the private palace quarters of Firuz's children, Mala's face slowly began to heal, yet her broken nose would forever betray a remnant of Malik's violence; the very bridge of it taking on a flection, not remarkable but noticeable. Also, the violet of her facial and arm bruises had begun to pale and her broken cheek bone had reformed itself nicely, but her forearm emitted a nagging, throbbing pain where he had forcefully yanked her. Even Malik's brutal assault could not permanently mar her natural beauty. On the mend, if nothing else, the changes gave her reblossoming face an added hint of character.

It was then and there Mala rediscovered hope, thinking Christophe would indeed survive and that they may, by the grace of God, lay eyes on Tristan once again before going to be with their Heavenly Father. Finding comfort in this, she explained to Benito, for the first time, her actual relationship with Bishop Saint-Germain, the history of it, and its current state. "In the wake of everything he and I have endured, years of hardships and separation," she explained in private, "I was on my way to see him in the crusader camp when Christophe and I were taken."

Her story shocked Benito guiltily to the core. He'd always suspected the young bishop of high crimes, to include murder of a mistress and her illegitimate child as a means of avoiding Church scandal and securing his rise up the Vatican hierarchy. "Oh, but Signorina," he apologized, "I testified against him during his trial by Tafur, DuLac, and the Peasants' Crusade at Civetot. Had it not been for the Turks arriving when they did, we would have hung him! I thought surely he'd been killed along with all the others by the Turks as they overran Civetot."

"Oh, he would have perished for certain," replied Mala, "if not for the courage of a young fellow named Innocenzo who sprung him from his cell at the last minute."

Hearing this name, Benito went cold. "In-nocenzo?" he stammered, faltering as his eyes turned to glass.

"Yes, Innocenzo," said Mala, seeing Benito's shoulder drop. "He was the young nephew of Peter the Hermit. Did you know him, by chance?"

"I-I did," said Benito, his memory digging deep, unearthing things. "And I loved him . . . dearly." Collecting a look of hope, he asked, "But then, like Bishop Saint-Germain, Innocenzo lives?"

"No. On retreating toward the fort of Nicodemia he was slain trying to help Tristan. All agreed that Innocenzo died a hero."

"I see," said Benito, dropping his head into his palms, choking back his sorrow. "Yes, I loved Innocenzo, a-and Innocenzo loved m-me."

Not understanding the full context of Benitos's words, Mala reached over to console him. "Oh, Benito, I'm so sorry to be the one to break such sad news," she said sadly. "I had no idea you two were close."

In saying this, she pulled her tunic low and latched a hungry Christophe to an exposed breast. Being less than six months old, Christophe's world, beneath the specter of impossibility lurking over him, consisted of suckling and sleeping. Since his relocation, he had shown nothing but contentment in the comforting arms of his mother . . . and Karine, who had developed the habit of doting on him, but at the same time did her best to provide consolation to Garik.

As to be expected, Garik's newfound surroundings and occasional summonses from Yaghi Siyan served only to unsettle him, but not half as much as the little blue man who, from time to time, popped in unannounced to check on the woman and baby. He also, at least to Garik, appeared to be checking on him and Karine, as though they were beneath his care, not that of Yaghi Siyan.

Nevertheless, Garik thought Ben-fazi unnatural, not of human breeding. In trying to figure him out, Garik turned to his limited exposure to the Koran's concept of the 'jinns.' These separate beings created from smokeless fire, who like humans could be good or bad (bad jinns being related to demons) but possess free will, unlike angels. Although Garik had been told that jinns were invisible, supposedly, and had limited access to the human world as governed by Allah, he decided that Ben-fazi was indeed a jinn, probably bad, that had broken restrictions put onto other jinns. In any case, whenever Ben-fazi arrived, Garik would go into another room, often peeking around the corner to investigate for magic.

During this period, Yaghi Siyan took immense pleasure in calling the two children to the palace hall; at times even inviting them to his living quarters where he shared conversation for hours at a time, often having them sit on his lap, caressing their hair, shoulders, and arms as one fawning over favored pets. The two beautiful siblings provided him a desired distraction from the war being waged beyond the city's walls.

Yaghi Siyan particularly enjoyed walking Karine and Garik through his fabled gardens where he housed his prized collection of exotic beasts from Africa and Asia, explaining in detail the instincts, behaviors, and feeding habits of his most beloved acquisitions, especially the large feline carnivores—lions, panthers, leopards and tigers. "You know," he would laugh, "many claim that I, myself, resemble a cat because of my hair, whiskers, and beard! But I think they mean an old fat one lying sideways on his haunches, not likely a panther or leopard!"

His new 'pets' gave him a deeper emotional satisfaction, a respite from death and destruction.

Karine enjoyed every aspect of residing in the palace, indulging in all its benefits and nuances, yet elicited not one iota of emotion, which was odd to all who encountered her. But Garik's incapacity to shed any anxiety over separation from their mother, a normal behavior to the children, baffled them. As a substitute, a surrogate of sorts, he accepted—no, he allowed his sister's indulgent care since she had been doing this for as long as he could remember. And, as young as they were, neither Karine nor Garik, either one, ever gave their missing father a second thought. No concerns. No questions. Nothing.

As days turned into weeks, Ben-fazi's clandestine housing of Mala and Christophe remained a secret, but such a secret could not hold indefinitely. A constant stream of servants, concubine, guests, and guards circulated daily within the confines of the palace, where tongues wagged freely. He had ordered extra locks put on the apartment entrance from inside and had prohibited servants from entering the apartment, as approved by Yaghi Siyan earlier. To further secure matters, Ben-fazi insisted that Karine and Garik keep the entrance to their apartment locked at all times, and should a knock arrive at their door, that Mala take Christophe to seek cover in the storage compartment that he'd cleverly constructed as a point of concealment within Karine's bedroom.

Despite these precautions, Ben-fazi could never quite get a handle on whether to completely trust the children. Garik's anxiety posed its own problems, but it was Karine who concerned him the most. Whereas it was undeniable that she adored baby Christophe, Karine appeared ambiguous about la Signorina herself. But then, Ben-fazi's depth of understanding the unusual girl, or any girl for that matter, was, well, shallow.

Ben-fazi was, of course, keenly aware of the fine line he was walking by taking on la Signorina, as well as the precarious situation he had created for Boros. Not only had Boros colluded with him about the fake order releasing Mala to the palace, he had done far worse by claiming to the guards that 'the woman' had been returned by Ben-fazi during the middle of that same night she had been taken. Refusing to trespass beyond Malik's so-called 'no-pass' line for fear of losing their immense pot of bribe money, the crooked guards took Boros' word, believing that 'the woman' was back in her cell, being tended to like the young girls, by Boros. And Boros pretended exactly as such, knowing full well the dire consequences.

Ben-fazi dreaded the inevitability of Malik's recovery; that he would avenge himself, making a bee-line for the prison only to discover his intended prey had escaped. Even beyond that, Ben-fazi knew the guards would quickly rat him and Boros out and that Malik would then report this subterfuge to the emir, even though he'd hidden young female captives for his pleasure without informing either General Ahmet or Yaghi Siyan.

In the end, regardless of Siyan's fascination and odd affection for his little blue man, Ben-fazi would suffer mercilessly from the wrath incurred by Yaghi Siyan's greatest single weakness: his expectation of blind, inviolable loyalty from the tiny number of people he trusted—first his sons, followed by his favorite and now elderly first wife, then Ben-fazi.

Clever and perceptive, Siyan, having mastered the game of survival, climbing over the schemes and bones of others, clearly understood his tenuous position in the 'real' world; that he was roundly ridiculed and disliked behind his back by his ministers, his military garrisons, the envious, his Seljuk neighbors, and everyone else on this earth whose intolerance demanded loathing anyone looking different, thinking different, or diverging in any way from the deeply rutted track of 'common expectations.' Actually, he even accepted this lonely reality. To him, there was but one dam blocking the flood raging against himself, and that was the unquestionable loyalty of his 'few.'

Knowing all this, Ben-fazi betrayed Yaghi Siyan to save la Signorina and her infant, not simply due to her having been good to him in Italy or the fact that he had always adored her, but because in his heart and mind, God now demanded it.

Nor did Ben-fazi consider his change of allegiance an act of treason. Being clever and uniquely like-minded to Yaghi Siyan, Ben-fazi had accepted his frail position handed to him at birth. He may be under Yaghi Siyan's protective wing at this time, but Ben-fazi existed merely as a temporary amusement, a slave whose entire continuance depended on Yaghi Siyan's whim. No, he had decided, if I must count on the whim of another to continue breathing, it shall then be by God's whim alone that I live or die.

In spite of Yaghi Siyan's order to cease delivering scraps to Christian prisoners, Ben-fazi stopped by on his own to visit Boros, primarily to remain posted on Malik's recovery. But one day, Ben-fazi received an unusual message from Boros, asking him to come quickly.

"And so, Boros," asked Ben-fazi, having slipped from the palace, "what is it? News about Malik? Is he moving about yet?"

"No, thankfully not," replied Boros. "But here's the latest, he's completely blind in one eye. The eyeball itself was sliced completely in half, come to find out, and they had to pull it. Yeah, they spooned the damn thing completely out just this week! Then too, of course, he's in a rage about what else he's now missing."

Hearing this, Ben-fazi winced. "Oh, but there'll be hell to pay, Boros."

"I know," agreed Boros shakily, "been thinking the same, which is why I sent for you. I've made arrangements to leave Antioch tonight. I want you to come with me."

"What? Tonight? But I've nowhere to go, Boros. But yes, by all means, you should get out tonight if you can."

"Look, I've been talking to my friend, Firuz, this past week. I've explained things and he said—"

"Shit!" interrupted Ben-fazi, alarmed. "You didn't tell him about la Signorina did you?!"

"No, no. Calm down. I gave him a different story but with the same aim in mind, getting you and me the hell out of here! Anyway, as captain of a guard tower, he said he'd help, though he didn't understand why you'd wish to leave." Here Boros raised his shoulders. "Firuz is none too keen on you, you know."

"I know."

"It's his kids. Can't blame a fellow who's had his kids taken from him. God only knows what that pervert Siyan's doing to those poor children . . . sexually, I mean."

"It's not how you think," sighed Ben-fazi. "I tried to explain that to Firuz the day I was sent to fetch them; that I wasn't his enemy; that I'd keep an eye to his children, but he shut me out."

"Damn right! So would I after everything that happened to him that day. His kids were taken, and that slut of a young wife he married! Ugh!"

"I know, I know." Ben-fazi nodded in benevolence. "How's Firuz doing, by the way?"

"Not worth a damn. Bad as things were back then, he had his ironworks operation hi-jacked, too."

"What?"

"Yeah, Yaghi Siyan, yet again. And just so you know, Firuz thinks you're complicit in it all, which is why he's none too happy helping you get out of the city. It confused him. He hates you."

"I can't help that. He doesn't understand, that's all!"

"Never mind all that. I explained to him what you've done for the prisoners and that you're a good Christian beneath that paint. Because Firuz and I have always been best friends, he's promised to help us both escape tonight. Damn Antioch, the Persian, Yaghi Siyan, and all this other horseshit scaring us and holding us down. It'll be good to get out!"

Ben-fazi shook his head. "I'm not going, Boros."

"But why not? Chrissakes! It'll be too late if we ass around much longer."

"I'm not leaving."

"What's here for you but a noose or the head of an ax?"

"I can't leave. I just can't."

Stepping back, Boros shook his forefinger at him. "It's that woman," he said, "and her baby, isn't it?"

Ben-fazi remained silent.

"Dammit, Ben-fazi, you've done everything for them short of putting your damn head on the block, and that, my little friend, is shortly about to happen anyway. Come with me, I say. You've done more than anyone else would have. Where the hell is she, anyway?"

Ben-fazi had refused to give Boros any details after taking her from the cell, not because he distrusted Boros, but in case Boros were to be caught and tortured. "She's in hiding. Let's leave it at that."

"That's fine," replied Boros, understanding. "But dammit, come with me tonight. Firuz'll slip us down on a rope and we'll be on our way."

But Ben-fazi shook his head, making Boros realize he would not budge.

"I'd say we could try to take the woman and baby along, but dammit, we'd attract too much damned attention on the ramparts. Hell, we could give it a shot though, I suppose. Neither of us has family or such. Why not?"

"No, things are shaky enough for them without going further out on the branch. One or two might make it down the rope in time, but four? Never. Especially an infant and a woman. Besides, Boros, things have gone well thus far, maybe fortune will hold."

"Not for long, my friend. When the Persian comes, it'll be over for you, for them."

"No," insisted Ben-fazi. "Not for them, at least. I'll never tell where they're hiding."

"They'll torture it out of you, Ben-fazi, whether by fire and rod, clipping your toes and fingers off one by one, or taking ear, nose, and tongue."

"I'll never give her up, ever," said Ben-fazi, his face tightening.

Looking at him, Boros gave up. "Damn. You love that woman, don't you?"

"Oh, but Boros, of course I do," replied Ben-fazi, his expression going awry. "But not in the way you suspect, which is always the worst, damn you. Look, she was the one person who had ever made me feel valued and professional, through all my other shit. Oh yes, I love her Boros, more than life itself, which in truth, for those like me, has scarcely been worth living from the start."

"I see," nodded Boros, knowing he really did not. The suffering of those living in such shoes as Ben-fazi's can be observed by others, but never felt, nor completely understood. "God be with you then, my friend. And when I reach the other side, I'll ask that a special mass be said for you."

"Thank you, Boros. You're a decent man, and you've been a good friend. Do one more thing for me, if you would?"

"Sure, Ben-fazi, anything."

"When you make it into the crusader camp, seek out a bishop there. His name is Tristan de Saint-Germain. Tell him who you are and that la Signorina was captured and brought into Antioch. Tell him what happened and that she's hurt, but that she and the baby are all right; that they're in hiding. He needs to know these things, Boros. He probably thinks they're both already dead. Will you do that for me, Boros, the last thing I will ever ask of you? And for la Signorina?"

"You can count on it," said Boros, patting him on his back. "And God speed, my friend. I'll miss you, dammit."

As dusk slipped into night and darkness overtook the city, Boros made his way toward the Tower of Two Sisters, the silhouette of which to Boros suddenly resembled a great scaffold awaiting its next victim. He was shaking a bit, knowing that those not in military uniform were not allowed to mount tower steps at night. Nonetheless, his faith in Firuz held firm.

Feigning the confidence of one on official business, he presented himself before two guards manning the tower approach. "Firuz has summoned me," he said, struggling against his nerves. "Something about a fissure that's developing along the south wall of his tower."

"Fissure?" questioned the guard. "But hold there, aren't you Boros, the jailer? What damned need would Firuz have of a jailer?"

"Yeah, I'm a jailer," said Boros, doing his best to act offended, "and long before you Turks arrived, I was the head-jailor here for nearly twenty years. As such, I oversaw all construction and repairs. But since you appear so damn curious, know that prior to that I was a stone mason, in the footsteps of my father and his father before him. But if you know all about stone and mortar, I'll turn around and make my way home to bed. It's been a long day already and I'll happily—"

"Amah, go on up then," said the guard, lacking all interest in Boros' past. "You'll find Firuz manning the tower entrance."

Arriving there, Boros found Firuz as told. "Dammit," hissed Firuz, "you're early, Boros."

"Hell yes," Boros whispered, trying to be silent and invisible. "I got word the Persian's up. Hasn't been able to talk for weeks since part of his damned vocal chords, larynx, or some other shit got cut along with his face and cock. Anyway, he's talking, kind of, anyway, and started asking right off about the woman that cut him. Hearing that, I ran and came your way."

"I see," said Firuz quietly, understanding. "I'll hide you inside the tower and keep you out of view until midnight when the rampart shifts are at half-count. There's a hidey-hole in the armory next to my overnight quarters. You'll be safe there. I'll fetch you before the count of the third toll . . . should all go according to plan. If I do not come, stay put."

For what felt like an eternity, Boris sat squatting within a small concealed break in the armory wall, until he felt himself nodding off. That is when the wall shuddered and the first deep knell of the midnight-bell vibrated from the adjacent tower. DONG! This knell was followed by five seconds of vibrating echo before the second. DONG! As the echo of that knell dissipated, Firuz shoved aside the trunk disguising the opening to Boros' cramped nest, and pulled him out. DONG!

"I've secured the rope to one of the ballista cleats," said Firuz, keeping his voice down. "All's ready. But no time to fool around, be quick!"

But as Boros squirmed out of his hole, he was shaking uncontrollably, wiping beads of cold sweat from his forehead and upper lip with the back of his hand. DONG!

"What's wrong, Boros?"

Boros whispered, rubbing his palms on his britches, "I've been thinking, it's a long damn way down that wall! You sure the rope's gonna hold? If it breaks, I'm a dead man."

"Yes, it'll hold. Christ alive, Boros! What wrong all of a sudden?" DONG!

"I-I'm scared shitless of heights, Firuz!"

"Damn fine time to tell me that!" complained Firuz in a hushed voice. "We've been talking about this for days and you haven't said a thing about heights!"

"Didn't really think about it because I was more scared of the Persian," hissed Boros. "But climbing up the rampart to get here and looking down into the darkness, I couldn't see the bottom! It's a long way, Firuz! What if I fall or the rope gives out?" DONG!

"Look, it's either go or stay, Boros. I've taken a big a risk for you. You're the only friend I have in this damned place, but I'll not push my luck, nor yours. What's it going to be?"

"I'll go," sighed Boros, having made up his mind. Falling to my death is better than facing Malik.

"Good," agreed Firuz, taking him outside to the wall and helping him mount the rampart. "Be careful," Firuz insisted, "and slide down quick as you can. At the count of twenty, I'll start pulling the rope back up. Understand?" DONG!

"Y-yes," said Boros, clenching the rope with white-knuckled dread, edging his feet over the wall.

"This is crucial, Boros, listen," said Firuz. "When you make it out, go to the camp of a man named Bohemud who's from Italy. Mention my name. Tell him I'm the Armenian tower commander who converted to Islam. He should remember me, I think, as he was surprised to find an Armenian along the ramparts. He can communicate with me here at this tower by note. I'll have a string hanging from this very spot, dropping all the way to the ground. He'll be able to tie a note to it under cover of darkness if he chooses to respond. To not attract undue attention, I'll check the string but once a week, every Sunday at midnight." DONG!

"For sure," replied Boros, hesitating, his attention fully focused on his feet, dangling straight down the upper edge of the rampart. "Oh, Christ but that's a long drop!" he murmured. DONG!

"Dammit, Boros, were you listening to me?"

"Yes, a Bohemian from Italy," quaked Boros.

"No dammit! A man named Bohemud, from Italy!" Firuz hissed, trying desperately not to be detected. DONG!

"Oh shit!" quietly wailed Boros. "I'm sl-slipping!"

"No, you're fine!" exhorted Firuz. "You're just sliding, and that's what's supposed to happen, Boros. Ease off on the rope and let yourself slide down. Quick! Get going! I've already begun counting! And remember, a man named Bohemud from Italy."

At that, Boros disappeared from sight. As Firuz stared at the base of the wall counting to twenty, he thought to see a shadow scrambling away toward the nearby tree-line. Then again, darkness plays phantom-movement tricks at night. Firuz peered hard but could not be certain it was Boros. DONG!

Be safe if that's you, my friend, thought Firuz, a measure of regret seeping into his heart. And dammit, perhaps I should have joined you!

DONG!

CHAPTER FORTY-FOUR

BOROS

Boros' point of descent down the wall by the Tower of Two Sisters placed him at the far southern edge of Antioch, which put him the greatest distance possible from the crusader camps, let alone that of Bohemud camped at the extreme northern quadrant of the blockade near the Saint Paul Gate. Worse, the only place to cross the Orontes river was a full kilometer downstream at the fortified bridge leading to the Bridge Gate. Downstream, in this case, was actually north, not south, because the Orontes originated in Lebanon and flowed northward before emptying into the Mediterranean Sea.

Making his way to the river, he followed its banks north trying to figure out how to get across the fortified bridge, it being heavily guarded by Turks. He was tempted to turn about, follow the river south without crossing it, and be on his way, but Boros was like a faithful old hound refusing to abandon his watch. He had promised Firuz that he would find the man called Bohemud and relay Firuz's message, for whatever purpose that might serve. Firuz had not divulged any details to Boros, other than what was said on the wall, so Boros had no idea why Firuz and the man named Bohemud would be communicating. In addition, Boros had promised Ben-fazi that he would locate the bishop named Saint-Germain to advise him about the woman and child.

Arriving near the fortified bridge, he sat for over an hour trying to determine his best course for getting across the river. Devising a plan, he waded waist deep into the river, crouching to maintain a low profile, and quietly made his way beneath the bridge at the point where its footings had been sunk into the banks of the Antioch side of the bridge. Though the only light afforded him was that of moon and stars, he gazed intently at the sub-structure of the bridge trying to figure out its design. Weighing his odds, he decided he might be able to monkey-climb his way forward by clinging to the framing struts in an upside-down position, inching himself forward. It would require a bit of courage and perseverance, but Boros saw no other alternative.

In all, the crossing took Boros nearly two painstaking hours of strain and exertion, and by the time he dropped to the opposite bank, he was spent. Sleeping through dawn and all that next day in the shadows of the bridge, he did not awaken until dusk. Having no specific idea where the crusader camps were located, he followed the river further north, in the pitch dark, until discovering what appeared to be a makeshift bridge formed of flatboats. Scared shitless of what both sides might do to him, he wandered about for another half an hour until spotting campfires and hearing foreign voices. Taking a deep breath of courage, he stepped into the outer edge of the camp's firelight. He had found Godfrey of Bouillon and the Germans.

"Bohemud! I'm looking for the man, Bohemud of Italy!" he shouted in Armenian as a swarm of Germans surrounded him, poking him with lances.

His pronunciation of 'Bohemud,' distorted as it was to the Germans, finally registered with a German knight standing nearby. "Hold there, back off you men!" shouted the knight. "This fellow's looking for Bohemud!" Stepping near, the knight pulled Boros by an arm. "Come with me," he said, mounting a horse, dragging Boros onto the saddle behind him.

Shortly, Boros was being presented to Bohemud who called immediately for one of his Armenian interpreters. After a brief but lively exchange with Boros, the interpreter turned to Bohemud and whispered, "Best you tell the German to leave, and anyone else within earshot except perhaps your nephew, Tancred, over there. This man just escaped Antioch last night. Seems he's come with a message for you from inside the city, but I don't believe you'd want word to get around about it."

"Tancred! To my tent!" said Bohemud, needing no urging. Then to the interpreter he said, "Bring the Armenian along and we'll talk in private."

That's how Bohemud and Tancred learned of Firuz, the disgruntled armormaker who had lost his trade, his wife, and his children to the Turks. As they finished speaking, Bohemud went to his trunk, withdrew a fistful of gold bezants, and told the interpreter, "Thank this man for coming to me and that the gold is his, but only if he gets as far away from Antioch as he can without ever mentioning Firuz, the Tower of Two Sisters, or me. And to speed things along, fetch him a ride so he can make tracks out of here."

Hearing the translation, Boros nodded with a smile, accepted the coins, and followed the interpreter to a mule.

As they were leaving, Bohemud said, "Tancred, tell no one of tonight's encounter. It's entirely possible that this could lead to me flying my banner over the ramparts and laying claim to Antioch."

"Certainly," agreed his nephew, "but we'd best be damn careful. The Tower of Two Sisters lies well south beyond our perimeter and under Turkish control. How might we know whether or not this is just a trick to lure us into an ambush at the bottom of the wall?"

"We can't know for certain, but the information is worth serious consideration. We'll say and do nothing for now, but as things develop and change, we'll probe about a bit; see which way the wind blows."

Though Boros had agreed to make a hasty departure from the crusader enclave, on his way out of camp, he inquired about the whereabouts of Bishop Saint-Germain. Just as he had kept his word to Firuz, he intended to be equally faithful to Ben-fazi. Coming across one of the many Antioch Armenians settled in the camps, he found a man who knew the bishop. "He's just beyond that second campfire down the line," pointed the man. "Follow me, I'll take you there."

Though it was late, they found Tristan seated alone by a campfire near his tent. The man assisting Boros happened to speak Latin, so he provided a brief introduction and turned to leave. Having dismounted, Boros stood holding the reins, listening intently. "Just as I don't speak French, nor do I speak Latin," objected Boros, pulling him back by an arm. "Please stay and help here, sir, for what I've got to say will be important to this man."

"Certainly," nodded the Armenian, taking a seat on the same log occupied by Tristan. Cautiously and respectively, Boros remained near his mule.

"Tell him," said Boros, "that his wife and child are alive and well. They're being hidden within Antioch, I do not know where, by a good little fellow named Ben-fazi. Oddly, he's painted blue and serves as companion and counselor to Yaghi Siyan."

As the Armenian translated, Boros was pleased at the effect his words had on the bishop. It was as if he had been instantly revived, transforming from what appeared to be a state of morose apathy to a state of jubilation.

"Oh, but praise God!" blurted Tristan, falling to his knees with clasped hands, feverishly reciting the Pater Noster as tears began to stream in rivulets down his cheeks. Even at that, his face then collapsed a bit and he began speaking quickly to the man translating.

"He wishes to know," said the Armenian, "that since his family is being helped by a member of Yaghi Siyan's court, is Yaghi Siyan involved in protecting his wife and child?"

"No," replied Boros. "Siyan knows nothing about them. If he did, they'd be executed like many other Christians in the city. It's entirely the blue man, Ben-fazi, hiding her, knowing his head could be next on the block. He's vowed, if need be, to even surrender himself to protect them both."

"But why? Who is he?" asked the Armenian. "The bishop will surely want to know."

"He's Yaghi Siyan's slave, a captured Christian actually, who, because of his deformities, has become an addition to Yaghi Siyan's collection."

"Collection?" echoed the Armenian.

"It's a long, twisted story that makes little sense to those of sound mind," said Boros. "Yaghi Siyan collects things, like flowers and plants from other continents, beasts from southern Africa and such, and people, too. In any case, I have to go. Simply tell the bishop that his wife and child are now in good hands, at least as long as their location remains undiscovered."

"But what is their location?"

"Awww," shrugged Boros, "now that I don't know. The blue man never told me."

As the two Armenians spoke between themselves, Tristan grew anxious. "What is he saying?!" he urgently enquired of the translator.

Turning, the Armenian explained as Boros began to climb upon his newly gifted mule. But Tristan rushed to him, throwing his arms about the man. "Oh, but thank you for coming to me, kind sir!" he sobbed. "May God bless you for all of your coming years!"

"Yes, yes, you are most welcome!" smiled Boros, needing no translation for what the bishop was emoting. "God be with you in these terrible times, my dear bishop, and may He keep your wife and child safe, as well as my little friend, Ben-fazi, whomever or whatever he may actually be!"

CHAPTER FORTY-FIVE

A NEW THREAT

As January dragged to an end, the future seemed bleak for the Christian army. Hunger prevailed, desertion was increasing, morale plummeted to its lowest point ever, and the crusaders' greatest weapon, heavy cavalry, had run desperately low of horses. The force of knights possessing mounts had by then actually dwindled to less than 1,000, but their mounts were not all war horses, nor even horses at all for that matter. It was recorded that some knights had been forced to actually ride into battle on mules and donkeys.

With circumstances turning so grim, Bohemud decided it was time to risk a visit to the Tower of Two Sisters. Without informing anyone of their destination, he and Tancred set out as soon as it was dark enough one night, secretly making their way toward the Saint George Gate far to the south. Dismounting within the tree-line located about a hundred yards from Antioch's wall, they squatted at the edge of the trees, spying on rampart activity.

"The Tower of Two Sisters is just there, by the gate," whispered Bohemud, straining to make out the silhouettes of guards along the ramparts. "It's there that I happened across this fellow, Firuz, months ago."

"I see guards down the line on both sides of the tower, but they're a good distance away. There's but a lone figure by the tower. Suppose that's Firuz?"

"Impossible to tell. And shit, it's open ground from here to the wall. If it's not Firuz, whoever it is will raise the alarm for certain, I wager."

"Whether it is or not," said Tancred, "we could get away before they could get archers above us, right?"

"Sure, unless that lone figure we see at the tower's armed with a bow and he isn't Firuz."

"It's worth the risk. Hell, what've we got to lose the way things are shaping up in camp? But, Uncle, wait here. I'll go it alone."

"Are you insane?"

"Yes, to attract less attention. Besides, I'm younger and quicker than you. Give me the note."

Fishing in his tunic for the note he had composed to Firuz, asking for details, Bohemud handed it to Tancred who had already tossed his helmet aside and was stripping his chain-mail down to his gambeson and breeches.

"Dammit, then," whispered Bohemud, "be quick and keep an eye to arrows from above!"

Scuttling out of the trees cautiously at first, Tancred dashed a short distance forward, coming in quick, as a lizard moves, to investigate the ramparts. This he did five or six times before finally making the wall. But once beneath its massive shadow, he was safely tucked in neat blackness. Despite this welcome advantage, Tancred could barely see. Undeterred, he moved along the wall's length, running his hand along the surface, hoping to feel a string. Just as he came almost directly beneath the tower, his fingers felt a feathery touch of resistance. Picking at it, Tancred pulled the end of the string into his palms. Fumbling about by feel, he determined that a small spike had been tied to the end of the string for weight, and to that spike was attached another loose string, presumably for purposes of attaching a note.

Minutes later Tancred was making a full dash back to the tree line, no stops. "It's done," he panted. "The string was there as promised, and the note is now tied to it. We'll come back Sunday to see if Firuz has fished it up and left a response."

"Good," said Bohemud, "let's get out of here!"

As unbelievably troublesome as things had been for the Army of God in January, February imported ominously dark news. Word arrived that Ridwan of Aleppo was marching to Antioch with 12,000 men. This meant the crusaders could well be caught in a pincer, crushed between Aleppo Turks coming in from the north and Yaghi Siyan's troops attacking from inside Antioch. Fortunately, having learned a bitter lesson about not posting scouts during Bohemud and Robert of Flanders' December foraging expedition, the crusaders had improved their intelligence and scouting system. Despite the bad news, they at least had knowledge of a new formidable Muslim army approaching, unlike at Jabal as-Summaq.

Regardless, the first question became evident: How do we counteract Ridwan's superiority in numbers, especially with insufficient heavy cavalry? Assembling on February 8th, the Council of Princes threw together a plan, deciding to split their forces to cover two fronts. Bohemud, Robert of Flanders, and Stephen of Blois were assigned to lead 700 knights in a frontal cavalry charge against Ridwan's army, while the remaining princes would hold in camp against Antioch with the infantry. Separating cavalry and infantry was a radical change of tactics. But in the end, it was determined that by not being encumbered by infantry, the cavalry could maneuver efficiently, effectively, and quickly, especially in the event of retreat. This was actually a lesson learned from the Muslims who capitalized on warfare deploying the speed and agility of light cavalry.

It had been boldly suggested by certain princes that the infantry, not being as 'brave' as the knights, might flee on being confronted by a vastly larger force. This was questionable, seeing as the crusader infantry was by this time a heavily experienced and hardcore band of fighters. Subsequently, infantry ranks had become populated with many knights who had lost their horses.

Sending an inferior force straight into the jaws of a mightier oncoming force may seem counter-intuitive, but being outnumbered, the princes had accepted the fact that a defensive stand would evolve into a grinding war of attrition, grossly favoring the enemy. In reality, they were left with little choice but to pray for divine intervention, hope luck was on their side, and catch the enemy by complete surprise.

To avoid the mistakes and oversights of double command, Bohemud was assigned as the unified commander of the heavy cavalry force, and under cover of darkness on the night of February 8th, he led the knights toward the Iron Bridge to establish position. To avoid encirclement, he selected a favorable spot between the Orontes and the foothills of Mount Staurin that would keep the Turks hemmed in, eliminating their ability to deploy wide flanking maneuvers.

At dawn, crusader scouts reported that Ridwan was marching straight toward the Iron Bridge, having placed two advance elements before his main army. As the Muslims approached, the Christian knights had but one chance to prevail since they could not possibly outlast the larger enemy force, and that one chance hinged completely on heavy cavalry shock tactics being unleashed with precise timing, surprise, and violent aggression. In preparation for this long shot, Bohemud once again demonstrated brilliant generalship by dividing his force into six squadrons, five of which were to attack the two Muslim advance contingents; the last to remain hidden in reserve to deliver, hopefully, a conclusive hammer blow.

On Bohemud's signal, the five squadrons of knights bolted forward in a wild and furious charge straight into the Turkish vanguard, catching them unaware. According to an eyewitness of the first moments of battle: "The din of battle arose to the heavens. All were fighting at once and the storm of missiles darkened the sky."

Shoving fear aside, the knights savagely pressed their attack, casting bravely, fearlessly, foolishly away its suicidal nature and their terror of being outnumbered twelve to one. Arising like banshees, crusaders began slicing through swaths of Turkish horse like men possessed. Consequently, the ground before them became a seething mass of horseflesh and clashing iron; faces streaming past in currents, one replacing another as the two forces smashed into each other; seemingly two onrushing rivers colliding in a mad wash of flesh, weaponry, and blood.

"Forward!" screamed Guillaume, pressing his horse to its limits, slinging his blade in a whir of destruction, taking heads, arms, and horses. Riding beside him, having abandoned his shield, massive Hroc charged head-on like an enraged bear tearing into a pack of dogs, swinging a sword in one hand, slinging a hammer in the other; a deadly pendulum meting out death with each murderous swing. Orla had recovered and was back in the saddle, and all the pent-up emotions that had built up over Crowbones' death was taken out on any Turk within his reach. Like Hroc, he had forsaken his shield in favor of swinging two weapons, bludgeon in one hand, mace in the other. Letellier, too, threw himself into the thick of things. Moving courageously forward, his spurs cut so deeply into his horse's flanks they began to bleed in long scarlet streams. As one formidable force they plunged from one fray into another, crashing into the advancing tide.

The sheer violence and shock of the Christian heavy cavalry assault terrified Ridwan's front, and their line began to break and scatter. Seeing them falter, Ridwan's trumpets blared, signaling his main force to advance into the mêlée and shore up the retreating front. This turned the tide . . . momentarily. Exactly what Bohemud was hoping for, the retreating Muslim front began to collide with the advancing main arm, spreading mass confusion and stifling movement into a complete bottleneck. Spotting his moment, Bohemud instructed his bugler to blow the code for the sixth squadron to show itself and attack.

The author of the Gesta Francorum, fighting in the very midst of this battle, later wrote: "So Bohemud, protected on all sides by the sign of the Cross, had charged the Turkish force like a lion having been starved for three or four days, which comes roaring out of its cave thirsting for the blood of cattle. His attack was so fierce that the points of his banner were flying right over the heads of the Turks. The other crusaders, seeing Bohemud's banner carried so honorably, stopped the retreat at once, and all our men in a body charged the Turks, who were amazed and took flight. Our men pursued them and massacred them right up to the Iron Bridge."

Bohemud's fearless leadership had, with that savage charge of heavy cavalry, changed the entire course of the battle. Within half an hour, Ridwan's Aleppan army was fleeing as one streaming mass in a chaotic rout.

In actuality, the crusaders chased Ridwan's dispersing force beyond the Iron Bridge as far as Harim, Yaghi Siyan's far eastern outpost. In defeat, retreating Turks set fire to Harim to keep it out of Christian hands, eliminating all possibility of using it in the future as a base of attack around the Iron Bridge area. And for the benefit of all, pursuing knights captured horses, food, and supplies from Ridwan's train, as well as plunder from slain Muslims and Harim. Undeniably, it was a spectacular victory.

As this battle at the Iron Bridge was raging, the infantry units remaining in camp successfully repelled a series of attacks coming out of Antioch's garrison, achieving for the day an astounding double victory just as Christian morale had ebbed to its lowest possible point and it appeared the crusade was deteriorating into defeat through starvation, the cold, desertion, exhaustion, and loss of morale.

Outstanding generalship and good luck aside, had Duqaq of Damascus and Ridwan of Aleppo joined forces rather than attacking individually, the Holy Crusade would have undoubtedly met its end by February 9th of 1098, but mutual hatred of one another prevented even a temporary show of unity between the two Muslim brothers. As a result, it was Muslim fracture in Syria, more than any other factor, that allowed the Army of God to resurrect itself from the ashes of certain defeat.

Many crusaders, of course, attributed this miraculous revival of the Holy Crusade to God's holy intervention, as did the high clergy, who began pounding this point over and over from the pulpit. 'Purification' had worked in the eyes of the true believers, of which, it must be remembered, there were many; men such as Adhémar of Le Puy, Fulcher of Chartres, Raymond of Aguilers, Peter the Hermit, Guillaume de Saint-Germain, Martin Letellier, Scule the dwarf monk, and a host of others. It is very possible, too, that the major princes believed that they had been saved by Holy Intervention, including Raymond of Toulouse, Bohemud of Taranto, Tancred of Hauteville, and Godfrey of Bouillon.

Then there was Bishop Tristan de Saint-Germain, who said ... nothing. During celebration of the daily mass and special liturgical rituals, he did not boast of victory, or slaying the heathen, or divine intervention. Rather, he encouraged praying for the less fortunate, treating civilians with honor and tolerance, and gaining the grace of God through decency, good deeds, and faith.

Privately, though, he had but one prayer, and that was on behalf of Mala and baby Christophe. Oh, Lord, he beseeched, should you spare my family, I shall abandon my space on this grand stage I have labored so hard to gain. I shall abandon the politics of the Pope and other great figures of Europe who have forgotten the poor, the disinherited, and the disenfranchised in favor of self-enrichment and conceited glory. I shall devote the rest of my life to teaching and spreading Your word to the humble, the scattered, and the obscure. Save my family, Lord, I pray!

CHAPTER FORTY-SIX

AN UNEXPECTED VISIT

One of the earliest strategies of the crusade before the first clash of arms at the battle of Nicaea was to ensure that the Fatimid Shia caliphate of Egypt did not ally itself with the Turkish Abbasid Baghdad caliphate, which was Sunni. In actuality, there was little chance of this occurring to begin with due to the pathological hatred existing between these two Islamic dynasties dating back to the death of Muhammed (June 8, 632 AD) when a blood feud broke out over succession. Muslims who became known as Shias or Shiites wanted Ali, the Prophet's cousin, to be the next leader; the remaining Muslims, becoming known as Sunnis, argued that the Prophet, on his deathbed, had chosen Abu Bakr to lead the prayer in his place.

Proactively, the crusaders sent an ambassador to the embassy in Egypt to ask the Fatimids for a 'non-interference' alliance in early 1097 before launching against Kilij Arslan's Turkish sultanate of Rüm in Asia Minor.

Having lost such vast tracts of territory, power, and influence to the Sunni Turks in Arabia, Syria, and south as far as the Levant (Jerusalem), the Fatimids were content to learn that their most hated Islamic enemy was soon be entangled in war against a formidable European invasion force. It is unclear whether the Fatimids actually rendered a formal response to either the Vatican in Rome or to the crusaders who were at the time gathering in Constantinople.

It was to the Army of God's good fortune that such irreparable discord had arisen within Islam between the Middle East and North Africa, creating a state of complete Islamic division. Compounding this Islamic Shia against Sunni fracture, other cracks were found to exist in the form of Sunni faction against Sunni faction, as evidenced by the failed individual efforts of the two Sunni brothers, Duqaq of Damascus and Ridwan of Aleppo, who despised each other too much to join forces to keep a foreign Christian army from overrunning Syria and vanquishing Antioch.

Having mostly forgotten about the Fatimids of Egypt since their initial overtures to Egypt, the crusaders received an unexpected visit from them on or around February 9th, the same time as their stunning victory over Ridwan of Aleppo. Egyptian ruler Vizier al-Afdal sent an unannounced delegation sailing from Egypt to the Syrian coast to inform the Christian army that the Fatimids were now prepared to enter into a formal pact of neutrality, guaranteeing that they would not interfere in the war between crusaders and Turks. It should be noted that the Fatimids may have lacked a clear understanding of crusader intent. Having heard the crusaders had been turning captured cities over to Emperor Alexius, the Fatimids may have thought the crusader invasion of Syria was merely the last phase of assisting a Byzantine campaign to recapture Antioch rather than a Western campaign to recapture Jerusalem.

In any case, the crusaders welcomed the Fatimids to Antioch with open arms, offering hospitality lasting nearly a full month. And when the Fatimids departed for Egypt, the crusaders sent along a delegation of their own to meet with Vizier al-Afdal and solidify the newly signed Fatimid/crusader pact.

This Fatimid/Christian liaison at Antioch was in itself remarkable because the crusaders had vilified all Muslims as dark, sub-human, and godless heathens posing a threat not just to Christianity but to all of Western Europe. Remarkably, even as the Fatimids arrived at Antioch, hundreds and hundreds of Muslim heads from Ridwan's defeat were being posted throughout the camps. But as history has testified time and again, necessity makes for strange couplings and unexpected forgiveness. This neutrality pact served Fatimid purposes against the Sunnis and, at the same time, the Army of God because it was the Fatimids of Egypt, not the Turks, who possessed a naval force large enough to disrupt crusader Mediterranean Sea traffic with Byzantium and the West.

Learning of this congenial gathering between the crusaders and Fatimids through his scout, Kareem, Abdul Azim became overly intrigued with the activities currently transpiring within the crusader camp. "Ah," he told Kareem, chortling, "it seems that despite what we've been told, these Christians will deal with Muslims if it advances their own interests!"

"Certainly, Sire, as do all enemies when mutual profit is in sight, or when danger threatens."

"I remember how we were treated in Rome by these Westerners, Kareem, as dark and ignorant savages, backward and unworthy of consideration. Cordiality these Christian crusaders may be extending to their Fatimid Muslim guests, but I dare say that in private they are gnashing their teeth."

"Certainly, Sire. The crusaders are but putting on a charade of false smiles just as the Pope did in Rome when we went there to negotiate with him and the men in the red robes."

"Cardinals, Kareem. They were called 'cardinals.' Like those birds with showy red plumage."

"They were showy, alright, but easy to see through. In the end, they managed to only fool themselves."

"Yes," agreed Azim, "and I'd wager these crusaders are making the same mistake the Pope and his cardinals made back then in Rome: underestimating their dark, backward Muslim guests. But just as we ignored the Pope back then, the Fatimids will play the crusaders."

"Oh? You think?"

"Oh, come now, Kareem," chided Azim. "Do you not see the game the Fatimids have put into play here?"

"For sure! They're getting back at the Abbassid caliphate for disassembling their Arabian empire. They hate us Sunnis."

"Yes, but like the game of chess, you must not dwell on the current move, Kareem, but on the move after the current move, and the move after that one, even. Look two or three jumps ahead in order to not fall behind."

"Oh, I would if I could, but I'm no good at chess as you very well know, humiliating me game after game. Besides, Allah gave me but a lone bag of tricks, remember? He didn't grace me with the same keen eye he blessed you with, Sire."

"Let's look closely at the board then, Kareem, and think a moment. You have heard talk in the Christian camps that their goal is Jerusalem. But do the Fatimids know that?"

"No. While wandering about the Fatimid camp, I learned they believe the crusaders are Byzantine mercenaries, and their objective is Antioch. If they take it, they'll return it to Emperor Alexius, get well paid, and go home."

"But they're wrong, we both know that. Once gaining a foothold, even a herd of elephants can't pull a badger from its hole. Consider that Baldwin of Boulogne has established a realm in Edessa already, and Mamistra now flies a crusader banner. And should Antioch and Jerusalem fall, the Christians will be here for the next thousand years. But another question, Kareem: Who once possessed Jerusalem for nearly 400 years?"

"The Fatimids, of course."

"And do you suppose they might like to grab the entire Levant back from our Seljuk brethren?"

"Ha, yes, in their dreams!"

"Another thing, Kareem. You and I know the crusaders have won a victory of late, finally, yet in truth they are still hanging on by a thread. The Fatimids don't know that either. Upon arriving, they found the crusaders celebrating victory, making them believe the crusaders are in a fine position, but they're not. Now we come to the next question, Kareem. With the crusaders tying up the Seljuks here in Antioch, having defeated Damascus and Aleppo, if the Fatimids themselves invaded Jerusalem, there would be no Seljuk help from either Asia Minor nor Syria, correct?"

As if unexpected fog had parted baring the landscape ahead, Kareem looked up. "Oh, but Allah has given you a circular mind, Sire! That 'jumping two or three moves ahead' you were talking about, it's the Fatimids taking Jerusalem back from us Turks!"

"Conjecture, Kareem, merely conjecture. But empires rise and fall on conjecture. If I were the Fatimids, I would shortly move an army against Jerusalem and reclaim it from my enemy, the Sunni Seljuk Turks. But I am not Fatimid, I am Sunni."

Changing expression, Kareem frowned. "But Sire, since we ourselves are Sunni and the Fatimids are our enemy, would it not benefit us to perhaps advise the crusaders of your conjecture?"

"Certainly not! These southern Seljuk tribes, in possession of Syria and the Levant, as you well know, Kareem, murdered my entire family line—parents, grandparents, uncles, aunts, cousins. If not for you, I, too, would be in a grave. No, I don't care whether the Christians take Antioch or lose it. I don't care if the Fatimids attack Jerusalem or leave it. This part of the world is my past, not my future. My main interest here hinges on but one man, the Persian, Malik. When that business is settled, and only when that business is settled, we shall turn north and return home."

"Ah, home," sighed Kareem, bowing his head. "I miss it, and my old wife, too, Sire. The hour glass is running short for my old woman just as it is for me. And I've been away for a long time, chasing Malik."

"We'll turn for home, Kareem, as soon as he shows himself. But while we wait, and when the Fatimids leave for Egypt, you and I will enter the Christian camp together to introduce ourselves. No disguise, no deception. Now that we know they will deal with Muslims directly, we will approach under a flag of parley as did the Fatimids, and we shall promise no interference. It is time for me to reconnect with a long-lost friend."

"Ah, I was wondering when you would get around to Little Brother!"

"I thought much of him as a boy, and now I'd like to see him as a man after these many years." Saying this, Azim turned, taking a long look at his old scout, almost as cataloguing every feature of his worn face. "Kareem, there is one last thing I wish to address with you," he said, taking on a look of affection. "Not only do I owe you my life, but much, much more. My debt to you has grown since that horrific day your bag of tricks got me out of Syria as a boy. So, I've come to a decision. From this moment forward, I ask that you address me simply as Abdul, not Sire, not Lord, not Master. You, my friend, have served as my most trusted scout and companion for years, you are as family to me."

Going motionless, Kareem stared into his lap. Looking up, touched beyond measure, he shook his head 'no.' "You would not require an old dog to jump high through a hoop of fire and do somersaults, would you, Sire?"

"What?"

"Then do not ask me to call you Abdul. Such a thing would surely disturb me, and those who respect age do not disturb old men."

"Ha!" Azim guffawed loudly. "But I thought you had a bag of tricks, Kareem? Are they so old you cannot turn a new one?"

"Yes, Sire, they, like me, are set in their limits. My time for somersaults is done."

CHAPTER FORTY-SEVEN

MORE VISITORS

Within two days of the Fatimid departure, Kareem and Azim donned their finest diplomatic garb and, with an accompanying escort of fifty riders, approached the northern camp of Bohemud. "Tristan de Saint-Germain! Nous cherchons Tristan de Saint-Germain!" hailed Azim loudly in broken French. "Est-il ici dans le camp?"

Startled at first on catching sight of Seljuk Turks entering the camp under a flag of truce, those crusaders in the path of the procession grew curious, following this second unannounced Muslim delegation with their eyes yet saying little. Hearing the name Saint-Germain, they pointed toward the direction of the Tuscan camp not far away.

"What the hell?" questioned Bohemud, recognizing Seljuk dress. "These are Sunni Turks, not Shia Fatimids!"

"I can't imagine," replied Tancred. "Sounds like they're looking for Saint-Germain though, and headed toward his camp. We'd best follow, I think; find out what's going on."

On arriving in the Tuscan camp, Azim dismounted, asking several questions and introducing himself and Kareem as visitors from Asia Minor, not Syria. "We come in peace," he declared to those gathering around, which included Scule, Christos, Guillaume, and Letellier. "To set you at ease, please know that we are enemies of Kilij Arslan of Rüm, and enemies of these Seljuk factions in Syria as well. Our purpose here is to locate a certain Tristan de Saint-Germain who as a young boy served as translator for Pope Gregory VII during my ambassadorial visit to Rome over sixteen years ago. Is he here?"

"I am," said Tristan, who happened to hear Azim's cry as he entered camp.

From their saddles, they could see the 'boy' had most certainly grown into a man, and even with his crown shaved in the traditional Benedictine tonsure, Kareem and Azim both recognized him immediately. "Ah, my young friend, but you've changed!" said Azim, changing from French to his native tongue.

Tristan balked, confused.

"Oh, but do you not recognize us, Little Brother?" laughed Kareem. "I'm Kareem! And that handsome fellow standing before you is Lord Abdul Azim. Surely you've not forgotten!"

Tristan had failed to recognized both men, but on hearing the moniker 'Little Brother' he knew instantly who the two men had to be. Looking again, his memory poked him and, in their language, he gasped, "Ah, but of course! Praise

God! I thought to never see either of you again, but here you are!" Upon opening his heart and mind, he ran to Azim, embracing him, then turned and went to Kareem who had just dismounted.

Azim looked exactly as Tristan remembered him, striking, impeccably dressed, carrying himself with dignity that did not suggest in any way the haughtiness of privilege. But Kareem, older than Azim, had not aged nearly as gracefully; his once dark hair had turned into a hoary sheen of speckled silver and his face appeared weathered, from what Tristan recalled, but his stilted smile had not changed one bit. As before, it betrayed a trace of bedevilment, as one knowing things not willing to reveal.

"Could we speak in private?" asked Azim, gesturing toward the tents. "What I have to say is for your ears alone. This is not a negotiation as you have just completed with the Fatimids, but a personal visit."

"The Fatimids?" echoed Tristan, surprised that Azim would know such a thing. "But how do you know about—?"

"Kareem keeps me informed," interrupted Azim, placing a hand to Tristan's shoulder. "He knows much about this camp, actually, and has been here several times."

"Yes, Little Brother," grinned Kareem, "as an Armenian, as a Syrian, as whatever I wished to be at the time. And I'm happy to say, your people are quite talkative." At this he tittered a bit, offering that shrug rule-breakers give when caught.

"But come," said Azim, "let us talk alone, Little Brother."

Hearing this moniker, Tristan smiled, feeling an odd comfort. It was as if an entirely forgotten but fond blanket from the past had wrapped itself around him. It was Azim who had first called him 'Little Brother,' but the others of the Seljuk delegation visiting Rome had taken up the label as well. For an entire two-week period, he was known affectionately as Little Brother by the visiting Turks.

"Certainly," said Tristan, directing with an open palm. "Come to my tent. It's just there."

That short walk began the rekindling of an old fire long turned to ash in the mists of time. Fond memories hold their warmth, and soon Tristan, Azim, and Kareem were sharing and laughing as kindred spirits who had shared a golden moment in time together. They replayed the Rome visit blow by blow, mimicking the dour looks of Pope Gregory's cardinals, recalling Tristan's introduction to hashish, and the night Azim led him into his harem where young caramel skinned young women marveled at Tristan's fair skin, golden locks, and startling blue eyes, and had done exotic, pleasurable things to him as a result of their wonder.

Within minutes, Tristan's woes melted away for the first time since receiving the bad news from Saint Simeon. Kareem and Azim became merry medicine for him. Although the information he had received from the Armenian jailer named Boros had substantially lightened Tristan's heart, he had not been entirely able to shed that lingering dread brought on by uncertainty. He feared that Mala and

Christophe could be discovered at any point, day or night.

Unbeknownst to the three as they jabbered, Bohemud had arrived at the Tuscan camp with his nephew and both were pacing about outside the tent.

"Who are these Turks and what're they doing here?" growled Tancred.

"They're old acquaintances my brother met in Rome years ago," replied Guillaume, "yet I've never met them before."

"But they're Seljuks!" said Bohemud, staring at the closed tent flap. "Dammit, I'm going in," he said, as Tancred followed.

Rudely interrupted mid-word, Azim looked up as two knights shoved the tent flap aside, planting themselves before him with crossed arms, staring with frigid eyes. "What's this about, Saint-Germain?" demanded Bohemud.

"Aye," piped Tancred, "these two should've reported to us first on entering camp, asking permission to proceed."

Azim had never been one to tolerate rude behavior, and in an instant took disliking to both men, their posture, their tone. "I am Abdul Azim," he said, standing, moving close to Bohemud, nose to nose. "I am a Seljuk lord of Eastern Asia Minor and—"

"If you're Seljuk, you're not welcome here," said Tancred.

"He is welcome here!" snapped Tristan. "This is my tent! It is the both of you who are not welcome here, especially dancing in here as a pack of yapping hyenas displaying a total lack of civility."

"They're the enemy!" insisted Tancred, placing a hand to the pommel of his sword.

Old as he was, Kareem stood, slipped a dagger from his robe, and had it cocked over his shoulder so swiftly that Tancred failed to even see it until he realized the blade could be flung into his heart by the time his sword was but half extricated.

"Kareem!" shouted Azim, flagging him off, then catching Tancred's attention, staring directly in his eyes. "Don't be a fool, young man." Turning to Bohemud, he said, "You there, I recognize you. You led a force through the Ruj Valley a while back and engaged in battle there as well."

"Huh?" huffed Bohemud, chest stuck out. "How would you know that? Were you there with the enemy?"

"Had I been fighting with the enemy, you would be moldering in the ground at this point. No, me and my 1,000 horsemen were watching from a hillside nearby."

"Watching?" asked Tancred, aghast. "You didn't enter the fray?"

"I'm not your enemy," said Azim. "Had I been, yes, I would have entered the battle and both of you would be dead, seeing the battle was closely contested, as I recall. My thousand ghazis would have ground you two and your army to dust. I will leave it at that, and ask you both to leave until invited here."

This Azim said with such authority that Tancred took offense, but it was Bohemud who flagged his hand. "I see," he said, mulling Azim's story. "You have an army in the area, I surmise?"

"Yes, but my army is of no concern to you unless, of course, you create concern. I came here for a different purpose, to—"

Pausing, Azim looked over to Kareem who had coughed and whose eyes were boring in on him with obvious intent. 'Be careful what you divulge,' his eyes were saying.

"Go on," urged Bohemud. "What were you about to say?"

"I was about to say," Azim changed course, "that we are here simply to see an old friend. And we have found him here in your camp."

"And what about Antioch?" questioned Bohemud. "What are your intentions?"

"I have none. Antioch means nothing to me. I have my own realm up north, a large one. Besides, the Syrian Seljuks are enemies of mine from an earlier time, and we share bad blood."

Bad blood, pondered Bohemud, who like his father, Duke Robert Guiscard, had often turned feuding Muslim clans to the advantage by forging alliances with one side or the other while conquering Sicily and Southern Italy. "Might you hold any interest in avenging the past, then? You could be of use to us. You might consider joining our fight."

"No. Never. Besides, I shall be returning north."

Hearing this, Bohemud grunted, gesturing to Tancred that they should leave. This was a burr in Bohemud's saddle. He much admired Guillaume, but he and Tancred held his brother, Tristan, in low regard. "Very well then," he said, "I've learned what I need to know. We shall be on our way."

As they left, Tristan's eyes followed them. "This is my status here within the crusade," he exhaled, addressing Azim. "Because I speak straight, I am no longer trusted here by many." He paused then, offering a small shrug. "Before they interrupted, I was about to tell you that I was surprised to learn that you, too, were in Syria, coming toward Antioch just as I was. I feared at first perhaps you were coming to fight for Yaghi Siyan, which distressed me greatly. I could not imagine us being at war against each other. But then I learned you were chasing Malik, who had raided your kingdom. Is that true, then?"

"Yes," nodded Azim, surprised that Tristan would already know such details.

"Aha, but he always was sharp as a razor!" said Kareem, who was just as shocked as Azim.

"No, not that clever, Kareem, a young Greek boy told me. He was from the town of Despina, within Azim's realm. He and his grandmother were fleeing from Malik, trying to make their way to Byzantium."

Thinking back, Azim held up a finger. "Allah works the entire universe, yet also works in the tiniest of ant piles! I'm certain I met that very boy and his grandmother on the battlefield begging for food just after we'd put Malik to rout! She was coarse as grit, that one, and afraid of nothing. Ha, and bitter as vinegar! But then, I was about to tell you something as well, Little Brother." Azim returned to his camp stool, his face losing its lightheartedness. "It seems we are connected more than you realize, my young friend.

Despite the laws of your Church, you have a woman you love, we've learned, and a son."

Tristan sat back, slack-jawed, stunned that Azim would know such things. Nonetheless, he also knew neither Azim nor Kareem were judgmental about Christian Church law other than believing most of it was rubbish. "Yes, that is all entirely true," he mumbled under his breath. "But how—"

"Her name is Mala the Romani," divulged Azim, "known as la Gran Signorina on your continent, but in Asia Minor we know her as 'Mâh of Genoa,' the Moon of Genoa."

"Because," added Kareem, "the moon is an important figure of our language and culture, and Mâh is a feminine word, too, sometimes personified as a goddess or 'queen of the night' in Zoroastrian tradition. Your Mala is treasured within the world of maritime trade in Asia Minor."

"Very much," said Azim. "She has been the major Western trading presence within the northern Seljuk Empire for the past decade." Pausing, his brows came together. "You did know she is heavily engaged in commerce with the Muslim world as well as Western Europe and Byzantium, yes?"

Tristan was indeed aware. "Yes, it gave me pause at first, but then, commerce is her trade, not war. Nor religion for that matter."

"Yes, and as such," pointed out Azim, "she and I have become close these past years. And I must confess, she has long owned the better portion of my heart." Here he chortled slightly. "I asked her to be my wife within months of meeting her."

Shaking his head, Tristan's voice dropped, "No, I never knew such a thing. It seems she must have neglected to tell me anything about that."

"No need to worry, Little Brother, she told me quickly that she loved another, and had loved that 'other' since childhood; that he was a Christian holy man, but I had no idea it was you until recently when Kareem came onto her seemingly by accident in Antioch."

"Recently?" Tristan straightened up with a start. "Kareem saw her in Antioch recently?"

"Yes," interceded Kareem. "She was captured leaving Saint Simeon by Mahmoud Malik and taken to a prison there. I saw her the day after she arrived."

"My god," whispered Tristan, his eyes going wide. "Oh, but I just recently learned she was there from an Armenian who had escaped the city! And I had no idea it was Malik who had captured her, nor that she was imprisoned. I received few details from the escaped Armenian. But tell, how was she, Kareem? Did she look well?"

"No, she did not look well at all," said Kareem sadly. "She'd been brutally beaten by Malik."

"B-but the Armenian I spoke with told me she was well!" asserted Tristan, growing confused.

"She may well look fine now," said Kareem, "but not when I saw her. The escaped Armenian who told you about Mala, was he by chance a fellow named Boros?"

"Yes. But how could you know that?"

"Ah, while nosing about Antioch I happened to befriend him. Few people know more about what's going on in town than the barber or the jailer. Anyway, I went into the prison with Boros and a little blue man they call Ben-fazi. That's when I saw Mâh of Genoa. The blue man said he would try to help her. And a funny thing, Mâh and the blue man knew each other from somewhere before, come to find out."

"What?" Tristan grew exponentially confounded with each new revelation. "But how was that possible?"

"I don't know, but great emotion passed between the two on recognizing each other, which they failed to do at first; she because of his paint, him because of her bruising."

"My son, Christophe, was he also injured?"

"No. He was untouched, and—"

Hearing this, Tristan closed his eyes, making the sign of the cross, and began a short prayer of gratitude.

Going solemn, Azim and Kareem accorded Tristan time to finish praying before speaking again. When he appeared to be finished, Azim said, "The last time Kareem was in Antioch, the jailer had disappeared, as had your wife and son."

"Yes," said Tristan, "the blue man put them in hiding, but I've no idea where. My only hope would be to find the blue man if I ever get inside the city. Until then, I fervently pray that Mala and Christophe remain safe. And that is all I think about day and night!"

"Ah, then we, too, shall pray, Little Brother," said Azim. "But the biggest problem is Malik. Mâh managed to cut his face severely and, in the same instance, removed his manhood during his attack and attempted rape. He has been completely demobilized, but for how long, we cannot guess. It seems she had a dagger concealed on her when captured, and Malik never suspected such. Poor bastard!"

"Yes, I know the dagger," said Tristan. "She has carried it on her since the age of fourteen when she used it to kill the boy who raped her aunt and butchered her mother's face."

Azim and Kareem exchanged glances, proud and surprised. "I could have never imagined such a thing," said Azim, thinking of the demure petite woman, "though I've always known her to fear no man, regardless of circumstances."

"Oh, what to do?" asked Tristan, his voice dropping to a whisper.

"Continue praying to your God as you have been doing," said Kareem, "and we shall beseech Allah as well."

"Aye," nodded Azim, "there is little else to be done, unfortunately, until your army breaks into Antioch. Then maybe you can find her and your infant son, Little Brother."

"I have fought against this siege from the beginning," said Tristan, wringing his hands. "And now, in a complete twist of circumstances, the only hope for my family is to pray for the success of the damn thing!"

"In the meantime," said Azim, "Kareem shall return to Antioch to learn what he can. And me, I shall put my mind to work. With the help of Allah, perhaps an idea will arrive. If there is anything I can do for our Mâh of Genoa, I shall move the earth to do it."

"The message," urged Kareem, looking to Azim. "Tell him about the message she sent, the one delivered to you by courier just before we crossed into Syria."

"Ah, yes, I nearly forgot, Little Brother. She sent a request, inquiring about the possibility of seeking political asylum within the protection of my realm, for her and her family. The request confused Kareem and me because we thought her to be unmarried, therefore lacking any family."

"Political asylum for her family?" Tristan stood mystified. "But asylum from whom?"

"Your Church, Little Brother, and the Vatican."

"What? But no, that cannot be. I do not understand."

"Oh," said Azim, "I was puzzled at first on receiving the message, but now I begin to see."

"See what?" asked Tristan.

"I saw how those two knights looked and spoke to you on bursting into your tent as we had begun to talk. Even though you are highly placed with your Pope, they treated you with insolence and scorn. And if they are leaders of this crusade, that does not bode well either for your safety or your future, I would think."

Kareem added, "There was hatred on their brow. And, too, you yourself mentioned that because you speak straight, you are not trusted by many in your camp."

"You said that you have fought against this siege of Antioch from the start, did you not?" prodded Azim. "And I know the power of your Church on your continent. It controls all that stands, all that lives, and even all who die. Does it not? It pokes its nose into every corner of your Western world, even those long-abandoned corners that seem to matter little. And you, Little Brother, as a man of high position in that web of spiders, have broken their law about holy men and women."

Tristan offered no reply, but Azim's words, like blood drying over a wound, began to congeal, becoming fixed.

"Yes, it becomes very clear now," Azim's one eyebrow arched, confirming his own words. "She intends for you to abandon your Church entirely, and every-thing in Western Europe as you have known it. She seeks a new world for you, herself, and your newborn son. You alone have step-by-step destroyed your chances for returning; burned your bridges. Do you not see that?"

"But she has never spoken to me of asylum," objected Tristan. "And she knows that my intention after Jerusalem is to return to Odo de Lagery, to report the atrocities of this crusade, and of the sinners!"

"Odo de Lagery?" Azim new no one of that name.

"Yes, Pope Urban II, Holy Father of the Catholic Church. He raised me at the Monastery of Cluny in France from the time I was seven."

"No, Little Brother. Going back to him would be like slashing your own wrists and throwing yourself on the altar of sacrifice. He may have raised you, but how many fathers have been forced to murder their sons for the sin of shaming family and name?"

"Indeed," Kareem caught his attention, "how many?"

"Mâh has decided to by-pass the Pope, the crusade, and any return to Europe," stated Azim with authority. "She loves you, Little Brother; wants to be with you and raise a family. Can you not see it though it looms huge before your own eyes?"

Too stirred for words, Tristan slumped, overcome.

"Should she not survive Antioch, it all means nothing. Nothing at all," sustained Azim with a flip of his bejeweled hand. "But if she should survive with your son, then you must come to a decision. You have much to consider then, Little Brother, so Kareem and I shall leave you to your thoughts. Should you weigh on the side of asylum, you know where we are camped. We will take you back north with us to my realm in Eastern Asia Minor, far, far beyond the reach of your Church, and your crusaders. You and Mâh, and your son, could have a fresh start there in safety and peace, never again to be crushed beneath the boot of your Church, or denied the right to be with the woman you love."

CHAPTER FORTY-EIGHT

MALIK

Malik's injuries were horrid, incapacitating him for longer than he or Hasan anticipated. In the interim, Yaghi Siyan had put Hasan to use, ordering him to take charge of Malik's ghazis and lead cavalry raids against the crusaders. Having little choice, Hasan carried out these duties, masking his hidden reluctance and misgivings about leadership. In truth, Hasan was a perfect number two man, content to follow and pass down orders but hesitant to devise them. Whereas another man in his situation might have begun plotting a takeover of Malik's army, Hasan wanted him to recover physically as well as regain command of the renegade mercenaries; a pack of violent misfits, unruly and rebellious, that only Malik could keep in line. Hasan lacked both the forcefulness and the will to accomplish such.

After weeks and weeks of confinement lying on his back, caused by extreme loss of blood, removal of his left eyeball, severe throat damage, a lengthy battle fighting off infection, and learning to endure the pain of urinating through raw flesh, Malik finally gained his feet, barely. "By damn, take me to the woman!" he bellowed in a furious animalistic yowl. The nicking of his larynx had perverted its ability to operate properly, so for the rest of his days Malik's voice would carry a bestial resonance.

"Yes, Komutan!" snapped Hasan, taking Malik by one arm and commanding a nearby ghazi to take ahold of the other. Leading him from the barracks toward the prison, the two released their hold on him on reaching the entrance. "What the hell are you men gawking at?" snipped Hasan at guards manning the door. "We've come to get the bitch that cut Malik's face! Fetch the key so we can open the cell!"

"Immediately!" said the guard, swallowing bile, sickened by Malik's deformed, oozing face. "Get the key," he ordered another guard, "and meet us at the end of the corridor." Gesturing then to Hasan, he said, "Get a good hold on your fellow there and follow me. It's dark back there."

Minutes later, as Hasan, his helper, Malik, and extra guards arrived at the cell, Hasan was the first to go stiff. Peering in only to find emptiness, he did what all men do when the impossible occurs—he refused to believe it. Scanning the entire width of the cell a second and a third time, his eyes settled on the straw heaped to the side, thinking the woman and child might have nestled within it. "Open the cell, dammit!" he shouted, palpitations striking hard and fast.

By this time the others realized the woman and child were not there. Watching Hasan dash for the heap of straw, they followed and within seconds the entire bunch was thrashing through it, grabbing it by fistfuls and poking its depths.

Nothing . . . except a shriveled, dried-up penis, which none dared mention.

Malik had been left outside the cell, holding himself erect by the bars; the searing pain between his legs almost unbearable. Seeing too poorly from his one eye to understand what was happening, he called, "Hasan, what's going on in there? What's taking so damn long?"

Having turned white, confounded by this impossible turn, Hasan yelled at the guards, "Where is she?! What've you done with her? Tell me or every damned one of you shall be dead within the half hour!"

"Nothing!" cried one of the guards, backing away from Hasan who'd drawn his saber. "We've done nothing, damn you!"

"It was the blue man! Ben Fazi!" shouted another. "Aye, he came with an order from Yaghi Siyan to bring her to the palace! For questioning, he said."

"Boros said she was brought back here, weeks go!" added another voice. "He's been tending to her per your instructions since her return because we're not allowed near these last two cells. Boros—"

Here he halted, as did the objections of every other guard within the cell.

Silence, each guard searching the others' eyes for an answer. Then a collective howl rung out, "Boros!" echoed throughout the cell as guards vacated in a mad dash, knocking Malik aside. "It was Boros!" they were shouting. "Get that bastard, Boros!"

Shocked that the bitch had escaped, Malik went berserk. Cursing, kicking, inadvertently smashing his fist against the iron bars of Mala's cell, his already maimed vision was doused completely by blind rage and his throat began to bleed; the internal wounds bursting from the straining and demonic roaring.

Horrified, the young girls in the adjacent cells watched Malik's dance of rancor as might a nest of cornered mice watching a king cobra writhing about just before hungrily attacking. Crying, falling into fits, clinging to each other, castaways to spars in a raging sea, they feared he would break into their cell, slaking his hostility by turning them into a blood bath.

But that did not happen. Malik collapsed onto the stone corridor floor, splitting his forehead open. This tumble, in turn, jolted the healing that had begun to scab over the entire run of his face from brow to throat; the elongated scab erupting in spots, pursing open, oozing blood and pus. "Oh, but I shall have her yet!" his horrid voice rumbled, then all turned black and he lost consciousness.

As this drama played out in the prison, Mala and Christophe were tucked safely within the apartment of Karine and Garik. Garik had finally lost his fear of her and over time actually became a bit entranced by her beauty. He had even taken to holding baby Christophe on those rare occasions that Karine did not have him nestled in her arms. Mala found comfort in Karine's attachment to Christophe, despite finding Karine to be extremely distant. Amazingly, the girl possessed mothering instincts, strange as they were, in light of her aversion of people. "We owe you our lives," Mala would say to her time and time again, only to at best receive a quiet tilt of Karine's head.

Mala had often attempted to inquire about their parents, but on family matters Karine remained secretive compared to Garik. At least Garik would speak about their mother, albeit rarely. The only topic Mala was able to extract responses about was Benito, or as Karine called him, "the Little Blue Jinn," in reference to Garik's interpretation of Ben-fazi. Mala had even tried to explain Benito's true identity and origin, but neither Karine nor Garik seemed interested. They preferred their own interpretations of Ben-fazi. As concerned Yaghi Siyan, Karine did deign to offer bits of information here and there, but selectively. This created suspicions in Mala's mind that the old emir's interest in the two children was unnatural, possibly even perverse. Yet, Karine never gave the impression of being either molested or abused. Rather, she treated Siyan's periodical summonses as a duty, nothing less, during which she accorded him courtesy and deference, but poor Garik remained frightened of him. Unknowingly, or maybe not, both steadily denied him the one thing he craved from them—affection.

Fortunately for Mala and Christophe, Siyan's contact with the two children diminished with each passing day due to the ongoing conflict beyond his gates. Balancing this was an increase in visits from Ben-fazi checking in on all four within the apartment; his greater interest lying with la Signorina, of course. Like everyone else but Garik and Christophe, Ben-fazi had not been able to penetrate the fortress known as Karine, either. Subsequently, he held private concerns that she might betray la Signorina, mainly because the girl had become tightly bound to Baby Christophe and might not mind eliminating competition for the infant's attention. The only thing that could possibly hold her back was the fact that she was not able nurse him.

Voicing this concern to Mala one day, he said, "You and I are at the mercy of that one, Signorina. You do know that, don't you?"

"Most certainly," agreed Mala. "But I keep my faith, not in her, but in God, Benito. I've never encountered anyone like her, but her guardedness about all things may be, in the end, our salvation. She adamantly refuses to talk freely. Rather, she labors at remaining tight-lipped, divulging nothing to anyone. I've no idea what made her that way, but she's been very attentive to my little Christophe, and that endears her to my heart. Poor little Christophe, he finds comfort with Karine as he does with me, but has no idea of things, especially that all of our lives hang by such a fragile hair!"

CHAPTER FORTY-NINE

BATTLE OF THE BRIDGE

As March approached, the crusaders had endured a horrid winter of hunger and despair. Yet with Ridwan of Aleppo defeated, several victorious repulsions of Turkish attacks coming out of the Bridge Gate, and the recent neutrality pact signed with the visiting Fatimids, some felt that by surviving Syria's winter they had successfully walked through the burning fire of 'purification' as an army and were now cleansed. As written by the knight Anselm of Rosemont: "The Franks were strengthened by that ordeal (purification). Growing stronger and stronger, therefore, from that day, our men took counsel with renewed courage."

This 'cleansing,' however, had taken a terrible toll; the weak had died of hunger and disease, the fearful had deserted, and many had been slain in battle. As an illustration of the toll taken by the winter of 1097–98, it must be noted that the Holy Crusade had begun with 100,000 crusaders departing Europe, but had dwindled to 35,000 survivors, and the battle for Antioch remained stalemated.

In the Tuscan camp, time slipped into of joy and celebration! Guthroth the Quiet had ambled his horse into camp.

"God's spine!" roared Orla, elated to see his younger cousin. "Where have you been these last two months?"

"H-healing," said Guthroth, dismounting and embracing one by one the men who meant the world to him.

"Good to see you up and about," said Tristan, giving him a hug, "we were worried about you!"

"Indeed," agreed Guillaume, slapping him on the back. "And being in battle with you not there guarding our backs has taken some getting used to!"

No one was more thrilled to see Guthroth than Hroc, of course. Embracing him, Hroc said in a low voice, "I've told them about the Oasis of Sparrows and to hold any mention of it around others."

"D-did you t-tell them about H-Haya?" whispered Guthroth, during the embrace, concerned.

"Only that she and Papa Daba rule the oasis and that old Daba has two other daughters. Oh, and I did relate that Haya was acting as your physician; that she knows about herbs and salves. I know you respect the privacy of others, so I chose to respect yours."

"G-good lad." Guthroth gave him an extra bear hug in appreciation of Hroc's consideration. Although Haya was on his mind, it was good to be back with his companions. They had been extremely fretful of one another. But looking about, his cousin was missing. "Wh-where's Crowbones?" he asked. But seeing faces drop with his question, he immediately suspected something had gone wrong and braced himself for bad news. He was not callous to war, but understood the unforgiving toll it took from anyone, and everyone.

"He's gone," said Orla, shaking his head. "Ivar is gone, Guthroth, killed on Mount Staurin during our northern scouting probe. They're all gone. Crowbones, Beltrane, Pierre Gustave, even DuLac, I think."

"Y-you think?" asked Guthroth, astonished.

"Ja, he took off when we ran into Turks coming down the mountain, nearly a score of them. But hours later, as I was carrying Crowbones' body down the trail, I came across him stranded on a cliff ledge he couldn't escape, and left his ass there. Unless he sprouted wings and flew off, he's been dead since November. And I hope thirst and sun took their good time punishing him for all the misery he's bred in our lives, eh, Guthroth? The dirty bastard!"

"Ja, the b-bastard," agreed Guthroth, feeling Orla's angst in reliving the mountain ordeal. Guthroth had never been one to emote, but the news of Crowbones wounded him deeply. "I w-will miss C-crowbones in battle . . . at my side, and b-by the campfire. But as the P-pope promised, C-crowbones is in . . . Heaven now, for s-sacrificing himself to th-this crusade."

"Or Valhalla," said Orla. "Either place would be good, no?"

"J-ja, either p-place," said Guthroth, who had abandoned the Nordic religion in favor of baptism. Nonetheless, he saw no point in arguing and did what he had always done, clamped shut.

"But are you fit to fight, Guthroth?" asked Guillaume, concerned. "Don't press yourself. Arrow wounds rupture even months later, you know, especially if they strike an organ."

"J-ja, I'm good. I want to f-fight, not stay behind w-with the women in c-camp, you know!"

"Ass of Loki!" clucked Orla, grinning. "There are no women in camp anymore!"

"Huh?"

"Ja," explained Hroc, "the camp has been purified, so we crusaders had to be purified."

"And we're pretty damn pure all right," snarked Orla. "Pure of food, pure of morale, and pure of hope."

The idea of running off the women of camp made little sense to Guthroth. Shaking his head, he asked, "Th-things have ch-changed since I l-left, ja?"

"Oh, yes," said Orla, grateful his cousin was back. "And I hope you were eating well at that other place, because we're starving here in camp. Shit, just look at us. I've had to cinch my belt three times in the last two months!"

"It's been a difficult run for all in camp," said Tristan. "It might have been better had you waited things out to the south. You may want to turn back. And I'm not poking, Guthroth, I mean it with all my heart."

"What? And l-leave all of y-you helpless?" jested Guthroth, surrendering a full, unreserved grin.

Damn, thought Orla, surprised, but what's this?

Hroc caught Guthroth's expression, but did not let on. Guthroth looks good, he thought, and happy. Happy.

March 4th provided an unexpected windfall as an unannounced but substantial English fleet anchored at Saint Simeon laden with supplies and craftsmen. Oddly, no records, documentation, or letters have ever been found indicating that the crusaders were awaiting such a shipment, so it is uncertain whether this fleet was actually sent by King William Rufus of England or whether it was part of an organized effort by others to reinforce the crusaders. As history shows, William Rufus was the third son of William the Conqueror and the oppositional brother of Robert of Normandy. He had refused to participate in the crusade for two reasons. First, because he felt Pope Gregory VII and Pope Urban II had disrespected his father by chastising him for being overly violent, and second, because he and his brother, Robert of Normandy, had become estranged while fighting for control over sections of Normandy.

Irrespective of the fleet's origin, hearing of its arrival and recognizing the huge significance it could play, Bohemud and Raymond of Toulouse were dispatched by the Council of Princes to secure the new supplies and get them safely back to the crusader camps. Since the crusaders had been unable to block the Saint George and Bridge Gate, Antioch had continued to resupply itself through them, at times via Saint Simeon and Alexandretta whose roads were intermittently controlled by Turks and Christians.

Bohemud, Raymond, sixty knights, including the Danes and Guillaume, and 600 footmen reached Saint Simeon without incident. The fleet was unloaded, supplies were packed onto mule and oxen trains, and the caravan struck out for Antioch. The princes had sent a good-sized force for the venture and appointed two of the most significant princes of the crusade to lead it, which testifies to the value of this cargo as well as to the fact that the thirty-kilometer road to Saint Simeon could be a perilous proposition.

Moving such a caravan was an arduous task, just as it had been with the cargo of the Genoa fleet arriving earlier on November 17th of 1097. Weighed down by large amounts of tools, stone, and lumber, the train was forced to move at a snail's pace. This lengthened the one-day journey back to camp into two, causing separations and gaps in the marching order, exposing once again the problem of miscommunication posed by dual leadership.

Guthroth complained about these breaks in the caravan within five kilometers of leaving Saint Simeon to Guillaume who passed along the concern to Raymond.

"Dammit, there's nothing that can be done about it!" replied Raymond, already irritated by the slow pace of the return trip. "Shit, we'll just have to take our chances, that's all."

When Guillaume passed Raymond's response back to Guthroth, Guthroth rebelled, "The infantry is up fr-front and exposed wh-while the c-cavalry protects the slower w-wagons. Who'll pr-protect the infantry if M-Muslim c-cavalry attacks? There are b-but four h-horsemen with them!" Miffed, he signaled to Orla and Hroc to advance with him from the midpoint of the caravan to the front with the infantry.

Trusting Guthroth's instincts, Guillaume followed along.

The date was March 7th as the train neared the vicinity of the fortified bridge leading to the Bridge Gate. Turkish light cavalry had hidden there in position to spring an ambush. On signal, they swarmed out in full attack against the crusader infantry. As described by a footman surviving the onslaught: "The Turks began to gnash their teeth and chatter and howl with very loud cries, wheeling round our men, throwing darts and loosing arrows, wounding and slaughtering them most brutally. Their attack was so fierce that our men began to flee over the nearest mountain or wherever there was a path. Those who could get away quickly escaped alive, and those who could not were killed."

Making scraps of crusader infantry by first hitting them with compound bows fired from fleet horses, the Turks next began running over them on horses. The original four knights placed with the infantry, along with Guillaume and the Danes, were the only salvation keeping every footman in the entire brigade from being slaughtered. Dashing here and there, swinging swords and axes furiously, they did their courageous best to defend the men on foot, but the Turkish numbers were simply too overwhelming. The crusader death toll of the ambush included 500 of the 600 footmen on the advance line, but only two knights, reviving once again two bitter lessons of the past: there existed a lack of cohesion between cavalry and infantry, and men on horse fared much better than men on foot.

Just when it appeared the rout was complete, Bohemud and his knights dashed forward from their position as rear guard, with Raymond remaining in position guarding the train. Simultaneously, hearing the clash of iron and cries of war, Godfrey of Bouillon and his Germans rushed into the fray from their camp.

Catching sight of this, Yaghi Siyan poured in additional troops from the city, locking the Bridge Gate behind them, forcing perish or fight. Within minutes, what appeared to be a deadly skirmish ruptured into a full-fledged war of attrition as Muslim and Christian slammed into each other, wreaking bloody havoc in an unrelenting clash to the death, driven by hatred and blinded by invidiousness.

In the midst of this mayhem, it was the weight of Godfrey's Germans that began to shift momentum. Falling into panic, Turks began leaving the bridge in disaggregated packs at first, then in streams, scrambling toward the Bridge Gate, which Yaghi Siyan was frantically trying to re-open. As documented by a French knight: "They fled swiftly across the middle of the bridge to their gate. Those who did not succeed in crossing the bridge alive, because of the great press of men and horses, suffered their everlasting death with the devil and his imps, for we came after them, driving them into the river or throwing them down, so that the water of that swift stream seemed to be running red with the blood of Turks. And if by chance any of them tried to climb up the pillars of the bridge, or to reach the bank by swimming, he was stricken by our men who were standing all along the river bank."

When the blood fest ceased, Guthroth rode back and forth fuming, surveying the piles of dead infantrymen being gathered by Bohemud's men. Spotting Raymond pulling in an hour later, Guthroth spurred his horse toward Raymond, confronting him. "L-look yonder at the d-dead footmen you've p-put in the grave!" he cried angrily. "Fool!" Kicking his horse in the flanks, he galloped away to help stack the dead.

In the end, it was estimated that Latins and Turks suffered equal casualties, about 1,500 men per side. But the Christians claimed victory, insisting they had 'invoked the name of Jesus Christ and, being assured of the journey to the Holy Sepulcher, joined in battle with one heart and mind as knights of the true God, protected on all sides by the sign of the Cross.' Afterwards they clothed their dead in white and gave them martyrs' palms, declaring them martyrs bound for Everlasting Heaven, the whole time insisting the Muslim dead were doomed to Hell to suffer at the hands of the imps.

Though both the Damascus Turks of Duqaq and the Aleppo Turks of Ridwan had been turned back by the Army of God during its five-month entrenchment around Antioch, the Battle of the Bridge held new significance. It was the first time that Yaghi Siyan's forces had been repulsed. The death toll being even, Yaghi Siyan's garrison had begun the siege with 5,000 men against a vastly larger Christian force. Attrition, then, favored the crusaders. Yaghi Siyan had gambled on an ambush catching Raymond and Bohemud alone, and failed only because Godfrey of Bouillon unexpectedly joined battle from his nearby camp.

Of additional significance to the crusaders was the plunder of the dead and capture of horses acquired after the battle. This was celebrated during a special mass offered up by Raymond of Toulouse's chaplain, Raymond of Aguilers. Victorious knights paraded newly acquired Arabian stallions back and forth through camp, whereas other men-at-arms displayed before their tents fine silk garments, jewel-encrusted weapons and shields, and other valuables taken from slain Muslims.

That very morning the Turkish troops clandestinely returned to the battle field to bury their dead near the crumbling remains of an old deteriorated mosque located not far from the bridge. As by custom, they buried their slain brethren with gold bezants and silver coins, jewels, fine cloaks, tools, and weapons.

Learning of this, angry crusaders later gathered in that area, unearthed the dead, destroyed their tombs, and dragged the dead from their graves, robbing them of all valuables. Afterwards, they dumped the corpses in a large pit, cut off the heads and carried them back to camp to post on lances before their tents.

Horrified as Muslim heads were being mounted everywhere but in the Tuscan camp, Tristan turned to Guillaume, Letellier, and Scule, saying, "Watch and wonder, for this is what we have become."

Standing nearby, Christos said, "But Bishop Saint-Germain, the Turks do the same thing, don't they?"

"Yes," replied Tristan, "but it is us who are the Christians, not the Turks!"

As a finale to this episode, the Council of Princes decided to make a gesture of friendship to the Fatimids of Egypt. Taking four horses the visiting ambassadors of the emir of Cairo had brought to the crusaders as gifts, the princes loaded them up with Turkish heads. These horses were then sent to the coast to be shipped to the emir of Cairo as a gift to Egypt. Along with the horses and heads was attached a note: "To our Shia friends in North Africa, we present 200 Sunni heads as a return gift."

CHAPTER FIFTY

LA MAHOMERIE

Seizing the advantage after the Battle of the Bridge, the crusaders mobilized the building materials and craftsmen from the English fleet, deciding to construct a siege fortification on their own side of the Orontes across from the fortified bridge leading to the Bridge Gate. This was perilous territory. Rather than beginning from scratch, the crusaders decided to take advantage of a deteriorating mosque standing on the hill facing the Turk's fortified bridge; the same mosque where the Antioch garrison had buried their dead and the crusaders, in turn, dug up, defiled, and robbed.

In essence, this new fortification was to be similar in purpose to the fort that had earlier been built near Mount Staurin, but the new one was to have a greater impact due to its objective of blocking the Bridge Gate. Beginning on March 10th, the crusaders dug a double trench around the mosque, stationing a brigade of archers nearby to defend from attack. Within the center of these trenches, a stone-and-lime mortar wall was erected to create a defensive perimeter, and beside the mosque, two makeshift towers were raised.

The Danes had volunteered to help build the fortification, but when assignments were given out, they were handed shovels. "For helvede!" groaned Orla, swiping sweat from his face with a full pass of his forearm. "When I said I'd help, I meant with rock and mortar, not turning dirt!"

"D-dig and be h-happy," poked Guthroth, exchanging grins with Hroc. "Y-you're a laborer, Orla, n-not a craftsman. If y-you d-did the rock and m-mortar, the w-wall would fall d-down and k-kill m-me and Hroc!"

"Dammit, Guthroth," said Orla, "you've turned into a regular shit stirrer since I saw you last. What's happened to you?"

Saying nothing, Guthroth filled his shovel with dirt, signaled Hroc, and both of them pitched dirt over the back of Orla's neck. "Oh, p-pardon!" brayed Guthroth. "Our m-mis-take!"

The next crusader issue centered on which prince would man La Mahomerie, due to cost. Some princes balked, a few others volunteered their services, but only for pay. It was Raymond of Toulouse who finally agreed to take the job. As usual, his motives were less than pure. To begin, he had been ill and incapacitated during much of the siege, which bred resentment amongst those feeling he had not done his part. Raymond felt that by stepping in with La Mahomerie, he might reclaim authority. He, of all the princes, possessed the wealth to take on such a burden. Most likely, his primary motivation was the simple fact that should Antioch fall, La Mahomerie would probably be the point of attack, which would give Raymond first access to entry, and subsequently the ability to be the first to mount his banner over the city. Agreeing to pay all expenses involving the safeguarding and maintenance of La Mahomerie, Raymond claimed exclusive ownership of the new fort.

Disturbed at watching such construction occurring across the river, Yaghi Siyan realized the new fortification could hamper future sorties against the Christians from his favorite point of attack, the Bridge Gate. As March came to a close, he decided to test the makeshift structure by assaulting it directly in a surprise dawn attack.

As La Mahomerie had been hastily constructed in only a matter of days, it was never intended to be permanent, nor was it intended to repulse sustained attacks. Its purpose, in theory, was to buy enough time for Raymond and his troops to stave off attack long enough for reinforcements to cross the Bridge of Boats and circle the enemy from behind.

On the morning of Siyan's attack, to the horror of those within, La Mahomerie was nearly overrun. As planned, the din of battle caught the attention of other camps and they rushed into the breach, crossing the Bridge of Boats. In the end, the Turks were driven back, but barely. The crusaders, as before during miraculous turn-abouts in battle, credited the intervention of God. Whereas God's touch was indeed possible, nature itself provided help by hurling down torrential rains the night before the attack, filling the double trenches with water, hampering the penetration of La Mahomerie's defenses. Of additional note, the crusader plan was solid to begin with, in that Raymond's defenders did manage to hold out long enough for reinforcements to cross the Bridge of Boats, though only by a whisker.

The crusaders finally blocked the hemorrhaging Bridge Gate, forcing the Turks to use their last avenue of outbound access, the Saint George Gate. But even this became dangerous for the Turks as learned when they trotted out half of their horses to pasture on the rich spring grasses along the slopes of Mount Silpius. The crusaders had been astute enough to at least start patrolling this area, and in an unexpected coup, one of these patrols came onto the small Turkish force pasturing many of the city's horses. In all, the crusaders claimed to have captured nearly 2,000 mounts from the enemy in this venture, but that number was likely an exaggeration, as was often the case when contemporary witnesses described events of the crusade.

Now seeing the Saint George Gate as the 'nose-bleed' of the Antioch siege, the Council of Prices concluded it wise to convert an old monastery near the foot of Mount Silpius into a military outpost. But once again the problem of financing such a venture raised its ugly head. Being of the secondary, poorer ranks of the crusader hierarchy, it was Tancred who stepped forward this time, but only if he received 400 marks of silver in payment. Raymond put up a fourth of this bounty while the other princes combined to fill the purse.

Tancred's nose for acquisition paid off. Just days after settling into the old monastery his forces captured a large Armenian and Syrian caravan headed toward the Saint George Gate. Spoils of the assault included corn, barley, oil, wine, and other valuable foodstuffs.

Further improving the rising fortunes of the crusaders, a large train of horses and weapons arrived from Edessa. Baldwin of Boulogne, brother of Godfrey of Bouillon, had abandoned the crusade to enrich himself by establishing the first crusader realm in the Middle East. He accomplished this by taking and declaring himself ruler of the 'County of Edessa.' He had voluntarily left the Army of God, yet Baldwin maintained a cordial communication with his brother, Godfrey, promising to contribute to the crusader march toward Jerusalem with his newfound wealth. Hearing of crusader woes during the difficult winter of 1097-98, there is evidence that Baldwin did send assistance to them, but records seem to indicate that it came only in trickles. In any case, his April shipment of horses and weapons was substantial.

So, it came to be that the Army of God found itself showered with a series of unforeseen blessings, whilst the earlier bounty of Antioch had run its course. In a reversal of fortune, it was now Antioch's turn to experience shortage, hunger, and deteriorating morale.

CHAPTER FIFTY-ONE

OH, ANTIOCH

April and May dropped over Antioch, a dark specter arising from the once flagging camps of the crusaders. All city gates had been blocked except the Iron Gate, all roads of resupply were cut off, and the once plentiful stores of food, grain, and feed were nearly exhausted. Yaghi Siyan began to feel the noose tightening, and began making daily inquires to General Ahmet. "Have we heard from Mosul, Ahmet?" he would ask, his face straining with hope each morning before calling court into session.

"No, Emir Siyan," Ahmet would reply, his face heavy with discouragement. "No pigeons from Mosul, no word from the emir there, nor from his general, Kerbogha."

"With Duqaq and Ridwan both failing to save us," Siyan would then say, wringing his hands, "Kerbogha is our last hope! Otherwise our end is near, and woe to Antioch for the Christians have lost much here. They will show no mercy and our blood will flow in rivers!"

This daily strain began to extract a toll from Siyan, disassembling the one attribute that had elevated him to power through the most impossible of circumstances: patience. He had learned through adversity that those who stampede, crumble from within, leading one to foolishly leap over the edge rather than being pushed by another. Nonetheless, the fortress walls of his renown patience were now growing weak, as manifested one morning when he summoned Ben-fazi. "I want you to accompany me to the ramparts," he said. "I'm negotiating a prisoner release for ransom shortly, and I want you there to translate between Bohemud and me, since you are from Italy."

"It would be my honor, Master Yaghi," said Ben-fazi, lying through his teeth. He had come to notice, in private, that Yaghi Siyan's notorious composure had begun to fray. As such, being around Siyan developed into a contest of nerves for Ben-fazi. Fortunately, he had thus far managed to keep la Signorina's presence in the palace unknown. But when Yaghi Siyan began taking to fits of anxiety and distrust in others, Ben-fazi began to suspect that even he may have fallen under suspicion, though Yaghi Siyan had said nothing directly. In constant fear, Ben-fazi suspected at times that Siyan was watching him of late.

The wartime concept of ransoming prisoners was common practice in both Europe and the Middle East. It happened frequently, actually, and worked to the mutual benefit of both sides. The success of such a transaction, of course, hinged on a completed money transfer and release of the prisoner being actuated as promised. But evidenced during the earlier ransom incident with the young Turkish prince being publicly executed before the city walls, anger itself could sabotage negotiations, usually to no purpose other than satisfying frustration.

In this particular case, Yaghi Siyan was negotiating the ransom of a crusader captured at the Battle of the Bridge, a certain Rainald Porchet. Taking Porchet to the ramparts in chains as Ben-fazi followed, Siyan issued instructions, "Ben-fazi, I want a fair price for this fellow. Make that clear to Bohemud. I hear he's a hard case. But warn him, I'll not spend all morning haggling! Either I end up satisfied or the unfortunate crusader ends up dead. Understand?"

"Certainly, Master. As you wish."

Rainald Porchet was well-known and highly respected within the Christian camps. Being among the most devout of crusaders, the pious of the pious, his joining the Holy Crusade had been purely altruistic. To him, everything centered on the Holy Trinity: God the Father, God the Son, and God the Holy Ghost. His blind faith and devotion to Christ never had impinged his ability to laugh, carry on, and endear himself to others. This had, over time, caused him to become a particular favorite of Bohemud. But unlike others of Bohemud's inner circle, Porchet held huge admiration and respect for Bishop Saint-Germain; making no apologies about the fact. Consequently, Tristan set aside his own bitterness at Bohemud and accompanied both him and Tancred to the city wall, hoping that Porchet might spot him standing in support of the ransom parley.

Waiting beside Yaghi Siyan and Rainald Porchet atop the ramparts, Ben-fazi shouted out to the crusader assemblage exactly what Siyan had told him minutes earlier, ending with, "I know this emir personally, and I advise you to make this quick and agreeable. I beseech you on behalf of this poor Christian soul standing next to me in chains!"

The appearance of a little blue man with an elfin voice took the crusaders by surprise.

"What's this shit?" asked Bohemud. "I feel I'm in the midst of a damned fairy tale."

"Hell if I know," muttered Tancred, equally baffled. "But the little shit speaks perfect Italian, so he must be one of us, or was at least, at some point."

Listening, Tristan knew immediately who had just delivered the opening declaration from the rampart. It was the blue man described by Kareem who was courageously sheltering Mala and Christophe. May God bless you, little man, he thought, whoever you might be.

"Tell Yaghi Siyan that we shall meet his price . . . within reason!" shouted Bohemud. "We want our friend Porchet back!"

As Ben-fazi translated this to Siyan, Siyan nodded with satisfaction. "Good, I shall be reasonable, and we'll be done with it!"

Siyan had barely finished when Porchet's voice rang out, addressing his companions below. "My lords, it matters not if I die. I pray, my brothers, that you pay no ransom for me. But be certain in the faith of Christ and the Holy

Sepulcher that God is with you and shall be forever. You have slain all the leaders and the bravest men of Antioch; namely, twelve emirs and fifteen thousand noblemen, and no one remains to give battle with you or to defend the city!"

Surprised, Siyan looked to Ben-fazi. "What is he saying?"

"Nothing good concerning you was said," replied Ben-fazi.

"Well then, Ben-fazi, ask him whether he might wish to enjoy living honorably with us."

On hearing this translation, Porchet looked at the blue man and replied, "How can I live honorably with you without sinning?"

Ben-fazi passed along the question to Siyan. "If I take money for this Christian knight," said Siyan, "he will just keep attacking my men. He's worth more to me alive here in Antioch than out there. Besides, if he were to convert to Islam, it would be a blow to the crusaders and a coup for me. Tell the prisoner this: Deny your God, whom you worship and believe, and accept Mohammed and our other gods. If you do, we shall give to you all that you desire—gold, horses, mules, and many other worldly goods you wish, as well as wives and inheritances. And we shall enrich you with great lands."

Hearing Ben-fazi's translation, Porchet replied, "Give me time for consideration." Clasping his hands in prayer pointing to the east, he went to his knees. "Oh God, my father," he said, "I humbly ask that You come to my aid. Transport with dignity my soul to the bosom of Abraham!"

This brave action seared Ben-fazi to his core, forcing him to remember how cowardly he had been at his own moment of truth. A tear began streaming down his cheek, mixing with blue paint, creating salty streaks.

Seeing that Porchet appeared to be praying, Siyan demanded to know what he was saying.

"He completely denies your god," replied Ben-fazi, "and refuses your worldly goods."

This irritated Siyan. "He has damned himself by his own doing then, not by mine!" he shouted. Signaling the executioner who had accompanied them up the rampart, he burst into a short fit of profanity, then said, "It seems this man prefers death over life. Move closer, executioner. Should he not agree to my terms, then clip his head!"

Siyan made two supplementary efforts to persuade Porchet that converting to Islam would be his salvation, but Porchet, a man of God, rebuffed both. "Pay nothing!" he shouted from the rampart. "I am not afraid! Nor shall I abandon my god, and yours!"

Hearing this, knights and footmen alike began pleading with Porchet. "Save yourself!" they cried. "Denounce God to save yourself, then recant!"

Tristan stood watching, praying that Porchet might survive this ordeal, yet suspecting that the cold reality of circumstance would not sanction such an outcome. Floundering in doubt and fear, his heart remained firmer in the camp of God than in the camp of mortality. Stay strong, Rainald! God awaits you, Tristan prayed. His almighty reach is but minutes away. Hold firm, dear friend, eternity is but one step further ahead. Do not falter! You are ever closer to leaving this dreadful earth and finding eternal glory beside the throne of God!

Pushed beyond the limits of tolerance by Porchet's iron will, Siyan shouted, "This is your last chance, heathen! Renounce your God and Christianity and convert here in front of your own army, or be decapitated on this rampart!"

Upon translating this to Porchet, Ben-fazi looked at him hopefully. "What's your answer?"

"NO!" shouted Porchet.

Yaghi Siyan needed no translation, nor did the executioner.

Spreading his legs, the executioner sucked in his breath and raised the ax high over his head, straining for height, then swung downward in one swift chop. Rainald's head dropped against the stone floor of the rampart and tumbled a good three feet, in its wake spewing a trail of blood emanating from the point of severance. It rolled to a stop lying flat on his cheek and ear, tissue and gore pulsated gruesomely, effusing the last of his life.

Ben-fazi began to vomit, and with each heave his heart admiration for Porchet grew. Oh, you brave Christian, he thought. I should have been but half as brave when facing my own trial, but cowardice saved me, which only led to my current misery! Next time I shall follow your lead.

Among the crusaders below the wall, an unidentified monk stepped forward, holding both palms open to the sky. "I see that swiftly the angels have come," he announced, "joyfully singing the Psalms of David. They are bearing Porchet's soul and lifting it before the sight of God for Whose love he has undergone martyrdom!"

Stung by the act of cruelty just committed, crusaders went to their knees, making the sign of the cross and reciting the Pater Noster.

Tristan alone remained standing. "Oh, Rainald, valiant and virtuous warrior of God!" he shouted. "If only these other men here possessed your virtue, your honesty, and your love of God over every other temptation this world sets before them, this would indeed be a Holy Crusade!"

Such words galled those on their knees, especially Bohemud. "Shut your damned mouth, Saint-Germain!" he barked; his grief over Porchet squelching any further response, but others began to grumble aloud about Tristan's epithet to Porchet.

Alas, the drama was far from finished. Having a fit over failing to make Porchet turn apostate, Yaghi Siyan screamed at the guards surrounding him, "Gather every damned crusader captive from the jail and bring them here!"

"Master Yaghi!" pleaded Ben-fazi, knowing that a dreadful demon had arisen and taken control of Yaghi Siyan's mind. "Don't do anything rash, I beg!"

"Indeed," agreed General Ahmet, "it will only make things worse should the crusaders break over our walls!"

Disregarding both, Siyan shoved them aside and vehemently ranted to the guards. "When you get them here, strip them naked and surround them with wood piled to their heads!"

Guards scrambled toward the prison, extracting every crusader within its walls, dragging them to the rampart for all to see. Binding them per Siyan's instructions, the guards surrounded them with any combustible material they could find. Oil was then dumped over the circular wall of flammables, saturating it from top to bottom.

Yaghi Siyan shouted, "Now in the name of Allah, set them afire so those heathens below can watch their friends scream for mercy!"

Guards shoved torches to the total circumference of the underbrush, igniting the tinder. Instantly smoke rose, choking the prayers lifted to Heaven, blessedly killing most beforehand. Then fire engulfed the entire cluster of Christian prisoners, leaping twenty feet over their heads.

That day, Yaghi Siyan's temperament and frustration colluded in a show of rage as Christian witnesses wept for their scorched brethren. Ben-fazi dropped to his knees in tears, Bohemud swore everlasting vengeance, and Tristan de Saint-Germain closed his eyes in prayer.

As recorded by a secondary papal scribe hours later: "The Christians, those knights of Christ, shrieked and screamed so that their voices resounded in Heaven to God for Whose love their flesh and bones were cremated, and they all entered martyrdom on this day wearing in Heaven their white stoles before the Lord, for Whom they had loyally suffered in the reign of our Lord Jesus Christ, to Whom is the honor and glory now and throughout eternity. Amen."

Documented afterwards by Peter Tubolde, a Latin contemporary: "Then Yaghi Siyan, in a towering rage because he could not make Rainald turn apostate, at once ordered all the captive crusaders in Antioch to be brought before him with their hands bound behind their backs. He ordered them stripped stark naked. And as they stood in the nude, he commanded they be bound with ropes in a circle. He then had chaff, firewood, and hay piled around them, and finally as enemies of God, he ordered them put to the torch. The Christians, those knights of Christ, shrieked and screamed so that their voices resounded in Heaven."

CHAPTER FIFTY-TWO

PEACE?

The fortunes of Antioch deteriorated to the point that by May the Turkish garrison became crippled with doubt and fear. General Ahmet continued to support Yaghi Siyan, but many of his commanders began whispering in clandestine huddles, agreeing that the collapse of Antioch was inevitable. On May 20th, an envoy slipped from Antioch, appearing in the camp of Bishop Adhémar and Raymond of Toulouse. "I have here an offer of surrender signed by a conglomerate of ten generals," declared the envoy, producing a document translated into French, containing ten signatures at the bottom.

"Bah, but where's the stamp and signature of Emir Siyan?" complained Raymond, eyeing the document suspiciously.

"Oh, but the emir is a proud man," replied the envoy, an Armenian who had converted to Islam decades earlier to make a good living in the service of Arabs, then Turks. "He's in full agreement with this document, but his pride does not allow his name on any pact of surrender. Being men of war and of high prestige, surely you can understand?"

"Certainly," agreed Adhémar, shushing Raymond's objections. "We should like to send several representatives into Antioch on an agreed date. I am certain they and Yaghi Siyan's representatives can quickly come to a suitable agreement. If he surrenders, I vow that we shall be fair and merciful to the general population."

"Ah, but, sire," replied the envoy, "the ten generals wish to know specifically how the Turkish garrison itself shall be treated."

"Fairly. I vow it," nodded Adhémar, giving Raymond a cold stare. 'I, Pope Urban's appointed leader of the Holy Crusade shall handle this, not you, Raymond,' the stare said.

The following day, the Armenian envoy returned. "All is ready within the city. The generals await the arrival of your own embassy to write out the details. They wish to surrender as quickly as possible. Tomorrow morning, just before light, is their choice of time."

"This damn early?" demanded Raymond.

"Hush, Raymond!" contravened Adhémar. "The hour is of no importance here. Rather, it is the agreement itself that counts!"

"The generals simply wish to avoid arousing panic," interceded the envoy, attempting to defuse Raymond's evident discontent. "Our population includes Christians, Muslims, Arabs, Greeks, Syrians, Turks, and Armenians. With such a volatile mix, best that we handle all this quietly for the moment. Does that not make sense?"

Raymond said nothing, so Adhémar spoke, "Most certainly it makes sense. Come fetch our delegation an hour before dawn. They will be waiting for you at the fortified bridge leading to the Bridge Gate."

As agreed, the Armenian envoy went to the bridge and welcomed a crusader contingent of twelve, representing the Provencal camp of Adhémar and Raymond, the Northern French camp of Robert of Normandy, Robert of Flanders, Stephen of Blois, and Hugh of Verminous, and the German camp of Godfrey of Bouillon. The appointed leader of this delegation was none other than Walo II of Chaumont-en-Vexin, the former constable to King Philip I of France.

But even as the envoy was heading for the Bridge Gate, Yaghi Siyan was astir, fuming within the palace. "Oh, but Ben-fazi, General Ahmet has just uncovered a rebellion within our very midst. Not amongst Armenians or Christians, but within the ranks of my own generals!"

"What?" This disturbed Ben-fazi greatly, not the suggestion of conspiracy but the look in Siyan's dark eyes deeply embedded behind their bushy eyebrows. They had turned to burning coals again, just as on the day of Rainald Porchet's beheading.

"Yes-s-s," lamented Siyan, launching into another world, "my own generals undermining me! I shall never surrender, come what may! I will not lose hope that Kerbogha of Mosul might arrive any day. He, of any Seljuk army in the entire Middle East, would grind these Christians to dust. He has never been stopped, nor ever suffered defeat!"

"B-but," stammered Ben-fazi, "what's to be done about your own generals?"

"There are crusaders approaching our gate as I speak, Ben-fazi, but no fears. Come along with me and watch."

Mere steps inside the portals of Antioch, the envoy and all twelve crusader delegates were snatched by over a hundred guards concealed in waiting as the Bridge Gate slammed to a close. "What's this?!" shouted the envoy, startled by the swarm of guards appearing from nowhere.

"Damn!" swore Walo. "But what foul form of treachery has been sprung this day!?" Looking ahead, he spotted a massive butcher's stump standing fifty feet from where he stood. Beside it stood the same executioner who had murdered Rainald Porchet. Gasping, Walo began to understand. "We're lost, men!" he shouted. "It's but a trick!"

As the Armenian envoy and the twelve crusaders were held in place awaiting the arrival of Yaghi Siyan, a different platoon appeared from the direction of the prison, marching ten Turks with hands chained behind their backs to the butcher block. Lined up in a file by the guards, the ten were bareheaded, barefoot, and stripped to the waist.

Of the first set of prisoners, only the Armenian envoy recognized this new collection of victims. It was the same coven of men who had enlisted him to contact Adhémar of Le Puy and Raymond of Toulouse about surrender.

"Who are these poor bastards?" asked Walo. "Are they to suffer the same fate as us?"

"Yes," swallowed the envoy, his throat going dry as sand. "It's the ten generals who signed the pledge of surrender."

"Then this was not a trick on their part to get us into the city?"

The envoy shook his head, tears filling his eyes, thinking of his wife and six children under the age of eleven for whom he had faithfully provided for over recent years. They would be disgraced, and everything his family owned would go into forfeit the moment the ax blade severed his head from his shoulders.

"Armenian," said Walo, "are you Christian?"

The envoy shook his head. "No, I converted."

"Then you believe in Allah?"

"No. I converted, but falsely."

"We've but minutes left to breathe, Armenian," said Walo, "best you pray hard to the real God, the only God, for forgiveness. Otherwise, you shall burn in Hell for eternity."

"Yes," said the envoy, tearfully dropping to his knees. Staring skyward, his lids closed in his struggle to remember the Pater Noster in Latin.

"Ah-ha!" shouted Yaghi Siyan, arriving with Ben-fazi. "One nest of traitors, and one nest of heathens! Both awaiting their end!" Signaling the executioner, he stood his ground.

This surprised Ben-fazi, who was expecting Siyan to spout a lengthy diatribe about loyalty and the price of disloyalty, Allah and the price of paganism. Instead, Siyan waited in silence as the generals' heads were taken. Then, continuing this silence, he nodded to the executioner who then axed the final thirteen heads. As surprised as Ben-fazi was about Siyan's calm, what came next chilled his blood.

"Come along, Ben-fazi," said Siyan, his voice nearly like the purr of a cat staring contentedly but not hurriedly at a meal it had killed an hour earlier. "I have something to discuss with you in private. Something that has come to my attention. Something that displeases me."

Swallowing hard, Ben-fazi's thoughts shot to la Signorina and baby Christophe. "Should you be displeased, Master," said Ben-fazi contritely, "and I am the cause of it, I beg your forgiveness with all my heart. Might I ask what I've done?"

Yaghi Siyan placed his long fingernails against the top of his upper lip, then sank them like claws into the bush of his hoary beard. "You know what you've done, Ben-fazi," his voice going low. "And you know how few people I have ever trusted, you being among that few. You know how I feel about trust, as just witnessed. Be quiet as we walk; just think, Ben-fazi. Yes, just try to imagine."

Feeling dread fill his heart, Ben-fazi waited for Yaghi Siyan to complete his sentence. When no words came, he said, "Yes, Master? What should I try to imagine?"

"Ah, I was so disturbed I failed to finish. Try to imagine, Ben-fazi, how I, Yaghi Siyan, must be feeling this very moment about you."

CHAPTER FIFTY-THREE

A MOMENT IN TIME . . . TELLING ALL

Arriving in the palace, Yaghi Siyan led Ben-fazi to the throne hall where court was held each morning. Twelve guards stood rigidly at attention, staring forward at nothing. "Sit right there where you always sit, at my right side," said Siyan, his look of agitation betrayed only by the tremor of his lips, which often occurs in old people when agitated or disturbed. "And do you know why your seat is to my right, Ben-fazi?"

His nerves jangling, Ben-fazi said, "No, Master Yaghi, though I do consider it a most precious honor."

"Ah, yes, an honor. Exactly," replied Siyan, deprecation slipping into his voice. "I am the only one on this earth that would honor one such as you, Ben-fazi. Have you ever been honored like this before? By anyone? But wait, no, don't answer. I know the answer. Now another question, why do you suppose a man such as me would honor a man such as you?"

"I don't really know." Ben-fazi was finding it difficult to look Siyan in the eye. "Perhaps because you collect things. Or perhaps simply because you can? And it pleases you to flaunt the unusual, because it disturbs others?"

"Oh, my clever little perceptive Ben-fazi. There is so much more to you than what people see, which is but your deformities. But your answer was close, very close indeed. Yes, yes, like in you, people see in me little of value. It's been that way since the day of my birth. My head too big, my ears too big, my face not symmetrical, born a slave. But someone elevated me, Ben-fazi, because of all things, he had eyes that could penetrate profoundly, not like the fools of this world, which is nearly every man alive. But I have eyes, too. That's why I elevated you, made you my counselor, to the dismay of my minsters and generals. And why did I do that? Yes, I knew it would disturb people, just as I disturb people. But you are clever, Ben-fazi. Like me, you are a survivor. Fools find an early grave, don't they my little friend?"

Here Siyan stopped. Ben-fazi was not sure whether to respond, and cautiously remained silent.

"Yes, they do!" said Siyan, answering himself. "In a moment I shall bring someone in, but before I do, I wish to say this. You are a fellow traveler on the underbelly of life, just like me. I scarcely trust anyone since I have been betrayed a thousand times. I find my pleasures not in reality, but in my mind. And it is my imagination that has saved me time and time again. It is my imagination that separates me from other men who have no imagination and are fools."

"I am a fool," said Ben-fazi tepidly. "I've been a fool, actually, until I stared death and Mahmoud Malik in the face. That frightened me into thinking right."

"Ah, funny you should mention Malik," said Siyan. Clapping his hands twice, the guard nearest the back of the room left to shortly return with the big Persian. "I know you are half blind, Malik," scoffed Siyan, "but come forward and stand with us. Poor thing, you look hideous; your mutilated face, I mean. Oddly enough, you seem much less frightening than before. Pitiful, actually. Talk slow for us Malik, since you are difficult to understand. Seems your throat was slit reasonably deep, no?"

His lone eye staring at Ben-fazi with pure hate, Malik advanced, ignoring Siyan's words.

"Now repeat what you told me earlier, Malik," requested Siyan.

Not hesitating, Malik began, though indeed certain words were hard to decipher, making him sound gruff, a little off. "That little bird sitting there next to you came to the prison and had one of my prisoners released," claimed Malik angrily, "and showed a document with your name and seal, Emir Siyan!"

"Hmmm," said Siyan, considering his words carefully. "But then, did you have permission to keep young girls, or a woman for that matter, in my prison?"

"No."

Turning slightly in his seat, Siyan addressed Ben-fazi, "Is what Malik said true?"

"Yes, Master Yaghi." Ben-fazi bowed his head. "His prisoner was a woman I knew in my previous life; the one person who treated me well in Italy, just as you are the one person who has treated me well here. Malik beat her and was about to rape her. She, too, is a fellow traveler. Beautiful beyond compare, but unlike us, she is a survivor and sees things differently than the vicious masses."

"Hmmm," replied Siyan, tapping his chin with his forefinger . . . but then stopped and pointed at Ben-fazi. "But you forged my name and stamp?"

"It was the only way I could get the guards to release her."

"But why didn't you simply ask me to have her released?"

"I was afraid. For her, not me." Here Ben-fazi gathered his breath, trying to steady his hands. "But I brought her back to the prison, Master Yaghi, and turned her over to Boros, the Armenian jailer."

"That's a lie!" shouted Malik, the rawness of his throat making his voice crack; the pain shooting from his bandaged crotch making him grunt out his words through clenched teeth, at least those that were left. "You and the jailer conspired together!"

"True?" purred Siyan, staring him down.

"No," replied Ben-fazi, looking coldly into Malik's one eye. "Boros knew nothing. Besides, a Turkish guard who could read looked at my document and gave the go ahead. I took the woman out for but a short time, to soothe her injuries and her heart that was breaking for the peril her infant son was in, then I returned her and the child to Boros. After that, I've no idea what he might have done with her. He felt sorry for her. Maybe when I returned her late in the night, Boros simply let them go. He's a good one, you know, that Boros. But my hands are clean, I swear it!" Saying this, he felt perspiration beading over his brows and lips, loosening paint.

"That's a damn lie, I say!" retorted Malik, spittle flinging from his deformed lips.

"But the jailer ran off," said Siyan, "which makes him look guilty, not Ben-fazi."

Turning purple, Malik began to shake in fury; rivulets of oozing pus running down his face.

"Ben-fazi, to whom do you talk or associate with in this city besides me?"

"No one. Only you."

"Ah, but I beg your pardon. It seems you have been spending time with my beautiful Karine and Garik. No?"

"Yes, but only because they are dear to you, Master Yaghi. You've been so occupied with this war, I thought it best to check on them from time to time, that's all."

Siyan clapped his hands twice and the same guard as before left and returned with Garik and Karine. Seeing them, Ben-fazi's face went hot, and he began to perspire profusely. Malik knew not what to think.

"Come, come, my dear children," urged Siyan, motioning the children forward. "I have a few questions for you. And I'll begin with you, my sweet Garik."

Looking to Karine, Garik's shoulders slumped. And as so often when nervous, he stood there shivering, standing awkwardly with one foot atop the other. In response, Karine glared at him sternly. "Stand straight," she said crossly, "and answer Master Yaghi. Don't be afraid, Garik, Master Yaghi adores you and will not hurt you."

"Garik," began Siyan, peeking through the bush of his brows, "have you, by chance, heard Ben-fazi mention anything about the prison?"

Saying nothing, Garik shook his head 'no,' but the gesture lacked conviction, suggesting uncertainty.

Siyan leaned forward a bit to better dissect Garik's expression. "And have you heard him, by chance, mention a man by the name of Boros? An Armenian here in the city."

Shaking his head 'no' again, he maintained his silence, but his eyes began shifting back and forth from Karine to Yaghi Siyan, and his shivering escalated.

"Well then," Siyan adjusted his seating position, "just one more question, Garik. Have you heard Ben-fazi mention anything about a woman or a child?"

Even before Siyan had finished his sentence, Garik began to bawl and howl, and within moments his sobs caught in his throat, making him gasp and sputter between breaths; the anguish blaring from his throat as if he were being prodded with a red-hot iron. Doddering, unable to see through his tears and squinted eyes, he groped for Karine, hiding behind her, his blubbering growing intolerably poignant.

"Stop it," commanded Karine, collaring him. "Stop it now, Garik."

Chortling a bit, Siyan did not get angry but just looked over at Ben-fazi. "A beautiful boy," he mused, "but frightened of his own shadow, poor thing. But that's his nature and he cannot help himself. I, too, have been terrified by the world, though I hide it. Garik, on the other hand, trumpets it!" Pausing a moment, he looked at Karine, tilting his head in a motion to step forward.

"Yes, Master Yaghi?" she said, neither smiling nor scowling, but presenting that same blank face that had become commonplace to the old emir.

It was a face that mystified but pleased him. He appreciated that a mere child could effectively mask such emotion. He himself had developed that identical skill by the time he was her age. "The same question to you, dear one," urged Siyan. "I know Ben-fazi spends time with you and your brother, Karine. Although in public he says little aloud because people mock his voice, I know in private, he very much enjoys conversation around those with whom he feels comfortable, few as they may be. Do you believe he feels comfortable around you, my dear?"

"I wouldn't know, Master Yaghi," she replied, staring directly into his eyes, daring him to doubt her words. "One never knows what another really feels, do they? They can only imagine what another feels, and imagination is often misleading."

"Ha! But you are precious, Karine!" twittered Siyan.

"I heard your question to Garik, Master Yaghi," said Karine, her eyes widening, making her appear more ambrosial than she already was, which pleased the old emir immensely. "Ben-fazi does not come to our apartment much, because Garik believes he's an evil jinn and is afraid of him. I think it's the paint. But Ben-fazi isn't that bad at all."

"Karine," said Siyan, enlarging his own eyes to respond to hers, "you have not heard him mention the prison, nor a man named Boros, nor anything about a woman or a baby?"

"No, Master Yaghi. He's said nothing about any of those things. He only talks about you, worrying about what this war is doing to you, or what might become of you should the crusaders get in our walls. He would not wish to see you injured or captured. Nor would I, Master Yaghi."

"Ha, you marvelous little prize!" replied Siyan, taking on a look of assurance, even smiling a bit, though his long hoary mustache and beard concealed it.

"Master Yaghi, may I take Garik back to our apartment?" asked Karine, offering that smile of supplication perfected by young girls just before turning into women. "When he gets this way, he sometimes goes into seizures, you know."

"Yes, of course," he said, patting her on the head like a pet, then without pausing or looking up, "and Malik, you are also dismissed."

This fueled Malik's fire. Dismissed?! I'll show him who's dismissed. His disdain growing to an uncontrollable level, he slightly bowed in mock reverence and headed for the door; every inch of his body throbbing in anger and pain.

As they left, leaving only Siyan, Ben-fazi, and the guards, he leaned over to the little blue man. "We are fellow travelers, you and me, in a world of scaffolds and executioners. I trust you. But should you ever violate that trust, bond or no bond, your head will be in a basket."

"Yes, Master Yaghi, I would expect so," said Ben-fazi, his cheeks streaming with perspiration. He had been sitting on edge, holding his breath, each time Karine opened her mouth; his pounding heart flushing straight to his face, fouling the daily delicacy of his face paint. "With your permission, Master Yaghi," he implored, "I should like to make my way to my quarters. I'm not feeling well."

"But what is it, Ben-fazi? Why do you suddenly appear ill?" asked Siyan, carefully judging his pet's demeanor.

"It's being in this room like this, Master, with Mahmoud Malik," lied Ben-fazi. "He was nearly my executioner, and each time I see him, I feel the axe blade coming down."

CHAPTER FIFTY-FOUR

A SPECTER ARISES FROM MESOPOTAMIA

Kerbogha was known in Mesopotamia and Syria as 'The Great Atabeg of Mosul,' atabeg being a Seljuk hereditary title of nobility, indicating a governor of a nation or province who was subordinate to a monarch and charged with raising the crown prince. If a Seljuk prince died leaving minor heirs, a guardian was appointed to protect and guide the young princes. This guardian often married their wards' widowed mothers, becoming a surrogate father. And in the Seljuk hierarchy, the rank of atabeg was senior to that of a khan. Being known as a 'dreadful man,' Kerbogha became the most feared figure of the Middle East through a hard-earned combination of military might and sheer mercilessness.

Yaghi Siyan had, the previous October, sent his son Muhammed with a delegation pleading for assistance from Duqaq of Damascus. After Duqaq's defeat and failure against the crusaders, Muhammed's delegation then traveled the lengthy 800 kilometers east to Mosul, in Mesopotamia. Believing that Kerbogha had little interest in faraway Syria, it was paramount that Muhammed make an impression on him.

To shore up his case, Muhammed and his delegation turned to drama to show the severity of Antioch's position. As reported by sources in the Mesopotamian court: "They took their hats off and threw them to the ground, they savagely plucked out their beards with their nails, they pulled at and tore their hair by the roots with their fingers, and they heaved sighs in great lamentations."

This wanton display of despair was impressive enough to earn its intended effect. "Oh, but call my magicians, summon our prophets and soothsayers!" declared Kerbogha after the Antiochian delegation had expressed their pleas. "Gather them all so they might tell us whether a great victory awaits us!"

Later crusader accounts, undoubtedly fabricated, insist that after deciding to march against Antioch, Kerbogha went to his mother to share his news, who sternly warned him, "Do not fight the crusaders. They are protected by the Christian God. If you join battle with these men, you will suffer great loss and dishonor, lose many of your faithful soldiers, leave behind all the plunder which you have taken, and escape as a panic-stricken fugitive!"

That crusaders could be privy to such a conversation in the first place is absurd, yet it must be remembered that fanciful interpretation and play on mysticism was very characteristic of events, as later translated by Muslims and Christians alike.

Muhammed was, of course, overjoyed that he had convinced Kerbogha, the final Seljuk hope, to come to Antioch's aid. He fancied that his theatrics had won the day. But in the cold world of reality, truth is always mercenary, less than fanciful. In reality, Kerbogha had been eyeing Syria, in particular Antioch, with envious eyes. Unbeknownst to Muhammed and Yaghi Siyan, Kerbogha had decided that if he marched as far as Antioch to save it, he had every intention of claiming it as his own. By accomplishing this, Kerbogha would then be powerful enough to even take on the great power of Baghdad. In the end then, the image of leading a 'sacred struggle against the ravening Frankish horde' provided Kerbogha with the perfect cover to thieve a kingdom; exactly the same 'sacred struggle' ploy being manipulated to advantage by certain crusader princes.

Kerbogha spent six months adding to his own formidable army by enlisting a vast array of allied forces, including Turks, Arabs, Saracens, Paulicians, Azymites, Kurds, Persians, and Agulani. As owed to hyperbole, many said that 'the army was so numerous that the troops could not be counted.' More specific estimates of the time claim 800,000 cavalrymen accompanied by 300,000 infantry, but that was undoubtedly an exaggeration. Realistically speaking, Kerbogha probably commanded a force of about 40,000-45,000, a massive army nonetheless. It must be noted, however, that Kerbogha's answer to Antioch's plea in no way represented a united Islamic front sanctioned to save the Sunni world from Christianity. Instead, most of Kerbogha's allies mustered to his side out of fear of Kerbogha himself.

Hearing vague reports of vast military activity forming far to the east from passing caravans and traders passing through the Ruj Valley, Lord Azim sent Kareem to the crusader camp to pass these rumors along to Tristan. Tristan, in turn, went to the camp of Adhémar and Raymond to advise them of such.

Bohemud happened to be there by chance, and after Tristan shared his news, both Raymond and Bohemud ridiculed him.

"Ha, that's preposterous!" jibed Bohemud.

"Aye, he's but pressing us to openly attack Antioch to save his precious Signorina!" claimed Raymond.

"And this scare has been perpetrated by that Seljuk friend of his who came for a visit a while back?" added Bohemud. "Horseshit, I say! And just why would he care about our position?"

Frustrated, Tristan looked to Adhémar, but Adhémar said nothing, walking off muttering beneath his breath. He had completely washed his hands of the younger bishop after their last bitter encounter.

"Very well then," said, Tristan, disgusted. "Lord Azim has gone beyond expected and carries himself with more honor than the three of you combined. Alright, have it your way. I shall extend my prayers to the bunch of you, for you shall need them!"

As time progressed, the Council of Princes, by mid to late May, had begun to intercept reports of Kerbogha's movement west. Dispatching scouting parties east to Artah, south of the Ruj, and north to Cilicia, the crusaders' worst fears were confirmed when scouts returned with reports on May 28th saying: "We saw the Muslim army swarming everywhere from the mountains and different roads like the sands of the sea, marveling at their infinite thousands and totally unable to count them!"

Alarmed, the Council of Princes met that very next morning. "Damnation, it seems we're about to be caught in the middle and crushed," remarked Raymond.

"Aye," agreed Robert of Normandy, "when Kerbogha's force arrives, Yaghi Siyan will sally his cavalry from behind his walls and we'll be caught in a vice!"

Looking about the table, Bohemud said to Guillaume loud enough for all to hear, "Though we are in serious trouble, I don't see your brother here. Does he not care?"

Guillaume and Bohemud were close, but he was displeased with the tone of Bohemud's question. "Yes, my brother cares about the situation," he replied calmly. "It's you and some of these others here he can't abide by, Bohemud. He's been ostracized and belittled and this council has ignored every counsel he has contributed; all of it being right from what I can see. Should that be done to me, I, too, would refuse to attend meetings."

"And I also," interjected Letellier.

Robert of Normandy, Robert of Flanders, and others of the Northern French army appeared to agree. "Fair enough," gestured Stephen of Blois to Bohemud, "let the subject of Bishop Saint-Germain be and attend to the matter at hand!"

"Very well then." Bohemud cleared his throat, making no further issue. "It doesn't look good, my friends," he said, shaking his head. "My first suggestion is we not spread word in camp about Kerbogha. It would only frighten them, kill morale, and fuel panic. Agreed?" There came no objections. "As things stand, we either run or we stay, and—"

"My ass!" shouted Raymond, incensed. "Having come this far, lost many, many men, and wasted a mint, I'll be damned if I'll run!" Looking about the table, most agreeing, his sights landed on one man. "Well, Bohemud, what now?"

Gauging the expressions of the stares aimed his direction, Bohemud answered, "Very well then, I've no wish to run from the calamity facing us either. But a question, one I've brought up before . . . that was rebuffed. If, by some miracle of chance or stroke of God, if I were able to take Antioch, would the rest of you relinquish it to me?"

Silence followed until Raymond of Toulouse, rolling his shoulders, cackled a bit, elbowing Adhémar. "Ha! But damn you, Bohemud. What the hell are you talking about? I don't give a shit what happens. I'll not consent to handing Antioch over to you!"

"I would!" decreed Tancred.

"Of course, you would," snarled Raymond. "Chrissakes, you're Bohemud's goddamn nephew!"

"I would as well," said Robert of Normandy, standing firm, offering unsolicited agreement to Tancred.

Because the Northern French had remained united in all Council decisions, others at the table swiveled in their direction, already supposing future responses from the group.

"Aye, me, too," joined in Robert of Flanders.

"Aye." Stephen of Blois raised his hand, followed by Hugh of Vermandois.

Seeing momentum wash into Bohemud's favor, Godfrey bit his tongue and acquiesced; his own visions of claiming Antioch fading from view. Bohemud taking the city at this point, in his mind, was a far stretch. With battles staring them in the face from two fronts and possible extermination to follow, Godfrey clung to a single hope. "If Bohemud can take this city either by himself or with others," he said, "I believe we should give it to him gladly, save for one condition: if the emperor and Taticius should show up as promised, we will return the city to him because it's the right thing to do!"

This, more than anything, was purely a stall tactic. Yes, Godfrey hoped that Taticius and Alexius might show up at the eleventh hour and swing the balance back to Christian advantage, but any army they brought would not outnumber the crusaders themselves. In the end, the crusaders could overwhelm Alexius' force and take Antioch for their own, splitting it rather than handing it over to Bohemud alone.

Hearing Godfrey's declaration, all at the table including Guillaume and Letellier agreed, except for Raymond of Toulouse. "I'll do no such thing, damn the lot of you!" he snorted indignantly, looking to Adhémar. "What do you say as the Pope's man?"

Shrinking a measure, cut to the bone at setting aside decades of friendship with Raymond, Adhémar's voice went meek as he turned away from Raymond, not wishing to look him in the eye. "If Bohemud should muster such a miraculous recovery from our current state," he said, "then, yes, the city goes to him save for the lone condition reserved by Godfrey of Bouillon."

Furious, Raymond slammed the table top and stalked off shouting a string of profanity at the top of his voice.

"Very well," said Bohemud, contentedly. "There remains one tiny hope in our black future, my friends." Getting their undivided attention, he cleared his throat and began, "I've been secretly contacted by someone inside the city, an Armenian who, unbelievably, happens to command the tower adjacent to the Saint George gate to the far south. It's near the old monastery where Tancred has taken up his blockading position." Here he paused, assessing the stunned expressions of the men who, like slipping from the edge of a cliff, suddenly spy an exposed root they might yet cling to. This pleased Bohemud immensely. He had their full attention. "Tancred, at a sizable risk, has been in communication with this insider and may be close to arriving at an agreement. We've promised this Armenian the moon if he carries out his part, but the high price he demands is well worth our lives, I say. But then, what do you say?"

The reply came quickly and unanimously. "Aye!"

CHAPTER FIFTY-FIVE

THE OXEN-HIDE LADDER

Moving east, Kerbogha became distracted along his long march by the idea of conquering the County of Edessa, now ruled by Godfrey of Bouillons' brother, Baldwin of Boulogne. He assumed, at first, Edessa would be an easy conquest, but Baldwin's force combined with thousands of Armenians heroically held Kerbogha at bay. Kerbogha had not yet amassed his full army; many having been sent south and east of Edessa, and to Syria. Knowing that time was of the essence, Kerbogha abandoned Edessa after three weeks, vowing he would return with his full army after taking Antioch.

Kerbogha's failed effort bought time for the crusaders. Having finalized plans with Firuz through Tancred, Bohemud set his strategy into play on June 2nd. Parading a large force of cavalry and infantry before the Saint George Gate, he had them march off, vanishing from view to set Antioch at ease. Under cover of darkness, the knights dismounted and returned by foot, remaining hidden, while the infantry made a wide circle to later rendezvous with the cavalry at the Saint George Gate. By 3:00 a.m. of June 3rd, over 700 crusaders were assembled along the slopes before the Saint George Gate.

Raymond of Toulouse's vehement rejection of Bohemud's conditions for taking the city went unheard, yet he agreed to the plot since all the major princes of the Army of God were taking part . . . except Stephen of Blois. Stephen, with a large company of crusaders from Blois-Chartrain, chose to desert the crusade that same day of June 2nd, traveling north over the Beleb path to Alexandretta, never to return. News of desertion by such an important prince devastated the rank and file of the crusader army, boding ill for Bohemud's plan. Reconnoitering, Bohemud and the other princes insisted that with Kerbogha coming, they had no choice but to carry out this perilous but final gambit.

Spotting Firuz's lantern at 3:00 a.m. sharp, and seeing that he had lowered a rope by his tower, a small band of crusaders led by Bohemud and Guillaume tied an oxen-hide ladder to the rope and pulled on it three times. Firuz, in position, pulled the ladder up, securing it to a rampart battlement. Sixty men in all had been selected to mount the ladder, and as the moment of truth neared, it would be impossible to describe the level of terror rising within each, including even Bohemud. Most, in fact, were certain they had been lured into a trap. But oddly to his fellow knights, Guillaume remained serene. He felt that God would not allow this effort to fail, for if it did, God's War itself would fail.

The author of Gesta Francorum was in Bohemud's group and later wrote: "Bohemud encouraged his men saying, 'Go on, strong in heart and lucky in your comrades, and scale the ladder into Antioch! By God's will we shall have it in our power in a thrice!'"

Despite these exaltations, Bohemud did not see fit to be among the first to mount the ladder. "Then I shall be the first," said Guillaume, taking the hide ladder in hand.

"No," insisted Bohemud, pulling Guillaume back by the shoulders. "On this night, I want you at my immediate side at all times. Wait until I go, so we may remain together."

The risk of going first was claimed by a knight from Chartres named Fulcher. This Fulcher was not Fulcher the chronicler, but Fulcher the canon of Notre Dame de Chartres. Moving quickly, he began scrambling up the ladder, followed by other crusaders, armor and swords clanging in the stillness of the night. In their desperation, too many mounted the oxen hide ladder at once, and at the midway point where Fulcher hung, one man lost his footing, causing Fulcher to crash down on the man behind him and a fatal chain reaction occurred. In a single stunning moment, the mishap sent the entire file of men on the ladder tumbling to the ground, killing some, injuring others; the ladder itself falling to the ground.

"Goddammit! We're finished!" cursed Bohemud as quietly as he could under the circumstances. "They've heard us and shall raise the alarm. Run, men!"

Reaching out, Guillaume held Bohemud in place. "No, we'll hold and wait," he insisted. "If the bell is rung, we'll run, but first we wait!"

As scribed in the Gesta Frankorum: "The people of God shook with horror at this, thinking all these things had happened by Turkish trickery, and that now all those sent in had undoubtedly perished. No sound, no outburst was heard in the city nor on the ramparts, even though those who fell made a great noise. Lord God raised a strongly blowing wind that night. Firuz, obedient to the vow he had made to Bohemud concerning the betrayal of the city, once again let down the rope to draw up the ladder."

Those gathered at the foot of the wall had lost heart. In their removal of the injured and dead, their faith had wavered. If not for Bohemud and Guillaume commanding them to stay, they would have fled. But no bell was rung and no activity could be heard along the ramparts.

Gauging the ladder carefully after it had been hoisted and reattached, Guillaume said, "The first half of the climb will be more difficult to manage, but we can still make it if we don't overload the lower half of the ladder."

"You think?" questioned Bohemud, eyeing the ladder warily.

"I'm certain," answered Guillaume. "But we can't ask others to climb unless you and I lead." Not waiting for a response, Guillaume began to mount.

"Shit," sighed Bohemud, following, "you're right."

Either through God's intervention or extreme luck, the ladder held together as nearly fifty men maneuvered their way up the wall.

Firuz was waiting for them. "Quickly," he whispered, "kill the sleeping guards in my tower! I gave them all the night off, which they gladly took without asking questions! But don't touch the third bed, my brother is in it!"

What followed was like the wanton slaughter of lambs as crusaders hacked to death a dozen guards, half of them in deep sleep; a few, hearing the commotion, had no time to fight back nor even orient themselves to what was occurring. But by mistake, in the frenzy of their attack, Firuz's brother was brutally bludgeoned to death.

"Now, to the tower on each side of mine," directed Firuz with quiet animation, not knowing his brother had been murdered. A small fortune awaited him if this gamble succeeded, and certain death if it failed.

Splitting up, Bohemud led his group to one tower, Guillaume and his to the opposite. Several guards stood in their path, but were swiftly overcome. As in the Tower of Two Sisters, the sleeping guards in these other towers were caught unaware and murdered.

"Now to the gate mechanism!" shouted Firuz, having lost all sense of maintaining secrecy. "It's just there beyond that gate! Hurry!"

"Follow me!" directed Bohemud as he and Guillaume ran to the gate, only to be stumped by the opening mechanism. "Shit," he stammered, confused, "it's just dark enough that I can't see how to open the damn thing!"

"Here, give me a go," said Guillaume, shouldering Bohemud aside. With a bit of initial fumbling, Guillaume heard the lock slip, and he shoved the gate aside.

Seeing the path laying open to the gate mechanism, Bohemud rushed forward with his men. "Heave, fellows! Heave for your lives!" he cried, pushing with all his might, along with Guillaume and two others, their shoulders against the massive gear holding the gate shut. Then came a creek, followed by the groan of thick timber and rusting iron. "It's opening!" screamed Bohemud, his blood running hot and fast. "Bring me my banner, dammit, and blow the bugles to signal those on the slopes and in the woods!"

Bohemud planted his banner, blood red in color, and tearfully embraced Guillaume. "Damn you," he said, effusing unadulterated affection, "if ever God placed a hero on this earth, his name is Guillaume de Saint-Germain!"

Along the rampart, as the gate was opened, crusaders began dancing about, raising swords to the sky shouting, "God's will! God's will!" In turn, Godfrey of Bouillon and Robert of Flanders charged through the open gate to attack the citadel perched 500 meters above the city, while Robert of Normandy and Hugh of Vermandois swarmed through the gates, killing Turks who began gathering from other towers and streaming from barracks.

CHAPTER FIFTY-SIX

A RECKONING

By 4:00 a.m., the clang of iron and wailing of war brought Antioch fully awake as unmitigated chaos began its twelve-hour reign. Realizing what was occurring, Christians in the city began assaulting the Turkish garrison and opening other gates, the first being the Bridge Gate where Raymond of Toulouse was already conducting a full assault of his own. As the gates unexpectedly opened, he and his Provençals charged in on horseback, followed by thousands of footmen wielding lances and swords.

With dawn breaking across the horizon, what followed was the carnage that arises in all wars when troops have been bottled up for months, suffering from starvation, the elements, frustration, desertion by comrades, and flagging morale. War in itself is a rather simple proposition when conducted honorably: kill the enemy, spare the innocent. But war never follows this simple path because, men being different, don't allow it. It is at times like this that the 'true' nature of men reveals itself. There are those who stick to the task at hand, and there are those driven by bloodlust, which quickly goes blind, erasing all trace of humanity and conscience.

As the diverse population of Antioch bared itself to the streets, they were exposed to both types of men. Soldiers like Guillaume, Letellier, Orla, Guthroth, Hroc and others of such grain were directed to attack Turkish men-at-arms; men like Bohemud, Godfrey, Raymond, and those of their breed targeted anyone standing in their path, including men, women, children, and the elderly. Initially they murdered those wearing what they interpreted as Turkish or Arabic garb, but the mix of Syrians, Turks, Greeks, and Armenians often wore similar garb. Armenians tended to be darker in complexion than Western Europeans, therefore, many were mistaken for Muslims. What ensued, then, was a blood bath victimizing more innocents than Turks because the vast majority of those inhabiting Antioch were neither of Turkish origin nor Turkish blood. No matter, the killing quickly turned indiscriminate.

Then the true colors of God's Army spilling into Antioch began showing itself, blood literally began to stream through the streets. As related by an Antioch survivor: "They were sparing no Muslim on the grounds of age or sex, the ground was covered with blood and corpse and many of these were Christian Greeks, Syrians, and Armenians as well."

Another Antiochian eyewitness later wrote: "All the streets on every side of the city were full of corpses, so that no one could endure to be there because of the stench, nor could anyone walk along the narrow paths of the city except over the dead!"

Tafur and his peasant warriors were especially egregious in their brutality, viciously beating and murdering anyone in their path with primitive weapons of staff, club, and pitch-fork. Word of their barbarism had already spread throughout Muslim Asia Minor, but with their entry into Antioch, they established a reputation as sub-human beasts throughout Syria and the Levant. Their custom after battles was to openly roast severed body parts and gnaw at the flesh, a ritual performed for macabre theatre, not out of actual hunger.

As vicious as the Tafurs were, their bestial behavior would help spread terror south, causing minor Muslim kingdoms along the road to Jerusalem to decide that surrender and collaboration would be better propositions than opposition. In particular, news of the cannibalistic Tafurs spread swiftly and was verily over-exaggerated, which made many Syrian Muslims believe that all crusaders participated in it, an assumption that was far from true.

Seeing what was being wrought by Christian soldiers and Tafurs that day, women began hurling themselves and their children from the ramparts to escape the sword or rape and sexual perversion, running rampant throughout every structure in the city, as well as in the open streets. The hitherto 'purified' crusaders who had been denied the company of women in camp were lethally unleashing months of pent up hunger for female flesh, often even raping children, both male and female.

Malik and his renegade ghazis joined the fray late, having been among the last out of the Turkish garrison's barracks. They came out fighting and were at first able to turn back the crush of oncoming crusaders, but were overrun by sheer numbers within the half hour. Pointing toward the citadel sitting along the top of Mount Silpius, Malik grabbed Hasan and shouted, "Come along, up to the citadel! It's holding!" His fearsome reputation gone to Hell, Mahmoud Malik abandoned his troops, running like a rabbit to seek refuge above the city.

Had Yaghi Siyan been able to react quickly enough, he might have averted much of that day's horror, but the hour of the attack, the element of surprise, and the incoming flood of crusaders was too much to counteract in time. Forcing Ben-fazi to flee the palace with him, Yaghi Siyan joined his son, Shams ad-Daulah, and several hundred members of the Palace Guard rallying their way up the slope of Mount Silpius, shutting themselves into Antioch's last line of defense, the citadel. Spotting Malik, Yaghi Siyan gave him a look of scorn. "Oh, the big frightful man who makes other men tremble running like a frightened school boy!"

But Siyan's words escaped prematurely. Just then, in a moment of panic, certain the crusaders were about to breach even the citadel, he fled out the Iron Gate with his bodyguards, taking Ben-fazi with him. This stampede, so uncharacteristic of him, was a mistake. In the only Turkish victory of the day, Shams ad-Daulah managed to repel the attack against the citadel by Godfrey of Bouillon and Robert of Flanders.

Siyan's fleeing group managed their way down the treachery of Mount Staurin, but near the Iron Bridge, Yaghi Siyan was violently thrown from his horse. Thinking him dead, his guards ran, leaving Ben-fazi to tend to him.

Cradling the old emir in his lap, Ben-fazi was overcome by confusion. "Oh, but what am I to think, Master?" he asked aloud. "You've always been good to me, yet I've feared you from the start! I felt like one of those tiny nervous lap dogs, forever trembling, always fearing the worst."

Staring up with glazed eyes, Siyan struggled to respond. "B-but my little pet," he rasped, "there was nothing to fear. As with Karine and Garik, I could never allow harm to come to you. Oh, and in my haste, I failed to gather them up, or even say farewell. Check on them for me, Ben-fazi. I love them as I love you, my gardens, and my big cats."

As Siyan uttered these last words, an Armenian who had fled Antioch early on and taken up with the crusaders happened along the road, traveling north. Spotting Ben-fazi and a man on the ground, the fellow could not believe his fortune. "Ho, but what's this?! It looks like the little blue man, by God!" Coming closer, he recognized Yaghi Siyan. "Stars of God!" the Armenian cried, pulling a fabric bundle from his pack, unfolding it on the ground.

"I fear it's too late for bandages," bemoaned Ben-fazi. "He's nearly gone."

"Oh, I've no intention of helping, little man," the Armenian sneered, looking down at a full assortment of razor-sharp knives tucked neatly into place. "I'm a butcher by trade, so imagine my good fortune this morning!"

"What?" screeched Ben-fazi, alarmed, the man approaching in two strides. "What are you doing?!"

"I'm going to take the old bastard's head and present it to the crusaders! And I've a good mind to take yours, too, you little shit!"

Terrified, Ben-fazi gained his feet, preparing to flee. But torn with emotion, he turned and tackled the man. "You'll not take his head, damn you!" he screamed. "He'll be buried like any other decent human being!"

With Ben-fazi a miniature man and the Armenian four times his size, the struggle lasted but a minute. Kicking Ben-fazi aside, the man said, "A brave little piss-ant you are, but you'd best run. After I slice this old bastard's head off and tie it to my saddle, I'm coming for you!"

Knowing he had little recourse, Ben-fazi prepared to run again, yet paused, riveted in place, watching the butcher begin his work. He thought to hear a rasp of death when the blade, in a single swipe, went halfway through Yaghi Siyan's throat. On the next draw, the head separated entirely, tilting to the side.

Thus Yaghi Siyan, wily Turcoman, collector of beautiful and unusual things, and emir of the great city of Antioch, met his end at the hands of a common butcher who once feared him above all other men.

His eyes filling with tears, Ben-fazi, who now refused to be called anything but Benito, took off, desperately rubbing paint from his face and hands, knowing those within Antioch would be calling for his head should they spot the blue paint. Without it, as long as he kept his mouth shut and nobody recognized his voice, he might be safe.

Half an hour later he waded waist-deep into the Orontes, washing himself completely of the paint. Cupping water in handfuls, rubbing his skin clean as in those stories of baptism and rebirth, he immediately felt cleansed of the filth of slavery, helplessness, and uncertainty. I'm a new man, he thought, and from this day forth I shall devote my whole being to doing my Lord's work!

CHAPTER FIFTY-SEVEN

TROUBLE ERUPTS

Tristan, Scule, and Christos entered the Bridge Gate together, following the forces of Raymond Toulouse. Daylight had not yet broken, and confusion and chaos were running amuck, but Tristan was certain he could find the blue man in Siyan's palace, and that he would lead him to Mala and Christophe. Scule had promised to help, and was scuttling along in Tristan's wake, trying to keep up. They had both instructed Christos to stay back until after the attack, but the boy refused. "No, I shall help you find your wife and child!" he insisted, unaware that Bishop Saint-Germain and la Signorina were not actually married. Since Greek Orthodox priests were allowed to marry, Christos incorrectly assumed that Catholic priests could also.

"Very well," scolded Scule, "but for your safety, stick close to us! Real close!"

His warning was of questionable value. Tristan and Scule were both unarmed. Ecclesiastic law did not allow members of religious orders to bear arms, nor spill blood. Even Bishop Adhémar, a de facto leader of the crusade who'd ridden into battle, never violated this particular Church law.

"The palace! But where is it?!" cried Tristan, lost in the streets, head swiveling left and right, frustrated by Antioch's sheer size.

Running about, dodging incoming crusaders charging about on horseback and on foot, Scule thought he spotted it. "There!" he shouted. "That's got to be it!"

Breaking into a dead run, Tristan made for the entrance, vanishing within as Scule and Christos fell further behind.

"Do you suppose she's really here?" sputtered Christos, breathlessly.

"Yes, if God wills it!" shouted Scule, making the entrance with Christos on his heels.

They heard Tristan shouting Mala's name at the top of his lungs, but the palace had already been overrun by crusaders killing any men in sight, whether Turkish soldier, eunuch, or servant. Women from Yaghi Siyan's harem had been corralled and were futilely begging for their lives, before being gang raped and having their throats slit. Seeing men rutting these women about the floor or propping them up on their knees to violate them, Christos stopped a moment, confused by what he saw.

"Don't look!" shouted Scule, pulling the innocent boy toward Tristan's voice coming from a four-way meeting of corridors.

"Scule, I'll go this way, you try that way!" directed Tristan. "Shout her name, if she's here, she's bound to hear one of us! Hopefully she's got the sense to remain sequestered wherever she might be!"

Fortunately, that is precisely what Mala was doing. After securing all the locks to the apartment, she, Karine, and Garik had further barricaded the door with heavy furniture to reinforce the locks. From inside, they heard boots tramping up and down the corridor, crusaders bellowing, and women screaming in terror. On occasion, they heard men trying to break the apartment door down, but their efforts were short-lived and quickly abandoned. There were too many harem girls running about and too much palace loot to be taken to waste time on fortified doors.

Then, as in a dream, Mala thought to hear Tristan's voice over the din of plundering crusaders. It must be my imagination, she thought at first. But his cry came again and she knew for certain it was him. Setting baby Christophe in Karine's lap, she rushed to the door and began shoving furniture aside, to little avail. It had taken all three to move it into place. "Help me, Karine! Set Christophe on the floor! Garik, come quick before it's too late!"

Karine lay the baby on the rug and rushed forward to help, but Garik's feet remained nailed in place. Day and night, every minute, had always been frightening, therefore what was happening out in the corridor was too horrifying for him to even imagine. He reached down and pulled the wailing Christophe to his chest; one consoling the other to no avail.

"Tristan!" Mala screamed. "Tristan, I'm here!"

Hearing her voice, he rushed to the door, shouting for Scule and Christos a short distance away. When they arrived, all three fought the door but their effort was futile.

"Mala!" Tristan shouted. "I am here! I am here!"

"It will only open from the inside!" Mala yelled in return. "Give us a moment!"

Mala and Karine heaved, shoved, and moved the furnishings aside, then Mala put the key to the locks, but nervous, anxious, and elated beyond her capacity to bear, the key chattered about the lock opening uselessly.

"Here," said Karine, "give me the key."

Helpless, Mala handed it to her. Within the count of three, the locks clicked and Mala flung the door open. In that next moment, if ever a man and a woman over the millennia had melted into the arms of the other, Tristan and Mala's joy outmatched anything that could have come before. Sobbing, bawling, caressing each other with tear-driven jubilation, the two joined as one in an embrace for the ages.

Karine stood watching, perplexed at first. Mala had, without going into great detail, told her about Tristan. But seeing them together, Karine was unable to fathom that two people could mean even half as much to each other as these two standing before her. Contented, she issued a slight nod indicating that, yes, things for these two were finally just as they should be.

"Oh, my god!" exclaimed Tristan, in the excitement having forgotten their son. "Where is Christophe!?"

Garik, holding the protesting, squirming Christophe, stood frozen in fear. Overly cautious, he would not advance toward the stranger, the dwarf, or the other boy standing in the doorway until Karine cast him a hard look. One lead-filled step at a time, Garik came forward, handing Christophe off, as one hands an offering, to the man standing by his sister.

Paralyzed upon seeing Christophe for the first time, Tristan's tears came harder, and his throat began to lump to the point of overfilling his throat. Taking the infant, Tristan held him to his chest, then to his cheek. Disturbed, Christophe began to mewl a bit, then protest with shrill crying.

"Oh, but it's your father!" exclaimed Mala, wiping streams of tears from both cheeks. She sniffled back and swallowed hard. All of her prayers were being answered.

Entirely overcome at being reunited with Mala and Christophe, Tristan blurted, "I'm leaving this crusade and the Church, to spend the rest of my days at your side!"

Mala stared, eyes wide. How did he know? How?

"There remains but one task, though," Tristan, breathless, looked her in the eye. "I must return to Rome to face my father, Odo de Lagery. I must look him in the eye, thank him for all he has done for me through these many years, and explain why I can no longer represent the Catholic Church. Then, I shall leave Rome and go anywhere you wish, Mala. You, Christophe, and I shall start anew and—"

Suddenly three of Raymond of Toulouse's soldiers charged down the corridor in pursuit of a young harem girl who ran past them, screaming hysterically. Just as Tristan was about to finish his pronouncement, the biggest of the three halted, stunned by the beauty of the woman standing by Bishop Saint-Germain and the young girl at her side. "By damn!" he exclaimed, excitedly elbowing his two comrades, other Provençal louts from Southern France. "Look here what Bishop Saint-Germain has found! Two of the very finest from Yaghi Siyan's own pussy palace!"

Ogling Mala and Karine, the other two men threw down their swords and began stripping off their chain mail. The first man, already divested of chain-mail and gambeson, pulled his breeches to his ankles, and was flagging his stiffening penis at Mala and Karine; fully intending to violate both females right there in the presence of Bishop Saint-Germain, then pass them along to his friends.

Realizing what was happening, and well outsized, Tristan passed Christophe to Mala. Turning, he flung a fist into the man's face and jumped for his throat, both crashing against the marble floor.

Scule instinctively attacked the other two men at once. From his low position as a dwarf, he simultaneously grabbed each by a knee in a single dive, trying to throw them off balance. As the scuffle escalated, Christos jumped in, kicking whichever crusader appeared to be hurting Scule the most. Knocked back twice in succession, he refused to give up and kept advancing.

The stout and muscular dwarf was easily outmatched by the two men he attacked and now lay flat on his back taking a pummeling from both. Furious, Christos grabbed one of the men by the leg and bit down viciously, hoping to feel bone. Yelping in surprise, the bite victim swatted back at Christos, knocking him aside, then raised a boot and kicked the boy square in the mouth. Addled, Christos tried to shake his vision back into focus but then felt loose teeth rolling about on his tongue. Spitting them out, he leaped up and dove for the man, this time biting his other leg. But all of Christos' upper and lower front teeth were gone, causing the man to rear back with laughter. "Ha-ha, you little shit! That's what you get, damn you!"

But it was the man's last laugh on this side of Hell. Mala had handed Christophe to Garik and was pulling her dagger from her sleeve, thanking God she always had it. Without a word, she plunged it forward, sticking the point clean through the crusader's Adam's apple, severing his carotid artery. Gurgling and drowning in his own blood, the man's expression went blank as Mala withdrew the blade. Looking at her, not understanding at first what she had done, his eyes rolled back in his head and he crumpled in a dead heap to the floor.

Right when he fell, his comrade groaned aloud, trying to pull a sword from his back. As Mala dispatched the one crusader, Karine had quietly retrieved one of the swords off the floor and took a full run at the man straddling Scule, beating him. Turning to see what Scule was looking at, she gave him a brief but cold look of satisfaction, then wordlessly rammed the sword through his back, his heart, out the other side, then pulled it back out, finishing him off.

Seeing this, Mala's hand flew to her mouth, horrified that a young girl could do such a thing, but then her memory forced her back to the day she had stabbed LeBrun over twenty times in retaliation for what he had done to her aunt and mother.

The soldier beating Tristan was doomed without knowing it, unaware of what was coming from behind. Mala, with her dagger, and Karine with her sword, pierced the man's back simultaneously. But just as they withdrew their blades, a cacophony of bootsteps thundered down the corridor towards them; five more of Raymond's men, swords raised.

They, like many of the other soldiers penetrating the palace, were hunting harem girls and loot. But one happened to be the brother of the man Mala and Karine had just combined to kill. Stunned, the man bellowed his brother's name, "Mathieu!" Too late, already dead, his brother's head and shoulders slumped onto Tristan who was struggling to rise.

"Run!" cried Tristan. "Lock yourselves behind the door!"

Time short and distance far, the five onrushing men would easily get to the door before it could be closed and secured. "Oh, God! Savior! Where are You!?" Tristan wailed, knowing what was bound to follow.

Mala and Karine stood their ground over Tristan, protecting him, ostensibly, yet futilely.

Seeing the Provençals, Scule grabbed the two remaining swords on the floor, handing one to Christos. "I know you don't know what to do with this, lad, but do what you can!"

As the men came within yards of their targets, another herd of boots thundered down the corridor.

"Provençals! Get in the room!" screamed Tristan, realizing God was about to mete out His final punishment for Tristan's breaking of his vows. Laying his head back, too injured to rise, the memory of the first time he had set eyes on the beautiful young Romani girl along the Seine River flashed through his mind. Then, like the wild, gyrating spin of some mental kaleidoscope, other memories began flood his mind, scarcely keeping them apart: the Loire River, Marseilles, the Alps where their first son froze to death, Genoa, Bythinia Beach where Christophe was conceived, separations, reunions, joyful and heartbreaking episodes. Oh, but such a fool am I to think Mala and I had finally arrived! he thought, knowing this second arrival of Frenchmen was the knell of death.

And as this thought flashed across his conscience, he thought to hear that great cathedral bell of his past bursting in his ears; as it had when fleeing Rome with Odo de Lagery and Desiderius; as it had when he was standing atop Monte Cassino and the Church declared his catatonic state of prayer a miracle; as it had at each most salient point in his life. And here it was again, thundering back and forth in his head, swaying like a great instrument of destruction, tolling death and damnation.

But the great bell he heard was not in his head. It was the massive alarm bell of Antioch being rung by crusaders drunk with blood, hanging and swinging like schoolboys from the thick rope attached to its clapper. Nor was the second stampede that of Raymond's Provençals, but that of Guillaume, Hroc, Guthroth, and Orla charging down the corridor, knowing that Tristan would have gone straight to the palace to seek Mala and Christophe.

It was Guthroth who perceived trouble before the others. In the eyes of the soldiers standing over Tristan, he spotted that peculiar look that overcomes men just before spilling blood. "H-Ho there, y-you damned Franks! Stop!" he shouted, charging into their midst.

Trusting Guthroth's instincts, Orla, Hroc, and Guillaume joined the attack.

Angered to be accosted by fellow crusaders, the five Franks thought to make short work of these intruders, but they were ill-prepared to take on the likes of these four particular men. All five Provençals were dead within a single minute.

"Come quickly, and stay in our middle! It's become a madhouse out there!" warned Guillaume, pulling Tristan from the floor. The others gathered Mala and Karine, who refused to relinquish their blades, Scule, Christos, Karine, and Garik; Garik bawling and quaking like a child confronted by a pack of lions, yet faithfully hanging on to baby Christophe who was screaming at the top of his lungs.

Preparing to leave, a handful of Raymond's Southern Franks appeared. As it was Raymond's intent to claim the best part of the city, he had sent many of his men straight into the palace to abscond with its wealth of plunder before other crusader princes made their way to it. Surveying the scene before them and realizing that the men trying to leave had killed their fellow Franks, a hue and cry arose from this third set of Provençals.

Disregarding threats and drawn swords, Orla and Hroc launched their massive frames through the new arrivals, splitting them as one lops an apple in half.

"Ja, step aside you bastards or you too will be on the floor!" blustered Orla, forcing an opening for the remainder of their party.

Backing off, the angry Franks gave way, one of them shouting, "Raymond's going to hear about this, by damn! And he'll have every one of your traitor asses on a lance, including Bishop Saint-Germain there!"

CHAPTER FIFTY-EIGHT

CHRISTOS. FIRUZ.

By dusk of June 3rd, the butchery and indiscriminate slaughter came to a close. Unbeknownst to all, the great wheel of destiny had already set itself into a quiet spin and was about to discharge earlier machinations while devising new ones. Fate, therefore, took certain unsuspecting individuals by surprise. In addition, it was going to confound the Army of God in a fashion they never imagined.

Deep darkness descending, Adhémar discovered the Antioch prison bursting with prisoners, mostly Christians. "Release these lambs of God," he commanded, "but keep any Muslims behind bars!"

Weeping with joy, having escaped Yaghi Siyan's recent spate of daily Christian executions, the prisoners verily ran from the structure out into the streets, only to be horrified by death and destruction stretching along the streets and avenues before them as far as the eye could see. Their imprisonment during the attack, blessedly, had been their salvation. Among those being released were the Greek girls captured by Malik in Asia Minor.

"Oh, but this is as bloody as the day Malik attacked Despina!" remarked younger sister Agda, dumbfounded.

Equally shocked but older and hardened from suffering more beatings and rapes than her younger sister, fourteen-year-old Berna held her sister close, wrapping her in her arms. "Don't look, Agda," she said, shielding her sister's eyes. "Come along with me and we'll take a seat on that fallen timber there and gather ourselves. We're free, at least, and should be thankful. Nothing could be worse than what we've endured this past year."

Their senses too dull to dwell on what had happened to them during their incarceration, Berna and Agda stared vacantly at the burning buildings, crumbling structures, and corpses strewn along the streets, many of which were missing limbs, feet, or heads. Most of the women had been stripped and were lying flat on their backs, their breasts and genitals mutilated beyond recognition. Some appeared, at their moment of death, to have been reaching for babies or older children lying within their reach.

"That day in Despina, everything changed," Agda whimpered sadly, trying to recollect their lives before the arrival of the black banners. "The crusaders have saved us, Berna, but what shall we do? How will we live? We've no family, no friends, no money—nothing."

"Oh, we have each other, and we will move forward," said Berna with certainty. "No matter what, you and I shall live, Agda. Even should we have to find a man, or men, and spread our legs for pay, we shall survive, the two of us. We know what men want, and at least it won't be taken from us unwillingly or for nothing but bruises and beatings. Let's just rest a bit, Agda, and I will sort things out for us."

Sitting there drowning in despondency, a monk passed by; a dwarf, accompanied by a boy. The monk ignored them, but the boy happened to glance up. Seeing them, he appreciated how God had saved him on being taken from the road by Scule, and how blessed he was to have been spared the horrors these two Antiochian girls must have endured during the crusader attack. They look so filthy, helpless, and spent that I can scarcely see their faces, he thought, just like I must have looked during the flight with my grandmother and Vaso the beggar.

This thought unearthed in him the memory of Petros and his clan of females, who he and Anglaia had met during their flight, then flushed forward the memory of the sweet young girl, Anna. He and Anna were far too young to grasp the concept of love, but he had felt a strong attraction and kinship to her, and she to him, until Malik had caught up to Petros' clan and killed them all, mutilating poor Anna, leaving unimaginable horrors below her waist, between her legs.

"Come on, Christos," scolded Scule, "we're to meet Bishop Saint-Germain and the others near Saint Peter's Basilica where they've holed up, and you're poking along."

Looking away from the girls, Christos picked up his pace.

"Christos!?" a girl's voice shouted. "Oh, my god! But it can't be!"

"It is Christos!" cried a second.

Looking about, Christos recognized the female voices; each momentarily holding a distant, familiar ring. Then, before he could muster another thought, he was assaulted by two figures, embracing him, blabbering and weeping out his name. "Wh-wha-at?" he exclaimed, startled, bloody spittle spewing from where his teeth had been. The two filthy girls were all over him, hugging him tightly.

Flabbergasted, Scule pushed the girls away, not understanding what had overcome them. "Get away, you little wenches!" he warned, crouching with balled fists.

But the girls rushed forward again calling Christos by name. Taking one by the shoulders, Christos held her back, staring in her face. Woefully dirty and smudged, her eyes wide as saucers, he thought her demented at first. Relentlessly bawling his name, the voice registered. God! It's my sister Berna! Speechless, his legs began buckling. And Agda! "Scule, it's my dead sisters!" he wailed, falling apart just as had Berna and Agda, grinning from ear to ear.

Scule had witnessed much, but nothing like the sheer joy and abandon erupting before his eyes. Crossing himself, he tilted his head skyward and said aloud, "God in Heaven, how great are your miracles! How good your works, though in circles they may arrive!"

Huddling together in a circle, the three siblings intermittently talked, cried, hugged, and talked more. Although surrounded by a nightmare, they relished in the joy of God's grace. Weeping themselves dry, they shared details of the two different hands they had been dealt, and how they had, in their own way, survived them. Learning his own current circumstances far surpassed those of his lost sisters, he turned to Scule. "They have nothing," he said, "but me, and I have nothing but you. Could you help them, Scule? I beg it!"

"Aye." Scule, scratching his head, had no idea how to react or what to do. "Aye, I shall help one way or another, then set a course for all three of you."

Hearing this, Agda and Berna ran to him, burying his short stature within theirs, shedding tears of elation and freedom all over his brown robe.

As this drama played out, another reunion was unraveling just blocks away, this time involving Firuz. Running frantically here and there, searching every corner of the palace, he was calling for his children, hoping they had not been lost to raging crusaders that he had schemed into the city. By now he was aware of his brother having been slain within the Tower of Two Sisters by the very men he helped mount the wall. "Karine! Garik!" he squalled, ranging from the palace towards Saint Peter's Basilica.

The Saint-Germain faction had settled, along with the sparse remnants of the Tuscan Guard, into a building nearby. Mala was the first to hear the voice calling for Karine and Garik. With Christophe in her arms, she gathered the two siblings and took them to the doorway. "A man is calling for you," she said pointing below. "That fellow just there in the square, could it be your father?"

Seeing Firuz, Garik tensed, and began to shake. "Karine," he shuddered, grasping her hand, "it's him."

In reaction, Karine, who was directly behind him peering over his head, pulled him back to her, moving her arms over his shoulders, standing as one.

"But what is it, Karine?" asked Mala. "What's wrong?"

"Yes, that is our father," she said, her expression more reticent than usual. "But we don't want him. Don't make us go to him. We want to stay with you."

Perplexed, if not bewildered, Mala replied not, just searched one face then the other for understanding. Karine had never once indicated the least bit of affection for her, only to Christophe and Garik. "What? You don't wish to return to your father? Oh, but be happy, Karine, he's survived this horrible day and is now fretting for you two. Just listen to his voice, he's desperate! He must love you very much."

"Don't give us away to him," said Karine coldly, gripping her brother even tighter.

"But you're not mine to keep," objected Mala. "You have a father, and with him you are a family."

"No," said Karine flatly. "We have never had a family. And though Garik clung to our mother, it was only because he feared our father."

Unable to accept denying a grieving parent their children, Mala shouted out to Firuz, "They're here, with me! Come!"

As Mala said this, Karine's voice became frigid and her eyes flared. "We helped hide you and Christophe for months and months at danger to the blue man and to us. I had thought you to be the first honorable person in our entire lives, yet you betray us both in our time of need?"

Wounded by the bite of Karine's words, and the truth within them, Mala's decision suddenly felt . . . wrong. "Tristan!" she called, seeing that the man had changed direction and was but steps away. "Tristan, come quickly!"

Seeing his children, Firuz's eyes lit up and he ran to the door. "Thank God you're safe!" he exclaimed, attempting to embrace the two as they stood together. "Merciful Heaven, I feared I'd lost you both to the attack!"

Forming a fortress wall to repel him, Tristan arrived with Guillaume, asking, "What is it?"

Her eyes pleading helplessly, Mala told him what Karine had said, loud enough for Firuz to heard. When she was done, she said, "I'm not sure what to do here."

"Oh, there's but one thing to do here," contended Firuz, turning hostile, "and that's to give me my children, dammit! Do you know who I am? I'm Firuz, who worked with Bohemud to get the crusaders into the city!"

"But they don't want to go with you," countered Mala, her own eyes going dark, insistent, holding Christophe a bit tighter. "Something is wrong here, and I'm forced to ask what it is. Tell us, sir, what is going on here?"

"What's wrong is that you are withholding my children from me," countered Firuz. "If necessary, I will go fetch Bohemud and the men I laddered up the wall. They know who I am!"

Knowing better than to address the volatile Garik, Mala turned to Karine. "If you don't clear this puzzle, then off you two go, Karine. I've no rights to you, nor can I help if I have no explanation. Just as Benito told you the full truth so you would help me and Christophe, you must trust me, or leave with your father."

Remaining tight-lipped at first, Karine looked her father in the eyes, her own shrinking to narrow slits. "Signorina," she said, her defying focus never leaving Firuz, "don't you think that Garik and I know we're not like other children? And why do you suppose that is?" She shifted her gaze to Mala. "As there's a reason for everything, don't you think there's a reason Garik and I have no wish to go home?"

Having no idea how to reply and not wishing to misspeak, Mala held her answer. Indeed, she had always thought both of them to be peculiar, if not completely aberrant.

"No answer, Signorina?" sniffed Karine. "Very well, then. I shall give it. Garik and I have feared our father since growing old enough to understand things. Yes, our father loves us, not as a father should love his children, but in another way."

"What?" shouted Mala, rebelling against the thoughts being suggested.

"Our father loves us as he loves our mother. He touches us and does other forbidden things behind the walls of our home. Our mother has known about it since it began, but has been too busy luring other men into our house when father is gone. Do you understand, Signorina? Do you require the details?"

"That's a goddamn lie!" erupted Firuz, turning scarlet. "She's lying, dammit! Can't you see that? Just look at her face! Shit! Always staring at the world with that same cold, scheming look!"

"Garik," said Karine, remaining serene in the face of her father's descent into fury. "You are afraid. You have always been afraid, but talk for once. Am I lying?"

Listening to the exchange, his trembling had escalated to spasms. But in an obvious attempt to collect himself, he tried to speak. His lips began to move, but there came no words.

Shaking him, Karine said, "Very well, Garik, let's go with father, then he can play with us as he likes again!"

Hearing this, Garik screamed, "N-no! She's not lying! It's true! Please don't give us away!"

Numbed by what the children had said, Mala, Tristan, and Guillaume looked at each, their mouths ajar, then shifted their gaze to Firuz, then back to Karine and Garik.

Firuz erupted and grabbed for both children. "They're mine, damn you! Get out of my way!"

Springing forward, Tristan shoved him back and Guillaume pulled his sword.

"Children, into the house!" shouted Mala, pulling them from Firuz with her free hand and directing them inside, seeing Guillaume angrily advance.

"This isn't over, by damn!" shrilled Firuz, backing away. "My children have been taken from me once, but I'll be damned if I'll lose them twice!" Shaking his fist, he then stalked off, kicking at the ground, swearing.

And this is how the mystery of Firuz the armor-maker and his children came to light. Certain neighbors, females, had held suspicions, even addressing them to Adelina, who had kept them at bay, not wishing to jeopardize the amenities provided by her husband's adequate wealth. As such, two children were forced to regularly endure moral squalor and perversion being committed against them; desperately clinging to one another as Firuz and Adelina kept their mutual pact with the devil between themselves.

Hearing Firuz's echoing footfalls, Mala signaled Tristan into a back room, watching the children comforting each other. "But Tristan, what is to become of these two now?"

Taking a deep breath, Tristan shook his head. "God shall determine their future, just as he has determined mine and Guillaume's on being abandoned to the Black Monks."

"Oh, but unlike many lost children of this world, fortune smiled on you and Guillaume," besought Mala, "seeing that two lost brothers landed well—you with Odo de Lagery, one of the most powerful men in Europe, and Guillaume with la Gran Contessa Mathilda of Tuscany, the wealthiest woman of the continent. But what shall happen to this lost set of siblings, Tristan?"

Pondering her question, he had no answer.

"They saved me, Tristan," said Mala, "and they saved our son. God put them in my path at an impossible time, under impossible circumstances. Do you not agree?"

"Yes, there is no doubt," said Tristan, stroking her long ebony tresses, never taking his eyes from his son.

"If that is true, then why can you not accept that God has put us in their path?"

Not smiling but serious in his approval, Tristan tilted his head. "And what are you suggesting?" he asked, already suspecting her answer.

"We must help them," she said, but changed her mind, holding up her finger. "No, Tristan, we must keep them."

Overcome with uncertainty, but knowing there was but one proper path to take, Tristan agreed, "Yes, Mala, we must." He then enveloped his family in a reassuring hug, all three overcome in the moment.

As he said this, Scule and Christos appeared with Agda and Berna. "So," said Scule to Tristan, Mala, and Guillaume, indicating the girls with his head, "a strange turn of events just shortly ago." Introducing the bedraggled, shoeless girls, Scule recited the entire story, praising the improbability of it. "Just as God placed Christos in my lap, He's now presented two more surprises, but they're girls. I may be able to help, but it's impossible for me to keep girls, of all things. What am I to do?"

As he spoke, Christos had gone silent, his focus having fallen on Karine. He had never in his entire existence seen such a rare creature, not even Anna. Karine noticed Christos as well, but returned his mesmerized gaze with little warmth. Instead, she led Garik away to comfort him. "I will watch over you," she said. "From now on, look only to me."

Sniffling, Garik was too overwhelmed to find words.

A short discussion ensued among Tristan, Scule, Mala, and Guillaume, ending with Mala pointing to Agda and Berna, her heart bleeding for both of them. "I am a woman of means, great means. These two, along with Karine and Garik, are orphans. Tristan and I have decided just moments ago to keep them under our wing. But as you said, Scule, God has presented yet two new additions to our family." She looked to Tristan, who, closing his eyes, intuitively anticipated what she would say next. "Tristan?" she implored.

His eyes remaining closed, a weak smile overtook him. "Yes, Mala, absolutely."

CHAPTER FIFTY-NINE

THE SAINT-GERMAIN FACTION

Having witnessed the looting and rape of Raymond's Provençals, other troops butchering innocent men, women, and children along with Turks, and coming onto the rape-minded crusaders confronting Mala and Karine in the palace corridor, something began to stir within Guillaume and the Danes. It could have been objection, but it seemed the arrival of clarity. Discouraged, they quietly began discussing their involvement within the Army of God, weighing its true nature, motivations, and direction.

Tristan's position was already known to all. He had lost his fervor for the Holy Crusade with the advent of Peter the Hermit's Peasants' Crusade, and had subsequently reached a point of open rebellion against the 'real' crusade. But with what they had experienced in Antioch, even Guillaume began to feel tiny fissures cracking in his once inviolable loyalty to the Pope's holy war. Whereas he did wish to reclaim Jerusalem for Christendom, put a halt to Islamic aggression, and continue to place God above all else, occurrences of the past eight months had begun to push his compass another direction. In particular, the rape of Antioch had rattled him, pushing him toward a decision.

Orla's stance, too, was affected by the bloody victory over Antioch. Although war was all he had ever known and this crusade was simply another extension of the madness, Crowbones had begun to appear to him in dreams, urging him to set aside his sword. 'Have you not drunk enough blood, Orla, to be weary of it?' the pallid face of Crowbones would whisper in the night. 'Will your thirst for blood never slacken?'

More than anything else, it was Crowbones' death-confession about what the bones had told him back in Nicaea that began to disturb Orla, rattling around in his head over and over, 'The bones showed three different times that none of us in the Saint-Germain party would ever set eyes on Jerusalem! So, set your sword down, Brother, and make peace with the world, and yourself.'

Knowing that Raymond of Toulouse's shadow loomed near for killing Provençals in the palace during the assault, and the specter of Kerbogha's advance stood just ahead, Orla grew exceedingly anxious and felt compelled to share his brother's final readings of Grandmother Tuulikki's bones with the others.

Hroc simply objected, reiterating his stand on superstition. But Guthroth, Christian that he had become, grew unusually uneasy upon hearing Orla's story. Refusing to address Crowbones' prophecy, he'd retreated within himself and trouble filled his eyes.

"Well, what do you think, Guthroth?" asked Orla, catching a glimpse of uncharacteristic uncertainty in his cousin's gaze.

Shaking his head, Guthroth offered no words.

"Well, dammit," questioned Orla, "what about you, Guillaume, and you, Tristan?"

But it was Mala who spoke, "My Romani people are Christian, but have long delved into prophecy and foretelling the future by reading clouds, the moon, and the flow of fresh menstrual blood. Those prophecies often come true. And think back to my beloved old Duxia de Falaise, whom all of you despised and knew as Mielikki. It's impossible to count the times her predictions came true. I have been Christian since birth, yet like my people, I accept certain beliefs of my Romani ancestors. Why would any of you, being of Danish Viking blood, be any different?"

"To believe in omens and superstition troubles me," replied Guillaume, feeling the glue of his own unshakeable faith the tiniest bit. "I feel it's a denial of God in favor of paganism."

"That troubles you?" asked Mala indignantly. "And did what you saw along Peter the Hermit's crusade not trouble you? And do the recent actions of the major princes not trouble you? And what you've seen here in Antioch, does that not trouble you, Guillaume? You seem to accept those monstrosities yet object ancestral beliefs. What's more sinful, believing in omens or accepting the horrors you've already accepted? And, in the name of God!"

"Mala," interjected Tristan, growing uneasy, "step lightly. Guillaume's faith is all he lives by."

"Answer the question, Guillaume. It's very important," pressed Mala, dismissing Tristan's request, staring her future brother-in-law down, clutching her innocent baby to her breast.

"Yes, many things I have seen on this crusade have bothered me," Guillaume replied, turning several shades of red, "including my own sinful behavior in Pelekanum, of which I've disclosed to one other person on this earth, my own brother, during confession."

"Easy, Guillaume," said Tristan, shocked to the core by his brother's willingness to lay bare his most dreaded secret, unable to comprehend what had brought on such a turn.

"No, I wish to continue," insisted Guillaume. "Mala, you must surely be aware of what happened at Pelekanum between Queen Irene and me, due to your close association with her back in Constantinople."

"Guillaume, no need to go further," said Tristan, knowing that his brother was about to expose his open wound to Orla, Guthroth, and Hroc who might not understand.

But Tristan could not have been more wrong. The Danes did understand. Not only did they understand, they clearly understood Guillaume's evident descent since Nicaea; something he had kept to himself, only to be outed in battle during suicidal charges or taking overly perilous risks. The truth was, Guillaume had been taking risks as an act of spiritual contrition, promised by the Pope and the Church, "To die in this crusade will be to guarantee a seat in Heaven regardless of previous sins."

"Perhaps there is a need for him to go further," contended Mala. "Guillaume's thoughts are narrower, more profound than even your own, Tristan, on God, the Church, reality. At least you have opened your mind enough to trespass from time to time against the idiocy of men by crossing the line of your Church vows! Oh, I love you beyond description and beyond all human sense, my dear Tristan, but after all we've been through, the time has come for us, here, tonight, to make peace with ourselves. I suspect God has already made peace with us, though we refuse to acknowledge it due to what we've been told over and over and over. Each one of us sitting here has struggled mightily against a world shaped but by a handful of men wearing collars and crowns. Each of us has been made to feel unworthy and sinful by that same handful of men claiming to know everything concerning God. But that, I decided years ago, is impossible. Only God Himself is all-knowing. Men, on the other hand, are frail and fallible."

Tristan had clashed with Mala over God and Church before, but this particular night she was speaking with certainty and authority, prompting him to bare his own secret. "I learned from Lord Azim and Kareem, Mala, that you have inquired about political asylum. You may not know this, but they are both here in Syria as we speak."

Mala's disposition changed completely. "No, I had no idea they were here. But how perfect!"

Even though Azim had offered Tristan asylum, he could not believe his ears. "Perfect? But Mala, you may have sent a message to Azim, but you've never heard his response unless, of course, he sent it by carrier pigeon to your hiding place in the palace!"

Now it was Mala's turn to reveal her secret. "I already knew his response when I sent my inquiry," replied Mala confidently. "Azim loves me, and has since we first began trading together. But he's always known I loved another, not him."

Tristan could not help but smile at her candor. "That's exactly what Azim said."

"Really?" This pleased Mala greatly. Smiling, she swayed to and fro to pacify Christophe. "Well, well, but isn't this a night for revelations all around, amongst we few here who have been linked together, one way or another, and who may enter eternity together as well. So yes, Tristan, I did ask Azim about asylum for my family, although you are the one in need of protection, not me."

At this the Danes agreed, nodding quietly amongst themselves.

"I am independent and possess an intercontinental trading empire," Mala continued, "and the Church has no claim on me. It's you who needs asylum, Tristan, especially since you've decided for certain to stay with me and Christophe and help me raise these four lost children we've taken on. It seems all of us here tonight stand together at the edge of a crumbling precipice with Kerbogha on the horizon. Tristan, I must tell you the truth, here in front of what remains of your family on this earth." Mala had always been iron-willed, but right then she was steadfast and resolute.

"You are right about these men, Mala, they have been my family since my birth. Please do speak your mind before all if they themselves do not object."

Looking to each other, Guillaume and the Danes expressed only consent; Scule and the children stood back, mere observers.

"Tristan, it has been me who has ceaselessly pursued you since childhood," began Mala, shifting the baby to her good arm, "yet one moment you're choosing me, the next falling back on the Church. I have never once been unsure about you, yet confusion has clouded your path about me since the night we first met as children. Even now you teeter between me and this foolish, suicidal idea of returning to the Vatican to report to your 'father' in this life, Odo de Lagery. But even as Pope, he can never accept you telling him that you're leaving the Church to be with me, Tristan. Nor can he reconcile attacks that surely will flow from Adhémar, Raymond, Bohemud, Tancred, Godfrey, and God only knows who else." Looking to the others, she asked, "Am I right, or am I mistaken?"

"You're right!" said Orla.

The others retained their silence, especially Guillaume who had early on objected to Tristan and Mala's relationship, concerned his brother would end up in Hell, and Tristan's recent decision to leave the Catholic Church, just as he feared his own repercussions for sinning in Pelekanum.

Hroc, too, was struggling with the thought of Tristan, a high bishop, leaving the Church even though he had readily accepted his long history of breaking Church vows with Mala. "But Uncle Tristan," he said, "how can you in good conscience deny God?"

"A p-poor question," said Guthroth, elbowing his nephew.

"No," disagreed Tristan, "it is a good question and I shall address it. Hroc, I have never denied God, nor shall I ever. I have been torn by certain ecclesiastic pronouncements that seem to come and go, not by God, but by papal regimes. It was Pope Gregory VII whom I denied, and Odo de Lagery thereafter, not God. Can you not see that?"

"I c-can!" professed Guthroth, looking at Guillaume and Hroc, both. "B-But should you re-return to Rome to f-finalize all this? Y-you are d-done! Don't b-be a f-fool, Boy."

"But Odo is my father," objected Tristan. "He pulled me from shame and abandonment. Do I not owe him a face-to-face explanation, at least?"

"Shit, write him a letter," snarked Orla. "You're good at such things! But if you insist on going back, why not save the effort and simply slash your throat here and now?" Reaching to his belt, he pulled out his dagger and offered it to Tristan.

"As I said before," Mala touched Tristan's sleeve, "our love has always hinged on your timing, Tristan, but no more." She shook her head, eyes locked on his.

"Christophe has changed the equation. And you and I have accepted four more children—Garik, Karine, Agda, and Berna—all of whom have struggled through things too hellish to fathom. If you return to Rome, we are done, Tristan. I shall simply return to Genoa and resume as before, but with five children to rear. But if you stay, I shall stay. Even in the Middle East I can easily manage my trading Empire from Asia Minor, coming and going at will. You could even travel with me, except when I return to Europe!"

Too many thoughts colliding at once, Tristan felt his head was about to burst. "You have never given me such an ultimatum," he fumed. "Yes, I've agreed to give up everything for you, for Christophe, for these orphans, but Odo is my father and—"

"He's not your father!" insisted Mala. "He's a man who helped you, never losing sight of how you could help him, and the Church!"

"I think she speaks right," stated Orla, backing up Mala.

"J-ja," muttered Guthroth, his expression turning cross at Tristan.

"I have risked all for you, Tristan, even this time risking dear little Christophe coming to Syria, and nearly losing him! I've been half a year living in abject fear, never knowing which knock at the door would be my last, or Christophe's. And during that terrifying time, I began to see what's important and what's not, where the truth stands and where it doesn't. The answer, I discovered in my trembling fear, is what lies ahead for us, you and me, Christophe, and these children!"

"What lies ahead?" echoed Tristan. "But we never know what lies ahead, Mala. Only God knows such things. In imminent peril awaiting Kerbogha, we might never leave these wretched walls of Antioch."

"Agreed," replied Mala. "But God may have another plan, Tristan. He may have reserved a future for us. If that is the case, we must at least attempt to navigate our own ship in our own direction. God gave us free will, but it's far easier for some to only hear the chatter of other men, such as Guillaume who's spiritually controlled by popes and cardinals. You, you are spellbound to some foolish sense of loyalty to a man who shall have no choice but to throw you to the lions because he's obligated—no, shackled to 'play-acting' as God's direct representative on this earth despite being just another man! Just like these damned crusaders acting at saving Jerusalem for Christianity. Play-acting, they are, just like Adhémar of Le Puy. Ha! Adhémar, Mister Holy of the Holy! Do you know what I learned hours ago? He will be celebrating a victory mass in the morning. Imagine that! A holy mass in honor of murdering thousands and thousands of innocents here in Antioch. Oh, and I assure you that the murderers have by now washed the blood off their hands just so they can take the sacred sacrament of communion in the morning. Guillaume, Tristan, I want you both to think about that tonight as you say your prayers."

"I shall," said Guillaume, staring at his boots. "Your words have been harsh, but I thank you for your honesty, Mala, whether I know what to make of it or not."

"Very well then." Mala, looked from one face to another. "I'm tired and it's been a long day. You men continue to sort out your woes and insufficiencies. We are retiring." She shooed them away like a fly on her supper, then waved her arm in an arc to all the children and snuggled Christophe to her breast, him rooting for milk. Before turning away, she looked the man who had always had the keys to her heart directly in the eye. "As for you, Tristan, or I should say as to us, I will await your answer about returning to Rome and Odo de Lagery until tomorrow morning. Either you proceed to Jerusalem and stay with this horde of fools leading the crusade, then return to that horde of fools running the Vatican, or you think about me, Christophe, and our new sons and daughters, which means never showing your face within reach of the Vatican and certain retribution ever again."

"Good night, Mala," said Tristan. "You have always been the blood of my blood, the heart of my heart. We shall talk in the morning about Rome." But as he said this, the last word was said with high inflection, nearly making the statement a question.

At this, Mala shuffled Christophe and bid all a goodnight, indicating for her children to follow. Lacking certainty in Tristan's answer, a smile still blossomed on her face, as if things had already been settled. "I love you, smart boy," she said, blowing Tristan a kiss. "I always have, and always shall."

"Well, damnation!" grunted Orla, his eyes following Mala and the children as they left the room, "if you walk away from that to make a final trip to Rome, Boy, you're the greatest fool the world has seen since creation!"

"J-Ja," agreed Guthroth, "th-the greatest f-fool ever."

"Yes, Brother," said Guillaume, carefully picking his words. "I have always opposed you and Mala being together because of the Church. But on this night, before the Danes as witnesses, I extend you, Mala, and baby Christophe my heartfelt blessings, along with the four other children. On your returning to Rome, I have decided, no. You've done too much, said too much, crossed too many bridges, and made too many enemies."

"Well, shit," whistled Orla, "I never thought to hear such words from Guillaume of all damn people! Odin's ass! This seems to be a night for baring secrets, I'd say, after all these damn years of being too manly to talk straight. Now, I've got something to say." At this he revealed cutting a lock of Crowbones' hair, putting it on a boat, setting it afire, and shoving it off into the Orontes. Ending his story, he said, "Yes, Crowbones may have wished a Christian burial because, yes, I confess, he did abandon his bones. But a word to you good Christians sitting here, I don't wish to be buried. Should anything happen to me, I want to be laid on a boat, and I want that boat and my body shoved to sea, fully afire!" As he talked, he had become insistent and the tone of his voice had risen. He meant every word he had just said. "Is that understood?"

Looking at one another, nobody answered.

"J-Ja," ratified Guthroth, moving on. "Orla, you s-said a while ago th-this is a night for s-secrets." Looking about to ensure nobody was listening but those within the circle, he lowered his voice, gathering an expression none of the others had ever before seen on Guthroth. "I w-will add m-my own secret . . ." he said, taking a long pause, his eyes skirting from one to another.

"Well, dammit," complained Orla, "if everyone else is going to ignore my request, what's your damn secret, Guthroth?"

"I'm m-married," said Guthroth proudly, smiling broadly.

Nothing he could have said would have shocked Orla, Hroc, Guillaume, or Tristan more.

"What?!" cried Orla and Hroc within the same moment.

"I don't believe you!" laughed Guillaume, leaning forward, gawking.

"Oh, but Lord in Heaven!" exclaimed Tristan, equally stunned.

"Ja," said Guthroth, a look of sheepish pride swelling his face. "That H-Haya, I love her." Guthroth had never in his entire existence uttered the word 'love,' and hearing it in reference to himself, he felt especially awkward. Nonetheless, he leaned toward them and repeated the words softly so no others ears could hear but those intended, "Y-yes, I love Haya, and m-married her at the Christian ch-chapel at the Oasis . . . just before returning to c-camp. It w-was a beaut-beau-ti-ful—" Here his tongue became twisted and he stopped.

"A beautiful ceremony?" urged Hroc, trying to help him.

"Ja!" grinned Guthroth, nodding his head up and down with the embarrass-ment of a boy caught absconding with a merchant's pie at market. "Haya d-didn't want me to c-come back here. She said th-this war is a f-fool's game."

"Ha! She may be right," agreed Orla, slapping his thigh.

"Aye," agreed Tristan ruefully, "I've been saying that for the longest time." He closed his eyes in regret, and lowered his voice in reverence. "Yet, as you all know, it was me as much as anyone else who helped start it. This war sickens me."

"I am l-leaving it," admitted Guthroth. He straightened his shoulders and dared anyone to contradict him.

"Huh? What did you say?" asked Orla.

A slacked jaw was the only response from Guillaume.

"What did you say?" repeated Hroc.

"I am l-leaving it," repeated Guthroth. "As soon as th-this thing with Ker-Kerbogha is done, I'm g-going back to H-Haya . . . for good."

"But," snorted Orla, "why wait, you fool? Go now, Guthroth. We might every damned one of us get killed fighting Kerbogha! Ja, just like Ivar's bones predicted. I now do believe none of us will ever set eyes on Jerusalem."

"N-No, I won't l-leave you," replied Guthroth, grinning a bit. "You f-fools n-need me!"

"Indeed." Hroc put a hand on his Uncle's shoulder. "Oh, but the many, many times you've saved one or another of us, Uncle Guthroth. But then, are you saying you will never return west should we survive Kerbogha?"

"Truly," asked Tristan, "is that your intention?"

"Ja. I w-wish to be happy at l-last. I w-wish to l-live for just me . . . and H-Haya.

You c-could join me, Hroc." His grin broadened at the thought. "Haya has tw-two younger sisters, remember? They t-talk my ears off asking about y-you. Ha! You c-could marry them b-both!"

Braying, Orla objected, "Hell no! He can have only one! Maybe the other would accept an old shit like me, eh? Then we could live as one big happy family!"

Hroc, Guthroth, Guillaume, and Tristan joined in Orla's laughter together, all four jesting and egging Hroc about the two sisters for another hour, finding fraternity and comfort in each other's company, and solace in each other's smiles.

And indeed, after all these years, as Orla had said, this tightly-bound band of brothers finally laid down the shields closely guarding their hearts from one another, from the very beginning of knowing each other, to finally open and share their innermost thoughts.

CHAPTER SIXTY

AFTERMATH . . . THE ARMY OF GOD

Raymond of Toulouse had intentionally chosen to attack the Bridge Gate head-on in order that his men could take control of it, the palace, and other major swaths of the city in his name, once the Armenian Christians opened the gate for him. In this, he succeeded brilliantly, ignoring Bohemud's banner already hanging on the parapets. Raymond now controlled his own Provençal stronghold within the city and fully intended to keep it.

This infuriated Bohemud, of course, who had taken all the risks associated with breaking into the city, but there was little he could do other than militarily turn against Raymond, which would be a tall order due to Bishop Adhémar of Le Puy and the size of Raymond's army. Even in the afterglow of a great victory, black blood between the two most powerful crusader princes began to deepen.

As to the other thousands of crusaders not of Raymond's camp, once their thirst for blood was finally sated, they began to focus on sacking the city—breaking into homes, shops, cathedrals, and any other structures that might provide plunder—yet ended up bewildered, having come up empty. They failed to comprehend that their siege had dried the city up as starvation and shortage depleted food supply, grain, and livestock. Even most of the personal wealth of individuals had been expended during the earlier months of the siege when price gouging caravans made their way into Antioch, feeding like parasitic spiders on Antioch's fear and anxiety. Frustrated, they looked with envy at what Raymond and his Provençals had acquired from the palace and other significant buildings in the same quarter.

Next came Raymond's fury at Tristan, Guillaume, and the Danes. Learning what had happened within the palace, he accused the entire Saint-Germain faction of treason and murdering sanctified soldiers of God, Raymond began enlisting support from anyone that would listen. "I demand justice!" he howled.

"Damn you, Raymond," retorted Bohemud, "while robbing the city, some of your country goons were about to rape la Signorina and a young Armenian girl who's but eleven or twelve, for God's sake! Did you not find one of your dead men with his breeches down to his ankles and his staff in hand? Chrissakes, what do you suppose he was doing like that, masturbating for a goddamned audience!"

"That was staged!" insisted Raymond, commanding that a trial be conducted by Adhémar and the Council of Princes. "It was murder of my own men, plain as day, and for no damned reason. And if I can't get a trial, then I and my Provençals shall settle the matter the country way! And that, I vow!"

This threat only further angered Bohemud, who cared none for Tristan but would go to the wall for Guillaume who had three times saved his life. He also favored the Danes as fearless fighting additions to his own camp. "If anyone's a traitor here, it's you!" he said in retaliation to Raymond. "You disrespect my banner flying yonder and you've claimed much of the city for yourself, you wild boar! And whereas my men were risking their lives, yours were thieving and plundering, laying claim to this and that for you! But touch a hair on Guillaume's or the Danes' crowns and my army will turn on you in a blink, Raymond! And that, I vow!"

Bohemud's idle threat was made easier by the fact that the Northern French princes, being among the most rational of the entire army, supported Guillaume and the Danes and had not turned against Tristan. Consequently, Robert of Normandy, Robert of Flanders, and Hugh of Vermandois refused to support Raymond.

As this feud between the two crusader Goliaths gained heat, Tristan, Guillaume, and the Danes remained silent rather than inflaming things, knowing that Raymond had in essence passed along to them a certain death sentence if and when the opportunity presented itself. Without a doubt, in the midst of war, that opportunity would arrive sooner or later.

With internal conflicts simmering, the wheel of destiny cast down an unexpected twist onto the Army of God after vanquishing Antioch. The crusaders had taken Antioch on June 3rd, not by siege but by the treachery of Firuz, who had been wronged by Yaghi Siyan, teaching yet another bitter historical lesson on how a tiny grain of discontent from below can out-match the destruction of a raging tempest above.

The Army of God indeed captured Antioch, but the course of war was about to take one of the most bizarre and monumental reversals of circumstance in the annals of wartime history. Having been shut out of the city and trying to break in for eight arduous months, then winning the city for a day, the crusaders found themselves locked in the city just twenty-four hours later, suddenly turning them from besiegers into the besieged.

Kerbogha's armies began to arrive.

CHAPTER SIXTY-ONE

KERBOGHA'S ARRIVAL

Kerbogha's advance scouting party of 300 ghazis arrived at Antioch on June 4th. Thirty of this number advanced in a small mobile group to closely reconnoiter the city, and were spotted by a renown Norman knight named Roger of Barneville. Flush with victory from the day before, and unable to resist the temptation of Turkish blood, Roger selected fifteen of his most capable knights and issued pursuit. Outnumbering this crusader force two to one, the Turks turned tail and fled as Roger took up hot pursuit, completely forsaking his characteristic military wiliness and experience. But it was a trap! He had fallen for the classic Muslim tactic of the 'feigned retreat.' Having lured him from the safety of the city walls, the entire force of 300 ghazis pounced. Turning about, Roger and his men desperately made for the city, even coming into full view of those manning the ramparts. But too late. Roger fell from his horse, pierced by an arrow from behind, puncturing his lung and liver, and all his men were slain. Watching from the walls, crusaders then witnessed Muslims decapitating Roger and sticking his head on a pole as a war trophy.

The death of such a prominent knight was a blow to the crusaders, but would pale in comparison to the arrival of Kerbogha's full army that very next day. This new Muslim force was double the size of the entire Army of God. On top of that, the crusaders' reversal of position had happened so quickly that they had left food, supplies, and even many horses in their camp, unable to reclaim them. This was further compounded, of course, by the near famine conditions already existing within Antioch.

By count, the crusaders had only 150 horses within the city, plus 400 captured from the Turkish garrison. These Turkish horses had been neither broken nor trained, thus were incapable of commands or of responding to signals or spurring. This eliminated the crusaders' most effective and dangerous weapon, the heavy cavalry assault. This left them with but one tactic in their arsenal, to fall back on the mighty fortifications of Antioch just as Yaghi Siyan had. But there remained a thorn even in this strategy. Shams ad-Daulah, Yaghi Siyan's son, was still in control of the citadel overlooking the city. In an attempt to contain it, Bohemud built a camp directly to the south of it along a ridge such that Christian and Muslim were separated only by a tiny valley and could look directly at each other.

Despite his innate advantages, Kerbogha played caution over bravado and pitched his main camp three kilometers north of the city at the intersection of the Orontes River and a smaller tributary, the Kara Su. Base in place, he 'initiated' contact with Shams ad-Daulah via the back trail leading up Mount Staurin to the Iron Gate, placing one of his commanders in charge of the citadel; simultaneously demanding title to the city. Shams ad-Daulah was, of course, in no position to deny either of these demands. Then Kerbogha began massing troops along the eastern, gentle slopes of Mount Silpius, blocking the Gate of Saint Paul.

Having abandoned the makeshift fort of Malregard near Mount Staurin, and Tancred's converted monastery to the south, the crusaders did their best to hold onto the substantial and strategically located fort of La Mahomerie, which controlled access to the city's single line of supply, the Bridge Gate leading to the road to Saint Simeon. Although Raymond of Toulouse had taken claim and paid for manning La Mahomerie after its construction, the duty to defend it had, oddly enough, fallen to Robert of Flanders. This being the only Christian stronghold outside the city walls, Kerbogha immediately began testing its strength by throwing 2,000 troops against the fort in direct assault.

Robert of Flanders and his 500 defenders fought valiantly, but after three days of vicious attack, under cover of darkness, they set La Mahomerie afire and withdrew back into the city. Watching Kerbogha continue massing troops along the lower slopes of Mount Silpius for a direct attack, the crusaders audaciously decided to make a pre-emptive attack on June 10th to harry the Turks. Using a small postern gate along the southern edge of Silpius, they sent out a force, taking a Muslim camp by complete surprise, routing all within it. Rather than making a swift retreat back to the city, many within this crusader force decided to loot the amply supplied camp. But greed exacts a toll. These plunderers were caught in Kerbogha's counter-attack. Trapped on open ground, their ill-fated dash back to the postern gate was overrun by swift moving ghazis firing deadly compound bows.

Following this slaughter, Kerbogha launched a double offensive in an effort to eliminate Bohemud's new upper camp. As one massive Muslim force attacked from the outside by assaulting the walls south of the citadel, his commander in the citadel poured troops from the inside against Bohemud. Battling on two fronts, the crusader defense of this area was woefully stretched because other crusaders had to hold position defending all the other gates of the city. Nonetheless, crusader heroism held out for two full days; clashes raging from dawn to dusk, fighting off wave after wave of Turks assaulting them from outside the walls and smaller numbers from inside the citadel. As later recalled by many crusaders: "While the battle raged, if a man had food, he had no time to eat, and if he had water, he had no time to drink."

Such was the ferocity of this battle that many crusaders who stood fast began to lose hope by the end of the second day, whereas others openly fled, lowering themselves from ropes at the uncontested northern and western points of the wall. Especially disheartening was the desertion of well-known crusaders such as Bohemud's brother-in-law, William of Grandmesnil, his brother Aubré, Guy

Trousseau, and Lambert the Poor, who after the battle along the southern wall became frightened and saw no possible way to hold off Kerbogha's endless onslaught. With these renowned crusader deserters went many of their followers. Reaching the ships at Saint Simeon, before boarding, they reportedly told the sailors: "You poor devils, why are you staying here? All our men are dead and we barely escaped death ourselves!" Terrified, all sailors in port started boarding ships and fluffing sails. But before half could get away, the Turks attacked, stealing cargo, then setting remaining ships on fire and slaughtering those left behind.

Those who remained in the city defending the southern wall held out for two more days, stretching their minds and spirits to the absolute limits of human endurance. Such, then, would become the stuff of legends, recorded in later years. Bohemud remained in the thick of the fight, and at one point was completely surrounded by Turks, only to be rescued at the end by Robert of Normandy and Robert of Flanders. A Southern knight named 'Mad Hugh' single-handedly defended an entire tower by himself, breaking three spears in the process.

Guillaume and the Danes stood in the midst of the fighting, alongside Letellier and his brave troops. Guillaume and Letellier especially put up a devastating defense in the midst of this battle. Guillaume had already become a crusader legend within the ranks of the Christian army, but it was here that his stature elevated to an entirely new plane. Slinging his sword without mercy, holding Turks at the wall, hurling them backwards one after another into a deadly thirty-meter drop, Guillaume's very presence emboldened and inspired others to collect every ounce of courage they could summon and remain in the fight.

Guillaume could have never survived his own extraordinary efforts had he not had Orla, Hroc, and Guthroth protecting his flanks. Turks savagely poured forward in an undulating, seemingly unending mass. Guillaume knew this, and had always counted on the Danes. On this day, he was especially satisfied that Guthroth was back in their midst. Regardless of being smaller than either Orla or Hroc, it was Guthroth who was by far the deadliest in battle, owing to well-honed skills and phenomenal instincts.

On June 11th, in the midst of this chaos along Silpius, a priest named Stephen of Valence came to the princes and soldiers defending the wall. "I've received a vision of Christ and the Virgin Mary, you brave warriors!" he declared. "You are admonished for your sins and charged to purify yourselves for five days! I swear upon the cross that this is true and am willing to cross through fire or throw myself from one of these towers!" History has never recorded whether Stephen of Valence actually had to carry out proof of his vision, nor whether his story was true. And although this moment on the ramparts was not a major event in the Battle of Antioch, it was the precursor of things to come; a burning need to believe in Godly and heavenly intervention on behalf of the Army of God.

As things happened, during Stephen of Valence's dramatic presentation of his vision to the defenders of Silpius, another was watching and listening carefully, taking meticulous note of Stephen's effect on desperate men fighting against all odds. That man was Peter Bartholomew, the former close friend of Peter the Hermit. Embarrassed by the Hermit's desertion, and despite his earlier adoration of the Hermit, Peter Bartholomew had since disassociated himself from the wild-eyed little evangelist, believing to have learned enough from him to stand on his own, declaring himself a new spiritual presence.

In the face of exemplary crusader courage on the Silpius wall, understandably, there were those who cowered. On receiving word that many crusaders had taken to hiding within a church, Bohemud went into a rage and ordered it set on fire; many burned inside, but those who ran out agreed to return to their positions. The fire spread out of control, burning other buildings, almost reaching the Basilica of Saint Peter and the Church of Saint Mary.

As the blazing fire approached the Saint-Germain faction's nest, Mala held Christophe in her arms, and poor Garik cringed at her waist. Brave children forced to grow up before their time and experience such horror, Agda, Berna, Karine, and Christos had already joined the bucket brigade and were boldly fighting the lapping infernos, sloshing water forward in the face of blazing heat. Intent on safeguarding their new albeit temporary abode, it would have been impossible to tell which of the four was more fearless.

"Faster!" cried Christos, keeping an eye to Karine in case she should need rescuing, not realizing that if anyone in their bunch was likely to rescue another, it would be Karine.

Karine noticed that Christos appeared to be hovering, but was not put off by it. The two had spent some time together, and after a point, Karine actually deigned to speak to him. This delighted Christos beyond measure, but in his heart, he knew Karine could never replace his dear, sweet, innocent Anna.

Agda and Berna, being older than their brother, in turn, hovered around Christos. They had never thought to see him again, and therefore considered him a newfound treasure, one they'd refuse to relinquish under any circumstances. Mala had washed their faces and cleansed Agda's and Berna's bodies, and within a single day in her company, the sisters had rediscovered their smiles. Even now, in the face of raging fires, they smiled at each other from time to time, often pointing to Christos who was completely lost, not to the fire, but to Karine. "Ha," snickered Berna, "he's too young to be looking at girls, especially one older than him, eh, Agda?"

Grinning, Agda sniggered back. "Yes, all us four fighting the fire are older than our years, especially that girl. She's nearly a woman, but our brother has no idea. Poor Christos!"

CHAPTER SIXTY-TWO

PETER BARTHOLOMEW

Having failed to break into Antioch after four days of extremely intense fighting, Kerbogha decided on June 4th to re-deploy his troops. This may have been a mistake. Crusader resistance was already at the end of its rope by the end of that fourth day. But rather than continuing to concentrate his army for an attack from the south, he spread them out, blocking the Bridge Gate and the Gate of Saint George, maintaining a strong force within the citadel. In essence, the crusaders were now cut off from the world.

On the night before this deployment, a strange light appeared in the sky, probably a comet, which many crusaders interpreted to be a heavenly sign. As recalled by one of Bohemud's followers: "There appeared a fire in the sky, coming from the west, and it approached and fell upon the Turkish army, to the great astonishment of our men and of the Turks also. In the morning, the Turks, who were all scared by the fire, took flight in panic." In truth, the Turks had not fled the southern slope of Silpius, they had simply redeployed and repositioned per command by Kerbogha. Nonetheless, this was another indication that the crusaders hungered for spiritual signs from above.

Learning about the sparse rations and conditions within the city from Shams ad-Daulah, Kerbogha began a policy of containment, eventually starving the crusaders out. And indeed, lack of food within Antioch quickly began to take its toll. Prior to taking the city, both crusaders and Antiochians were already on the verge of starvation. Kerbogha simply extended this problem. The little food that was available within the city was exorbitant in price; a loaf of bread costing a full gold bezant, a hen fifteen shillings, and an egg two shillings. Needless to say, most crusaders and Antiochians had no money. Men began to boil and eat grape leaves, vines, thistles, and any other foliage they could get their hands on, and stew hides of horses, donkeys, camels, and oxen, which, in desperate times, became a precious commodity. At any rate, each day bodies were carted away, stacked in piles, and set afire. It must be remembered that due to Kerbogha's quick arrival, there were already thousands of corpses strewn throughout the city from the crusader assault. Most of these had not been disposed of, therefore the collection of the dead became a gruesome daily ritual, and the nights were lit by funeral pyres.

Exhausted, starving, lacking horses, their ranks thinned by desertion and battle, seeing no escape, the Army of God faced their blackest hour. They had thought their conditions over the previous eight months had been difficult, but realized that those days had been far, far more tolerable than what they were presently enduring. Indeed, they were facing the end, and from the look of it, the entire expedition would go down in history as having a glorious beginning only to drown in the tarpit of Antioch, never making it to Jerusalem.

History is filled with grandiose campaigns, failing for one reason or another, and the graveyards of time are filled with their casualties; men following a vision, chasing a cause, righting a wrong, or pursuing some quixotic quest to mend the world or re-shape it. One can only imagine the thoughts of these last 30,000 crusaders, counting their final days, thousands of kilometers from home, knowing they would never see either their families or homelands again. The very thought of taking their last breath in such a barren, remote, and distant landscape must have been crushing to the spirit.

Above all, there were still those who held out hope amidst the stark impossibility of circumstances. And hope, you know, is what has kept humanity crawling forward from the darkness into the light. When all else has collapsed and withered, hope is the flagging remnant of the human heart, and when hope itself collapses and withers, only 'the end' remains.

It was at this black hour that Peter Bartholomew, bedraggled peasant from Provence, requested an audience with Raymond of Toulouse and Bishop Adhémar. "I've something remarkable to relate to the two of you," he announced, entering their company, appearing as if he had been touched by a great light; glowing, elated. "Beginning on December 30th, I've been visited by two men clad in brilliant garments, on no fewer than five occasions."

Raymond was aghast, rising in a defensive stance. "Here, in Antioch?"

"No," replied Peter, closing his eyes, chin tilted up, holding his palms out, raising them skyward, mimicking a favorite spiritual pose of the Hermit. "Not in Antioch itself, rather in visions. They've been coming to me as apparitions. The older visitor had red hair sprinkled with white, a broad bushy white beard, black eyes, and an agreeable countenance, and was of medium height. His younger companion was taller and fair in form beyond the sons of men."

"Indeed," said Adhémar, who was willing to acknowledge miracles and embrace the spiritual, but only if such was authentic and validated by specific processes ordained by the Church. This peasant, however, was already raising Adhémar's skepticism. "And just who were these two men?" he asked.

"I believe them to be Saint Andrew the apostle, accompanied by Christ," replied Peter, who then launched into great detail concerning the visits, what was said, and who said what.

"And how long ago was your latest vision?" asked Adhémar, watching Raymond who appeared intrigued by Bartholomew's tale.

"My final vision came to me," replied Peter, "as I was sitting dejected and listless on a rock, having barely survived the fighting along the southern wall of

Mount Silpius. But know this, even from the very first visit, Saint Andrew had one very specific message for me. He reminded me about the Roman soldier, Longinus, who had pierced Jesus in the side with his lance as He hung dying on the cross. And you know very well, Bishop Adhémar, that Longinus' lance became known as the 'Holy Lance.'"

"Yes, yes, of course," said Adhémar, crossing his arms in a show of apparent knowledge. "But what of it?"

"Ah, yes, let me get to the reason I've come to you and Prince Raymond," said Peter, closing his eyes and extending his palms again, but without lifting them. "Saint Andrew revealed to me that this most holy relic is buried right here within the very walls of Antioch. And he showed it to me."

"Chrissakes!" cried out Raymond, overcome. "You mean to say the Holy Lance is here in the city?! God in Heaven! But quick, tell us where!"

"Before we conquered Antioch," Peter went on boldly, "Saint Andrew spirited me away one night still in my nightshirt. Oh, and right past the Turkish guards we went, and into the Basilica of Saint Peter."

"Ah, the Basilica of Saint Peter!" sighed Raymond, riveted to every word coming from Peter's mouth.

"Yes, that's where the lance is buried. When Saint Andrew showed it to me, he charged me with the task of informing the Council of Princes of its where-abouts once we captured Antioch. Saint Andrew said, 'It's to be used as a stan-dard in battle, for he who carries this lance in battle shall never be overcome by the enemy.'"

Scratching his head, Adhémar scowled. "Peter, you claim that his message to you from the very beginning was about the Holy Lance, and that the first visit came on December 30th, which was six months ago. How is it that you are just now revealing these visions to us?"

"Oh, but I feared you wouldn't believe me, Bishop!" replied Peter without hesitation. "I was frightened and intimidated even though Saint Andrew kept pressing me to approach you and Prince Raymond. I am but a ragged peasant, like Tafur and his wild bunch, yet in no way do I approve of their savagery!" He cast his eyes to the floor. "And with you two, our leaders, grand royalty to us, yes, I was simply afraid to come forward."

"Oh, but be frightened no more!" exclaimed Raymond, taking Peter by the arm. "Come with me! You shall henceforth be in the private care of my own chaplain, Raymond of Aguilers. And when we find him, I want you to tell him the exact thing you told us, word for word, mind you!"

"Certainly," said Peter, turning to look at Adhémar who had not moved from his chair. "Aren't you coming along, Bishop?"

"No, no," said Adhémar, flagging the back of his hand at Peter and Raymond, gesturing for them to go on without him. Adhémar waited until they left, then went straight to his knees in prayer. "Oh, Lord in Heaven," he prayed aloud, "I wish to believe this man, but doubt and uncertainty are blocking my way. Guide me, I beg, as word is spread that the Holy Lance is buried here within the Basilica of Saint Peter. I pray it is, Lord, for if that be the case, it is surely a direct godsend from Your very hands at our darkest hour. Amen."

CHAPTER SIXTY-THREE

THE HOLY LANCE

It was ardently believed in the 11th century that saints, or the sanctified dead, could intercede on behalf of those living on earth. Their usual role was to petition God for aid for a particular person or group. Visions, too, were an important aspect of Catholicism, as were miracles. Special reverence was given to relics, tangible evidence, and foci of sanctity; the highest grade of relic being those articles having belonged to or touched Christ, then descending to major saints/disciples, then minor saints. Relics held special powers, too, in terms of calling for God's intercession during critical times of need.

It would be a mistake to believe that such credence in visions, miracles, and relics were the realm of the poor and the ignorant because the clergy, being the most educated element of society during the Dark Ages, promulgated and espoused beliefs in these three aspects of Christianity. Then, too, kings, queens, counts, and other royalty piously venerated these beliefs also. Relics were often placed in monasteries or in cathedrals beneath the altar, but some people carried them on their body, especially during times of travel, war, or tribulation.

Adhémar of Le Puy had brought along on the crusade a small piece of wood that he believed had come from the cross on which Jesus had been crucified, and Raymond of Toulouse brought a chalice that once belonged to Saint Robert of Chaise-Dieu, celebrated saint and founder of a Benedictine monastery. A priest in the service of Robert of Flanders actually stole an arm of Saint George from a Byzantine monastery during the crusade, and when he died it went to Robert of Flanders who began venerating that particular saint to the point he began stylizing himself as 'the son of Saint George.' Authenticity was important, of course, and it was the Church that made rulings on whether an object was a true relic or not. In the case of visions, these rulings were generally based on whether the individual claiming the vision, usually an individual of social stature, was willing to swear a sacred oath. At times, they were even asked to undergo a physical ordeal of some sort that was relatively dangerous, like walking through fire.

Hearing Peter Bartholomew's recitation of his visions of Saint Andrew and Christ, Bishop Adhémar held deep reservations about Peter, as documented when he gave voice to these to Raymond of Toulouse and Raymond of Aguilers, both of whom were convinced that Peter Bartholomew was telling the truth.

Adhémar's hesitancy and part of his objection to accept Peter Bartholomew's story was undoubtedly based on the fact that the young man was but a lowly peasant and there was already one Holy Lance ostensibly located in

Constantinople. There could not be two. Telling no one, and setting aside the long-brewing bitterness he held for Tristan, Adhémar made his way to an out-building near Saint Peter's Basilica where the Saint-Germain group had settled for the time being.

"Bishop Saint-Germain, could I have a word with you?" enquired Adhémar, with unusual awkwardness when Tristan answered the door.

Surprised to see Adhémar, and in little mood to get into another fiery exchange with the old bishop, Tristan barred entry by standing in the middle of the doorway, filling it. "Mala and my son are inside, Adhémar, and I know they offend you, just as I do. These are impossible times already. I need no more drama. Nor does my family. If you have something to say, say it out here."

"I've not come to argue, Saint-German. But very well, that suits me fine," replied Adhémar. "Besides, I intend for our conversation to be private, and I ask that you respect the confidentiality of it. Do you vow it?"

Unable to guess what Adhémar was after, Tristan did not answer immediately. "Yes, I vow it," he said finally.

"I know things have been difficult between us, but I need your expertise for a moment. Hopefully for the purpose of reinforcing my own."

Curiosity peaked, Tristan asked, "Very well, what is it?"

"Could you tell me the location of the Holy Lance?"

"What? Adhémar, you know very well the Holy Lance rests in Constantinople."

"Yes, yes, I'm certain I do. But most in Western Europe have little knowledge of the status of the Holy Lance other than it was used to wound Christ. And with you actually being one of the most studied Church historians of our times, I would like to hear from you not only where it is but how it got there."

Shaking his head, puzzled, Tristan began, "The Holy Lance was discovered in Jerusalem by Saint Helena in the 4th century. Then, 400 years later, it was moved to Constantinople, the center of the Eastern Roman Empire, which, by that time, had become Christianized. From what we know, the Holy Lance is currently part of the relic collection of the standing Byzantine emperor, Alexius Comnenus."

"Thank you, Bishop," said Adhémar, turning and disappearing down the street without another word. But by the time he got back to find Raymond of Toulouse, Raymond of Aguilers, and Peter Bartholomew, they were gone. Not only were they gone, but they had already informed the other crusader princes that the Holy Lance was in Antioch. Bearing such knowledge, the princes had begun telling their men, who were repeating the news throughout the city.

As Peter Bartholomew's story spread like wildfire, crusaders began clanging their shields and shouting praise to God in the streets, quickly joined by the general populace. "We're saved!" they shouted, drunk with jubilance and euphoria. "The Holy Lance is here! We're saved by a sign from God!"

On witnessing this outbreak of exultation washing through the streets of Antioch, in a dubious act of self-interest, Adhémar decided it best for him to say nothing else about the Holy Lance. But this gave rise to a new concern: What shall occur should a lance not be found?

It was Raymond of Aguilers who feverishly documented the actual search for the Holy Lance, as cited in his record: "On 14 June, twelve men and Peter Bartholomew collected the appropriate tools and began to dig in the church of the Blessed Peter, following the expulsion of all other Christians. The Bishop of Orange, Raymond of Aguilers, author of this work, Raymond of Toulouse, Pons of Balazun, and Farald of Thouars were among the twelve. We had been digging until evening, when several gave up hope of unearthing the Lance. In the meantime, the Count had gone to the citadel and persuaded fresh workers to replace the weary workers, and for a time they dug furiously. But the youthful Peter Bartholomew, seeing the exhaustion of our workers, stripped his outer garments and, clad only in a shirt and barefooted, dropped into the hole. He then begged us to pray to God to return His Lance to the crusaders, to bring strength and victory to His people. Finally, in his mercy, the Lord showed us His Lance, and I, Raymond, the author of this book, kissed the point of the Lance as it barely protruded from the ground. What great joy and exultation then filled the city."

The Holy Lance, extracted from the digging site, was nothing but a shard of metal. But as it was brought out of Saint Peter's Basilic, a full celebration by thousands broke out in the streets and anxious crowds jockeyed about, shouldering their way forward just to get a glimpse of the sacred relic.

"Ho there, you people of the Lord!" cried Peter Bartholomew triumphantly. "Right when we face annihilation, here is the Lance! Proof of God's renewed support for the crusade!"

CHAPTER SIXTY-FOUR

"COURAGE, YOU CHRISTIANS!"

The discovery of the Holy Lance took immediate effect throughout the entire city, which had been dropped in a black hole of hopelessness, teetering to the edge of surrender. In particular, it was the crusaders who caught fire, rejuvenated in their belief that God was with them and convinced that heavenly intervention was just an arm's reach ahead.

This was just as well. They were completely blocked in by Kerbogha and under threat of attack from within by Shams ad-Daulah and Kerbogha's commander who held a firm grasp on the citadel above the city.

The Holy Lance was unearthed on June 14th, and what followed was two weeks of celebration and preparation, yet starvation mercilessly, persistently gnawed at the bones of the city. Inspired at discovering the Lance, resurrected crusader morale should have directed them to charge out of the city to attack Kerbogha immediately. However, it is presumed that the Army of God remained hopeful that Taticius might return with Emperor Alexius and his Byzantine troops, therefore the two-week delay.

Peter Bartholomew, meanwhile, had another visit from Saint Andrew and Christ, announcing to all who would listen, "All crusaders, turn from sin to God and offer five alms for the five wounds of Christ." Cocky Bartholomew felt overly protected in the care of Raymond of Toulouse and his chaplain, Raymond of Aguilers, who then organized this collection of alms, and in the process amassed a small fortune.

As to Taticius and Alexius, they fell victim to one of unforgiving foibles of history. To begin, Alexius was exploiting the damage the Latins had wreaked against the Turks in Asia Minor. That spring, he sent a Byzantine fleet into the Mediterranean to the west coast of Smyrna and the city of Ephesus to finish off pockets of Turkish resistance. This fleet was commanded by Alexius' brother-in-law, John Doukas. The Byzantine vessels then sailed to Philomelium to await Alexius who, by early June, had marched an army from Constantinople to rendezvous with Doukas and Taticius. The emperor's intention was to arrive at Antioch after the crusaders vanquished it, then appear only to have the Latins turn the city over to the Byzantine Empire as they had done with previous cities. Taticius argued that they should arrive in time to reinforce the crusaders, but his pleas fell on empty ears.

Then came the twist. On June 20th, a ragged band of crusaders appeared in Philomelium traveling from the east. The crusaders were being led by none other than William of Grandmesnil, Bohemud's brother-in-law, and Stephen of Blois; both of whom had deserted Antioch at a critical moment. In talking to Emperor Alexius and Admiral Doukas, Grandmesnil and Blois claimed that, "The Franks have been reduced to starvation and a position of the utmost danger." Stephen of Blois expounded on this story by predicting, "I tell you truly that Antioch has been taken by the crusaders, but the citadel has not fallen and the crusaders are besieged on all fronts by the vast army of Kerbogha of Mosul. That was how William and I, having separately abandoned Antioch, happened to meet along the way here. But by now, I expect every crusader to be dead. Go back to Constantinople, therefore, post haste in case Kerbogha finds you and your followers!"

Alexius' first priority was protecting his empire, not trying to get to Antioch to save the crusaders, especially if they had already been overrun. Accordingly, he ordered a complete evacuation of the area, initiating a scorched earth policy in his wake back to Constantinople. He wanted to prevent any pursuing Turkish armies from being able to forage in case they showed up to chase him back west. Setting Anatolia aflame, Alexius and the Byzantines left the Latins in Antioch to their fate, and turned their backs on them.

Whilst the Army of God awaited Alexius, they sent two envoys into Kerbogha's camp, Peter the Hermit and an interpreter named Herluin. The Hermit was none too keen to perform this embassy, of course, but as a noted deserter was given no choice. His mission was to threaten Kerbogha, even though the crusaders were on the edge of collapse themselves. Dutifully, the Hermit delivered an ultimatum as instructed, saying to Kerbogha, "Our leaders, as one man, require you to take yourselves off quickly from this land, which belongs to God and the Christians, for the blessed Peter converted it long ago to the faith of Christ by his teaching. But they give you permission to take away all your goods, withersoever you may choose. If you choose not to abide by this offer, our princes then propose that rather than a full-scale war, leaving tens of thousands slain, a small war by five, or ten, or twenty men from each side could be waged. The party that overcomes the other shall claim the city with no further controversy."

Hearing Herluin's translation, Kerbogha fell into a fit of laughter. "Ha!" he proclaimed, "I promise you that either death or captivity awaits every one of you heathens unless you surrender immediately and convert to Islam!"

Herluin translated this reply, and the Hermit indicated that they should leave immediately, which they did, to report Kerbogha's answer. The question remains, of course, what this was all about. It could not have been a serious negotiation by the Council of Princes. The Latins were in no position to negotiate anything, let alone threatening Kerbogha that he should abandon Antioch and make haste back to Mosul. And the challenge of one small group against the other was absurd! Kerbogha outnumbered the Latins, therefore it would be madness for him to agree to such a scheme.

The supposition, therefore, is that the Hermit's mission was either an attempt to buy more time for Alexius to show up, or a show of sheer bravado and defiance.

With time running out and the fever of the Holy Lance burning ever stronger, the Council of Princes were down to their last option. They decided by June 25th that their only hope would be to plan a profoundly audacious break-out from Antioch, taking Kerbogha's forces head-on. Bohemud, most likely due to his battle record, was chosen as temporary commander-in-chief, and in preparation for this last-ditch effort, the Army of God spent three days fasting, processioning from one church to another, confessing their sins, and receiving the body and blood of Christ through the holy sacrament of communion.

CHAPTER SIXTY-FIVE

THE FINAL BATTLE FOR ANTIOCH

It was now June 28th. With everything on the line, knowing it would be victory or death, galvanized and stirred by the Holy Lance, the Army of God was ready to fight. At the break of dawn, clergy stood along the ramparts offering prayers to God. Other priests and monks, carrying crosses, chanting and praying for God's help and the protection of the saints, marched out of Antioch with the crusaders, advancing head-long toward the enemy. Tristan was amongst them, marching forward, lost in prayer, hoping that defeating Kerbogha might finally put an end to his and Mala's lifelong quest to be together, raise a family, and live in peace. Part and portion of that hope was woven into leaving the Catholic Church and finally setting Pope Urban II aside, despite the gratitude and love he felt for him.

It was Raymond of Aguilers who actually carried the Holy Lance, surrounded by the Southern French, as they followed the lead of Bishop Adhémar of Le Puy. All knew exactly what stood before them, impossible odds numerically, and the harsh reality that those odds worsened in terms of the Army of God's shortage of both horses and knights. Of the 20,000 tattered men marching out of the city, noncombatants included, the Latin cavalry was only able to muster about 200 mounts trained for war, and these were, in fact, feeble from near starvation.

In light of this grim scenario, the crusaders did hold several elements in their favor. Whereas they marched out to attack as a single, unified force, Kerbogha's camps were scattered in an effort to block six of the city's gates. Kerbogha's headquarters were one kilometer to the north of the Saint Paul Gate, with the remainder of his huge army lined in a long shoestring extending from his camp all the way around the southern perimeter of the city.

The lack of horses denied the crusaders their most dreaded weapon, the heavy cavalry charge, forcing knights to fight on mules, donkeys, and other pack animals, including oxen. This bleak disadvantage greatly boosted the infantry in that thousands of knights had been reduced to joining the footmen. Knights were known to be far more aggressive and courageous than footmen, therefore their presence within the ranks turned the Christian infantry into a vastly hardened and dangerous fighting unit.

But the crusaders had Bohemud. Irrespective of his nature or selfish motivations, he was a brilliant military strategist and leader. His generalship had time and again saved the day as proven at Nicaea, Dorylaeum, throughout the long march, and against both Duqaq of Damascus and Ridwan of Aleppo. Bohemud was confident, fearless, and had been fighting since early adolescence by the side of his father, Duke Robert Guiscard the Wily. He possessed more experience fighting Muslims than the combined leadership of the entire Council of Princes.

There was a final domino assisting the crusaders, one of which they were not even aware, actually. The Army of God, bearing the history of frequent in-fighting and internal fractures, was entering this battle with one mind, one hope, and one objective only. Kerbogha's, on the other hand, had been cobbled together hastily from all parts of Mesopotamia and Syria; many volunteering strictly out of fear of Kerbogha. Although he had not been involved in Syria until now, his brutal reputation had preceded his name. In the end, these factors combined to jeopardize one of the most critical factors in war—loyalty.

There was one other factor flagging in the wind. Many of the Muslim lords heeding Kerbogha's call had little heart for risking their lives, their men, and their resources in Antioch, knowing that Kerbogha would claim the city for himself and refuse to share the spoils of war. Then understandably, the Syrian element of these Muslim lords actually feared that with Kerbogha owning Antioch, he would then come for their own realms, attacking their own families and friends. Kerbogha demonstrated on a daily basis behavior that alienated others—selfishness, monstrously narcissistic pride, and he treated others with disdain and scorn.

The issues just cited were certainly not lost to Kerbogha's disparate army, as behind his back many of these very things were being hotly debated among different Seljuk clans. There were even those among the Syrian generals who hoped Kerbogha might fail.

Kerbogha, notwithstanding his many advantages, had to hope that the fickle, swift-moving currents of battle remained in his favor. Otherwise, his fractured alliances might disband and leave.

Bohemud's battle plan was exceptional, all things considered. He chose the Bridge Gate as the sally-point, placing his troops along the west bank of the Orontes. In doing so, the Latins would meet a limited force at first, and the barrier of the river would impede Muslim advancement from other gates. To ignite the battle, Bohemud assigned Hugh of Vermandois to dash out of the gate with a full squadron of archers charged with lying down a heavy aerial shock-attack. This brave act would allow the entire crusader army time to exit Antioch and form as one on the Antiochian plains without being taken apart piecemeal in their attempt to get out of the city.

Within the full crusader army, Bohemud created four sub-armies: Northern French under the command of Robert of Normandy and Robert of Flanders, Germans under Godfrey of Bouillon, and the Southern French under Adhémar of Le Puy, while he himself held the largest army, as was often his custom, in reserve. His reserve force was made up of Norman-Italians and an assortment of troops from other armies to boost its size. Their duty was to hold place until the need arose to plug gaps or respond to Turkish break-throughs. As an historical note, Adhémar had been placed in command of the Southern French for this battle only because Raymond, as had often happened before, was ill. He remained in the city with a contingent of 200 crusaders.

Once Hugh of Vermandois cleared the path of the Bridge Gate, the Northern French marched behind Hugh of Vermandois' archers and deployed left, after which the next two armies repeated the maneuver, forming a semi-circle. Despite Bohemud's acute generalship, had Kerbogha actually sent his full force against the Latins precisely when the Turks in the citadel raised the black flag warning of attack, he would have easily crushed the Christians.

But at this most crucial of moments, the snare of 'assumption' took hold. As messengers raced to inform Kerbogha of the black warning flag, he was engaged in a game of chess. Having listened to the message, never taking his eyes from the chess board, he reflected a moment.

Uncertain whether he was actually reflecting on their message or whether he was contemplating his next chess move, one of the messengers said, "Some of the generals insist you should go up to the city and kill the Christians one by one as they come out of the gate. They say it would be easy to pick them off now that they're waiting on each other and are split up."

"N-o-o-o," replied Kerbogha calmly, slowly, moving his rook to attack his opponent's bishop, pinning it, "we'll wait until they all come out, and then we will kill them all at once. But then, how many are there?"

"Doesn't appear to be a large force, Sire, from what we can tell. Nonetheless, they're on the move and coming out!"

"Few in number? Bah! Then my troops posted before the Bridge Gate shall easily dispatch them. Besides, I doubt they're actually attacking. That'd be beyond imagination! Most likely they've begun to flee, in which case, I'll let them go. No need to lose men and horses if not necessary."

The entire time this exchange was being conducted, Kerbogha had never once lifted his eyes from the board.

Immediately upon completing the formation of their semi-circle on the Antiochian plain, the crusaders were attacked by Turks camped in the immediate vicinity to blockade the fortified bridge and Antioch's Bridge Gate. Minutes later, Turkish bugles blared and additional troops rushed in from the north, leaving their positions at the Gate of the Duke and the Saint Paul Gate. Then the pincer closed its claws from the south. Turks guarding the Saint George Gate began flooding into the battle, moving to outflank the crusaders and attack them from behind. This maneuver by the Muslims, washing in from the Saint George Gate, surprisingly forced the most decisive event of the crusaders' opening attack.

From his reserve position, Bohemud was watching this particular Turkish maneuver unfold with Guillaume and the Danes who sat astride their horses at Bohemud's side.

Growing alarmed, it was Guthroth who first suspected the crusader line was going to break with the arrival of Turks surging into battle from the Saint George

Gate. "Th-They're circling be-behind the l-left flank of our s-semi-circle!" he shouted, nearly springing from his saddle. "N-now! We g-go now!"

"Hold!" commanded Bohemud, thinking it best to allow more Turks from the Saint George Gate into the snare before sending in the reserves.

"N-no, I w-won't!" snapped Guthroth, charging forward to the back of the semi-circle, driving south and charging headlong into the Turks surging in from the Saint George Gate.

"Guthroth! Get back!" screamed Hroc, furiously spurring his mount forward into Guthroth's wake.

"Shit!" cried Orla, in a panic for both their lives, and hotly spurred his horse, galloping into the fray defend them.

Bohemud screamed at all three, "Hold, I said! Damn you! Get your asses back here!"

The words had barely escaped his lips when Guillaume took off, shouting, "Guthroth's right, it's now or never!"

In reaction, Bohemud dispatched Reinhard of Toul with a squadron of Northern French and Germans to follow, stepping in as rear guard.

But Guthroth, having been the first to charge, and having charged in alone, found himself swamped by both Muslim footmen and cavalry engulfing him from every direction, closing off all hope of escape. Refusing to falter, he spun his horse around, swinging his bludgeon with one arm and his sword with the other hoping to open a swath to what had just seconds before been his rear.

But then a mass of arms and hands came at him, like aroused tentacles, pulling him from his saddle. "Arghh!" he groaned, knowing his time had come. "H-Haya!" he shouted, tumbling blindly to the ground, his eyes obstructed by a swarm of arms, legs, boots, and the flash of scything saber blades.

Ah, this is death, thought Guthroth; things spinning and swirling fast and furiously, he had but time left for a single flickering emotion: regret over Haya.

Unimaginably, the crushing weight began to dissipate suddenly, causing Guthroth to fail to even notice at first. Then came fragmented glimpses of daylight breaking through as figures attacking him were tumbling or being flung one way and another. Hroc and Orla, quickly followed by Guillaume, burst through, hacking and slinging Turks off Guthroth in a mad effort to free him. Wasting no time, Guthroth, although beaten a bit, sprang to his feet, wildly adding his bludgeon and blade to their already savage onslaught against the Turks.

For three deadly minutes the four fought heroically to repulse the augmenting swarm of enemies arriving, but the momentum refused to turn as the left flank of the semi-circle of infantry they had tried to save began to collapse. Guthroth, Guillaume, Hroc, and Orla, all fighting afoot, clustered together back-to-back like a ring of bulls facing a pack of wolves.

This was the point at which ten Turks rushed en masse against Hroc, knocking him to his back. Glancing up, he saw an entire thicket of spearpoints raised over him that, within a blink, would perforate every inch of his body. As happened in the brutal and unforgiving face-to-face murder of war in this era, Hroc had no time to react, nor even time for hope. Closing his eyes, he thought of God, and commended his spirit to Him.

But Orla caught sight of Hroc's dilemma. Screaming his son's name, he bulled forward, heaving his massive frame over Hroc head-first, just as the wall of spear-points were being thrust down, in unison. Impaled head-to-foot from the back, Orla gasped, staring straight into Hroc's eyes, not even having time to call out his name, or even wail in agony.

Swarming again as men possessed, Guthroth and Guillaume drove into the Muslim lancers, clearing a swath around Hroc and Orla. Hroc, in what he thought to be his last moment, had exchanged a fleeting glance with his father. With his eyes closed, he had begun to keen, wrapping both arms around Orla, squeezing him to his chest.

In haste, Guthroth and Guillaume both began jerking lances from Orla's back, the shape of their tips hindering them greatly. With each extraction, Hroc felt his father's body pull away from him for an instant, then relapse, which made him hold Orla even tighter.

Removing the last spear, Guthroth and Guillaume then fought to free Hroc's grip from his father. Guthroth screamed, "G-Get up! G-get up, Hroc! Th-they're still coming!"

But Hroc refused. He had a vice grip and would not let go. "Leave me!" Hroc shouted. "Let me be, damn you!"

Having no time to argue, Guillaume and Guthroth turned against the fast-approaching wave of Muslims washing forward.

Gasping for breath, incredibly, but utterly helpless, Orla could move nothing but his eyes. He blinked slowly, staring down at Hroc screaming in his mind to a god his father had been denying yet now embraced with his last breaths, No! Oh God, this can't be! Oh, Father, dear Father!

In the midst of a churning bloodbath, Hroc had but one thing in his heart: the impossibility of his father's death.

Then Orla blinked no more. His eyes froze. Watching, Hroc caught a glimmer, at that final moment, emanating from Orla's sky-blue eyes—pride and ... and ... peace. A single rasp and dead weight signaled Orla Bloodaxe's Continuation Day.

Guthroth had seen Orla's heroic sacrifice—his heart had dropped to his belly—but there was no time for grief. Shortly, like Orla, they would all be dead, unless there came a miracle.

Back to fighting, he noticed Guillaume had moved away from him, slashing, screaming, wading into the enemy, an invincible single force lost to all reality. Then, before Guthroth could assemble another thought about it, Guillaume, his face streaming with the blood of the many Muslims he had already slain, vanished into the sweeping currents of blood, men, and horses raging toward him.

This, oddly, is when Crowbones' prophecy struck him, reaching up from the grave, throttling him. It's true, shuddered Guthroth, none of us from Saint-Germain-en-Laye shall ever set eyes on Jerusalem! Crowbones is dead, Orla is dead, Hroc is soon to be slain, lying helpless under Orla, and Guillaume has charged off to his own execution, and I shall not survive either. Not a one of us will lay eyes on the Holy Land.

Then Bohemud arrived.

Seeing what Guthroth had seen earlier, he realized that the Latin line, being taken from behind from the south, was the arrival of doom, ending all crusader hope. Jolted by reality, Bohemud and his reserve drove into the mob of oncoming Muslims with crazed abandon, taking heavy losses in a show of ferocity nearly matching that of Guillaume and the Danes.

Kerbogha's men had never in their war-torn years encountered such suicidal savagery coming from so few men. Frightened, the Turks from the Saint George Gate fell to fighting at a crouch, slowly backing away. Then, as when a dam bursts, packs of them turned, breaking into a full run. Seeing this, the entire Turkish line stalled, then erupted into flight, setting the ground behind them on fire to impede Christian pursuit. Simultaneously, the other two factions of the crusaders' semi-circle held rock-firm, repulsing charging Turks with a furor of their own, while Bohemud's deadly reserve force cut into the routed Turks, and mercilessly. This phase of the battle was recorded as such: "As was their custom, they (Turks) began to scatter on all sides, occupying hills and paths, and, whenever they could, they wished to surround us. For they thought they could kill all of us in this manner. But our men, having been trained in many battles against their trickery and cleverness, and God's grace and mercy, came to the forefront so that we, who were very few in comparison to them, drove them all close together. Then with God's right-hand fighting with us, we forced them so driven together to flee, and to leave their camps with everything in them."

Unable to break the crusader line, the surge of Turks blocking the bridge fell into sheer panic, fleeing in one mass. Kerbogha, realizing the Latin threat was more dangerous than he had anticipated, quickly gathered his much larger secondary force and charged into the raging battle. To his shock, he and his troops ran straight into the chaos of thousands and thousands of his own fleeing troops running from the bridge, in full rout. Utterly complete was their terror in their flight, they scattered Kerbogha's advancing formation.

What followed was pure bedlam as Kerbogha's mighty secondary army fell into disarray. Any general commanding loyalty and admiration might have been able to rally his troops under such failing circumstances, but Kerbogha commanded neither. Those armies that had answered Kerbogha's call from afar, one by one, abandoned the field, retreating to their prospective realms. Seeing this, realizing he had lost the day, Kerbogha fled, returning to Mosul in shame and disgrace, never to return again to Syria.

The field slowly cleared, sporadic movement here and there, then as always after battle, crusaders began seeking out brothers, cousins, uncles, nephews, and friends, praying they had survived this murderous man-made hell of their own devise. Hroc lay motionless under Orla, appearing dead, like his father. Seeing this, Guthroth took a knee beside the two. Shaking his head, he felt tears welling in his eyes, something he'd never felt before. Ten yards away, Guillaume's actions caught his attention, shocking him to his core. Bloodied head-to-toe, he was standing astride the corpse of a Muslim, holding the pommel of his sword with both hands, stabbing the dead man relentlessly, viciously.

Then Bohemud approached on horseback. He had been seeking Guillaume, actually, to make sure he had survived the blood fest. What he came upon was almost beyond belief. The Muslim's torso was pulped—guts, blood, organs flying left and right—yet Guillaume kept heaving his sword up and down, as if the dead Turk yet resisted. Guillaume, saturated in gore, mumbling incoherently, admonished himself; tears streaming down his cheeks in endless rivulets.

"Guillaume!" shouted Bohemud, dismounting, coming to his side, grasping his hands and arms from behind. "That's enough! Stop! The heathen's dead, and long been so!"

But Guillaume wrestled his arms free and started in again, until Bohemud pulled the sword from his hands. Guillaume, in another world, muttered as if no one else was present, "Knud, Handel, Crowbones, Orla . . ." over and over and over. "Knud, Handel, Crowbones, Orla . . ."

Looking at one another, Bohemud and Guthroth shook their heads, both knowing something was terribly wrong.

"He's b-been fighting l-like a demon since l-leaving Nicaea," said Guthroth, before turning to look down at Orla staring blankly back at him from the ground, now flat on his back. He offered Hroc, who was attempting to rise, a hand and a mournful look, his heart swelling to bursting. "I'm s-sorry," he said, bringing Hroc to his chest, embracing him with the strength of a bear. "G-God's w-will, Hroc. I d-don't understand it, b-but it is God's w-will."

Motioning to men passing by, Bohemud called out, "Come gather up Guillaume, take him into Antioch immediately for medical care! He's been wounded in four or five places, dammit! See to it he's taken care of, and clean him up, too. He's swimming in blood, and half of it isn't even his, but that poor devil he's turned to mush."

Moments later, Tancred showed up. Ensuring his uncle was not injured, he watched those taking Guillaume away, covered in gore, blabbering with glazed eyes.

"Take a good look, nephew," said Bohemud, "and a damn good one at that. I know you and Guillaume have no heart for each other, but accord him respect today. If not for men like Guillaume, we'd have never made it to Antioch, we'd have never taken Antioch, and we damn sure wouldn't have overcome Kerbogha this bloody day. Guillaume de Saint-Germain is a goddamn hero! He's fought harder than any man I've ever seen in any war I've ever fought. I think maybe it's been too, too much. Pray he recovers. I've seen this before and some never come back as they once were. Fact is, we need him for Jerusalem, but I think he should quit. I'd be worried for him if he fought again. He's killed a multitude for our cause that whatever demons were driving him before, they've now turned and are trying to kill him."

Tancred pivoted and gave Guillaume a stiff salute. "Aye, Guillaume, damn you," he said. "You are the true crusader, while the rest of us are but just crusaders. May God keep you well."

Shaking his head, Bohemud went to Guthroth and Hroc, extending his hand. "I want to thank you both," he said, "as well as Crowbones, who we lost on the mountain, and Orla, whom we've lost today. You Danes have been a force to reckon with, and we owe you much." At this, he shook both their hands and left, disappearing across the field of the dead where thousands of men lay slain, and thousands of others gasped and wailed for assistance from the bloody ground strewn with corpses stacked high as cord-wood, one atop the other in crossed and endless heaps. The madness just barely ending—a scattering of men gathered their spoils, limping spent off the field of death—the buzz of flies had already descended, and flocks of crows and vultures had begun their bountiful feast on the mountains of carrion before them.

Incredibly, in yet another complete reversal of fortune, a collection of circumstances had coalesced and colluded to deny Kerbogha an Islamic victory at Antioch. In the end, the crusaders had benefitted from a stroke of luck, combined with the masterful deployment of a shocking frontal attack fortified by inhuman resolve and naked courage.

At the end of this unexpected victory, crusaders discovered the fleeing Turks had abandoned their camps hastily and left everything behind, including pavilions, gold and silver, exotic furnishings, horses, oxen, mules, wine, flour, and many other things Antioch lacked. The crusaders, in fact, could not believe that any army could be so luxuriously accommodated in war.

Then began the looting, plundering, and robbing of the dead, which ran rampant for two full days. As to the hundreds and hundreds of abandoned harem wenches and concubine left behind by the Turks, Christian clergy records insist: "They were not sinfully raped or abused, but only pierced in their bellies with lances."

The great Battle of Antioch was the bloodiest war of the entire First Holy Crusade, ending the lives of tens of thousands of men, both Christian and Muslim, dying in the name of God and Allah. But in reality, they sacrificed themselves for a fistful of dominant leaders on each side possessing the most ungodly of intentions.

But then, such is the path of men . . . and all wars.

CHAPTER SIXTY-SIX

MALIK

Watching the entire battle unfold from the ramparts of the citadel looming high above the city, Shams ad-Daulah began to argue with Kerbogha's commander. "I see but few crusaders down in the city," he insisted. "We should attack immediately from here! We can easily overcome their small numbers, rush out the gate, and surprise their line from behind! It'd throw them into confusion and chaos within minutes!"

Kerbogha's commander had noticed that the crusader presence in the city had thinned to nothing, estimating less than 100-200 Christian troops milling in sight. Had he made a decisive move then, or even later when the Turks from the Saint George Gate began trying to slip behind the crusader semi-circle out on the Antiochian plain, the thousand troops manning the citadel, as Shams ad-Daulah predicted, could have created sheer confusion from behind, completely neutralizing Bohemud's reserve force from delivering a crushing blow at the last minute out on the plain.

But battles are won and lost in a blink, and on the deadly swing of momentum. To pause is at times judicious in one instant, but fatal in another. The fact was Kerbogha's commander, aghast at watching the aggression of the crusaders marching out to battle, lost his nerve. "No," he said, already seeing a lack of matching Turkish aggression on the plain. "I fear it's too late. In fact, I think it wise for all of us to withdraw out the Iron Gate and make our way down the mountain, and quickly." Turning, he gestured to his officers to muster their troops.

"Damn you!" groused Shams ad-Daulah. "Don't you see how easy this can be!?"

"Do as you wish, Shams," stated the commander indifferently. "Me, I'm withdrawing from the citadel."

Because 700 of the 1,000 troops manning the citadel belonged to Kerbogha, Shams ad-Daulah would be too short of manpower to risk a rear attack. Infuriated, he cursed Kerbogha, Kerbogha's commander, and all of Mesopotamia in a single breath as they saddled up to leave. He refused to abandon the city, his home, the only thing he had ever known or cared for; had no heart for fleeing Syria in exchange for a marginal existence in Mosul. Here he had been a prince; there, he would be nothing. Accepting the calculated risk of remaining, he hoped to throw his fate at the feet of the Christians, perhaps even agree to collaborate with them as they spread their influence over the land.

As Shams ad-Daulah and his force stayed atop the wall, Kerbogha's commander and his Mesopotamians withdrew from the citadel. Watching, Mahmoud Malik grabbed Hasan and pulled him toward two nearby horses. "Come, Hasan," he said, rasping, "best we slip into their ranks and get out of here. Once we make the bottom of Staurin we can make for Jerusalem!"

"Jerusalem?" Hasan was shocked. "But that's where the Christian army's headed."

"Maybe, but they control everything to the north already."

"But what about Mosul? We could follow Kerbogha back to Mesopotamia."

"Ha, and what's there for us, Hasan? I've lost Kilij Aslan in Asia Minor and I've lost my mercenary force here in Antioch."

"But the Christians will be attacking Jerusalem," objected Hasan.

"Oh, I've no intention of staying there," replied Malik. "It'll take the crusaders months to move their entire army south. Once you and I get to Jerusalem, we'll recruit another army and head for Egypt. There'll be work there amongst the feuding Fatimids, just as there's work everywhere."

"Very well," agreed Hasan, lacking conviction.

Unbeknownst to both Kerbogha and the Latins, Lord Abdul Azim had stationed his army of 1,000 horsemen near the Iron Bridge to the north, intentionally blocking the bottom of Mount Staurin. He had already learned from Kareem that Shams ad-Daulah and Kerbogha's commander controlled the citadel, but once the battle went against Kerbogha, Azim was convinced that the entire citadel force would escape down Mount Staurin rather than surrender. Specifically, that should Mahmoud Malik be alive in the wake of the Christians overrunning Antioch, he would likely be among those fleeing. Malik may have a formidable reputation, but Azim knew he had a history of fleeing the moment the tide turned against him.

As the Mesopotamians began reaching the bottom of Staurin, they trickled out in single file due to the narrowness of the lower half of the path to the Iron Gate. Azim signaled his men to advance, blocking the path.

Seeing that progress had stopped ahead of him, the Mesopotamian commander advanced to the front of the file, spotting Lord Azim whom he had never met before. He was vastly relieved that these were Seljuk Turks and not Christians. "But why are you blocking my men?" he demanded. "And who are you?"

"I am Abdul Azim of Eastern Asia Minor," said Azim, trying to assess the number of troops coming down the mountain in case violence broke. From where he sat upon his Arabian, he could see they would be bottle-necked trying to get off the mountain through his men. "I'm seeking a Persian, Mahmoud Malik, who's been hiding there in the city this past half year. He may be dead already, which would be fine with me. But since you are the last Turks leaving Antioch, I wish to check your ranks to be certain."

In a hurry to get off the mountain and head for home, the commander said, "I don't know any such man, but if he's in my ranks, take him. We've got to be on our way!"

"Pass then, and lead your men out. My men and I shall watch for him."

In acknowledgement, the commander rode through Azim's ghazis; his men following in a slow file. It took nearly half an hour to get to the final thirty odd men. "I've seen no sign of him, Sire," said Kareem. "He may well have been killed in the city when the crusaders broke through."

Malik happened to be the last man in line, with Hasan riding just in front of him. Neither had any idea that Seljuk's from Asia Minor stood at the bottom of the mountain, nor that they were being led by Abdul Azim. With all that had transpired these past months, Malik had, in fact, forgotten about Azim entirely. But as he descended the mountain and reached the beginning of the Asia Minor Seljuk gauntlet, a voice shocked him from his thoughts.

"You there with the monstrous face. Halt!"

Looking up, what was left of Malik's face fell slack and his heart dropped into his belly. There in his path, Azim sat proudly astride his sleek stallion . . . smiling at him.

"Have you nothing to say to an old enemy?" asked Azim calmly, icily. "Come now. After raiding and plundering my kingdom, murdering thousands of inno-cents, both Christian and Muslim, and kidnapping Greek children for slavery, you must have something to say now that we meet again?"

Malik glared, his blood beginning to run cold. He knew he was already breathing his last few breaths.

Azim would have never recognized Malik if not for the great gash separating one side of his face from the other and the missing eye, as earlier described by Kareem. Scrutinizing that wound, Malik appeared deserving of pity, not the bitter retribution Azim had been patiently waiting for this past eight months. "After looking at your hideous face, and thinking of the many women and girls you've raped over your black history, I understand that you finally met your match. Allah's justice, I say."

"What would you know of my face?" hissed Malik, hoping no one had mentioned his genitalia. "And what would you know of Allah that I don't know? You kill using His name believing it, I kill using His name as my excuse. But in the end, the dead are the dead. Don't waste my time nor yours, and kill me, then. And do it in the name of Allah whether you mean it or not!"

"Oh, but I'm in no hurry," said Azim. "And I've got a question for you. The woman who rearranged your face, she was beautiful, yes?"

Sneering, Malik refused to answer.

"Before you meet the devil," Azim the cat said, enjoying his mouse, "let me tell you about that woman. She has known and loathed your dark, parasitic breed of men since they began noticing her by age nine or ten. But even then, she steadfastly refused to bow to their lust and threats, holding firm even until this very day. In my realm we call her Mâh of Genoa, but in Genoa they call her la Gran Signorina, for she is no ordinary woman, as you fatefully learned attempting to violate her. She is a rare creature, Malik. Far, far beyond your feeble reach, and far, far stronger than yourself, no matter how much ample muscle, neck-flesh, brawn, and bluster. While you prepared to feast on her, she cut you to the quick when no other has been able to even approach you. Such is her strength."

"Preach on if you wish," retorted Malik, "I'm not afraid to die. I've killed enough men, women, and children in my time to understand the 'long sleep.' It does not frighten me."

Taking a look at Malik's eyes, one intact and the other an open, gaping socket, Azim stared at the top of Malik's forehead where Mâh's knife had cut to the bone of it, then followed the angle of the gash to what was left of the bone crossing Malik's nose. From there the cut turned deep, slicing all the way through Malik's cheek flesh to his gums. And finally, Azim's gaze ended where the dagger blade had done its best work, where he sat in the saddle. The wound was grislier even than a war wound, and had disfigured Malik's face to the point of revulsion, but knowing he would never rape and feel that power through his penis again, a slight smile curled Azim's lips.

"Pass," gestured Azim.

"What did you say?" grunted Malik, not comprehending, a shock wave shooting through his whole body.

"I said 'pass,' Malik," replied Azim. "Be on your way quickly before I change my mind."

"Sire?" objected Kareem.

Saying nothing, Malik kicked his horse in the flanks and disappeared down through the gauntlet of Azim's ghazis. Vanishing from sight, Azim looked at Kareem and said, "Think how repulsive Malik's face is, Kareem, and decide whether you should wish to go through the remainder of your years carrying such a look, much less enduring what it takes for Malik to ride a horse."

"But, Sire," protested Kareem, "you've come so far from home with blood on your brow for Malik! How could you just let him ride away?"

"Allah's justice, Kareem. Malik has behaved like a ravenous beast since attaining manhood, and now Allah has made him look like one. Killing him might have satisfied me for a few minutes, perhaps even an hour, but I shall be satisfied the rest of my years knowing that as Malik moves among people, he shall be repulsing them, forcing men to look away and women to flee. Ah, for him the years shall stretch into everlasting shame and humiliation."

"Oh, I see," Kareem said with great uncertainty, in no way understanding Azim's mercy. "May we return north now?"

"Yes," replied Azim, "as soon as we find out whether Little Brother and Mâh of Genoa shall accompany us. Let us give the crusaders a day to quell their blood, then we will approach the city under banner of truce."

CHAPTER SIXTY-SEVEN

HAYA

As extraordinary as the crusader victory against Kerbogha was, contemporary writers explained it away as a miracle; the Franks having been saved only by the palpable intervention of the hand of God. Raymond of Aguilers recorded that as the Army of God had marched out of Antioch for battle: "The Lord sent down upon His army a divine shower, little but full of blessing."

Others professed: "On seeing the relic of the Holy Lance, Kerbogha was paralyzed."

Another witness fighting in the battle went further, stating: "There came out of the mountains, also, countless armies with white horses, whose standards were all white. And so, when our leaders saw this army, they were entirely ignorant of what it was, and who they were, until they recognized the aid of Christ, whose leaders were Saint George, Saint Mercurius, and Saint Demetrius. This is to be believed, for many men saw it."

Whereas it is true that the entire crusade was wrapped in spiritual fervor and intent, it was especially the Battle of Antioch where this came to a peak. Finally, twice defeating Kilij Arslan in Asia Minor, surviving an impossible trek through the hardships of Anatolia, and a grueling eight-month siege ending in the capture of Antioch, the road south was open and the Holy City of Jerusalem awaited.

On the first day after the battle, to Guthroth's surprise, a small caravan showed up from the Oasis of Sparrows, guarded by twenty armed men accompanying Haya, her two sisters, and a number of servants. Spotting Guthroth, Haya came toward him in a slow walk, smiling the least bit. "Guthroth, you've been gone five months and no word. I became worried. And this last month I began having dreams that you were slain, which is why I've come, to seek your grave, to pray over it. But you are standing in front of me, so God must have wished it."

At this, she embraced him warmly but not passionately. Guthroth returned the embrace with equal lassitude being in the company of Tristan, Mala, Hroc, and Mala's brood of new-found children. Formal as their greeting of each may have appeared to other, in truth, both Guthroth's and Haya's hearts were afire. Neither having ever missed the absence of another their entire lives, this particular separation had been excruciating for both.

Having heard very little about Haya from the closed-mouth Guthroth, Tristan and Mala introduced themselves along with Christophe, in his mother's arms, Christos, Karine, Garik, Agda, and Berna. Tristan and Mala thought her to be attractive enough, but with time, they began to notice there was an alluring presence about her, though she made little of it. Nonetheless, after twenty minutes of conversation, or rather, pulling conversation from Haya and Guthroth, Tristan and Mala decided that Haya and Guthroth were perfect for each other.

"You've done well, Guthroth," said Tristan. Turning, he said to Haya, "And you also, Haya. Guthroth is one of the finest men I've ever known."

"Yes," said Haya, offering that reserved smile she brought out when pleased. "I've missed him very much."

"We're staying in a rather humble structure at the moment," said Mala, "and the cupboards are bare, except for a few items that were brought to us by our Tuscan friends when clearing the Turkish camps. Thankfully, tea was included in that treasure. Would you care to have some?"

"Certainly," replied Haya, watching her two sisters from the corner of her eye, who were oblivious to anyone or anything but Hroc. "Would you mind if my two sisters joined us?"

"No, not at all," smiled Mala, handing Christophe to Karine, asking her and Berna as the oldest to keep the other children occupied.

Entering their building, Mala made tea and the seven sat down to share conversation, where Tristan and Mala did most of the talking. Guthroth and Haya sat there quietly lost in each other most of the time, while Haya's two young sisters refused to loosen their focus from Hroc, who had become practically paralyzed the moment the two sisters arrived.

An hour later, Haya stood. "We brought our own bedding and such, it's packed in the wagons, which is where we will be sleeping. But I have a request. It is actually Guthroth's request, but as you probably know, he was hesitant to insist that you respect the request. On the other hand, I am not."

As she said this, Guthroth's ears had pinked and he appeared apprehensive.

"Very well," replied Mala. She and Tristan waited with bated breath what was to come.

"Guthroth and I have married. Has he shared that news yet?"

"Yes, but only recently." Tristan nodded respectfully. "And I've passed it along to Mala. He's also shared that he intends to leave the crusade. He said after the Kerbogha issue was settled, which it has been as of yesterday, he wanted to return to the Oasis of Sparrows with you and your sisters."

"Precisely," replied Haya.

"But you said you had a request," said Mala. "One that you would insist on?"

"Yes. Guthroth says he shall probably never see any of you again, though he loves you beyond measure. Thus, he would like you to come for a visit to the Oasis of Sparrows, to see his new home, where he shall spend the remainder of his days . . . and be buried."

Tristan and Mala simultaneously turned toward Guthroth, who had said nothing to this point.

"Is that true, Guthroth?" asked Mala, concern and love flooding her.

"It is but two and half days from here," Haya answered for him, not allowing Guthroth to speak; knowing his desires as if they were two in one body. "And I insist that you take time to visit, to satisfy Guthroth's request. He is very upset, you know, about losing you."

Both confused and surprised, Tristan and Mala smiled and nodded 'yes.'

"But we are about to part shortly for Asia Minor," said Tristan. "We, too, are leaving, which leaves only Hroc and my brother with the crusade. We have told no one, of course, so we ask that you not share that information during your stay."

"My sisters and I shall say nothing. But a question to you both. Is Asia Minor going anywhere?" asked Haya, half smiling. "Will it not be there next week, or next month?"

Haya's bluntness embarrassed Guthroth, but in this case he appreciated her resolve. Finally speaking, he gave a look of supplication. "Please," he said.

"Yes, for you, Guthroth, anything," said Tristan, squeezing Mala's hand.

"Well, that's settled," agreed Mala. "And as Haya suggests, Asia Minor shall be there next week."

Turning to Hroc, Haya said, "Hroc, we will want you to come also. As the man who brought Guthroth into my life, I insist."

"Oh, oh, yes," he said. "I've been there and it will be a fine place to recover after Kerbogha!" His eyes quickly cut to her siblings.

This much pleased Haya's sisters and they began to twitter, turning Hroc's cheeks and ears crimson.

Addressing Tristan, Haya said, "You mentioned a brother, we should like him to come as well."

"He's in the infirmary at the moment. If he is well, he would want to come, I am certain, but I can't promise anything," said Tristan, with a touch of concern in his tone.

"Fine, it's settled then," said Haya, her face broadening into a full smile that matched Guthroth's. "My sisters should like to spend a day or two visiting the churches here in Antioch, and then we would like to make a trip to Saint Simeon to enjoy the sea, taking Guthroth with us to meet a favorite aunt of mine; one who swore I would never marry for being too particular about men. Will leaving on the fifth day from now give you and the children suitable time to prepare?"

"Yes, of course," answered Mala, actually growing excited about taking a sojourn beyond Antioch before departing for Asia Minor.

When Tristan and Mala told the children, they were going on a trip in three days, they were overjoyed. The only traveling Christos had ever done was fleeing his hometown with his grandmother, Aglaia, as a refugee, followed by the march from Armenia to Antioch with Scule. Berna and Agda had been similarly limited in travel, experiencing only the horror of being sex slaves during their travels with Malik. As for Karine and Garik, neither had ever been beyond the walls of Antioch.

Tristan visited Guillaume, who appeared dull and lethargic as he sat on his cot by the far wall of the brimming temporary infirmary; the best they could do under the circumstances. He had agreed to go to the Oasis of Sparrows only because it was Guthroth's wish.

"As long as I've known Guthroth," said Guillaume, "he's never asked for anything, ever. He has always, always supported each and every one of us. And seeing as we are about to go our separate ways, we need to support him, his marriage, and his new life, even if it's here in this godforsaken land of sand and rock, of which I've had my fill."

"You've a way to go, though, if you plan to make it to Jerusalem," Tristan reminded him. "Bohemud says you should not fight anymore, at least for a time. He thinks you need a rest."

"Yes, I know. He's been to see me twice just today. He wants me to stay with him here in Antioch."

"What?" Tristan was shocked to his core. "Is he not marching to Jerusalem?"

"He wasn't exactly clear, and my mind . . . well. He and Raymond are fighting over Antioch, and I've no idea which direction the wind shall blow. It was all—I—" Guillaume focused on the wall bearing a single sunbeam the shape of the cut-out window. "Tristan, things are coming and going. Strange thoughts and ideas. I'm not sure whether I'm losing myself or what. I've been doing a lot of thinking, too. A lot. Perhaps my head will clear by getting away from this nightmare we've experienced here in Antioch." He closed his eyes envisioning; a lone tear of remorse sliding from one corner to etch a wet line down his cheek. His voice lowered, head moving slightly left to right, "Hardship and hopelessness, disappointments and . . . blood." With that, he tilted his face to meet his brother's eyes. "But yes, Tristan, I will travel south with you, for Guthroth."

"Which brings me to a question about you," said Tristan. "Are you going to be all right, Guillaume? They told me what happened to you at the end of the battle, and it frightened me. I know you've been driving yourself along this long march, and I was the only one who knew why until you opened your heart the other night. God forgives, Guillaume, but there are things at times for which we do not need God's forgiveness since they are not trespasses against God but trespasses against men; men claiming to know what God demands of us in this temporal existence. But being men, they are often wrong; just as I was wrong about this crusade back in Italy and France when I was preaching it. I was listening to men, Guillaume, not God."

"Yes, I'm beginning to understand. A little anyway, and for the first time. It was good listening to Mala the other night. Things she said made much sense. She has a clear eye for things. But Tristan, I'm tired. I need to sleep." He lay back and turned to the wall, pulling the woolen blanket about his shoulder. "Tell Guthroth I will gladly go south, just for him." Guillaume's wounds were extensive, both physically and emotionally, extracting their toll deeply on many levels.

CHAPTER SIXTY-EIGHT

LOOSE ENDS

On the first day after the battle, Raymond of Toulouse again began to harp about the incident in the palace corridor involving Tristan, Guillaume, the Danes, and the slain Provençals. "Am I to have my justice, or not?" he demanded, lobbying Adhémar and the Council of Princes.

"Leave it be!" argued Bohemud. "Had you not been in an infirmary bed, you'd have seen how they fought like lions against Kerbogha's heathens! And remember, touch a hair on their heads and it'll be war, Raymond."

As stated before, the Northern French Princes had no interest in Raymond's revenge. After gathering the facts, even Bishop Adhémar advised that Raymond drop the issue. "You're doing yourself no favors, Raymond," he insisted, "nor are you doing the Holy Crusade any favors. Your men were wrong! They were not doing God's work, but raping and pillaging! And I'll say no more about it, so say no more about it to me! Besides, you've taken control of half of the city, what else do you want?"

The morning of the second day after Kerbogha's defeat began as 1,000 Seljuk Turks showed up at the Saint Paul Gate causing great alarm, until the banner of truce was spotted. Bohemud had the gates opened, but only allowed entry to Lord Azim and Kareem.

Finding Tristan, they shared the morning together.

"Now then, Little Brother," said Azim, "you, Mâh, and Christophe are coming north to build a palace within my realm?"

"Yes," replied Tristan, "but there shall be four more children coming as well."

Kareem sniggered. "You two have been together but such a short while and have produced four more offspring already!"

"It's a long story," grinned Tristan, "but I'll share it later. This tale has twists."

"And no one yet knows you are leaving the crusade?" asked Azim.

"No. And for many reasons."

"I understand. We are beginning to break camp and shall be departing in two days. Can you be ready?"

Tristan shook his head. "There has been a promise that cannot be broken. Mala and I must take a trip in two days, south with the children. And it is timely. The princes know about the trip and will be expecting us back in about a week. But after leaving our southern destination, Mala and I shall head straight north for Asia Minor. There will be no suspicion on this end until we are well away."

"Excellent. But it's a long journey, Little Brother. You will need an escort going that far. Which road shall you be taking for your trip south?"

"The road to the Saint Simeon fork, then due south."

"And when shall you leave?"

"On the third morning from now."

"Very well. I will have fifty of my men meet you at the Saint Simeon fork. They will accompany you south, then escort you back to Asia Minor. Kareem and I would not wish any harm to come to you, Mâh, or the children."

"Your generosity is overwhelming!" exclaimed Tristan, embracing Azim and Kareem both.

"Ah, now we must go, Little Brother. I see Bohemud and his nephew eyeing us from the gate. Ha, we know when we are not welcome! In any case, we shall see you in Asia Minor within the month."

"Yes, certainly," replied Tristan. "And many thanks for all you've done for us here in Antioch." Pausing, he asked, "But then, Lord Azim, did you ever find Mahmoud Malik?"

It was Kareem who answered out of turn, "Yes, we found him, but Lord Azim let him go, of all things, which I shall never understand!"

Giving a wink to Tristan, Azim smiled, mounting his horse. "Ah, there come times when the thing you think you want most unceremoniously falls aside, replaced by something else, something better. Good-bye, Little Brother, and safe travels."

The afternoon of that same day marked Orla's funeral. A full high mass service was served within Saint Peter's Basilica with Tristan celebrating the mass and delivering the eulogy. Although Raymond and his Provençals refused to attend, the cathedral was filled to bursting, crusaders even spilling out the door into the square. When the service was done, Hroc, Tristan, and Guillaume put Orla, wrapped in a shroud, on a wagon and traveled the thirty kilometers to Saint Simeon where they met Guthroth, Haya, and her two sisters.

That evening, Orla was laid in a small skiff stacked high with dried kindling and hardwood cut to size. Tristan, Hroc, and Guthroth each said a few words over Orla's body about his early days, his wife and deceased son, Knud, his mix of humor and ferocity in war, and his tragic end, then the skiff's sail was raised, the vessel put aflame and shoved from shore, catching the wind and receding tide.

The four companions sat together on the beach, watching until the skiff slipped into the distance on the current, its fire dissipating to embers and slowly sinking into the sea. It was an emotional adieu for all, especially Hroc. Seeing the final flame extinguished, the four remained quietly huddled for another three hours, sharing memories of Orla, Crowbones, and the old original Danish Guard, including Sigurd Fair Hair and Halfdan Straight Limbs, though Tristan and Guthroth were the only two who knew them.

CHAPTER SIXTY-NINE

AS GOD MIGHT WISH?

After times of want and adversity, the simplest of things take on an entirely new significance. For the four newly added children, the trip south was a magical interlude, erasing the blackness of their past. The same could be said of Guillaume in one sense, and of Mala and Tristan in another.

For Hroc, however, the trip signaled the end of all as he had known it. Having lost his Uncle Crowbones and just recently his beloved father, Orla, he was now on the cusp of losing his Uncles Tristan and Guillaume. Breaking his heart the most was the fact that the one man who had taken inordinate time and demonstrated unbelievable patience with him from birth would soon to depart forever, Guthroth the Quiet. Their bond had been the glue of Hroc's upbringing, and the cement of his manhood. Guthroth's departure was already forming a gaping hole in his emotions, and the time for farewells had not even arrived. He could not imagine life without him.

In preparing for the trip, Christos had begged that Scule be allowed to accompany them, and with no grounds for objection, his presence was gladly accepted by all. Besides being a monk, Scule had been a bit impish since early childhood, which had subsided little during his difficult religious novitiate and taking on the heavy responsibilities of joining the Benedictine religious order. But he had not once, since joining the Black Monks, ever had occasion to take time off for leisure, let alone take a fanciful trip for purposes of pleasure. This trip, then, had him on the edge of giddiness as he horsed about with Christos, Berna, and Agda. Garik, of course, was terrified of him, convinced that the dwarf was just another jinn in the fashion of the blue man.

As to Benito, upon fleeing the Iron Bridge, he was torn between making his way back to Italy, his dream since his enslavement, or returning to Antioch to seek out Mala and baby Christophe. He had no idea whether they had survived the crusader attack on the city, or whether Malik might have finally managed to get his scabrous claws on her and the baby. In the end, his faithfulness won out as he made his way into the city.

On spotting him, wandering about the avenues making inquiries about her, Mala ran to him in tears and grasped him in her arms. "Oh my god!" she cried, falling apart. "My brave little Benito! Christophe and I owe you our lives!"

This, for Benito Fazio, ever the hapless misfit in a world that had shunned him since birth, may have been the happiest day of his entire life. He, too, was unable to hold back tears as Mala dragged him to the nest of the Saint-Germain faction where he was hailed a hero by all, even melting for a moment the ironclad reticence of Karine. Berna and Agda did not recognize him at first without paint, but when he spoke, his voice unmasked him quickly.

Looking about, he saw trunks and bags being assembled, and this saddened him. "It appears that all of you are leaving?" he asked, his voice dropping.

"Yes, yes," replied Mala excitedly. "We're going on a holiday!" Hearing this, the children began to outshout each other for Benito's attention, each wishing to be the one to explain the trip. But seeing the expression of regret that had swept across Benito's face, and owing to the profound debt she owed him, she said, "Benito, when were you last on holiday?"

"Never," he replied, without having to even for an instant ponder the question. "No, not even once."

"Ha! Then you, too, shall come along with us, Benito! And during our travels, you and Tristan can finally make peace with each other."

Overjoyed, Benito began to tremble with gratitude. Inclusion he had rarely experienced, and the warmth of it confused him.

On the morning of departure, everyone assembled and Haya directed them to different wagons. "Guthroth," poked Hroc, "you'll not have to think much anymore. She'll be doing it for you, won't she?"

Grinning, Guthroth shoved a finger in Hroc's belly. "Y-you should b-be so lucky! Now leave m-me alone and g-go sit with Haya's s-sisters. H-Haya is about to m-make you anyway."

"What? I'm to be in a wagon with them?"

"Ja," grinned Guthroth. "Haya h-has it in her m-mind that you sh-shall marry one or the-the other. She just hasn't de-decided wh-which one."

Guillaume was feeling better, but there was a vacancy in his eyes that worried Tristan. "Are things well for you, Brother?" he inquired along the road.

"Yes, yes, more than ever, possibly," he replied, his thoughts elsewhere, searching the landscape from his seat in the wagon. "You know, all this," he waved the back of his hand, "takes on a different appearance when not scarred by war, men charging about with murder in their eyes, driving horses forward, wielding death in their hands. There is a beauty in peace, but I've rarely had time to think about it." All at once his countenance clouded with shame. "Tristan, how many men do you think I have killed? And in the name of God?"

Tristan was not prepared for such a question, especially from Guillaume. Reflecting, and answering carefully, he said, "It is not what happened in the past, with God, Guillaume, but where a man goes from his point of awakening."

"And that's why they called you the Wonder of Cluny when we were boys." Guillaume patted him on the back appreciatively, then pulled him in close.

After two and a half days of travel, punctuated with chatter and unbridled contentment from all, the caravan arrived at the Oasis of Sparrows. As the wagons made the ridge shielding it from the north, the idyllic, pastoral site below opened as an unexpected desert blossom might unfold, one petal at a time. It would have been impossible to adequately describe the expressions of surprise sweeping over those who had never been there, nor to detect which of them was the most impressed.

"I've traveled the world," sighed Mala, "and this is such a simple setting, but look Tristan, just look! So green, so lush, so peaceful."

His breath taken, Tristan uttered, "Yes, lovely, but mainly because of the barren landscape surrounding it."

"Ha! Much like yourself, then!" snarked Mala sarcastically, eager to explore.

Taking charge, Haya gave instructions to the small army of servants appearing as the wagons pulled through the palace gate. The servants were followed by Papa Daba, hobbling his way to the newly arrived troup, assisted by a young boy guiding him. "Ho! But welcome, welcome!" he rasped. "Oh, and how many all at once!"

And what a greeting this was for a tight band of family and friends who, in the Year of our Lord 1073, was forced to abandon a small feudal manor tucked into the gentle forests of Saint-Germain-en-Laye, cast into the wild winds of uncertainty by a tiny coven of privileged men who cared not a single farthing about the future of others, unless they could serve an underlying purpose. Upon departure, each would be hurled into turbulent currents and circumstances beyond their control, and nearly beyond their ability to repel. But the human spirit of certain tenacious men and women is indomitable, as demonstrated by Tristan de Saint-Germain, Guillaume, the Danes and those whom they loved.

But such is life, directed by fate, the hand of God, or most likely, the privileged few who orchestrate the grand stage for those of us who can but watch.

OUTCOMES

Ah, Scule, the dwarf monk. Above all things, his heart burned ever hotter for the Holy Crusade and the reclamation of Jerusalem for Christendom. After leaving the oasis, he threw himself back into the tenuous grasp of the Army of God. He made it to Jerusalem and celebrated a Christian victory there, albeit a bleak one, that would change him forever. Returning to France, he became an ever-relenting force of Church reform, fighting abuses of the Church as well as abuses of an utterly rapacious Medieval aristocracy. He became a beaming beacon of light for the poor, the disinherited, the diseased, and the elderly.

He would die of leprosy while establishing a Benedictine leper's colony in Southern France, but at a ripe old age, surpassing that of most men of the era. Having lived fully, despite his deformity, he managed to impact fellow travelers more succinctly than most ever born to this earth.

When Scule departed the oasis, he did not depart alone. Christos Laskaris accompanied him. The two had developed one of those rare and spiritual bonds between boy and man, learner and mentor. As Christos matured, he followed Scule's path into the clergy, actually completing his novitiate at Cluny Monastery in Burgundy, just as Scule himself had done. From there, he managed to rejoin Scule and the two worked side by side on behalf of the less fortunate. Christos was there on Scule's deathbed, in fact, and administered Extreme Unction, the final rite of death in Catholicism, to Scule as God's dwarf took his last breath.

Berna and Agda remained under the care of Tristan and Mala in Asia Minor for a brief period, striking back out together to Antioch. Their mutual dream of finding a good husband, having children, and enjoying a quiet life was realized when Berna wed an Armenian farmer at age sixteen, the normal age for marriage at that time. She and her husband had a son and daughter, who they named Christos and Agda.

Agda also married a farmer, a Syrian Christian, and had two children, both sons; the first they named Phillipos, after Berna and Agda's father, and the second they named Scule. The two farms sat four kilometers east of Antioch and were within sight of each other, ensuring the sisters saw each other every week, and their four children grew up as playmates. Having had their girlhood ripped from them by Mahmoud Malik at tender ages, it is likely that both Agda and Berna were trying to recollect the shards of their shattered early years, reshaping them into the image of the deceased village of Despina where all things had seemed simpler.

Garik, incredibly, eventually overcame his private terrors with much support from his sister and additionally from Mala and Tristan, who served as his parents from the moment of Kerbogha's defeat. He grew into an incredibly handsome young man and, after learning a bit about commerce from Mala, developed a thriving caravan trade extending through Asia Minor, Syria, the Levant, Egypt, and even at times reaching into the western edges of China. Miraculously, with much love and support, the fearful young alarmist and hopeless invertebrate evolved into an adventurer for whom there were no barriers.

Karine maintained her distant exterior, grew to be a stunning woman, but never married. Tying herself to Mala, who recognized within her a phenomenal level of intelligence and decision-making, Karine built an economic empire within the Middle East rivaling even that of Mâh of Genoa. The two remained ever close and often partnered on grand financial ventures.

Benito Fazio, of all people, became Karine's primary financial agent. Having mastered both the Persian and Arab tongues, and having in earlier years commandeered 'street savvy' as the most ingenious of informants and spies, Benito served Karine's purposes brilliantly. His greatest asset, oddly, became his deformity of size and elfin voice. Others under-estimated him vastly, and he exploited their short-sightedness as a chess master easily exploits less clever opponents.

Papa Daba died within Guthroth's first year of abandoning the crusade, leaving Haya and Guthroth as operational heirs to the Oasis of Sparrows. To be more accurate, because Guthroth had no knowledge of trade and had little interest in learning, Haya operated the entire oasis, which suited them both perfectly. Guthroth and Haya enjoyed a more than comfortable marriage, insulating one another with love, compassion, and intimate companionship. The combination of their similarities was actually complemented by their differences; Haya commanding in public, Guthroth instinctual. Two people, who transcended culture and circumstances, discovered each other and what matters most across two continents at war with each other. Such is the wheel of destiny . . . or perhaps the hand of God?

Hroc became a bit of a surprise, especially after his visit to the Oasis of Sparrows, following Kerbogha's defeat. In discussing Crowbones' final reading of the bird bones at Nicaea, Guthroth asked Hroc to leave the crusade. "I be-believe the bones," said Guthroth, "and I be-believe Crowbones. This crusade is and w-was n-never for our Saint-Germain-en-Laye family, and d-deep down, Crowbones kn-knew it, but d-didn't know h-how to tell us. P-please, please stay here with me and H-Haya, Hroc. There is n-nothing for you b-back in Europe."

The weight Guthroth carried with Hroc had always been immense, which inclined Hroc's ear to him. Guthroth had earlier joked about Hroc marrying both of Haya's sisters, and that is exactly what he did. Until now in this tale, Haya's sisters have always been mentioned in one breath, and without names. But they had names. The eldest of the two was Hroc's age and her name was Ciri. As things happened, Hroc and Ciri fell in love, married, and had a son they named Orla, but Ciri refused the addition of the moniker "Bloodaxe" to follow the name. Unfortunately, three years after baby Orla's second birthday, Ciri fell ill from an unknown disease and passed. Two years later, Hroc married the younger sister, Zaria; him two years her senior. In time, Hroc and Zaria had a son whom they named Ivar. It was Hroc this time who refused adding the moniker since 'Crowbones' inferred paganistic prophecy, which Hroc, being a pious Catholic, rebuked.

But as to Ivar Crowbones and the prophecy that befell him in Nicaea . . . it indeed came to pass. But how and why? The answer is simple, actually. Each person possesses, through the bounty of God, certain gifts we shall call perception, anticipation, foresight, and intuition. That being true, as the dynamics of these four endowments mature, intermingle, and clash, each individual spends a great deal of time thinking, worrying, imagining, and projecting. Therefore, many things that one supposes might happen, actually do happen, but most things one supposes might happen, never occur.

All things being equal, we, as humans, dwell on the former, not the latter. We pass off the many, many things that do not occur like falling raindrops interfering with our vision. Ah, but when those things one predicts do happen, the entire equation is given new meaning, and new weight. Of course, most people keep such things to themselves, hiding and hoarding them in the hidden backwaters of their minds. But then there are those brave souls who announce and prophesize aloud, and to the entire world, such as Peter the Hermit and Peter Bartholomew. Wrong much of the time, these men were idolized and revered for the few things they did get right but rarely castigated for the many things they missed, unless they were outrageous and offended human sensibilities, such as Peter Bartholomew's final vision, which shall be revealed later on.

But back to Ivar Crowbones, who, whether by luck, coincidence, or true intervention of the Nordic gods, correctly prophesized the forthcoming reality, interpreted through the raven bones, that, "Not a single member of the Saint-Germain-en-Laye faction would ever set eyes on Jerusalem." This actually came to be. But any conclusions one might draw would have to revert back to the original roots of: perception, anticipation, foresight, and intuition. This, of course, means there is no 'real answer' since all four of those qualities are based on feeling, not fact.

Now, Guillaume, one of the most stalwart and virtuous men of the entire Holy Crusade, and perhaps of the entire period known as the Dark Ages, during the bloody engagement against Kerbogha, had been hurled into a state of complete emotional and mental crisis, or so he and others thought. In truth, everything he had believed in and fought for had suddenly come crashing down on him, drowning in the blood of a man he had just murdered. This event completely restructured his once immoveable frame of mind.

As often happens when one is reborn through fire and blood, Guillaume was struck by a new light. Upon leaving the oasis, Guillaume abandoned the crusade entirely, telling no one but Bohemud, who gave him his private blessings. Sailing from Saint Simeon, Guillaume made his way back to Italy to spend time with his great mentor, la Gran Contessa Mathilda of Tuscany, enjoying a most pleasurable summer sojourn.

Departing Canossa and bidding her farewell, he announced, "I shall now make my way to Burgundy."

"Burgundy?" asked Mathilda. "But what's there for you?"

"Everything," replied Guillaume, his face taking on a different light.

"Everything?" echoed Mathilda.

"Indeed," smiled Guillaume. "It's in Burgundy, as you know, that one finds the Benedictine monastery of Cluny where Tristan and I were raised."

"Ah, I understand," sighed Mathilda, "you're going to revisit your youth."

"No," kicking his horse to leave, turning in his saddle, the horse galloping forward, Guillaume shouted back, "I'm going there to become a monk!"

Alas, the brother who really should have become a monk, finally became one.

At last, we get to the heartbeat in this epic saga. Tristan did indeed finally marry Mala, in a beautiful Greek Orthodox ceremony celebrated in their new home of Asia Minor. The wedding was officiated by the Bishop of the Hagia Sophia (Church of Holy Wisdom in Constantinople) who had been sent by Emperor Alexius and Queen Irene, who would have, in fact, attended, but the crusade and Christian-Muslim hostilities did not allow it. After the Christian ceremony, Lord Azim then officiated a second marriage ceremony for Tristan and Mala in an elaborate Seljuk rite more lavish than any had ever seen.

After a chance encounter as children along the Seine River and nearly three decades struggling against one obstacle or another, including Gregory VII, Odo de Lagery, the Vatican, the Church, continental war, the death of their firstborn son in the Alps, separations, and the Holy Crusade, the wheel of destiny finally saw fit to allow Tristan de Saint-Germain and Mala the Romani to find peace together in a loving relationship that would endure until the end of their lives. One of their most blessed endeavors, of course, was watching baby Christophe grow to manhood. In their old age, it was Christophe who eventually took over Mala's vast trading empire, ending by enjoying the easiest, most peaceful, and most prosperous life of the entire Saint-Germain lineage.

Tristan remained, as promised, true to God, albeit not within the Catholic Church. He was ordained a Greek Orthodox priest and preached throughout Byzantium, Cyprus, and even many Muslim territories when and where allowed. Many Muslim areas were extremely tolerant, but as news of the Holy Crusade spread, that tolerance began to diminish greatly everywhere except within the realm of Lord Abdul Azim.

Mala's great wealth did not influence her and Tristan's construction of an oddly humble home in the country, ten kilometers from the palace of Abdul Azim. Tristan designed it entirely. Wracking his memory for months, he tried to recall every tiny detail about that stone farmhouse he had fallen in love with nestled at the foot of Canossa Mountain. Accordingly, the site he chose for the new cottage was located at the foot of yet another mountain, a vista both pastoral and verdant. The architecture was Tuscany-agrarian built in stone. Water was sparse there, but Mala's great fortune easily allowed for engineering a large, running brook through the property, flowing over a rock dam just fifty yards from the farmhouse. Tristan acquired sheep, goats, donkeys, pigs, swans, ducks, and chickens. Had one seen this home, then gone to the foot of Canossa, one would become disoriented, for one farm looked like an exact replica of the other.

The moral of Tristan and Mala's story, of course, is that dreams do come true, especially the simple ones. Having overcome the complex obstacles and obstructions that Tristan and Mala encountered along the way, their dream, in truth, had always been quite humble from the very beginning. But a tiny number of men driven by ambition and pride disassembled and dissected the simplicity of that dream. It just took Mala and Tristan half a lifetime to reconstruct it.

Their love was so enduring, as described by others, that when Mala died at age eighty-five of illness, Tristan died two days later, although he, in every aspect, was quite well at the time of his passing.

Most concluded, whether true or not, that Tristan de Saint-Germain simply died of a broken heart.

THE HOLY CRUSADE

To believe that the ending of this tale is 'happy' would be a grievous mistake. In truth, the ending of the First Holy Crusade was one of the most horrific and tragic events in human history. To begin, historically, the city of Jerusalem was but a two-week march from Antioch, but the crusaders, incredibly, would not see Jerusalem for over a full year!

As predicted by Bishop Saint-Germain, Antioch became a tarpit. First through the eight-month impossible siege of attrition and the chronological arrivals of Duqaq of Damascus, Ridwan of Aleppo, and Kerbogha of Mosul, then it extended for an additional year as Bohemud of Taranto and Raymond of Toulouse descended into ceaseless feuding over title to Antioch. Raymond controlled half the city, Bohemud the other half, including the ever-strategic citadel overlooking the city. Further complicating this stalemate, the two princes extended their feud out into the neighboring territories of Southern Syria.

Unfortunately, only one month after Kerbogha's flight, a deadly disease struck Antioch. Bishop Adhémar of Le Puy was among the early casualties, dying on August 1st. It mattered not whether this man was an extraordinary cleric or, as accused by Tristan de Saint-Germain, "a man play-acting at religion," Adhémar had served as the glue holding the Army of God together. His absence, therefore, became a crippling blow.

One of the most critical figures in the crusader victory over Yaghi Siyan and conquest of Antioch was the Armenian armor-maker, Firuz. His early history was shadowy, but less so than his later history. Having changed the entire course of Medieval history through his betrayal of Antioch, he simply vanished into the dust of passing time, never to be heard of again, nor even mentioned other than within bloody tales of his dubious actions during the great Battle of Antioch.

Next, unexpectedly, the stock of Godfrey of Bouillon began to rise exponentially due to assistance from his brother in Edessa, Baldwin of Boulogne, and a series of other circumstances. Godfrey's new rise, of course, further complicated an already complex two-way struggle over Antioch.

Then, precisely as predicted by Lord Abdul Azim, the Fatimid Empire in Egypt decided to capitalize on endless crusader in-fighting and Sunni defeat in Syria. Six weeks after the crusaders defeated Kerbogha, the Fatimids attacked Jerusalem, vanquishing Sunni Seljuk rule and ownership of the Holy City (August, 1098). This meant that Jerusalem now had a new master, and if the crusaders were to ever attack Jerusalem, they would not be fighting Seljuk Sunni Turks, but Fatimid Shia Egyptians.

During this same period, to further challenge both Bohemud and Godfrey, Raymond began using the Holy Lance as spiritual propaganda. Since he had been the one to take in Peter Bartholomew from the beginning, Raymond was in possession of the Holy Lance and exploited it to develop a large 'cult' around it. His primary agent, of course, became Peter Bartholomew, who conveniently began to have new visions, each becoming more audacious than the one before, and all being in support of Raymond's claim to Antioch.

In particular, Peter's visions began to involve Adhémar of Le Puy, 'speaking' to him from the grave. Nonetheless, by January 13th of 1099, seven months after Kerbogha, Raymond marched out of Antioch and headed for Jerusalem with Robert of Normandy, whereas Godfrey, Robert of Flanders, and Tancred remained in the city with Bohemud, who finally took full possession of coveted Antioch.

Without Godfrey, Bohemud, Tancred, and Robert of Flanders, there was little prayer of taking Jerusalem. Consequently, Raymond launched a four-month campaign to feed his frustrated territorial ambitions, starting fights with many Turkish cities along the path, successfully claiming some yet repulsed by others. This meant more war, considerable gains for Raymond, and Jerusalem still not in sight.

On April 5th, Peter Bartholomew, who had at this point eclipsed Peter the Hermit as spiritual leader of Raymond's army, claimed to have had a vision in which Christ, Saint Peter, and Saint Andrew came to him proclaiming the presence of 'many sinners within the army' that needed to be rooted out in the following manner: Raymond was to muster his entire army as if preparing for a siege, after which Peter would 'miraculously find them aligned in five ranks. The first three ranks would be devoted followers of Christ and the last two ranks men committing the sins of pride, envy, gluttony or cowardice.'

"God has command me," Bartholomew then declared to all, "to oversee the execution of all men in the last two rows!"

The utter absurdity of this development had finally become too much for many crusaders to stomach, causing an uproar challenging the credibility of both Peter Bartholomew and Raymond of Toulouse. In a state of fury, Arnuf of Chocques, chaplain to Robert of Flanders, denied the validity of Bartholomew's recent visions, as well as, by association, those of the Holy Lance.

Peter Bartholomew replied, "I not only wish, but I beg, that you set ablaze a fire, and I shall take the ordeal by fire with the Holy Lance in my hands. And if it is really the Lord's Lance, I shall emerge unsinged. But if it is false, I shall be consumed by fire."

To purify his soul for the ordeal, Peter fasted for four days. On Good Friday, in the presence of thousands of crusaders, he walked into a blazing inferno of olive branches stacked four feet high and arranged thirteen feet in length. Those watching provided conflicting accounts of the outcome, depending on whether they supported the Holy Lance and Raymond or whether they opposed them. In the end, the most accurate account was written as such: "The finder of the Holy Lance quickly ran through the midst of the burning pile to prove his honesty, as he had requested. When the man passed through the flames and emerged, they saw that he was guilty. His skin was burned and they knew that within he was mortally hurt. This was demonstrated by the outcome. On the twelfth day he died, seared by the guilt of his conscience."

This event cost Raymond of Toulouse dearly, spelling the end of his reign as self-proclaimed commander of the Holy Crusade. Henceforth, he would have to share equal footing with all other princes. Raymond's collapse did finally prompt all the crusader armies to join together on May 16th and head for Jerusalem, excluding Bohemud and Tancred. Arriving there with 1,300 battle-hardened knights and 12,000 infantrymen, and princes arguing among themselves, the Army of God launched its first direct attack against Jerusalem on June 13th of 1099.

Having endured many trials, tribulations, failed tactics, and bloody assaults, the crusaders finally took Jerusalem on the 15th of July 1099. Charging into the city, they unleashed one of the most horrifying events of the entire Dark Ages, surpassing anything that had come before. As recorded by Raymond of Aguilers: "After a very great and cruel slaughter of Saracens, of whom 10,000 fell in that same place, they put to the sword a great number of gentiles running about the quarters of the city, fleeing in all directions on account of their fear of death. They were stabbing women fleeing into palaces and dwellings; seizing infants by the soles of their feet from their mothers' laps or their cradles and dashing them against the walls and breaking their necks. They were slaughtering some with weapons, or striking them down with stones. They were sparing absolutely no gentile of any place or kind."

Christians and Jews were slaughtered alongside Muslims. Of Jerusalem's Muslims, scarcely few survived except Fatimid commander Iftikhar as-Daulah and remnants of his Egyptian cavalry, who were later escorted out of the city and allowed to return to Egypt. During the slaughter, looting broke out as related by one witnessing crusader: "Our men rushed around the whole city, seizing gold and silver, horses and mules, and houses full of all sorts of goods."

Another account related: "How astonishing it would have seemed for you to see our squires and footmen after they had discovered the trickery of the Saracens, splitting open the bellies of those they had just slain in order to extract from the intestines the bezants the Saracens had gulped down in their loathsome throats while alive."

When the carnage subsided and Christian bloodlust had been satisfied, 'the crusaders turned their hands, still covered in mostly civilian blood and loaded with plunder, back to devotion and worship, rejoicing and weeping from excessive gladness to worship at the Sepulcher of our Savior Jesus Christ.'

Thus, in the name of God, the Holy City of Jerusalem was freed from the claws of Islam and returned to Christianity after 400 years of Muslim control. As to disposition of the Holy City of Jerusalem, Godfrey of Bouillon was appointed "Advocate of the Holy Sepulcher" and charged with ruling the city, not as king, but as "protector," remaining subordinate to the Church.

As fate would have it, or perhaps as God willed it, Pope Urban II (Odo de Lagery) died on the 29th of July 1099, just fourteen days after the fall of Jerusalem. Owing to distance, modes of travel, and communication of the era, Pope Urban II never learned the outcome of his Holy Crusade, nor that his "Army of God" was victorious in the end, against hopeless odds from outside, as well as from within.

To place the First Holy Crusade in realistic perspective, and in testifying to the sheer futility and human folly of such grandiose endeavors, the Christian victory during the First Holy Crusade was but a fleeting moment in time. Islamic military might quickly resurrected itself through unification and resolve, and as a result, the First Holy Crusade (1097–1099) would become but the first of eight more crusades, one unfolding after another over the next two centuries.

The final crusade, the Ninth Crusade, began in the Year of Our Lord, 1271, and ended in the Year of Our Lord, 1272. Of the nine crusades, the Islamic armies won all but the First Crusade (1097–1099) and the Sixth Crusade (1228–1229), which entailed very little actual fighting.

Today, nearly one thousand years later, Christianity and Islam continue to struggle against each other in a bloody, unforgiving war of wills, hate, religion, and race, as cities named Baghdad, Mosul, Aleppo, and Damascus continue to echo and rage, albeit unheard by many, in the deaf and blind stream of human consciousness.

Not, as God wills it, but as man wishes it. Amen.

ACKNOWLEDGMENTS

In releasing *Cup of Blood . . . Bread of Salvation* (the fifth and final novel comprising my series entitled The Dark Ages Saga of Tristan de Saint-Germain), I wish to, without reservation, give full acknowledgment to my agent, Jeanie Loiacono, President of Loiacono Literary Agency. Jeanie introduced me to the world of writing and publishing as I submitted my first novel (Contrition, JournalStone Publishing, 2012), and has since that time counseled and navigated me as a novelist. Jeanie, I thank you profusely, and sincerely appreciate your time, interest, and efforts on my behalf. You encouraged a wandering literary soul and life traveler, long in search of realizing a childhood dream, who became a story teller/writer of poignant drama and the human struggle to overcome life's darkness, which at times, unexpectedly, hurls each of us into raging currents well beyond our capacity to repel.

BIBLIOGRAPHY

THE DARK AGES SAGA OF TRISTAN DE SAINT-GERMAIN

Asbridge, Thomas, *The First Crusade: A New History* (2004)

Clark, James, *The Benedictines in the Middle Ages (Monastic Orders)* (2011)

Cobb, Paul, *The Race for Paradise: An Islamic History of the Crusades* (2014)

Cole, Teresa, *The Norman Conquest* (2016)

Douglas, David, *William the Conqueror: The Norman Impact Upon England* (1964)

Frankopan, Peter, *The First Crusade: The Call from the East* (2012)

Gesta, Francorum (Deeds of the Franks), anonymous (1100–1101)

Lewis, Brenda Ralph, *A Dark History: The Popes* (2011 ed.)

Medieval Sourcebook: Urban II 1088–1099: Speech at Clermont

Mullins, Edwin, *In Search of Cluny: God's Lost Empire* (2006)

Rosewell, Roger, *The Medieval Monastery* (2012)

Rubenstein, Jay, *Armies of Heaven: The First Crusade and the Quest for Apocalypse* (2011)

Runciman, Steven, *A History of the First Crusade*, vol 1 (1987)

Smith, Katherine Allen, *War and the Making of Medieval Monastic Culture* (2011)

Tyerman, Christopher, *God's War: A New History of the Crusades* (2008)

ABOUT THE AUTHOR

Robert E. Hirsch was born in Pusan, Korea, in 1949. In 1953, Hirsch's mother sent him to the United States to live with his biological father due to Korea's harsh wartime conditions. He spent the next thirteen years as a military dependent, traveling all over America and passing three years in France, where he attended school at a French lycée.

Hirsch graduated from Cameron University in Lawton, Oklahoma, and began teaching French and social studies. He retired in 2012 after forty years, having served during his career as a teacher, principal, and superintendent. Hirsch has lived with his wife, Melissa, in Ocean Springs, Mississippi, along the Gulf Coast, since 1980.

THE DARK AGES SAGA OF TRISTAN DE SAINT-GERMAIN

FROM OPEN ROAD MEDIA

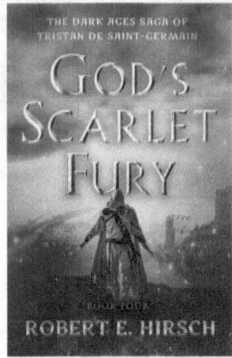

OPEN ROAD

INTEGRATED MEDIA

Find a full list of our authors and
titles at www.openroadmedia.com

FOLLOW US
@OpenRoadMedia